CRITICAL
RANDAL

"I will not compare Randall to King, Barker or any other writer in the genre today. This is Randall Boyll, a unique and individual voice."—J. B. MACABRE of *Rave Reviews*

"Imagination and talent!"—*Mystery Scene*

MONGSTER
The horrifying story of a boy and his mummy . . .

"*Mongster* was the most fun I've had reading in a long, long time . . . Fantastic!"—*Scream Factory*

"Exciting . . . A satirical, ripping good time . . . Makes the reader question who the monsters really are."—*Rave Reviews*

DARKMAN
Based on Sam Raimi's electrifying horror film . . .

"Tense, dramatic but compassionate."—*Fear*

"Effective . . . a good read."—*Mystery Scene*

"I like Boyll . . . Great book . . . You can't go wrong, so buy it already."—*Scar*

SHOCKER
Based on the terrifying Wes Craven thriller . . .

"I am continually amazed at how good Boyll is."—*Scar*

AFTER SUNDOWN
A novel of snowbound terror . . .

"Absolutely terrific . . . If you're the sort who kicked him- or herself for not picking up a first edition of *Carrie*, maybe you should take a cue and stash a few extra copies of *After Sundown*!"—EDWARD BRYANT, *Locus*

"Four stars . . . Fascinating . . . It speeds toward an exciting conclusion!"—*Rave Reviews*

Books by Randall Boyll
from The Berkley Publishing Group

AFTER SUNDOWN
CHILLER
DARKMAN
MONGSTER
SHOCKER

CHILLER

RANDALL BOYLL

JOVE BOOKS, NEW YORK

CHILLER

A Jove Book / published by arrangement with
the author

PRINTING HISTORY
Jove edition / April 1992

ISBN: 0-515-10836-7

Jove Books are published by The Berkley Publishing Group,
200 Madison Avenue, New York, New York 10016.
The name "JOVE" and the "J" logo
are trademarks belonging to Jove Publications, Inc.

PRINTED IN THE UNITED STATES OF AMERICA

10 9 8 7 6 5 4 3 2 1

And no Grand Inquisitor has in readiness such terrible tortures as has anxiety, and no spy knows how to attack more artfully the man he suspects, choosing the instant when he is weakest, nor knows how to lay traps where he will be caught and ensnared, as anxiety knows how, and no sharp-witted judge knows how to interrogate, to examine the accused as anxiety does, which never lets him escape, neither by diversion nor by noise, neither at work nor at play, neither by day nor by night.

—Søren Kierkegaard
The Concept of Dread

For Sam Raybould and Mike Timko
The Two Smartest Son-of-a-Bitches in Clay County

ONE

THE FIFTH DAY

ONE

PETER KAYE DROVE HIS RUSTY GRAY CHEVETTE TO THE FRONT of the Citizen's First Bank in Effingham, Illinois, and stopped. He did not turn the engine off, but surveyed the building for a moment, squinting through the yellowed windshield of the old car. It looked just fine, a great building, a great bank. He leaned forward on the seat and patted the back pocket of his jeans to reassure himself that the pistol was still there. He had been sitting on it for five days now and it had become a part of him, not much different from his fingers or toes. Satisfied that it *was* still there, he took a small notebook off the dashboard, located a pen from the litter of Coke cans and McDonald's bags between the bucket seats, and began to write.

His daughter Darbi was on the seat beside him. "Daddy, I'm cold," she said fretfully.

He nodded, intent on his writing. In the July-in-Illinois heat his black T-shirt sported big sweat rings under his armpits and a tornado-shaped runner of it on his chest. He was a tall man, too tall to be the owner of a Chevette, but the car was stolen anyway and would soon be ditched. After this heist, maybe. They had driven the car all the way from Indianapolis and the cops were sure to be snooping around for it.

"Daddy?"

"Baby, I know," he said. Sweat dripped off his eyebrows and made splotches on the paper. He brushed them away with the side of his hand, wiping the words THIS IS A ROBBERY into an illegible smear of ink. He flipped the page and began to write again. When he was done he ripped the page out and stuffed it in a pocket. The notebook went back onto the dash. The pen followed.

"Daddy?" Darbi whined. "Do you have to do it again?"

He turned his head and stared helplessly at her. She was packed from foot to neck in bags of crushed ice. There was one draped atop her head, but it was mostly water now and looked like a droopy brand of see-through Mickey Mouse ears. Not for the first time Peter Kaye felt an almost unbearable rush of love for her, followed by a surge of despair and horror. His pills were supposed to cure that, but under these conditions even a man with all his mental nuts and bolts tight would be ready to weep.

"You know I hate to, Darbi, but we've got a long ways to go. Now help me lean your seat back."

He heard her hand work its way out of the burden of ice bags (Mr. Frosty, they all said in blue print) and ratchet the seat release. He pushed it back as far as the seat would allow while she sat up straight, shivering. There were bags of ice on the back floor, and he dragged two forward, noticing with dismay that they were for the most part already melted. He stuffed them behind Darbi's back, then pushed on her forehead lightly to make her lie down. She grunted from the sudden sting of new cold. "Sorry, babe," he said, and dragged another bag from the supply in the back. "Face," he said.

She clenched her eyes shut. He laid a bag gently across it. "Feel okay?"

"Cold." Muffled under plastic.

"Put you hand back."

Ice crunched and shifted. Peter checked her over, this thin and wispy six-year-old wearing a soggy pink dress, hoping the damage to her backside had been minor. One of the bags she had been sitting on had burst a while back, so as he drove he had desperately shoveled ice and ice water from the bucket seat down her back with one hand. He wondered how many hours it had been since she was fully protected. His watch told him it was almost five o'clock now. They had left the motel in Ohio about ten A.M. That meant seven hours, which was seven hours too many, but they were on the run from the Indiana Mounties and nothing had ever felt so good as crossing that brown-muddy Wabash River, getting the hell away from Hoosier hospitality and into Illinois, the Land of Lincoln. He estimated it would take three to four hours to make it to Missouri. Between here and there were a hundred towns, a hundred banks, a thousand stores that sold ice. But they would be wise to him very soon; the Illinois cops were doubtless as hell-bent on catching the new John Dillinger as all the others had been. Perhaps, Peter thought dismally, they think I am really Dillinger and am in my nineties. Or perhaps they know I am a twenty-nine-year-old grad-school dropout who had not known which end of a gun was which just five days ago.

He took a few deep breaths, steeling himself for what was about to happen. Cars droned past on this hazy Friday, people intent on their own business. He watched traffic through the cracked rearview mirror. It occurred to him to light a cigarette, maybe eat a handful of pills. Something for his nerves, which were as taut as spring steel about now, something to make him feel that all this torture had a purpose. Anxiety was clawing at his guts and churning in his brain. The damn pills were supposed to stop this particular demon, but they seemed to have deserted him. It didn't matter just yet. Darbi needed ice. The black Hefty garbage bag in the back on the cargo floor had maybe a hundred thousand dollars in it. And this was already the fifth day.

Peter opened the door to a furnace blast of heat and humidity. The Chevette's air-conditioning had been working overtime just to keep the temperature at the bearable level; still, the ice kept melting, as ice will often do when it's ninety degrees outside and eighty inside a car that is in need of a few cans of Freon or a quick one-way trip to a junkyard. He made sure the butt of the revolver in his pocket was hidden by his shirt, took a last deep breath of air that smelled old and soggy-summer putrid, and got out.

"Daddy?" Darbi said. "Daddy?"

He leaned back inside. "Yeah?"

"Please don't kill anybody?"

He bit his lower lip, a habit picked up during sleepless nights in the Duchess County Mental Health Center in Poughkeepsie. He forced himself to stop; his lip was chafed and flaking already. He wished he could answer Darbi's request with a simple yes, nobody's going to do any dying today. But would he kill someone if he had to? Could he actually pull that trigger?

Yes. Yes, he thought he could.

"We're just playing cops and robbers, Darbi. Don't you worry. And tallyho. Okay?"

The bag of ice on her face nodded slightly. Through the melted Mickey Mouse ears on her head he could see the top of her scalp, which was covered with a short and comical stubble of blond hair. Funny stuff, that chemotherapy. Every hair on her body had sifted off like the needles of a dry and aging Christmas tree. Peter gave her a smile she could not see and eased the door shut, knowing she didn't believe the lie about cops and robbers. What had started out as a curious game had gotten serious pretty quickly.

He made his feet propel him toward the Citizen's First Bank. He hesitated at the doors, which were huge glass affairs with brushed aluminum handles and signs above them that read PULL. Peter was able to reach out a hand that felt heavy as granite, and pulled. Cold air hit him in the face like a breeze from an iceberg. He stepped inside and let the door swing shut, wishing this kind of cold could be available in the car. Last night in the motel in Ohio (what town was it? Cleveland? Cincinnati? He could not quite remember) he had cranked the air conditioner to full blast and left Darbi in a tubful of cold water while he hauled courtesy bucket after courtesy bucket from the ice machine and loaded Darbi's bathwater up for the night. It was a tricky business that he had not yet mastered; either from too much heat or too much cold, the tip of her right thumb was already gone, sloughed off to reveal the pinpoint of ivory-white bone inside. It had taken a lot of Band-Aids and a lot of lies to calm her down. He supposed the thumb could be repaired. It was her head he worried about most; there would be no way to replace *that*.

"Pardon me, young fella," someone said behind him.

He came to himself with a start. "Sorry," he mumbled, and let the old man pass. He forced himself to walk into the maze of red velvet theater ropes that guided customers to the tellers, and stood awaiting his turn. He noticed that everybody here was busy. Muzak drifted out of hidden speakers. There was a hum of politely muted conversation. Compared to the terrifying chaos waiting outside, this was the inside of a church.

"I can help you over here," a teller far to the left called out to him, smiling. Peter hesitated, battling a gigantic urge to simply turn and run. The girl was young, maybe nineteen, and did not deserve what was coming to her. In Pennsylvania two days ago a teenage teller-in-training had fallen over in a dead faint and wet herself when Peter presented his note. It was the bank manager himself who'd hustled over to hand Peter all available cash when the teller collapsed, his Hush Puppies squishing in the urine-soaked carpet as he worked between her legs.

Peter felt himself moving toward the girl. He was on automatic now, operating by rote while the real Peter Kaye worried about the college he had abandoned and his unfinished doctoral thesis. He thought of his wife Brenda, but that was an old memory, a picture on the screen of his mind that was yellowed and curling with age. She was currently occupied, and had been for the last six years, with being dead. Eighteen and dead.

Peter found that he was in front of the pretty teller. She said, "Howya doon?" Then Peter's hand reached into his pocket and brought out the notepaper. It was wadded and damp. He handed it mutely over while his mind reviewed logarithms and their usefulness to trigonometry in the age of hand-held calulators, a subtopic of his thesis that was now a useless pile of typewritten paper in an apartment being ransacked by a vengeful Saudi Arabian landlord who, like John T. Braine, expected his money on time.

She read it and looked at him with a bit of smile hanging on the corners of her lips. "Joke, huh?" she whispered. "Fraternity initiation?"

Peter's dark side gave her a flat, muddy stare. "In July?"

The color washed out of her face. She took a breath that sounded like a distant whistle. "You mean you've—you've got a—"

"Gun."

Her face twisted up. "But see," she whined, "the bank has a policy. About these things, I mean. There's a button near my feet and I'm supposed to—"

"Push it and die," the other Peter, the one born some days ago, said in a voice that sounded very Clint Eastwood-ish. "Didn't you read the note?"

"Well, yeah, sure. So what am I supposed to do?"

"Give me all your money. Do it quietly and without fanfare. Ask each teller in turn to fill up your sack. If it takes more sacks than one, get another. If you get out of my sight, my men and I will kill everyone in this building." He reached out and took her chin in his hand. He eased her jaw shut. "Dig?"

For a moment he believed himself to be very dashing, very daring, but such thoughts did not belong to Peter Kaye. They belonged to the other personality that had recently taken up residence in his mind, the strange tough guy who was so unlike the real thing. He was a sham, a braggart. Peter was a tired and frightened wreck whose knees were threatening to unlock and dump him on the floor. But the teller was doing as she was told, loading up a dirty white canvas bag with all her paper money, and then the change as well.

"Good, so far," he managed to grunt. "Now work your way on down the line."

She moved off, a robot without direction, thudding into things and people. When she found her mind again there were whispered conversations that resulted in the outflow of cash. The bank ran on like precision German machinery. The four security cameras mounted in the ceiling corners swiveled back and forth without hesitation, seeing everything. Peter's alter ego bared his teeth at one of them, and almost laughed aloud. Nothing seemed to be happening that might disturb the serenity of the Citizen's Bank of Effingham, Illinois. Best of all, there was no armed guard as in days of yore.

The teller came back. She was pale and shaking, but she had three bags stuffed full of cash. All the other tellers were staring; Peter had no doubt that a lot of feet were pressing secret buttons. Behind him, upper-echelon employees were looking up from their desks or hanging up their phones in mid-conversation. Automatic dialing machines were phoning the police with a recorded cry for help. The game of cops and robbers was about to begin in earnest.

Peter disengaged the bags from the girl's fists, cast her a good-bye wink, then made his way through the maze of theater ropes with the bags in one hand and the other free to go for the gun if necessary. Save for the Muzak, this cool and neat-smelling bank was now quiet as a mummy's tomb. Heads swiveled to watch him pass. Unblinking stares and bulging eyeballs tracked him to the door. Outside, the heat dumped itself on him like a bucket of hot water, nearly making him gasp. It had to be a hundred out here. As he jogged to the car he hoped to hell that Darbi was all right, but of course she was, she always was, though with each passing day something new slipped away from her. Yesterday it was the thumb. Today it might be an ear falling off. With each new horror she seemed to fade from the world a bit, slipping into some dark region between sleep and death.

He was opening the door of the Chevette when the police siren made itself known over the murmur of traffic. His heart jumped a little as Peter the Second deserted him and went to wherever multiple personalities reside while awaiting their turn at bat, leaving Peter the Only to deal with the rest of this mess. He crunched himself into the little car, tossed the money in the back, gave Darbi a quick once-over, and dumped the gearshift into drive. The Chevette had no spirit whatsoever, but it did belch silver smoke into the dead air and creep forward. Peter urged it on, wishing he had something with more power to it. Why had he stolen this particular slowpoke? Because some incautious Indiana Hoosier had left it running in a grocery store parking lot. The car before, the one he'd exchanged his own ancient Gremlin for in Ohio, had likewise been left unattended, that one at a gas station while its owner used the rest room and the bored attendant watched a mini-TV with his back turned.

"Daddy?"

Peter shook his head. "Not now, babe. I have to concentrate."

"But my face is cold."

"No buts. Sorry." He forced the car into moving traffic and got honked at. The siren was getting close. The light up ahead turned red and the traffic became a lineup of cars that was a colorful, wavering mirage above the baking asphalt. Peter blinked sweat out of his eyes, looking for escape avenues, an opening to dive into and disappear. There were none. The light seemed permanently stuck on red, but he knew it was a trick of the mind, part of the paranoia and anxiety he had endured since the year after Brenda died giving birth to Darbi, Brenda impossibly dead in childbirth.

The light changed to green. Peter shut the memories off because they were the enemy and because he had to think of escape now and nothing else. If the cops chose to shoot through the back window, they would get Peter but not Darbi, for Darbi was lying down almost horizontally and would be safe from any bullet. Darbi would survive for a while. Peter only hoped that the fatal bullet with his name on it would be quick and painless, and that Braine would take pity on the new orphan named Darbi Louanne Kaye.

Traffic began to move. Already some drivers were swerving over to the curbside as the siren and flashing blue and red lights came into earshot and rearview-mirror range. Peter crunched the tiny accelerator pedal hard to the floor, filling up the gaps in traffic, knowing the cops would need at least a minute in the bank to get a description of the robber and his car. Tall, sweaty, nervous, driving a gray Chevy. And see here, Officer, I believe the man is insane. He winked at me. Then the APB would go out, and everybody would be on the lookout for a rusty gray Chevette with Indiana plates and the driver with the greasy blond hair and the purple bags under his eyes, name currently unknown, but with the aka of The New John Dillinger, the casual robber of over sixteen banks in five days.

The next light was red. The lone car in front of Peter, an ancient Rambler driven by some dwarf with white hair, cruised through as if no light existed here at all. Way to go, old lady, Peter thought, and performed a similar easy cruise through the intersection. One car honked, then two, and suddenly Peter the Second resurfaced long enough to flip them the bird. Then he was gone, leaving the real Peter Kaye shaky and anxious and wondering just how far sanity could stretch before it broke.

That was self-pity, he had decided long ago. All of this mewling helplessness served no purpose. He had cracked, and the therapy and the pills had patched him back together, but it was a loose threadwork and the seams were shoddy. He had asked his appointed psychiatrist not long ago if he was crazy.

"Crazy is a euphemism that describes many conditions, yet describes none at all," the doctor had said while exercising his habit of rolling his pencil in and out between his fingers like a baton. Talk about crazy. "Insanity actually comes in many forms, Peter, but for now, we'll use the term mildly psychotic for you, with a possible manifestation of multiple-personality disorder. And panic disorder compounded by depression, of course, for which you are taking the medication."

"But the pills don't work," Peter had lamented. "And I

can't live this way much longer. Really. I never know what's going to happen next."

The shrink, one Dr. Fredrickson, had ducked his head, almost apologetically. "Of all the psychiatric miseries available to man, you unfortunately chose three that are the most distressing. Your psychosis is the generator that sets certain parameters to your brain activity."

"Huh?"

"I mean your afflictions are not your fault. Your brain has undergone an inexplicable chemical or electrical malfunction, possibly both. But we can hardly cut out a brain sample and analyze it, now can we?"

Peter had frowned, not lying on a couch as was endlessly portrayed in movies, television, and newspaper cartoons, but sitting in a chair while sunlight streamed through the office windows and formed cheerful squares on the floor by his feet. "Why not?" he had said with a shrug.

"Well, first of all, we don't yet know the chemical composition of a healthy brain, so we would have nothing to compare yours against. The chemicals of the brain are present in such minute amounts that they are virtually undetectable. As for electrical activity, we can map it in groups, but your condition most likely occurs in a very tiny area of your brain, perhaps microscopic in size, and one bad link makes a weak chain, as they say."

Peter had thought about this for a while. "Will I get worse?" he'd asked, wishing very much that Dr. Fredrickson would give him nothing but good news, even if he had to lie—but it was not to be.

"The chances of it simply going away are remote. More likely, you'll remain the same, or the psychosis will progressively worsen until you are very much debilitated."

"Debilitated?"

"I know the prospect of requiring permanent hospitalization is not pleasant. Perhaps new drugs will be found soon. Maybe even a cure. That's about the best I can come up with, but for the remainder of this session I'd like to talk about your daughter Darbi, and how you are going to cope with her—"

Peter had slipped as easily as if greased into a state of panic, and the matter of Darbi and her impending death got rerouted when he began to jitter out of control. What his condition boiled down to, as Peter saw it in his state of misery and fear, was that he was psychotic and unstable and prone to being someone else once in a while. That might explain why he was trying to become the new John Dillinger by robbing sixteen banks in five days and keeping his daughter packed in ice. Wonder what the shrink would think of that? Peter believed he would never see him again, and Peter was very right.

He stopped at the next light, knowing that the police were at the bank by now and that he had precious little time to act. His modus operandi up to now had been to simply get out of town and onto some forgotten back road, where he could blend in with the scenery and the silence and hopefully not be conspicuous. It had worked so far, but the cops were no fools and only needed a map to tell them that the crime spree was branching westward. Eventually there would be an observant farmer or passing county Mountie, maybe a roadblock, and the party would be over.

The light turned green. Peter started forward, but Peter the Second decided to return long enough to make him turn right. Usually Number Two's instincts were good; this time they stank. As the real Peter spun the minuscule steering wheel in obedience to that inner man, the little car swayed on its ruined springs, making ice shift and nearly spilling Darbi out of her seat. Somebody on the right honked loud enough to make Peter jump; a second later came the rubbery scream of tires on hot pavement, followed immediately by a loud and ominous bang. The Chevette was dragged sideways and the dashboard was suddenly full of red lights. The noisy blast of the air conditioner faded off.

Peter sat in stunned dismay, barely realizing he had thumped his head against the door window hard enough to put a spiderweb nest of cracks there. Automatically he reached to check Darbi over, shoving the ice back into place, packing it tight around her once again. The bag over her face had slid down onto her lap, and even though this strange new situation reeked of cops and strangers on the way, he paused for a moment before covering her face again.

It was Brenda the dead wife minus twelve years, with a dash of Peter thrown in at the shape of her nose and the curvature of her mouth. Her eyes were open and blue. Her hair was white peach fuzz. The left half of her face was black.

"You okay, babe?"

She nodded. "What just happened?"

"Looks like we've had a fender-bender." He cranked the key and got no response. The dash lights faded to black. Peter hung his head, shaking it wearily from side to side, aware now of the smell of gasoline from somebody's smashed tank, no doubt the Chevette's.

"What's a fender-bender?"

"A wreck, I guess." He raised his head and summoned up a desperate smile. "Do you suppose our insurance will cover it?"

She deliberated; outside, a small crowd was forming to inspect dents. "I sure hope so," Darbi said earnestly.

"Okay." Peter picked the bag up off her lap and lowered it across her face. "Sit still and let Dad handle everything. Got me, Darbi-Darbi?"

"You're got, Daddy." She worked a hand out of the bags and squeezed his arm. Peter let his smile fall. Cold, those fingers were, as cold as, well—ice. Black too. And why not?

"Tallyho," she said through the ice.

"Yeah, babe." Peter stuck her hand back where it belonged. "Tallyho."

He got out, already reaching for his pistol, waiting for Peter the Second to take charge and get him out of this new mess, but Peter the Second, only five days old, had a peculiar personality. He could feign courage, do a nifty Eastwood imitation, scare bank tellers, flip people the bird. But when the going got really nasty, he could park himself in some dark corner of Peter's mind and wait placidly for things to cool off. As Peter came out of the car into the heat, Number Two ducked a little deeper down the back roads of his mind, letting Peter know that no, no way was he coming out until everything was safe. For Peter this was almost a physical experience, this desperate search for new identities in a mind ravaged by five years as a certified nut; he felt his vision go haywire, saw the people clustered behind the Chevette as sparkling apparitions, had a sensation of being sucked away from reality, and all the while his heart was pumping out of control in his chest. He was suddenly dizzy and he had to hold onto the car's rain gutter to keep from falling.

One of the sparkling people came over to him. "Ya get hurt, bud? Huh? Are ya bleeding anywheres?"

Peter shook his head. His lungs wanted to keep pace with his racing heart, but that would lead to hyperventilation and a fainting spell. He might be out for ten minutes; plenty of time for the cops to arrive.

"Got any broken bones?"

Peter pushed away from the car while the world spun and rocked around him. Now pinpoints of light were corkscrewing across his vision like shiny gnats, and there was an unbearable whining in his ears. He staggered drunkenly to the front of the Chevette and sprawled across the hood. The shakes were hitting him. He knew that anyone looking would be convinced he was epileptic, and there were plenty of people looking.

The hood was too hot against his cheek. He raised his shaking head and forced his eyes open. He saw Darbi through the windshield. She was waiting, trusting, freezing. The man who was hot on the trail for blood and broken bones was leaning inside to check out this strange mound of melting Mr. Frosty ice. He was wearing bib overalls and a red cap, a regular Farmer Brown.

Peter shoved himself upright. The world had become a Tilt-a-Whirl, pitching and rocking. The noise of passing traffic and people chattering thundered in his ears, competing with that strange, high-voltage whine that seemed to emanate from the bones of his skull. The smell of gasoline was huge and overpowering. He stood swaying, knowing what was going to happen, knowing that Farmer Brown was about to take the tip off the iceberg named Darbi and scream bloody murder when he saw her black and white face. Peter took an awkward step and nearly fell over; once again the rain gutter came in handy. He passed around the open door like a man on a shaky tightwire, his eyes squinched to slits against the monstrous glare of the sun.

The man leaning in the car lifted the ice bag off Darbi's face. Sheet metal bonged as his head jerked up and hit the Chevette's wobbly ceiling; ice slapped wetly against ice as the bag fell from his surprised hands. Peter heard the old farmer's lungs scoop in a terrified breath. Sure, Peter thought, sure. She isn't pretty to look at but by God she's mine and I love her and no damn Effingham Illinois farmer is going to take her from me.

He worked the pistol out of his pants. His jeans were tight and it hung up. He jerked it with both hands, turning in a clumsy circle and almost falling over. During this ordeal Farmer Brown did not scream; instead he jerked out of the car and turned to face his sizable audience.

"Jesus!" he shouted. *"Jesus Christ in heaven! Look at this!"*

People surged forward. Peter got the pistol out and dropped it on the street. No one seemed to notice. One man in a yellow suit with a preposterous pink tie pushed his way to the front and confronted Peter. He began howling about fuckhead Indiana drivers and the damage done to his front bumper. He appeared to Peter as a flat painting of a man, not human at all, an idiotic hallucination. Everything was shimmering, unreal. Peter realized this was the last stage of the attack. Soon the overheated cauldron of his brain would cease bubbling with noises and visions from hell, and he would be all right, after a fashion.

"Show me your license," the pink and yellow man shouted above the noise. Peter squatted down and searched the hot street with his hand. His eyes were still slitted against the light; his pupils would return to normal size in a few minutes, but for now he was as good as blind. One probing finger touched warm metal. He snatched the gun up just as the siren noise renewed itself in the east. The cops had gotten what they needed at the bank, Peter knew; the manhunt was on.

He managed to get himself upright, and pointed the gun at the sky. The crowd and the cars and the man in pink who was screaming at him were a jumbled, crazy picture. The siren warbled high-low, high low, speeding closer. Peter pulled the trigger of his stolen pistol, the one he'd acquired at the start of this ordeal when he'd thumped a cop on the head with a chunk of broken sidewalk cement and snatched the gun out of his holster.

The crowd fell back at the sound of the shot, the perimeter dispersing like ashes in the wind. Peter had barely heard the report over the noises in his head. A puff of gray gunsmoke drifted skyward, scattering itself to reluctant tatters in the hazy dead air. Mr. Pink and Yellow had shut up in a hurry and was backing up toward his car, his hands held high like Nixon proclaiming victory, his shirt parting between the buttons to reveal the naked white skin and potbelly of the heavy drinker. Perhaps he was drunk right now, Peter thought—who else would plow into a car making a sudden and only slightly illegal right turn? The cops wouldn't care how drunk he was, of course. He had managed to do what the law had not. He had laid the new Dillinger low.

Peter slumped against the side of the car, making it rock. More ice bags slithered off Darbi and slapped to the floor inside. Peter let himself fall into the car. The pistol, fired only once in the hands of its new owner, clattered to the hot street and lay there, its calm black bore pointing somewhere that no longer mattered nor made sense.

TWO

KIM MARDEN DIDN'T KNOW WHETHER TO LAUGH, CRY, OR smack her roommate, Nina Patterson, over the head with her ridiculous new Ouija board. Nina had gotten the board for her twenty-second birthday yesterday, and quickly decided she was some kind of talented psychic. Kim was watching without much interest as her future and the rest of her life were laid open by this amateur soothsayer, knowing that both of them should be doing some housecleaning instead of this stuff. Their small apartment on Beech Street in St. Charles, Missouri, a virtual suburb of St. Louis, was still littered with colorful wrapping paper, strung-out ribbons, paper plates and plastic spoons slimed with old cake and ice cream, and a sprinkling of confetti. A look at the clock told Kim it was five in the afternoon, and both of them had to be at work at the freeway Holiday Inn at six.

"Please," Kim said, strangely tired—or maybe, she thought ruefully, deservedly tired. "Let's call it quits." Liquor had flowed freely at Nina's party yesterday; Nina's eyes as she stared down at the Ouija board now were threaded with bright snaps of scarlet and she was still in her pajamas. Kim was dressed and ready to go, sitting at the kitchen table of their apartment with her fingers resting lightly on the Ouija board's pointer while Nina the Hungover Birthday Girl did the same on the other side of the table. The pointer was having no trouble moving around on the board to spell out its mysteries; Nina knew how to make that sucker go.

"You'd better get ready for work," Kim said, very bored

with this. So far she had learned that her future husband's name would start with an R, that she would have three children, and would die at the age of 206. Her friend Nina (which she pronounced *Neena*, supposedly the name of some distant grandmother) had tried her best to push the pointer to a more plausible number, swearing that she was not moving it at all. She believed the spirits were working through both of them. Somehow Kim found it odd that even when she lifted her own fingers imperceptibly off the plastic teardrop-shaped indicator, it still slid around on its three padded feet, but Nina would go to her grave swearing she hadn't moved it. She was a pushover for the occult and just about everything else. Rumor had it that her grandma had been a certified fortune-teller possessed of amazing accuracy; Nina liked the idea, and thought herself a bit of a crystal-ball artist too.

"We don't have to be there till six," Nina said, intent on the board and Kim's future that was there to be read.

"Have you even ironed your uniform yet?"

"All in good time, my pretty. All in good time. Wee-Jee!" she called loudly. "Will Kimberly Marden ever be promoted to manager?"

"I don't want to be a manager," Kim said.

"You never know what you want, and you are famous for it. Hush."

Kim hushed. Since there wasn't really anything else to do right now, except maybe clean up this dump, she went along with Nina and her fascination with this fraudulent thing. For her birthday Nina had received a remarkable number of goodies from her friends: sweaters, T-shirts with semi-obscene logos on the front, bottles of white wine, an expensive makeup kit (from Kim), a set of chrome designer dumbbells, a stuffed bear, a ring with a microscopic diamond (from her boyfriend, Jerry), the Ouija board (from who knows who), and other bric-a-brac. The apartment had thundered with rock music and shouted conversations and clinking glasses until two, when Mrs. Gimble downstairs in

Apartment Three had nearly punched a hole in her ceiling and their floor with her broomstick. Everybody had finally left, except the hard drinkers clustered around the keg, and Nina's Jerry, and Kim's own boyfriend, Wayne Abel. By the time she'd had him and the drunks pushed out the door, Nina and Jerry had vanished into Nina's bedroom. Sometime in the night he must have left, because he wasn't here now.

"There it goes," Nina said, pushing the pointer around, heading it for the big YES stamped on the bottom right of the board. Kim was glad it was all fake, because the last thing she wanted was to be promoted from Holiday Inn desk clerk to Holiday Inn manager. Life was tough enough as it was.

The pointer stopped on YES. Nina clapped her hands. "Now let's see if *I'll* ever be in management."

"Somehow," Kim said dryly, "I think you will."

Nina put her hands back and the pointer wandered around. Past her head, on top of the refrigerator, Kim saw that Wayne had forgotten his hat. Hats were, of course, utterly out of vogue in these early nineties, especially a preposterous black derby, but Wayne Abel claimed to be his own man, unaffected by fashion. That may well be true, she often thought, but he should be affected by the embarrassment the damn thing causes when we go out.

"Oh, God!" Nina said. "It's headed for YES! God!"

"Do tell," Kim murmured, still staring at that idiotic black derby on the fridge. In a way, she thought, that hat might stand as a symbol of her relationship with Wayne, though he would never know it and it was quite possible she was being absurd. He thought he was daring and dashing because he had eight ounces of oddball hat on his head, but his cockiness whenever he wore the damned thing was repulsive, as was the way he would stick his hand inside it and twirl the hat on his finger while he talked. When she'd met him ten months ago in the lounge at the freeway Holiday Inn, the hat had been a mere curiosity parked between the ashtrays, and when she had asked him about it, he'd said, "I keep my personality in it." She had actually laughed, having no idea that he was right without knowing it.

"YES!" Nina screamed. "God, gag me! Noxious! I'm going to quit my job tonight!"

Kimberly Marden pulled her hands away, and rubbed her shoulders with them. "This is wearing me out," she said. She looked at her watch. "It's ten after, Neen. Get yourself ready."

Nina made a face and drew her knees up, balancing on the rickety chrome chair that was all rust and popped rivets. "I wonder what it will be like as a manager. I'd have to transfer, and then I wouldn't have any friends."

Kim stood up and stretched, hearing a series of pleasant little crackles from her backbone. When she drew back together she could have been a picture straight out of a Holiday Inn brochure: sensible blue dress cut just a tad too high (for the benefit of the male customers), light blue blouse, gold vest. Her almost-blond hair fell past her ears and was curled under in a flip; her bangs brushed her eyebrows. Nina had told her once that with a hairdo like that she could hop into a time machine and come out in 1960 and finally be in style. Kim didn't mind. She had some kind of strange fondness for Patti Page, famous singer of the fifties, and if the style had been good enough for her . . .

"One more," Nina said, looking over at the clock set in the stove's control front. "Time for just one more."

Kim shook her head. "It kills my shoulders, Neen, and you're still in your silly Garfield pajamas."

"Silly?" She tilted her head back, and laughed. "Aren't you the same girl who was cavorting around last night in the same bathrobe *President* Garfield wore in 1822? Correct me if I'm mistaken."

"It's all in the eye of the—"

"Beholder. I know. How did Wayne's eye behold you last night? Can he even get a decent boner when you're in bed with him dressed like that?"

"Oh, be quiet." Kim felt her face reddening. Nina might

never know it, but Wayne seemed to be in a state of perpetual horniness. Maybe for a twenty-five-year-old man it was normal, but she had to draw the line somewhere or spend the rest of her days on her back. He had even tried wearing his derby to bed one memorable time; Kim had tossed him and his hat out together.

Nina settled down to business and put the pointer back in the center of the board. "Come on. One more question."

"I don't think so, Neen."

"Come on. This will be the last one. Please?"

"Okay, okay." She sat back down and put her fingertips on the silly pointer. "Go ahead, Madame Zarathustra."

"Madame who?"

"Just do it."

"Okay." She cleared her throat. "O magic Ouija, reveal to us one more secret. Is Kim Marden ever going to decide what she wants to do in life?"

"You dope."

"Shh. It's moving."

"I'll notify the press."

"Shh. O magic Ouija, tell us the answer. Will she spend the rest of her days handing out room keys, or finally get a real life?"

Kim pulled her hands away. "This is dumb. Ask if it will mind when I set it on fire."

Nina had her eyes clenched shut. The pointer was moving in small circles. Kim cast the ceiling a weary glance. "Neen?"

"Shh."

"My hands aren't on the pointer anymore."

She opened her eyes. "It's still moving!"

Kim laughed. "See how far it moves when you take *your* hands away."

She shrugged. "All right then, here." She put her hands in her lap and stared at the pointer. Kim had a quick vision of the board magically slamming itself shut on her nose. It didn't.

Nina gasped suddenly. "It moved!"

Kim gave the ceiling another glance. "Alcohol has pickled your brain, dear," she said, but Nina was staring at it as if attempting to move it with mental force. A thin blue vein began to pulsate on her forehead above her left eye. Kim frowned, having another vision, this time of Neen falling to the floor with a cerebral hemorrhage while blood squirted out her ears, a victim of too much thinking. "It's not going to move, Neen. Take a shower and get yourself dressed." She checked her watch. "Quarter after, Neen, and we have to leave by quarter till. Neen?" She cocked her head, trying to make contact with Nina's eyes. They might as well have been glass.

"Neen?"

Nina looked up then, frowning. "Your life is so dull it even puts the spirits to sleep."

"Why, thank you. But perhaps the board is defective."

"Skeptic."

Kim kept her face neutral; no sense arguing about this psychic crap when there was no way to prove it one way or the other. She checked her watch again and saw the minute hand marching patiently on toward the deadline. "Well, you can be late if you want to, but don't expect me to cover for you," she said, already wondering where her handbag and the car keys inside it might be in this zone of demolition. No doubt buried somewhere amongst all the party mess, she assumed.

Nina grinned. "You always cover for me, Kim old pal. Tell the boss I'm in the basement fixing the furnace."

"In the summertime?"

"The air-conditioning, then."

"They're in the windows."

"The roof? It's been known to leak."

"Jesus God, go take your shower. I'll dream up *something* to say."

Nina put on an exaggerated frown. "My dear lady, lying is a grievous sin."

Kim picked up the Ouija board and slid the pointer off, then slammed it shut with a bang. "So is premarital sex."

Nina nodded, looking suddenly glum. "I guess we're both bound for hell. Has Wayne proposed to you yet? Or does he want to continue this shameless life of sin and debauchery?"

"He's hinted around."

"Will you say yes?"

Kim stood up and smoothed her skirt, uncomfortable with this. "I don't have the slightest idea."

"Perfect!" Nina unfolded the board. "The magic Ouija will guide you. Come, child, and behold its powers."

Kim squeezed her forehead, massaging it against the headache that was coming on. "I am going to kill you in your sleep, Swami," she growled, and began to scout around for her purse and keys, vaguely worrying that she might not find them and would be late for the boring night shift at the motel, or that the manager, Gwendolyn Stone—already there running the show and probably anxious to leave—might snoop around too much and find a certain little secret of Kim's, and fire her on the spot.

Hidden in a drawer under a stack of phone books in Gwendolyn's office was a sheet of paper Kim had been working on for several nights. What was written on it was excruciatingly short, but it was something to do to while away the quiet hours between two and six in the morning, when the whole world seemed to be asleep. It was her resume, which showed a dismal record of eight menial jobs in the three years since she had graduated from high school. Kim had already toyed with the idea of making a thousand copies when it was done, and mailing them to every big city in every state, anything to get out of this town and this rut and an apartment that was really too small for two people and cost really too much for one. The only thing she thought might be holding her back was Wayne, who had started making noises about getting engaged, getting married, maybe living together first. By the looks of her pitiful resume, it didn't seem like a bad offer at all.

Mercifully, Nina wandered off to the bathroom. A minute later the shower started up with a rattle of old pipes. Kim finally found her handbag on the floor under the box the Ouija board had come in, which was under a pile of discarded birthday wrapping paper. She picked up her rather unpromising and nearly empty purse, shook it to see if the keys were inside, which they weren't, and dropped it on the table. The Ouija pointer got knocked slightly aside on the open board and came to rest showing nothing but a blank brown section through its plastic eye.

She stared down at it, feeling bland and lifeless. "Some future," she muttered tiredly, then set out to find her keys.

THREE

PETER KAYE FELL INTO THE STOLEN CHEVETTE WITH ALL THE agility of a rubber dummy, and in a groggy way realized that he had landed on the farmer. He was immediately bucked off and shoved out of the car. He fell heavily to his hands and knees on the overheated street, his knuckles and knees popping in unison, and he let out a yelp. His hair, which had not encountered a comb in nearly a week, fell across his forehead in greasy wet tatters. The shakes had him now, a result of the surprise of being tossed out of his own stolen car and the brief spurt of adrenaline that came with it. The part of his mind that was still able to think with any degree of clarity told him he must look more than casually like a drunk in the grip of the D.T.'s—spit drooling off his lips, his eyes clenched shut against the merry-go-round of the world, arms and legs wobbling, sweat standing out on his skin in a fine beadwork. As a capper his stomach decided to rebel and he threw up a bitter-sour blot of old cheeseburger between his hands.

A shadow draped itself across his own as the farmer worked himself out of the car and straightened. The siren was very close now; above its unlovely music Peter heard Darbi cry out. "Daddy! Daddy!"

He pushed himself up on his knees. Darbi needed him. Everything was a nightmare scramble of sunlight and colors, but Darbi needed him. He homed in on her voice, waddling in a half circle. Suddenly big hands were under his arms, hoisting him upright, more than upright, hoisting him off the ground.

"What the hell did you do to that boy?" Farmer Brown demanded. "I ain't never seen a bruise like that in all my years, and I've seen plenty." He shook Peter, putting out a sweaty aroma that was a blend of pig shit and onion breath. Maybe, Peter thought stupidly as he was rattled back and forth and the siren droned closer, our good farmer ate himself a burger with double onions for lunch. But what about dessert? What about dessert?

"Daddy!"

Oh, yeah, Darbi. Darbi without any ice on her face. Darbi on display like the two-headed lamb or the bearded lady in some cheap sideshow where the midgets walk around in cowboy outfits and the ground is all sawdust and pony manure. Yowza, yowza, step right up and see the amazing frozen black and white kid, only a buck, folks, one slim dollar, and you even get to guess its sex to win a free ride on the Ferris wheel.

"Well?" the farmer barked. Peter's hands had clutched the other man's forearms in a useless duel to set himself free, but it was like battling a tank. The good Mr. Brown was as big and solid as the John Deere tractor he probably drove.

"Let me—go," Peter coughed, batting at those stodgy forearms.

"The cops is a-coming and I want them to see this." He was blowing a fresh batch of onion breath in Peter's face to compete with the hot refinery smell of spilled gasoline. "We got child-molester laws in this state, and a goddamn gun-shooting-in-the-city law too!"

"It's not—what you—think!"

"We'll just wait and see about that."

"Darbi!"

"Daddy!"

"Tell him, tell him . . ."

He heard the sound of ice bags shifting, a couple hitting

the floor with a thud and a splash. Then: *"You let my daddy go!"*

Now Farmer Brown was wobbling around; Peter looked down and saw that Darbi had crawled across the seat and taken the kindly farmer's leg in a bear hug. Her black arm around his thigh gleamed wetly, shiny and loathsome in the sunlight. Side effect of the chemotherapy? She believed it only because Peter kept insisting that it was so.

"Hold on here, kid," the farmer said, trying to shake her off. "I'm going to rescue you."

The three performed a strange boogie-woogie, Mr. B. shaking his leg as if attempting to dislodge a pesky turd before it could slide into his sock, Peter jiggling bonelessly in his hands like a Raggedy Andy doll in the grip of an enraged tot. Darbi added fun to the situation by getting her foot jammed in the steering wheel and pressing the horn button with her shin. Everything was noise and mayhem and hot chrome winking savagely in Peter's eyes.

"Goddammit!" the farmer roared, and dropped him. Peter sank immediately to his knees and jammed his knuckles against his eyes to blot out the light. The panic was beginning to pass at last, releasing brain cells from the grip of a chemistry gone sour. The hissing cauldron that had been his mind began to cool, and with that coolness came the knowledge that he was in danger from more than imagined terrors. The cops were almost here. He dropped his hands and opened his eyes.

The pistol had gotten kicked out of sight. Peter bent down and saw it under the car in a broadening puddle of gas. He wormed under the car, glad for the shade, while hot asphalt cooked his stomach and arms. He got kicked in the side by the dancing farmer, whom Darbi had decided now to bite. His whoops of pain showed that she was getting more than a mouthful of baggy overalls. Peter got the gun in his hand and shoved himself back into the light.

"Whoop!" the estimable Mr. Brown screeched. *"Whoop! Quit it, ya goddamn kid you! Whoop!"*

Peter got up, dodging flailing work boots. His vision was back. He looked down the street toward the bank. Two blue-and-white cop cars were a block away and coming fast, their red cherry-tops winking and flashing, sirens howling. He swiped an arm across his forehead to dislodge the fresh sweat there, and jammed the gun against F.B.'s sizable belly. "Let him go, Darbi."

She disengaged herself from his meaty leg and fell back into the car, gasping. Her lips were smeared with blood as bright as lipstick; Farmer Brown had lost a few mouthfuls of Good Samaritan skin. The leg of his overalls was tattered in spots and wet with multiple blossoms of good Midwestern blood. He screeched and bellowed.

"Shut up," Peter said. "Where's your car at?"

Farmer Brown ducked down and grabbed his bleeding leg, cocking his head to stare into the barrel of the pistol with his eyes crossed. "Blue pickup just over there at the curb," he said, and pointed.

Peter shoved his open hand at him. "Gimme the keys."

He shook his head. "Ain't got no keys."

"You're not going to have a life unless you hand them over," Peter growled, and clicked the hammer back with his thumb while the old question resurfaced in his thoughts: Will I pull the trigger? Will I?

"It's still running," the farmer said, and pointed again. "Blue Dodge, so wore out you don't need a key anymore. You know, I pulled over as soon as I seen the accident but I never expected none of this. What the hell's wrong with the brat anyway? Birth defect?"

Peter ignored him, searching the crowded curbsides for anything that looked blue and running. He spotted the word Dodge on the tailgate of a truck that was more rust than blue. Oily black smoke boiled around it. "Darbi," he said, "grab the trash bag."

She scurried into the back, her pink dress pasted to her multicolored body in spots. She gathered up the trash bag and stuffed the recently added canvas bags inside it while

Peter got his notebook and pen, one eye on the farmer, whom he suddenly wished would go away.

"Beat it," Peter said, jamming things in his pockets.

"Taking my truck, then?"

"That's what it looks like."

The framer frowned suspiciously. "You got any insurance, mac? You ding up my Dodge and you'll be the one who pays, you know. Not to mention my leg."

Peter regarded him incredulously. The sirens were closing in fast. "Get out of my face," he snarled, and pushed him away. The man skidded in the broadening pool of gas and nearly fell over, then began to shout.

"You'll pay, sonny! Nobody steals from Archie Matthews and walks away! Nobody!"

Ah-hah, Peter thought sourly. The sodbuster has a name.

"Nobody!"

Peter helped Darbi out. Her bare feet encountered the broiling pavement and she began to hop from foot to foot, moaning. Peter took the trash bag out of her hands. It was amazingly light. Way too light. "Better take a hike, Archie," he said. "I just might toss a match in all this gasoline. Ever had a hotfoot?"

Archie's eyes got wide. Archie looked down and saw what he was standing in. Archie Matthews departed without so much as a whoop.

"Jump up," Peter said to Darbi, and bent over to offer his arms. She climbed up and he straightened, barely able to hold her with his hands occupied. He began to jog toward the cloud of smoke with the truck inside, Archie's pile of rust and bald tires that no sane insurance company would ever underwrite. The trash bag full of cash swung from his left fist, bouncing crazily against his knees as he ran. The gun felt greasy in his sweating hand. And even in her condition, Darbi was no lightweight anymore.

Tires barked on asphalt. Peter snapped his head around and saw the cops make a noisy halt at the intersection, the scene of thc newest crime. The familiar figure of Archie

Matthews hustled over to give them the news. The cops got out and aimed their guns at the deserted Chevette. This seemed to make Archie very angry. He pointed at Peter and Darbi, who had almost made it to the truck.

The cops jumped back inside their car, bouncing it on its springs. The front wheels cranked themselves to the right. The motor bellowed.

No! It isn't right! It can't end this way!

But it did indeed seem to be right, and seemed about to end. Peter lumbered around to face them, trying to aim his pistol while holding Darbi and the money. He popped off a shot, which punched dead center through the cops' windshield—most certainly not his target, but it made the car screech to a sudden stop. The doors were flung open and the cops crouched behind them. Pistol barrels glinted in the sun, black and deadly.

They shouted something. Peter fired again. The bullet hit the asphalt four feet in front of him, making an elongated crater. Smoke drifted out of it.

The cops fired. New craters burst into existence in front of him, one close enough to spatter his eyes with hot tar. Darbi crunched her face into the hollow of his collarbone, mewling. New fear welled up inside him, fear this time for Darbi. Would they shoot through her to get him? Were they that determined to end the mad crime spree of John Dillinger II?

He fired twice more, aiming toward the Chevette. People were scuttering away, some shielding their heads with their arms. The bullet hit something on the car and ricocheted off with a bright metallic buzz.

Two shots left. The Land of Lincoln was taking its toll. Peter shifted Darbi fully to his left arm, and raised the pistol. He was shaking so hard it nearly jittered out of his hand. He sighted it on one side of the Chevette, aiming low, desperate to get the sights lined up before the cops decided to fire again.

Something hard and hot drove across Peter's left thigh

then, a quick stab of pain followed by a curious numbness. He saw the cops crane around; the shot had come not from them but from a black car just off to the right of the wreckage. Peter saw a large gunmetal-blue pistol being aimed at him again, a regular Dirty Harry cannon with an incredibly long barrel, manned by someone in the car wearing mirrored sunglasses that flashed in the sunlight. Whoever it was—probably a police detective or the like, Peter supposed—shot at him again, a brief flower of hot orange fire blasting out of his huge gun. A fast, angry insect hummed past Peter's ear—a supersonic wasp that could have just as easily flown between his eyes—and crunched through the windshield of a car parked a block away. His leg gave out and he felt himself starting to fall. His only thought was that when he fell he would land on top of Darbi, and that some of her would come off on the hot and unforgiving street, some new piece of flesh that time and heat had turned to mush. He lifted his uninjured leg and stuck it out in front of himself as a prop. His wounded leg had taken on a life of its own and was jerking and spasming while blood drizzled down his Levi's and splattered on the street in ugly red splotches.

He raised the pistol one more time, clutching Darbi with the last of his strength, tottering and gasping. The pistol bucked, jarring his arm, and then fell from his hand.

Before it hit the street, what he had tried with four unsuccessful shots happened at last. The bullet found its mark against the thin sheet metal of the Chevette's rusting hide. On this windless day the fumes of the gasoline had not dispersed, and not enough time had passed for it to dry up. A single spark was what Peter needed, and that was just what he got.

The fireball seemed as huge as the street, as tall as the buildings. It came with a tremendous *whoompf!* that flapped Peter's clothes against his skin, a blast of concussion and heat. Peter shielded Darbi with his arms, hating the heat for her sake but welcoming it for the both of them. The cops and their cars were enveloped momentarily in the blossoming yellow flame, which quickly flared out, leaving a gigantic smoke ring to waft skyward. Someone screamed; Peter thought it might be one of the policemen, who maybe had just discovered that his hair and eyebrows had been vaporized. At any rate, the cops were suddenly too occupied with themselves to bother with any John Dillinger, First *or* Second.

Peter executed a shuffling turn and staggered to the truck. He had to put Darbi down to open the door, then swung it to the musical squeal of hinges that no longer recognized grease. Darbi hopped from foot to foot, her eyes wide with terror. When the door was open she scurried inside, moving faster now as she warmed up. Peter handed the bag to her and clambered onto the running board, grunting. Pain was saying hello to his leg—a mere whisper now, but soon it would be shouting. He plopped down onto the flaking remains of a seat and immediately sunk so deep he could barely see over the dashboard. It didn't matter right now. The truck was running, if you could call it that. At least it was rattling.

He was turning the oversized steering wheel away from the curb when the second explosion came, this one huge and loud, the sound of a blockbuster bomb. He looked back and saw the Chevette launch itself on a spray of flame like a bulky rocket, flip twice in the air trailing smoke in a giant figure eight, and slam upside down on the closest police car, which immediately popped its tires in unison, another terrific bang, and clunked down on its rims. The two policemen had hustled away from the heat and the noise and were beating out imaginary flames on their heads, whapping themselves with their hats. Hubcaps rolled down the sidewalks, rattling and flashing in the light.

Peter checked the steering column, hoping for another bit of luck, which he received. The ancient Dodge had an automatic transmission. No clutch-pushing for his bleeding leg, which was speaking up quite nicely now in a voice that was solid and true and spoke of new agonies to come. He yanked the lever into drive and pulled away from the curb, giving Old Bessie or whatever her name was all the gas she could take. Farting oil smoke, popping and chugging, Peter Kaye's new 1962 Dodge pickup rolled down Fairway Avenue toward its next destination, which would be another town and another store where ice could be bought so that Darbi could be packed tight, and the process of robbing every bank in sight could continue.

By nightfall they were tucked safe from the evening moonlight in a motel parking lot west of St. Louis, the St. Charles Holiday Inn. Darbi had dozed off during the tortuous ordeal of negotiating St. Louis's nightmare freeway system, and Peter was happy for her, worried only that the door she was leaning against in her nest of bags might pop open and spill her out. The day had been endless, like so many previous days had been. They had robbed another Citizen's First Bank in Vandalia, and another outfit called the Community Bank of Edwardsville. These had all been in Illinois, and they all had been successful. The fact that he no longer had a pistol in his pocket seemed to make little difference. Peter was amazed that the banks and the cops could be so blind to his westward progress, and that the God who smiles down on Hopeless Causes had cast some beneficence his way. His luck in the past had been notoriously rotten.

He turned off the truck, which died with a grateful wheeze, and waited in the silence for something to goad him to walk around the building to the front office and register under some hokey name. The truck smelled heavily of rotten foam rubber, gasoline, and dust, a decade of which had accumulated on the dashboard to a quarter-inch depth. There were two plastic quarts of Quaker State motor oil on the passenger-side floor, and Peter guessed he might be using them come morning. The Dodge's gauges were all broken but he had been able to sense the motor trying to bind up. No use being caught on the freeway in a dead vehicle.

He rested his forehead lightly on the bottom quadrant of

the steering wheel, staring at the dark between his feet, listening gratefully to that almost perfect silence, trying not to think about thinking. He believed it had been thinking that screwed him up in the first place, too many days of thinking hopeless, despairing thoughts that seemed to have sprouted like a foul mold from his brain, its roots and spores penetrating deep and deranging everything they touched. He remembered that once upon a time he had actually been happy at the simple joy of being alive and young, a college sophomore who drank an occasional beer now and then and liked to read Goethe in the original German. Major: mathematics. Minor: German language. Go figure it out. Some of the brightest mathemeticians ever to live had been born in that peculiar and baffling land. Modern times had muddled everything. Now international teams with truck-sized computers took calculus to its extreme and postulated new theories of math as it related to the universal constant, which of course it did; another subtopic of his abandoned thesis. But, he wondered, why worry about academics when the anvil of reality had been dropped off the nearest convenient skyscraper and hit the unwary academician named Peter Gary Kaye smack on top of the head? Who gave a shit if there was a universal constant? A bullet had a constant of its own, and there was no arguing with it. His leg, which he had wrapped with a greasy rag he'd found under the seat, barked at him with a regular throb—a constant pulse beat. The rag was drenched with blood, but it was old blood already turning brown. The officer's bullet had scraped a deep trench, hardly fatal, which was sloppy police work, in Peter's judgment. Commissioner, reprimand that man.

He almost grinned. Five states terrorized in five days. Not bad for an imitation crook. He leaned sideways and dug a hand through the cash in the bag on the floor, got a fistful, and opened his door slowly, letting the squeaks escape in rusty twangs that wouldn't awaken Darbi, although she didn't awaken easily. Hers was more like a coma than sleep. After a few shouts into the ear and a few shakes she built herself slowly back together, conscious thought by conscious thought, a dazed See-Threepio reassembling itself chunk by chunk into a recognizable robot entity. He had listened to her breathing during more than one sleepless night on a motel bed and found that she would quit for spaces of five minutes, give or take, but invariably start in again with a pronounced snore. The ice would slosh in her bathtub. Sometimes she would mutter in her sleep, dark, mysterious words that made no sense, a language of the dead and the dying. The smell of her breath was becoming more and more putrid, something like the stink of old potatoes rotting in a damp cellar. No surprise there; it was, after all, the end of the fifth day.

He eased himself out, clutching the steering wheel until he found his balance, able to feel a drowsy sort of heat gently cooking out of the parking lot, that nearly overwhelmed him with a need to sleep. With a gentle push he shut the door, letting the squeaks out one at a time, knowing that Darbi would sleep through them but not sure enough of it. Sometimes when she woke up she screamed, God only knew why—and she didn't know either. Perhaps she was dying bit by bit, her soul shuttling itself off to heaven or hell one slice at a time; he had no way of knowing. Perhaps John Braine knew—he was, after all, the director and producer of this show—but most likely he didn't. Like he'd said, this procedure is awfully damned new, and you'd better be very sure you want it.

Peter had been sure. He didn't like the idea of letting them drill a hole in Darbi's head, didn't like having to borrow three grand from his dad and floating a two-grand loan at the university credit union that would never be repaid, but the alternative was to stick Darbi in the ground in one of those horrifying kid-size coffins that had no right to exist in a universe that had a constant, and water her flowers with tears—then trot off to the funny farm, where insanity got your ticket punched to free room and board for life.

When the door latch had clunked into place Peter buried the wad of money in a pocket and hobbled to the motel sidewalk, almost glad for the pain in his thigh as a distracting agent against the more serious pains in his head, which fortunately had quit trying to kill him since the incident at the intersection in Effingham. Panic attack of the day over with, all systems go, he thought dourly as he walked. Tomorrow we will rehearse the act again. He made his way along the long stretch of sidewalk that bordered the three-story motel, glancing around himself with the cautionary eye of the unpracticed criminal. The air was heavy with the scent of fresh summer flowers that were putting off pollen in a nearby field, honeysuckle overriding them all, sweet as sugar. Peter breathed deeply as he walked, and pretended he was okay, nothing had happened, he was twenty again and Brenda was eighteen and they were checking into the motel in Vermont and snow was on the ground outside. The bus that took them there had had chains on its rear tires and smelled like the in side of an ashtray. Not romantic, but being a student on the dole of the student-loan program tended to keep the Mercedes and Cadillacs where they belonged.

I'm so nervous, she had said.

Here's the threshold. Number Two Twenty-one. Hop on, my love, and I will transport you to heaven.

This promise he had kept. Nine months later she was a corpse in addition to being a mother at eighteen, and Peter was headed for mental bankruptcy another year down the road. Darbi's turn would come later, when the preposterousness of cancer had swatted her out of childhood like some pesky fly and landed her here, in the truck, chilled to something approaching thirty-five degrees by fifteen dollars worth of bagged ice.

He came near the brightly lighted front of the motel, not particularly concerned that he was dressed almost in rags or that his left thigh was bound with a dirty red cloth. All he wanted was a room with a bed and a bathtub, and directions to the ice machine. At the front corner of the motel decency stopped him long enough to make him at least run his hands through his hair. They came away shiny with grease, and he rubbed them on his pants, which were likewise greasy. It hadn't taken long to learn that it was pretty hard to take a shower or wash his clothes with the bathtub full of Darbi and ice. He decided that tonight he would use the bathroom sink to finally unload the grime; his own smell was beginning to bother him. It had already occurred to him that his underwear would probably come off only with the aid of a paint scraper or wire brush, maybe some turpentine. Ouch.

Thinking of this almost made him smile. Another torturous day was over. He was not in jail and he was not dead. Darbi was still with him. And as always, come evening, the panic and the dread left him alone for a while, gave him time to rebuild his resources for the next session.

He went around the corner, squinting under the bright glare of the alcove's floodlights. A cherry-red BMW loaded with luggage was parked there while its owner was inside. It would be a fine car to steal, a sleek little machine that might even outrun police cars if it came down to that, but he was just too tired to be horsing around with grand theft tonight. First get a room, put Darbi in the tub, and then go find some grub and perhaps a small bottle of elixir to quiet the nerves. Kentucky Fried Chicken with a bourbon and Coke sounded nice. Hell, he thought, anything sounds nice after four days of hamburgers.

He came to the glass quadruple doors and peeked inside. It was all posh and potted palms, businessmen in suits amiably chatting about whatever businessmen in suits chatted about. A cocktail waitress wearing a black miniskirt breezed out of the lounge and disappeared down a hallway. He could hear muted music being played inside, no doubt in the dim poshness of the lounge, some obscure group nobody ever heard of crooning out lounge tunes nobody ever heard of. Nothing was unusual. No cops on patrol. He swung the door open and made his way to the desk, aware of the stares he was getting from the minor-league Rockefeller types. The BMW driver breezed past him as if he weren't there and went outside to his car. Well, Peter mused without humor, screw him and his cohorts. If they knew how much cash I have in the truck they would scatter rose petals at my feet.

He came to the desk and leaned on it, favoring his bum leg. Against the air-conditioned motel smell of fine carpets and deodorized air his body odor seemed to be rising off him like warm swamp gas. He swore he would wash himself and his clothes tonight. Then if he got gunned down tomorrow he would make a sweet-smelling corpse if nothing else.

He was looking down at the top of a young woman's head. She was busy writing something on a pad. Peter cleared his throat, and she looked up. "Hi there," she said in a sprightly tone, and stood up. "Can I help you?"

"Sure can," Peter said, and put on a big smile that he hoped didn't look as phony as it felt. This chick was pretty. "I need a single. Ground floor, close to the ice machine. I've got a bad knee, see."

"Oh, okay." Her eyes remained professionally calm, though he did see her nostrils flare a bit as his B.O. walked its way into her nose. She produced a small carbon form and shoved it at him. He got the pen-on-a-chain out of its holder and checked in as Albert Olsen, a name that drifted into his head from the great beyond of imagination. For type of car and license plate number he invented something about a 1989 Dodge with Wyoming plates. He signed the slip and handed it back.

She stuck it in a slot on the cash register, which began to jingle and make the giant-mosquito buzz of dot matrix printing. In a zip it was all done. "Forty-two-ninety," she said.

Peter dug out a fifty. "Keep the change," he said, broadening his smile. "I know they don't pay you enough in this joint."

She winked at him. "Tell me about it." She reached under the desk and brought out a key on a big hexagon of plastic. It bore the number 126 in gold letters. "Go back out the front, take a right, and another right. Twelve doors down. The ice machine is in the walk-through next to your room. Will you need a wake-up call?"

He shook his head. "The shape I'm in, I need all the sleep I can get. When's checkout?"

"Usually eleven, but I can get you extended till two."

"Do that, will you?" He dug out a damp and wrinkled ten, and shoved it over to her. "That's for being nice."

Her eyes widened. "Golly, thanks."

"Under all this dreck I'm actually a nice guy." He laughed without feeling, turned, and lurched away. He heard her call out to him.

"Mr. Olsen?"

For a moment it didn't register; the memory of writing that alias had already gone down the drain.

"Albert?"

It came to him then, and he shuffled around.

"Do you need any first aid for that leg? It looks pretty bad."

He looked down at the filthy rag encircling his thigh. "I don't think so. A bail of barbed wire fell off a truck I was loading and scraped me up. I'll survive."

"So you drive a truck? Sounds hard."

"Hard?" He thought about it. He couldn't make a big rig move one inch, not with its five hundred gears and engine the size of an elephant. "It isn't bad."

"As long as you're not hauling barbed wire, huh?" She laughed a little. He laughed a little with her. When they were done they were smiling at each other with absolutely nothing to say. To Peter's relief the doors burst open and another Holiday Inn girl breezed in. "Better late than never," the second girl called out, and Peter turned back to the door, glad for the interruption. He was about to open it when heels clicked on the tiles behind him and a warm hand laid itself on his shoulder. He flinched back with an unintended gasp.

"You can keep it," the first young woman said, handing him a blue and white Johnson's first-aid kit. "We've got a dozen of them."

"Thanks," he murmured, shaken. The old nerves were getting back into the act, making him skittish. "Thanks a lot."

She eyed him with remarkably pretty green eyes. "What's dreck, anyway?"

"German for filth. Yiddish too. Yiddish for the stuff I'm covered with."

She smiled. "You are a bit gamy right now."

He grinned at her, this time genuinely. "Catch me in the morning." He looked at her name tag. "See you later, Kim."

"Yeah. Well, bye-bye."

He went through the doorway, wondering idly what this Kim saw in him to be so nice, and why she even cared. Because he was a big tipper? Mr. Megabucks? Maybe. Maybe not. Maybe she had a thing for wounded veterans of the bank wars. It occurred to him that he might be handsome, even in this wretched state. What a laff riot. Beneath the bones of his face lurked a dark and ugly second self, perhaps two of them, though Peter the Third was a mere tickle in his brain, a mysterious, malignant embryo who would choose its own time and place to be born. Peter did not look forward to meeting him. Peter the Second was a loudmouth, a smug coward. Peter the Last might be a combination of Hitler, Stalin, and Jack the Ripper; he might be an angel. Whoever he was, he would show himself when the time came.

He came to the truck, started it, and parked in the slot marked 126.

By ten o'clock Darbi was in the tub, moaning softly as she always did. Peter had emptied most of the ice bags into a foot of cold tap water, put her in, and hauled four big buckets from the ice machine. She came awake a minute later. Up to her shoulders in ice water, she reminded Peter of a pitiful sea lion pup stuck in an ice hole in the Arctic; only sea lions had fur and fat and Darbi had none of those. He dunked his hand in the water and guessed it to be about forty degrees. Good enough. He sat on the edge of the tub and laid the last bag on top of her head. Her large blue eyes swiveled up to meet his.

"It hurts, Daddy."

He nodded grimly. "I know."

"Why do I have to stay in here? It's cold." She tried to sit up. Peter pushed her firmly back down. Water and ice cubes sloshed.

"You do what your dad says, girl. It's part of the cancer treatment. You do want to be well again, don't you?"

"But I feel fine," she whined. "Just frozen."

"No more pain? The old pain, I mean?"

"It's gone. My stomach feels okay. How did I get out of the hospital?"

"We've been through it before, Darbi. You were asleep and I carried you out."

"But the doctor said that—"

"Forget the doctors," Peter almost shouted. Every evening she went through the same rigamarole, asked the same questions. She wanted him to explain the impossible, and he would sooner cut his tongue out than tell her. "Now just sit still," he said more gently. "I'll turn up the TV so you can hear it. I have to go out and buy some things."

"What things?"

"Supper, for one."

She arched the fine yellow fuzz that was her new eyebrows. "Do I get some tonight? I haven't eaten for . . ." She frowned. "I don't remember. But I'm not hungry, Daddy. How come?"

"The medicine," he said—lying, of course, grappling with the guilt and the doubt. "The medicine is like food for you, but we're starving that cancer to death. Won't it be great when it's gone?"

She pondered that. "Then can I get out of this ice?"

He nodded. "A few more days, babe. Just a few more." It was not a lie. A few more days and she would be dead.

She nodded, and blew out a small sigh. "Few more days. Okay. Don't be gone too long, Daddy. I get scared alone."

He bent down and kissed her on the white side. No prejudice there. If he kissed the black side he might come away with a piece of her face stuck to his lips. And then she would scream like she had screamed the night the pad of her thumb dropped off, mad with panic, a tiny banshee struggling wildly to get away from a tub and a terror she wasn't able to understand. It's just the medicine doing its work, he had told her again and again as she kicked and screamed in his arms. It's fighting the cancer.

Somehow, she'd bought it. With the innocent trust of a six-year-old, she'd bought it. The Band-Aids helped immeasurably. Now they had sloughed off, and she seemed not to notice her ragged thumb and the twig of bone lying exposed inside it.

He stood up. "If somebody knocks on the door, you keep quiet."

"Standard procedure?"

He had to smile. "Right. Standard procedure."

"Okay." Her teeth were chattering loudly now. "Tuh-tuh-tallyho, Daddy."

"Sure, babe. Tallyho."

He went out, remembering to turn the television on loud enough for her to hear. The only thing worth watching was a rerun of *Family Ties,* and he knew she liked it so he left it on, blasting away for her benefit. The trash bag of money was stuffed under the bed—not exactly a strongbox, but what thief would expect to find a cool hundred grand or so under a motel bed? The first-aid box sat on the dresser, unused. He had snapped it open, scouted through it, but the aseptic smell of pure sterility had been somehow too strange. Maybe after he got washed up, he'd decided, and so there it sat.

He shut the door and locked it, tested the knob once, pocketed the key, then turned to where Old Bessie sat waiting. Only . . . Bessie wasn't waiting anymore. Her parking space was empty save for a sickly puddle of black motor oil on the pavement.

Peter gaped. Someone had swiped Old Bessie. Her battered ignition slot performed magically without benefit of a key, but no man in his right mind would steal an abomination like Bess. It had only been twenty or thirty minutes since Peter pulled the last melted bag of ice out and tossed it in the dumpster behind the building. Could a crook pull such a stunt right under his nose? He snorted. Sure, anything on this earth was possible nowadays. Even college grad students were turning to crime.

He found that he was growing immensely angry. Fine society this, he fumed. Everybody was out to stick the other guy. How could some sleazebag simply waltz up and steal another man's truck, especially one that had been such trouble to steal in the first place? Probably some teenage punk, some Midwestern James Dean. If there was any poetic justice in it, it was a pill too bitter to swallow. He turned and jammed the room key back in the doorknob, kicked the door open, and stalked inside, simmering with the righteous rage of a man who knows he ought to laugh at himself and his absurd situation but is too mad to do it.

Darbi was sitting on the bed wrapped in a big white Holiday Inn towel, watching TV. Her head snapped around at the noise and she stared at Peter with large eyes.

"Daddy, I . . ."

"Get back in that bathtub!" he shouted.

"But Daddy, it's too . . ."

"Now!"

She began to cry. "I can't do it anymore, Daddy, it makes me too cold and it hurts and I just want to sleep in a real bed and get warm."

He gave her a dark, flat stare. "You don't know, do you?" He slammed the door shut with a foot. "You don't have the slightest idea, do you? Do you think we're on a picnic? Do you think we're on this trip for fun and games?" He was boiling inside now, not so much at Darbi but at the lousy luck of having his transportation stolen by some Missouri punk. It came to him that old Archie Matthews might be just as mad, but at least Peter had given him the courtesy of letting him know who the thief was. Hell, the man was probably a celebrity about now.

"Just get in that tub, girl," he said as levelly as possible, and she went, slump-shouldered and sobbing. He heard water and ice shift as she sat down.

"Cover up your head," he barked, and heard more ice move. His stomach was a burning hole and his brain was screaming for a pill or a drink or both. He intended to oblige those urges even if he had to walk ten miles.

He went to the bathroom doorway first and leaned against the jamb. "Listen, Darbi," he said as the anger fragmented and reassembled itself into a vague burden of guilt. "Darbi, look, hey, you know I can't stay mad at you. Someday you'll understand all this, but for now, please, *do what I say*. Okay?"

She didn't answer. Peter nodded to himself, not surprised. She was entitled to moods of her own. He went back outside, stoop-shouldered and glum, eased the motel door shut until the latch clicked, and started the long, hobbling walk to the splash of color and noise that was downtown St. Charles. There was still so much to do tonight. Eat, get a little drunk maybe, steal a car or at least look for a likely one, and take a sponge bath. Then some sleep, if it came, and tomorrow it would all start over again.

FOUR

Less than ten minutes before Peter Kaye came out of his Holiday Inn room and discovered to his unhappiness that Old Bessie was gone, a short, scrawny-looking scarecrow of a man named Jared Brooks had crept purposefully up to her with nothing very legal in mind, making his way from a car hidden in the darkness of an empty field behind the parking lot, where honeysuckle grew in wild profusion, to the space in front of Room Number 126, and Bess. Jared Brooks had opened the door of the truck ever so slowly, patiently letting the squeaks come and go, had climbed in and found to his pleasure that the truck did not need his hot-wiring talents, and stolen it. At this point Darbi was sitting in a few inches of cold water with the tap gushing full blast, and Peter was in the walk-through shoveling ice into a small white container. Above the noise of the ice as he worked with it, and the hum of the eight vending machines that lined the walls, Peter heard nothing unusual. To some people Bess's grumbling, popping protestations would not have been recognizable as a motor being cranked; she sounded more like an iron lung gasping its last. Jared drove out of the parking lot and turned left toward the last businesses on this side of town, and the dark empty plain beyond in the south.

A moment later his partner, Steve Rafter, followed him in the shiny new Ford Escort they had both arrived here in, bouncing through the field with the headlights off, crushing honeysuckle under its brand-new Goodyear steel radials, tires that emerged onto the asphalt of the parking lot smeared yellow and green and smelling very fine indeed. Steve Rafter himself was not an impressive-looking man, no more impressive than Jared Brooks. Standing five-eight in his wing-tips, he had thinning brown hair lying lifelessly on his small round head, eyes that were perpetually squinted from spending too many years of his life under the sun, and a mouth that was turned down in a dissatisfied little frown almost all the time.

They had arrived here nearly on Peter Kaye's heels, had been, in fact, patiently following him from the day his bizarre cross-country crime wave began in New York State. In Illinois earlier today both Steve Rafter and his skinny partner, Jared Brooks, had nearly lost the trail when Peter exploded the car and all traffic ground to a halt for more than half an hour. A man wearing Osh-Kosh B'Gosh pinstripe overalls had been more than glad to tell them and anyone else within range which way Peter went, as well as the make of truck and the license-plate number and the depth of his indignation. He'd also given these interesting details to local cops, at which point the State Police had been called in and a very determined manhunt begun.

This was very bad news for the two partners named Jared and Steve. The last thing they wanted—the *very* last thing—was to see Peter Kaye get caught. Jared had asked two days ago why they didn't just run him off the road, ask him where in the fuck he was going, and report back to their field office in New York City that the guy with the kid was headed for Bumfuck, Egypt, and could we please come home, we'd like to see our wives and kiddies before we get old.

In reality five days on the road were not all that severe; both had tailed people, cars, and criminals much farther than this during the course of their careers as Federal Bureau of Investigation field agents. The bad thing about this one—the thing that made this case so maddening—was that they had to sit back and watch while the tall blond fellow popped bank after bank, then do their best to throw the cops off the trail. It was enough to make you sick.

It had been Newell Jackson, their immediate superior, who had called them in unexpectedly and handed them this case last Monday afternoon. Newell, big and robust and tall, a man who enjoyed working out with weights and flexing in front of mirrors, had invited both Jared and Steve into his office and had explained their assignment. Steve had always felt uneasy around the big man, both because he himself was shorter by half a foot and lighter by sixty pounds, and because Newell Jackson had been promoted ahead of him though he was younger. It had been based solely on physiques, Steve knew, and it galled him and woke him up nights with his pillow crushed between his hands and cool sweat shiny on his skin.

"This is a very old case," Newell had told the partners, sitting casually on the edge of his big desk and towering over them as they sat crunched in low chairs in front of him. He handed them each a bulky manila folder. "It started back in 1968," he went on, nodding to indicate they should open their folders and follow along. His office was big, his window (not many agents were lucky enough to have one) was big, even his secretary was big. Pretty too. It didn't take a Rhodes scholar to see that life had handed Newell Jackson a good brain and a body to match. Steve himself had barely squeaked through training, even punier then than he was now. It had not taken long for him to dislike Newell Jackson. "In that year we were swamped with more investigations than we could handle," Newell said. "Of course neither of you, or me for that matter, were with the department at that time. Myself, I was bagging chicks in high school."

He chuckled amiably, looking for a response, blue eyes sparkling whereas Steve's were a lackluster brown, muscles taut and healthy under his suit whereas Steve's were small and saggy, jaw firm and set whereas Steve's own was weak and prone to trembling without much provocation. How Steve hated him.

"Anyway, in 1968 a rich young fellow named John Thomas Braine—that's his name there at the top in capitals—John Thomas Braine was involved in a fledgling corporation called New Future Cryogenics, and—yes, Jared?"

Jared, who had raised a hesitant hand, cleared his throat and shifted in his chair. He was not much smarter than Steve, though neither man was stupid, and physically he was mercifully smaller than Steve, though this didn't seem to trouble him at all. "What's this crying—cryo—whatever it is, what is it?"

"Good question," Newell said, which he usually did no matter how stupid Steve happened to find the question. He suspected this was done simply to irritate him. "Cryogenics is a relatively new branch of science that I consider about two points up from a crematorium, and much less useful. What these cryogenic outfits do is freeze you after you die, keep you frozen for as long as your money is good, and pocket a handsome profit no matter what the outcome."

"Why freeze dead bodies?" Jared asked, and Steve was pleased to realize that he already knew the answer. He jumped in before pesky Newell had a chance to reply.

"Some people believe a frozen body can be successfully thawed when future technology advances far enough, and by then they hope man has invented a way to bring the dead back to life."

"Good answer, Steve," Newell said, nodding, which made Steve feel uncomfortably flattered. "There seems to be enough rich people in this country who can afford the huge fees that are charged to keep the cryogenics outfits going. In 1968 the technology was a little shaky, though, yet people were still willing to pay that fee. I guess when you're dead anyway it doesn't matter much where the hell your fortune goes."

"Right," Jared said enthusiastically, and Steve threw him a disgusted glance. What a suck-up.

"What happened to our boy Braine is this. He had eleven underground vaults in northern California, and three of them lost their ability to keep nitrogen cold and human bodies frozen. Something about failed compressors—it's in the reports. About thirty of the bodies were unrecoverable, something about high-pressure explosions—it's in the reports as well. We were called in by the local police investigators because many of the bodies had been shipped to California from all parts of the country, East Coast, north, south, whatever. Braine called them *clients,* to make himself feel more like a businessman and less like an undertaker, I'd guess. There was a lot of hubbub, some news coverage, but it was 1968 and there was still Vietnam, race riots, campus riots, the whole pile of shit. With two hundred boys dying every week in the jungles, who gave a shit if thirty corpses got frozen or dropped in a blender or sliced thin and put on whole wheat buns? As far as the FBI went, it was a matter for the D.C. lawyers to handle."

He paused to reach across his desk and get an 8 x 10 photo, which he held at his chest for Steve and Jared to see. "This is a shot of the interior of one of the vaults." He pulled a mechanical pencil out of a pocket and used it as a pointer. "These blotches of dark stuff on the walls are exploded corpses. All those metal coffin-things with all the bones and stuff are the containers where the bodies were kept frozen."

Jared leaned forward, squinting. He too had spent plenty of time on the sunny road. "The ones that aren't exploded look all bent and stuff, except that first one, the open one there," he said. "It's only a little crooked looking."

Newell moved his pencil to point at it. "Very good, Jared. This was the one coffin that got Braine in a pile of trouble. The forensic specialists knew what had happened right away, but it took Braine a while to admit it. See, that particular corpse housed in there was his own uncle. Thing was, Old Man Braine had been very much alive when he was frozen. After he thawed out he even lived for a few minutes, we think, but of course he was inside the container with no way out. He died, so the medical examiner's people said—it's in your reports—from a combination of lack of oxygen, damage from the freezing itself, and raw terror. His heart gave out."

"Blecchh," Jared said, making a face. "What happened after that?"

"Well, there wasn't much we could do to the younger Braine for all the dead bodies he'd collected. Everybody had signed a lengthy contract before they died, except, of course, the uncle. Technically, when Braine's machines went haywire and blew up, he was in breach of contract. None of the corpses had any complaints, though, so our D.C. lawboys built a case around the uncle. It was pretty tight. Braine hired himself a batch of good lawyers, and then they went at it.

"The case took years. Meantime Braine had gotten disgusted with the whole affair and handed everything over to his partner in Sacramento, whom I doubt very much wanted it all that bad. The partner and Braine held tight to their story meanwhile, and that story said the uncle volunteered to be frozen alive. Since there is no way to thaw somebody out and have them live for more than a minute or two, it was considered just plain murder. It was like somebody telling you they wanted to commit suicide, so you shot them to save them the trouble. You've still murdered the person."

"Right," Jared said, making Steve grit his teeth.

"But here was the catch. The uncle woke up before he was supposed to. It might have been the first documented case in history where anything other than an embryo or a test tube full of sperm was frozen and then thawed out alive. So the freezing hadn't killed the old man, the damned metal coffin had. And who made the coffin? The partner in Sacramento, natch, since he was the scientist and Braine was the financier. Suddenly the case was shifted to him. His name was, uh . . ."

Jared was digging through his manila folder. "Dr. Henry Austerwahl," he said proudly.

"Very good," Newell said. "The focus of the case was shifted to Austerwahl. Problem was, *he* didn't have any motive to kill the old guy, except maybe that Braine would inherit his uncle's millions and contribute more to the business, but that's pure conjecture. So this is what the lawyers had: Austerwahl with no motive, Braine without the technical know-how to do it alone."

Jared looked up from his folder. "Since the uncle wasn't actually dead while he was kept frozen, how did John Braine expect to get the old geezer's money? A will isn't good until you die."

Newell smiled. "Another good one, Jared. It seems the uncle signed his entire fortune to his nephew John Thomas Braine *two days* before they froze his ass. Lock, stock, and barrel, every bit of it handed over."

"Mighty odd," Jared mused. "Coercion?"

Newell shrugged. "Don't know. And to throw another monkey wrench in the works, it turned out a company named Bradforde Industries, which built the unreliable machinery in the first place, was at fault for the breakdown. But they sure as hell didn't have any motive, and lost their good reputation due to the press coverage the case got, which was limited, but still enough. Basically what was left was the finger pointing at three suspects, but the cases against them were weak."

Steve found that he was sufficiently interested in this to ask a question, even if it was the insufferable Charles Atlas named Newell Jackson who would answer it. "I assume the case never came to trial," he said. "So what's Braine up to now?"

Newell pushed an open hand toward him, shaking his head. "Hold off, Steve. The case actually *did* go to trial, in the winter of 1971. The defendant was John Thomas Braine."

"Huh?" Steve grunted, simmering inside a bit from the brush-off. "I thought you said the partner in California was the bad guy, and that company with the junky freezing machines too. How'd Braine get dragged back in?"

The corners of Newell's mouth curved up a bit in a dour smile. "It seems our lawmen in D.C. did some digging even though it looked like nothing was left to be dug. Guess who turned out to be the principal stockholder in Bradforde Industries?"

Jared snorted. "Our good Mr. Braine, I'd say. He had the old man tagged for death from two directions. If the freezing didn't kill him, the thawing out would. Did he hire somebody to sabotage his own machines?"

"It was never proven one way or the other, and you can bet Braine denied even *knowing* the company was his. But see, if he'd frozen thirty or forty people with the same machines *before* he froze his uncle, he would have been in the clear. Unfortunately for him, his uncle was the first human they froze. It was Braine's first underground vault, and Uncle Dearest was the first victim."

"Ah-ha," Jared said softly.

"It went to trial, the jury deliberated only twenty minutes, and when they came back the paper in the foreman's hand said guilty of murder in the third degree. Braine appealed, of course, but in the end he went to prison for a few years."

All three men thought about this in silence. Outside, eight stories down, life in New York went on about its noisy business.

Steve took a long breath and let it out. "How about my question now, Newell? What's Braine up to these days?"

"Well," Newell said, rocking a bit on his perch, "Braine's in his fifties now, busy running his empire, which I guess doesn't take a lot of running. He's the big chief who sits on his ass and makes big bucks for nothing."

Sort of like you, Steve Rafter thought bitterly.

"We've been doing periodic checks on Braine, and especially his one-time partner Austerwahl. During the years after the trial all of the Bradforde units eventually went haywire, and the business ceased to exist. Braine requested, and got, a new trial based on the fresh evidence that the Bradforde units were self-destructing and had not been monkeyed with. Braine won, and went back home. Austerwahl now lives somewhere between here and the Pacific Ocean, if you get me. Braine stays at his estate in Pennsylvania."

"Good boys now, huh?" Jared said.

Newell shook his head. "No, not good boys anymore. Six times in the last eighteen months Austerwahl has either flown or taken a bus to Harrisburg, P.A., where he spends his time at Braine's mansion. God knows what they're cooking up, or have cooked up. Probably cryogenics again."

"After getting burned like that?" Steve said with a frown. "He must be nuts."

Newell nodded. "You have to remember that cryogenics technology is a billion years ahead of what it used to be, thus not so unpredictable anymore. Someone in New Hampshire froze a rhesus monkey some months ago, thawed it out in premeasured stages, and brought it back to life for about ten minutes before it died of a zillion internal hemorrhages. It's only a matter of time before it can be done on humans, hopefully with more success, but we won't live to see it, I'll wager."

Jared slapped his folder shut. "So what do we do? Stake out Braine's place? What are we looking for?"

"Hold on," Newell said. "There's more, but first I'm getting me a cup of coffee. Jared? Steve?"

Jared got up and followed him to the corner of the spacious office where the Mr. Coffee sat on a small table sending out fragrant steam. Steve stayed where he was with an elbow on his knee and his chin propped on his hand, his fingers covering his mouth and a frown on his face as he thought about this cryogenic stuff. If it was really as advanced as Newell said, it would be a nice alternative to rotting eternity away in a coffin. Perhaps it would be easier to die if there was the hope of waking up someday, maybe even living forever if man had come that far, developed an injection or pill against aging. Something to consider, anyway. Maybe he'd even talk to Braine about it, if they happened to meet during this case. But one thing Steve knew for sure. If he got himself frozen he sure as hell wasn't going to have his wife Marilyn frozen with him. Talk about a nag.

The two men came back and resumed their positions, Jared in the chair to Steve's left, Mr. Hotshot Newell sitting on the edge of his desk in front of them. "Okay," he said, "here's what we know so far about Braine's and/or Austerwahl's latest moves. Like I already told you two, he and Austerwahl have started meeting each other for the first time in twenty years. We're safe to assume, I think, that they are both up to their old antics. Fortunately, there isn't an old uncle to murder this time—I still believe it was intentional—but now it may turn out to be even worse. We had no trouble planting a mole in the Braine corporate empire, and he feeds us tantalizing info once in a while."

Jared raised his hand. "How tantalizing, Newell?"

"Good question, Jared."

Jesus Christ, Steve thought, disgusted, why don't you two just kiss?

"A year ago Bradforde Industries changed its name to Acme Tool and Die. I know. How clever of them. They also began manufacturing and testing large nitrogen compressors of the sort necessary for a long-term installation in, say, an underground cryogenics vault. Eight weeks ago one was shipped to a secret location out West. We weren't expecting it and had no time to organize any kind of trace. And now, several of Braine's elderly friends, and some of his corporate people facing retirement, have disappeared from the face of the earth. I think we're safe to assume they've been frozen."

"Frozen alive?" Steve blurted.

"Yep. I would say Braine is tucking away some of his best people, who will, if you can trust my guesswork, be thawed out later to keep the empire rolling smoothly. Any day I expect to hear that Braine himself is gone, but it hasn't happened yet, not to him or Austerwahl, who's pushing seventy now."

"Okay then," Steve said, "I understand it now. We keep an eye on Braine's visitors, his business associates, everybody including his gray-haired mother. If he or they suddenly start heading West, we catch the same flight, and tail them. I'm right, aren't I, Newell?"

"Not at all, Steve. Braine is too crafty after his years in the pokey to be sloppy about this new operation. When those people vanished, I mean they *vanished*. No trace. Nothing. The only thing we find more peculiar than that is the fact that none of the missing people have any relatives to speak of. A man or woman with family would be crazy to go for the freezing routine—who wants to outlive their own kids, for God's sake? But even if we succeeded in locating these people, they'd be frozen and not biologically dead yet."

"Okay then," Steve snapped, tired of throwing mental darts and not once hitting the board. "What do we do?"

Newell stared into his coffee cup for a moment. "Braine visited Dutchess County Memorial Hospital in Poughkeepsie yesterday morning. Very unusual for him—a first, really—because he *never* leaves home anymore. He was accompanied by a man we've identified as one Peter Gary Kaye, whose daughter was in that hospital dying of cancer, and another fellow who could be Genghis Khan for all we know. Our civilian tag followed Braine back home, unfortunately, instead of following Peter Kaye. He vanished along with his daughter late last night."

Steve glanced at Jared, who was glancing at him. "So?" Steve demanded.

"His daughter died that afternoon at five o'clock. Her body was stolen from the hospital morgue in the basement, sometime between dark and dawn last night."

"Yuck," Jared said. "What did he do with her?"

"We can only guess, Jared, but you don't need to be Einstein's twin brother to figure it out. Kaye struck a deal with Braine to have his daughter frozen after she died. I didn't know at first *how* he was supposed to get her to the facility in secret, wherever it is, but after the First National in Poughkeepsie was robbed today by Peter Kaye and no one else, I began to figure things out. Kaye is—was—a graduate student at Marist College there. I had Akers drop by and talk to his landlord first—said Kaye didn't have a pot to piss in and was three months behind on the rent. Upstairs Akers found some kind of unfinished book or report dealing with mathematics, and not much else. There were some empty prescription bottles in the cabinets and the trash. Akers tracked down his doctor at home, a shrink. Said he didn't know anything, Kaye just had some minor troubles with depression, not a psycho and not to worry about him. But see, Kaye's already robbed three banks this morning alone. The cops have a positive ID on him and his car, a green 1977 Gremlin, of all things. I've already done my best to keep them from hunting him down like a dog, and I need you two to follow him and make sure he gets where he's going. It seems he's armed himself somehow but so far he hasn't shot anybody."

"Whoa," Steve interrupted. "You want us to *help* the bastard?"

"That's right, I do. Don't hold up the banks for him, but try to keep him out of other trouble."

Steve sagged deeper into his chair, scowling, while Jared perked up. "When he gets where he's going, we'll know where Braine's new vault is."

"Good answer, Jared, damn good answer. We use our influence and our muscle to keep the cops as far away as possible."

"Yeah? What if he shoots somebody?" Steve growled.

Newell shook his head slightly. "We'll deal with that when the time comes, which I hope it won't. Kaye is not a killer; if he decides to become one, we grab him and try to squeeze the info out of him with, ah, persuasion." He stood up, rubbing his hands briskly together. "We know where he is now, which is only about ten miles or so into P.A. on 80 West. You'll have plenty of time to catch up with him because he spends most of his time standing in line at the banks." He laughed. "Poor bastard."

Steve stood up with Jared, confused and not liking it. "What the hell is the guy robbing banks for? Recreation?"

"Hardly," Newell said. "That poor bastard is trying to get enough cash to pay Braine to freeze his daughter's corpse when he gets there. You gotta admit he's a dedicated daddy."

"Nuts," Steve grunted. "I thought he was supposed to get her there in secret, but now he's becoming very publicized. What happened?"

"That is a very good question, Steve, to which I have no answer. I can only guess that Braine is one scared man about now. Instead of being secretive, Peter Kaye is making himself one of the most notorious bank robbers of this new decade. When we get him I'm going to shake his hand and then put him in prison for a thousand years, if possible, and Braine along with him, if possible."

"Sounds like both of them have bats in their belfry," Steve said.

"Maybe so. If you have any more questions, read the files. Me, I'm going home early and get the barbecue ready for the office party this evening."

"Office party?" Steve said. "Office party?"

Newell laughed, then looked humorously apologetic. "The office party you boys are going to miss, I guess. I'm surprised nobody mentioned it to you, but then, you'll be on the road anyway." He started for the door, ushering them out with sweeps of his arm, when he suddenly turned and went to his desk. He opened the center drawer, pulled out two fat brown envelopes, and threw one to Jared and one to Steve. "Cash for the trip," he said. "I figured a grand each would do it."

"Great," Jared said, and went out.

"Absolutely super," Steve said sourly, and followed him.

They caught up to Kaye on 80 West, as Newell had predicted, with the aid of their police-band radio and Kaye's sluggish progress as he trudged his way westward. At a bank in Dunmore and twice in Scranton they were able to send the police in thc wrong direction via the radio and Jared's good imitation of a patrol cop hot on the chase. Steve could scarcely believe, that first evening, that Kaye simply stopped for the night at a motel in Wilkes-Barre after visiting the nearest McDonald's, a casual tourist with his ghastly lime-green Gremlin and its bright and criminal New York plates sticking out like a searchlight in the dark. While he snoozed the night away in comfort, Steve and Jared took turns sleeping on the back seat of the Escort, the other keeping watch while nothing happened.

They watched with a mixture of dismay and relief while he ditched his own car and stole a rust-diseased Plymouth in Columbus, Ohio, on the third day. They watched him steal a gray Chevette from a grocery store parking lot in Indianapolis earlier today. They saw, of course, the chaos he brought about in Effingham, and nearly lost him. The police radio told them the make and plate number of the junky truck he was driving, and they found him again, but the police were very much on the hunt for it and him, and it was only by a miracle, Steve acknowledged, that the stupid fool made it all the way to St. Charles.

Which was why Jared was now roaring off toward Nowheresville in the truck with Steve and a dense cloud of exhaust close behind. If Kaye didn't have enough sense to know how to keep himself hidden, the FBI would have to help him out, which it was doing courtesy of Steve Rafter and Jared Brooks, two disgruntled agents who would much rather shoot the crazy fucker and go home than put up with more of this bullshit.

Which was also why Steve Rafter of the FBI was now grumbling out loud in the dark as he drove the red Escort out of town: "Fucking office party? Fuck the goddamn office party. Aid and abet a crime spree? Fuck the goddamn crime spree. You too, Newell. Up your ass." And on and on.

After a few uneventful minutes Jared pulled the truck to the side of the road. He killed the motor and the lights, then wiped his prints off the steering wheel and door handle with a handkerchief. After he got out he tossed the keys in the weeds and got in the Escort, and both he and Steve drove back to the motel to spend another boring and uneventful night. Or so they thought.

FIVE

DARBI LAY IN HER MISERABLE BATH OF ICE AFTER PETER LEFT and while his new-old truck, Old Bess, was being abandoned by the roadside by two men who would rather be elsewhere. Darbi was almost in tears now that her dad had hollered at her so. What had she done wrong? Can getting out of a tubful of ice water to watch a little TV be such a terrible crime? Apparently so, she thought, because up to now Daddy had not once shouted at her, had not even been mad at her the slightest bit, ever since she got sick.

Sick. Oh, yeah, so sick. It hurt her brain and her memory to think of it: the stomach pains, those awful pains when her midsection would clamp up like a knotted rope, bending her over. She had to acknowledge that Daddy had spent a lot of money trying to deal with it, counting out coins or staring into the wasteland of his wallet where nothing green ever grew, his face pinched up, sweat standing out on his forehead because their apartment was on the second floor and all the heat rose, or so he had told her; Daddy sorting through a handful of coins with the light of a single overhead bulb painting his troubled face with blurry shadows; Daddy telling her to stay in bed, I've got enough money, I think, I'll go down to the drugstore and get some paregoric. Only the paregoric never worked, and after a few weeks of missed kindergarten she began throwing up bright red blood, little dots of it, and then streamers of it, and then she couldn't eat at all, and he had taken her to the hospital and spent the next three months kicking himself for having waited so long.

The staff there was very nice. They gave her balloons and stuffed animals, and even flowers. Daddy came seven or eight times a day, and she would ask him how the thesis was going, even though she had little enough idea just what a thesis might be. She only knew that her dad hated it, wadding up whole pages of it and tossing them against the wall to rebound into the wastebasket, but then back to the typewriter and books he would go, and she would fall asleep to the chitter-chatter of a used typewriter being beaten to death, key by key. But that was before the stomachaches came and ripped her out of her home and planted her in the antiseptic whiteness of the pediatrics ward of Dutchess County Memorial.

Yes, Daddy visited all the time while she was there. He would sit on the side of the bed and read his mysterious schoolbooks, frowning a lot, making pencil notes on a pad, glancing at her again and again with a reassuring smile or a squeeze on the shoulder. Sometimes he would have a piece of computer paper stuck in a book, and would study it for a while, frowning a lot. She would ask him what it was, and he would say, "Just another bill." She guessed it was the hospital bill, which had to be getting big by now, because she had been in the horse-pistol—as Daddy called it when he was feeling happy, which really did happen once in a while—she'd been in the horse-pistol almost three months.

The worst part came when they started putting weird, thick hot stuff in her veins. This was, as Daddy and everyone else reassured her, something called Keemo-Thairpee, and would make her well. She imagined that along with Keemo-Thairpee would come See-Threepio, and Ar-too-Dee-too. Sort of like all the fighters of the Star Wars rebellion working inside her. Well, what they did was make her sick as a dog, and then her hair started falling out and her fingernails quit growing (not that she cared about them). But the continual barfing, the tubes in her nose that hurt, the one between her legs that *really* hurt—this got old real quick. And she began losing energy, losing weight. Sometimes she would take *fifteen* naps a day, 'cause the barfing woke her up in the night, but when she was done she would fall asleep again.

Her arms started to look like twigs. Her thighs got curved and hollow. She was bald and tired and worse off than before. One time she heard Daddy almost grow angry at one of the doctors, and they had gone into the hallway to argue, but she had heard it, yes, she had.

"What the hell makes it inoperable?"

"A tumor of this magnitude is simply too large to attempt surgery with, Mr. Kaye. Also the fact that it has metastasized dramatically . . . it's already in the lymphatic system . . . inoperable. I wish I could give you a better answer. Perhaps a cure will be found in the meantime."

"*What* meantime?" Daddy had almost shouted. "Between now and the day she dies? Is that all I have to hope for? Is this what I owe you guys sixty thousand dollars for?"

Silence. Footsteps.

Daddy came back in looking like he had been beaten up in a fight, shoulders slumped, feet dragging. She tried to cheer him up even though *the day she dies* was printed on her mind in big screaming colors, but instead of cheering him up she fell asleep without meaning to.

And when she did wake up for a brief moment in the night, the time when all the lights were dim, she heard him snuffling and crying, could feel his tears soaking through the sheet and making her chest wet. She had patted his head, knowing that he was crying for the mommy she had never known, but when he looked up, if he ever did, she was already asleep again.

Now she lifted a foot idly out of the ice water, looking at it. This was the white one, the one on the right, but it wasn't exactly normal-type white. It was kind of like invisible white. She could easily see the green and blue veins that ran up and down the scrawny stalk of her leg from her toes to her thighs and back. She thought maybe that before they had been fatter, sort of swelling in and out to the beat of her heart, especially on the tops of her feet. Now they were dead, a network of color and nothing more. She let that leg splash down, and hoisted the other one.

Hmmm. This color stuff had been puzzling her since Daddy snuck her out of the hospital and started robbing banks all the time. He said again and again that it was the medicine, the Keemo-thairpee, working inside her with all the other Star Wars robots. Now, this seemed very plausible, because that stupid Keemo-robot had made her puke all the time, until it got tired of that, and now it had changed her left side into a kind of blue-brown-black. But the barfing was all gone—she didn't even eat anymore—and pretty soon this odd color business would go away too, she knew. That only left the annoying matter of the ice.

Daddy was acting *very* strangely, she had to admit. Robbing banks seemed like an unusual thing for a person to do every day. Keeping her packed in ice was even more peculiar. What had that smelly farmer said, back there in who-knows-where? He had looked at her and screamed something about her being beaten. That was certainly not true. But all the people there had looked and gaped and gawped as if she were some kind of monster. Hadn't they ever heard of that Keemo stuff, the stuff that was making her better? Dumb-dumbs. But like Daddy had said, what do you expect this far west? Everybody's weird.

Leg Number Two executed its splashdown. She looked around the bathroom, seeing only super-clean white and winking chrome. The switch-plate on the wall had three flippers—what for? She frowned at it. Curiosity did its underhanded work. She tossed her head to dislodge the ice bag on top, brought her knees up, and stood. Water and a zillion ice cubes slid down her shoulders and the pink dress, which at one time had been pretty but now looked like some kind of squishy pink second skin. Holding her arms out for balance, Darbi stepped over the rim of the tub onto the hard ceramic tile of the floor, sluicing cold water all the way to the door. She flipped the first switch, and the light went out. No good.

She flipped it back up. The Second turned on some kind of noisy motor in the ceiling somewhere. Number Three turned on a strange red light overhead. She looked up, squinting, shielding her eyes with a wet and wrinkled hand.

Heat. *Heat!*

She let it bake into her, standing in its wide red circle of light, feeling a smooth and welcome tiredness sneak through her mind, beginning to shiver just because it felt good. There was a mirror above the sink, and she turned to look into it. A black/white girl stared back, looking sleepy from the heat. Darbi leaned closer and stuck her tongue out at her. Her tongue was blue, like her lips. Good grief, she thought, that girl looks *funny*. 'Specially without hair.

She giggled at her reflection; Black/White Girl giggled back. She turned her face up to that wonderful red light again, her eyes pressed shut, still shivering with a delicious sort of well-being that she had not felt for so long.

But . . . what if Daddy came back? She could probably kill the red light and jump back in the tub, but he'd know, he always did. So that left only the matter of deciding to obey the law he had laid down, or not. She sighed heavily, thinking about it. One thing she knew as a fact. Daddy always won out in the end. But . . . for now, for just this one second, she'd stay under the lights and look at herself in the mirror.

She made funny faces. Black/White Girl did too. She pretended to kiss herself. Ditto for Black/White Girl. She pulled out her ears and made faces, looking like a goofy clown, and then her left ear tore off with a greasy *squiiiish,* the black ear tore free, and it was in her hand and the hand of Black/White Girl too, and both of them were screaming while a stinking fluid the color of molasses oozed out of the ragged trench where the ear used to be, and dribbled down their necks, and they screamed and screamed.

A few minutes before the man in 125 called the desk to inform Kim and Nina that someone was being killed in the next room, Wayne Abel had breezed into the lobby with his black derby perched at a rakish angle on his head, his light blue NAPA Auto Parts shirt dark with grime on the chest and stomach, his pants hanging a bit too low as usual and bunched on the tops of his shoes. He had made small talk with Nina at the desk, flashing the bad-boy charm he seemed to reserve for everyone but Kim, and eventually gotten around to asking Nina to please tell her that loverboy was waiting to see her for a minute.

Kim was inside the manager's office with the door closed, worrying her skimpy resume to death. When the door burst open suddenly she had a quick, ugly vision of Gwendolyn the Manager coming in, seeing what she was doing, and telling her to hit the road because loyalty was as important as grooming and punctuality in the Holiday Inn corporate mind. But it was just Nina, leaning in to tell her Wayne was here. Kim frowned, not expecting this (though it did happen with expectable frequency) and feeling, as usual, uncomfortable about it. It was just something about keeping her job separate from her private life, because on the job she could hardly be herself and felt stilted and wary whenever Wayne, or anybody else but Nina for that matter, dropped by to say howdy.

She hid her resume back under the phone books after Nina had spoken her piece and left, glad even that Nina still knew nothing about it. It may be silly, she had thought more than once, but she'd probably think I was betraying her somehow. She pushed away from the desk, got up and smoothed her skirt, and went out to see what was up.

Wayne was, obviously. His cheeks with their stubble of five-o'clock shadow were reddish, his brown eyes too shiny. She stood behind the front desk, squirming a little inside, and he leaned over, encircled her neck with his arms, and kissed her hard on the mouth. She ducked and pushed him away, spluttering. In one stroke his hands had made a shambles of her hair, probably gotten it dirty too, by the looks of his fingernails. For a moment she felt a brief and intense loathing for him. He had been drinking beer and she could taste its flat, metallic residue on her lips.

"How'd you get your hat back?" she asked.

"Nina was home," he said, grinning. He brought a hand up and flipped a finger against the stiff brim of the derby, *thok!* "It's Friday night, m'love, and the werewolves are loose. Not to mention me and Bill. Could you skip out for an hour or two, slug down a couple cold ones with us? Bill's friend Jason is at the Quarter Moon Tavern waiting for us."

"You've already been drinking," she said.

"Caught again. Neen? Run the show for a while? Sweetie?"

Nina giggled. "Sure, Wayne. I owe her a few hours anyway."

Kim glanced at Nina, speaking with her eyes, predicting mayhem and doom if she didn't shut up. The front doors wafted open and a knot of five or six men and women in corporate power suits ambled in, chatting and grinning. In the lounge someone was crooning things about San Francisco at night. Kim wished the world would simply leave her alone for a minute; in the office, gnawing the pencil, she had entered into a brief fantasy about meeting a dashing millionaire at the front desk and absconding with him to Vegas. No more jobs, no more resumes, no more Wayne.

She wondered now how she could love Wayne while disliking him at the same time.

"Aw, come on," he said, taking her wrists in his hands. The corporate people crowded against the desk while Nina dug out check-in slips and handed out pens. Credit cards were laid down. Kim noticed one man, maybe Wayne's age, in a nice blue suit. He looked calm, intelligent, even sensitive. She looked at Wayne while her arms strained to pull away from his grasp and saw only a beer-swilling auto-parts clerk with grimy hands and a ridiculous hat.

"Miss?" one of the women said to her. "Could I have something on the top floor? I like the view of the city."

"I believe so," Kim said, trying to jerk away to check the

roster, but Wayne held on. When he did let go he swiftly hooked an arm around her neck and dragged her head down until it was almost on top of the shiny veneer of the desk. He twisted her around and began slobbering kisses on the side of her face. "Dammit, Wayne," she growled, "you're drunk. Let me go."

"Noogies!" he cried, and scrubbed his knuckles against her scalp in a blur, hurting her and doing more damage to the Patti Page image. A faint odor of sweat came out of his armpit; his shirt was wet there and was cold against her ear.

"Hey, Kim," Nina said, "do we still have that discount on Visa Golds?"

The phone chirped.

"Miss?"

"Noogie noogie noogie!"

"Stop it!" She jerked free and shook her hair out of her eyes. "Wayne, get out of here. Nina, no discounts as of the fifteenth. And ma'am, just let me check the roster. I'm sure we have rooms still available up there."

The phone chirped again. Nina glanced over at Kim. You take it, baby.

"Just a few beers," Wayne said. "What's the harm?"

"Friday night is busy night," she snapped at him, and picked up the phone. "Front desk. May I help you?"

"This is James Fleming over in One-twenty-five," the voice said, sounding tinny. "Somebody's screaming bloody murder in the next room. Sounds like a kid. I tried banging on the wall but it hasn't stopped."

Kim frowned. "Screaming?"

"One lousy beer with us," Wayne said. "One lousy beer."

"This gentleman swears he was guaranteed a discount," Nina said. "Says he got something in the mail."

"What room is it?" Kim said into the phone. She tried to smooth her hair but it was in knots.

"Room?"

"I'll be in the lounge," Wayne said, and flipped a finger against his hat again. *Thok!* "I'll order you a beer."

She covered the phone with a hand. "I can't drink on duty!" she whispered fiercely at him. "Sir?" she said into the phone again.

"Just thought I'd let you know. I think it's Room One-twenty-six. If I was you I'd call the cops."

Nina touched her elbow. "About the discount?"

"Give him the damn discount!" she hissed. "Sir?"

Click.

She put the phone back together. "Emergency in One-twenty-six. You stay put. I'll check it out." She opened the little door at the base of the desk and got 126's management key, then made her way through the people in the lobby to the entryway. Her reflection in the glass showed a woman with exploded hair. She mashed it down as well as she could and went out. Squealing kids were nothing new around here, almost as common as drunks passed out in the hallways, or toilets where some jerk had shoved a towel down to see how fast he could flood the place. There were vandals and family fights and, yes, a screeching kid or two whose parents were in the lounge doing the mambo on the tables.

The screaming was dwindling down to moans when Kim got to 126 and pushed the key into the doorknob and turned it. She eased the door open and saw that the room was empty, the beds untouched, the lights off, the television on and blaring. A blue and white first-aid kid was on the dresser, and she remembered having given it to a man—Olafson? Osborne?—not too long ago. She stepped inside, so used to that familiar scent of micro-filtered and conditioned air that it didn't register, hadn't registered for months. Leaving the door open in case this was a violent domestic fight and a hasty exit was required, she walked hesitantly toward the bathroom, where white and red light spilled out, forming a glowing rectangle on the carpet. The moaning was coming from in there. Suddenly a gust of apprehension breezed through her veins, and she stopped.

If I was you I'd call the cops.

She cleared her throat nervously. "Hello? Hello?"

The moaning went on and on, sounding weak and somehow bubbly. She passed the TV bolted to the wall. *Family Ties* was just ending.

"Hello?" she called out above the noise of its theme song.

The moaning stopped. Water sloshed, grating strangely, the way ice and water in a large cooler might sound when it is moved or shaken.

She stepped into the light of the bathroom doorway, more curious than afraid. The floor was wet. A rumpled towel was soaking in a reddish sheen of water on the white tiles. Some dollops of brown stuff were dissolving in the water there too, dark against the whiteness of the tiles. A black human ear, a small one, was lying in the sink on the chrome pop-up drain, dribbling brown stuff. Kim hitched in a breath, ready to scream, ready to swoon, ready to do all kinds of things while her eyes grew huge, staring at that ear, but then the shower curtain was drawn aside slightly and a small bald head poked out, blue eyes bright and wet in the discoloration of its face.

"My ear fell off," the little thing said, and started crying.

For Kim, the world went gray, then black, and it didn't even hurt when she cracked her head on the sink on the way down to nowhere.

It didn't take very long for consciousness to return, and in those first few seconds Kim wondered just why in the hell she was lying on a bathroom floor, the sink looming above, the toilet two feet away (rust around the mooring bolts—better call maintenance), the entirety of her front section sopping wet and cold, her dark blue skirt rucked up too high and very black with water.

Black.

The little boy had half a . . .

Half a black . . . face.

She pushed herself up on her hands. They slipped on the tiles, nearly letting her fall again. There was a bright star of pain on the side of her head, and when she was able to get to her knees she dabbed at the lump with wet fingers, which came away tinged pink with blood. She got to her feet, holding the traitorous sink for support, her vision still rocking a bit from the blow. Never much of a fainter, she had made a stunning premiere on this balmy night. She looked in the mirror and saw a wet woman whose exploded hairdo had turned to mop strings and whose right cheek still bore the impression of the floor tiles, Holiday Inn's cold and precise white floor tiles. The dead black ear was still in the sink, shiny under the light. While Kim studied the shocked face that had been her own in the mirror, her shaking hands propped on the edges of the sink, the shower curtain slid aside again a little and her heart went cold as a breathless, hurried sort of terror swept through her mind. She turned her head slowly, hearing each vertebra in her neck click and creak, and when it had turned as far as possible, she lowered her eyes.

At the base of the white shower curtain, one lone blue eye peeked out. "Who are you?" a small, trembling voice asked.

"Kim Marden," she replied automatically.

"Have you seen my daddy?"

"I don't think so. Are you—are you okay, little boy?"

The voice was gently indignant. "I'm a little girl."

"Sorry. Why are you . . . why is your face . . . two different colors?"

"Haven't you ever heard of Keemo-Thairpee? I've got cancer."

Kim frowned, no longer scared, just concerned. An older cousin of hers had died of lung cancer not too many years ago, and he sure as hell hadn't turned colors. But now, with modern science taking giant steps, who could know what bizarre medicinal side effects were common? Kim wished suddenly that she had some kind of schooling in medicine or nursing; hell, even being a Candy Striper would beat this tub of ignorance she was swimming in right now. She noticed that there was a faint smell in the air of the bathroom, as if a very tiny mouse had expired in the wastebasket and was getting moldy there. Did that smell belong to the girl?

She chucked these unanswerable questions aside and took a step toward the tub. Gently, she eased the curtain aside.

She felt herself growing faint again. The tiny girl in the tub was black and white all over, skinny and scrawny and nearly hairless. There was an ear missing from the dark side of her head, a crescent-shaped trench where once an ear might have resided. Kim felt her stomach twist up. Doctor, nurse, Candy Striper—it didn't take a trained mind to know that something awfully strange was wrong with this girl. She knelt beside the tub. "Tell me what happened," she said levelly.

"I have cancer," the girl said.

"Okay. What's with the ice?"

"Keemo-thairpee, silly." She looked at Kim as if she were very, very dumb, and Kim, feeling a little embarrassed, responded with: "So anyway, what's your name?"

"Darbi."

"Darbi what?"

"Kaye. Darbi Louanne Kaye. Sometimes my daddy calls me Darbi-Darbi."

"Okay, Darbi-Darbi, let's get you out and dried off."

Darbi looked down to the floes of ice cubes bobbing in the water. "But, but Daddy says I have to do this until we get to Wyoming. It's a big state in the West, you know, where they have cowboys. When we get there I'm going to be cured of this stuff, and then I'll be okay."

Kim nodded without knowing it. Wyoming? It occurred to her that there must be some big cancer specialist there, maybe a clinic that specialized in childhood diseases. She shrugged to herself, deliberating, then stood up on legs that shook. "Out with you," she said, manufacturing a smile, inwardly afraid that she was meddling with the girl's medical treatment. But she had screamed for so long, and her ear was in the sink, and no matter what this treatment was, Kim could hardly make herself walk away and forget what she'd seen and heard. "Come on," she said. "I'll dry you off."

Darbi protested. "Daddy says I can't get out, even for a minute. If I do the medicine won't work!"

"Girl," Kim said firmly, "I wish I could believe that. We're just going to take a ride, let a doctor look at you, and see what he says. Believe me, I don't think it can hurt. Will you come with me?"

Darbi gave a small shrug. "If that's what you want," she said, and rose up to step out of the tub and its surface layer of dwindling ice. What Kim saw as Darbi stood was nothing more than a starving child, a structure of delicate bones held together by a wet pink dress. She draped her shoulders with a towel and let her stand under the heat lamp until her shivering went away, and then scrubbed the bristles of her hair with another towel and carried her to bed, tucking her tight under the sheets and blanket. She turned the noisy television off and sat on the bed beside her, staring at that pitiful little face against the crisp whiteness of the sheets. Nothing in Kim's twenty-one years as an earthling, and certainly nothing that had ever happened in this motel before, had prepared her for this—emergency—and she had believed she'd seen it all.

The sheets rustled. Darbi was running her wrinkled white fingers over the patch where her ear had been. She seemed lost in thought, frowning almost comically. Then her eyelids began fluttering up and down, trying to drag the mind behind them toward sleep.

Kim picked up the telephone and dialed the desk. "Nina?"

"Kim?"

"Yeah. Listen—I want you to page whoever belongs to Room One-twenty-six. I used to know his name but I can't remember it. Ask him to come to the desk, then send his ass back here pronto."

"What's up?"

"Little girl left all alone. She's . . . never mind. Just do the page."

"Gotcha."

The phone clunked as she laid it on the desk. Then, mutedly, Kim heard the page, which was piped through the restaurant, lounge, hallways, and rest rooms. After a minute Nina paged again, and then she was back on the phone. "No takers. Need help?"

"Nuh-uh. I guess I'm going to be gone for a while. This little girl here in One-twenty-six is—needs, uh, a hospital, I'm pretty sure. Can you hold the fort?"

"Sure," Nina said. "Want me to send Wayne back to help you out? He's waiting in the lounge."

"Wayne can wait forever, for all I care. For God's sake don't tell him I said that. I'll be back as soon as I can."

She hung up. Darbi was asleep, which Kim found reassuring. Take your average sick kid, she thought, and if she can sleep, she can't be in very much pain. Kim stood and tiptoed out, easing the door gently shut without latching it. Her car was around back. The nearest hospital was not very far away, just off the main drag, St. Mary's. Kim hurried to the employee parking area and tried to locate her car, squinting in the dusky light thrown this far by the motel. Her goal was a rust-eaten Chevy Nova that had rotted to little more than a motor and four wheels, a benefit of working for minimum wages. When she found it and yanked the door open, hinges that had not tasted oil in decades greeted her return with tortured screeches. She got in and pulled the door shut, found her keys under the floor mat, and offered a silent prayer as she turned the key. The engine belched, seemed to consider things, then ran. She dropped the shift lever into drive and the Chevy crawled forward on its bald tires. The headlights even worked, thanks to Wayne, who several weeks ago had spent an hour on his back with his head stuck under the dash, testing crumbling wires with some kind of electronic thing.

She drove around to 126, put the buggy in park, hopped out through the familiar cloud of burned-oil smoke, went inside, and came out with Darbi asleep in her arms cocooned in a blanket. She put her on the back seat, glad that she did not awaken, then drove away away farting giant blue smoke clouds and punctuating the night with backfires.

Once she was downtown and in the hospital lot, signs led her to the emergency room of St. Mary's. There was a carport of sorts overhead to keep the ambulance crews dry when the weather hit, capped by a sign proclaiming the maximum height to be nine feet three inches; a large pair of automatic entry doors were set into the wall of the old building. Kim parked underneath the giant awning and turned the motor off. She managed to get Darbi into her arms, and worked her way out of the car. There was some kind of squawk-box set in the bricks, and she wiggled Darbi around to get a finger free to push the red call button. A woman answered immediately: "Emergency."

"I've got a sick little girl," Kim said, reshuffling Darbi and her blanket to a better position. "I was wondering if someone would take a look at her."

"Is she ambulatory?"

"Huh? Wait. Oh, yeah. I mean, no. I'm carrying her. She's asleep."

"Come in." The doors slid apart, hissing. Kim hustled inside, hoping for a stretcher and a full team of masked surgeons. What she got was a walkway that went mildly upward. It turned a few times, reminding Kim of a maze built for a rat, and then the light was brighter and an orderly was standing near the top holding onto an empty wheelchair. Kim lowered Darbi into it. Her head slumped forward and she nearly tipped out. The orderly caught her shoulders and pressed her back. "Follow me," he said, swinging the wheelchair around while keeping a hold on Darbi, and walked to where the light was the strongest. A nurse was waiting there with all the shiny instruments of disease and pain arrayed on steel tables. In the center was a tall padded bench covered with white paper, with a large flexor light poised above it. The orderly stripped the blanket away from Darbi, ready to place her on the examining table. He bent down and hesitated, frozen in a half-kneeling posture with his eyes large and staring.

"On the table, Roger," the nurse said, and Roger came

back to life. When Darbi was laid out she opened a stainless-steel drawer and withdrew a stethoscope. She plugged it into her ears and listened to what Darbi's insides had to say, her face compressed into a caricature of stern attention.

She straightened and popped the stethoscope out of her ears, still frowning. "Are you her mother?" she asked, then answered her own question. "No, you're obviously too young. Are you two related?"

"No."

"Have you contacted the police yet?"

"I didn't know if I should," Kim said. "Do you know what might be wrong with her? She told me she has cancer."

"Told you? The discoloration indicates that she was lying on her side for several hours after death. Blood pools according to gravity, until it coagulates. Judging her from sight alone, the lack of hair and emaciated condition she's in, I would say cancer is a good possibility." She lifted one of Darbi's hands, the black one, inspected her fingers, and brought them to her nose. She shook her head. "She's been . . ." She put the stethoscope back into her ears and listened again. "She has been dead at least ten days, maybe twelve. Why is her dress wet? Was she found in water?"

Kim's jaw dropped. Dead? No, no. She was as alive as the nurse, as alive as the orderly named Roger, who had busied himself looking out the window at the dark and suddenly very bleak night. "She was alive just a few minutes ago," Kim said, feeling weak and light headed, as if she had stood up too fast. "Just a few minutes ago. I swear. I work at a motel and she was in one of our rooms, laying in a bathtub full of ice."

"Ice? Why?"

"She said it was part of her treatment. But she really was alive!"

The nurse shook her head. "Not likely. Do you feel—do you feel all right? Sometimes when a tragedy strikes it makes our thinking go haywire. Is she your kid sister, maybe?"

"No. I really did just find her in a bunch of ice. Really! She told me her name is Darbi. Shouldn't you be giving her mouth-to-mouth or something?"

The nurse turned away from her. "Roger, get the little girl a toe tag and wheel her to the . . . downstairs, will you? And add her to the coroner's pickup roster for tomorrow afternoon, which I'm sure the police will demand anyway. As for you, miss, I'm sorry but I have some forms you'll have to fill out, and I have to phone the police. Could I have your name, please?"

"Name," Kim said. Even her own voice sounded dreamlike. It finally came to her that the nurse thought she was insane, and for a tiny moment she wondered if she was. "My name," she said, not knowing if she was being slick, stupid, or just plain criminal, "is Margaret Mason."

"All right, Miss Mason, I'll phone the nurses' station and they'll have the forms waiting. There are vending machines in the waiting areas, and you could complete them there. Roger will take good care of the girl. Is she your niece, maybe?"

"No."

"Okay. I don't mean to be playing detective here, but you have to agree this is a strange situation. I don't think I've ever seen a person dead for as long as this Darbi has been."

She turned to another drawer and pulled out what looked like a large white tablecloth. She flapped it out and draped it over Darbi, then went for the black telephone on the wall beside the window. Kim was frowning hard enough to hurt her face. Dead for ten days? No way. Not fifteen minutes ago Darbi had been awake, alive, everything. Hadn't she? Kim reviewed what had happened since the phone told her screaming was going on in 126, then tried to doubt her own memory since doubting her sanity had not worked, but her mind insisted that she had never suffered lapses before, and tonight was no exception.

"Pardon me," she said to the orderly. He turned. "Could I

look under the sheet? If this girl is really dead she sure wasn't acting like it fifteen minutes ago."

He nodded, looking at her very strangely. Kim stepped to the table and lifted the sheet away from Darbi's face. That smell drifted up from her, that mouse-in-the-wastebasket smell. Kim pressed one of her eyelids up, and saw only a blue eye whose pupil was very large. She reached to the lamp and swiveled it to aim directly in Darbi's face, looking for a reaction.

Nothing happened. The eye, at least, was very lifeless. She put her ear to Darbi's slightly parted lips. No breath, just that unpleasant odor. Kim realized that she was indeed quite dead, and her heart began to beat too fast. Dead for ten days, maybe twelve? That was impossible. Yet, you didn't have to be a doctor to recognize that this was a corpse becoming ripe very rapidly. She covered her face again and looked at the orderly. "She was alive just a few minutes ago," she said, aware that her mouth was becoming dry, her lips trying to stick to her teeth. She swallowed against the heartbeat pulsing thickly in her throat.

"Sure," Roger mumbled. "Whatever you say." He went back to staring out the window.

"Really!"

No response. The nurse got done with her phone call. "They'll have the paperwork waiting for you," she said, hanging up. "Just go straight down the corridor and you'll see the nurses' station on the left." She pointed to the open doorway that allowed entrance to the hospital proper. Kim wandered through it, her feet running on automatic, her thoughts in chaos, able to see only the bright afterimage of a small human form named Darbi underneath a white sheet. In an offhanded way she was aware of the ubiquitous hospital smell of antiseptics, a smell not much different from that at the motel; the stronger aroma of floor wax drifted up from the linoleum squares here. The lights were dimmed for the night. Only the first-floor nurses' station was bright, and two or three nurses stood chatting with subdued voices. Kim walked to it, still dazed, strangely numb, and was handed several forms by one of them, forms which at first made no sense. Darbi was being admitted—a little late for that, Kim thought—and there were questions about insurance, which Darbi no longer needed, and payment plans for the unfortunates who had no medical coverage. Kim filled them out as if in a trance, inserting the name Olsen after the Darbi without realizing she had remembered the name at all. When she was done she went out into the warm night, totally forgetting that the police might mount a manhunt for Margaret Mason, woman of mystery, when they arrived and found her gone. She walked aimlessly through the parking lot that was spread before the hospital in a huge square that shined almost silver under the light of a rising moon. Then she remembered that she was parked beside the emergency room's entrance, found her car and made it run again, and went back to work with visions of a talking, walking corpse stamped on the inner screen of her mind, a vision that could not be. Already she had decided never to tell anyone about it, not even Nina, because she would surely think Kim was insane.

SIX

THOUGH HE OF COURSE HAD NO REASON TO ATTACH ANY IMPORtance to it, no reason even to notice it, Peter was passed during his hike toward downtown St. Charles by a backfiring, wheezing wreck of a Chevy Nova that contained Kimberly Marden and his own daughter Darbi. He was still fuming about the truck—what a stroke of wretched luck, spoke the tireless voice of his mind while the bright and colorful downtown area drew closer and he contemplated the unpleasant realities that awaited him there, which probably would turn out to be laden with luck even more wretched. Yes, what luck. His wounded leg ached abominably. Though he had eaten only once today, and could not remember where, his hunger had transformed itself into a sharp knot of apprehension in the pit of a stomach that had little desire for real food anymore. Limping down the weeded, dusty roadside, he checked his wristwatch as he walked, noisy traffic droning by on his left, drifting exhaust fumes tainting the air with bitter highway smells. He noted with a jolt of surprise that it was after ten. The fast-food joints would soon be closing, and he had no wish to eat in a real restaurant when his hunger finally did return. Dressed as he was, as dirty and smelly as he was, chances were slim, he knew, that any self-respecting restaurant would even let him in. As he walked through the sultry and almost suffocatingly damp night air he passed several taverns nested between the black faces of time-worn factories and abandoned buildings, and stopped once to look through the big window of a place whose stuttering neon sign proclaimed it was the Quarter Moon. He could dimly see heads inside, men parked at the bar slugging down the waters of euphoria, a few guys toward the back carrying pool cues; jukebox music was thundering country stuff, and the conversations were loud and full of laughter. He decided what the hell, he ought to eat a bag of chips or a pickled egg—*something*—and went inside to the noise and the fun. To his delight he found that the Quarter Moon had a small short-order menu. He got himself a steak sandwich and ate it while watching the local news on the wide-screen television behind the bar, wondering if he had made the headlines in Missouri yet, and feeling strangely betrayed when the news was over and he hadn't. Before he left he bought a pint—what used to be a pint before the liquor industry went metric, anyway—and came out with a flat bottle of Jim Beam tucked in a back pocket. Phase one completed, he thought, and walked on, picking his teeth with his tongue, wishing that some nice fellow would stop beside the road and ask if Peter would be kind enough to steal his car, preferably his Cadillac or Mercedes.

This did not happen, which was no surprise to Peter, and when he felt himself close enough to the residential area on this southern side of town he veered to the right on a street that called itself Johnson Avenue, an avenue where junky houses reposed on either side like the shattered ruins of war, and where streetlights did not exist. For the first time Peter was going to attempt to hot-wire a car—that, or spend the next two days watching Darbi disintegrate, still a thousand miles from Wyoming and salvation. Thinking of this nearly made his heart stand still. Darbi dead? Good-bye, cruel world. Peter Kaye has checked out with his daughter by means of suicide and is on the long road, that highway to heaven.

He wondered if it would really come to that, for at this moment his desire to live was sharp and clear. As he walked along Johnson he briefly tested car doors, looking for something unlocked in this darkness, feeling more and more like a criminal, perhaps even more so than when he robbed a bank. There it was impersonal, nobody's money in particular; here, he was horsing around with somebody's transportation, maybe even their pride and joy. One of the door handles he tried—a white car, some kind of Dodge—was unlocked, and he stopped for a look at the house it belonged to. It was an average down-in-the-dumps family house, but lights were on inside and from the look of the lawn there might be a dog around who had made a path in the grass beside it. Peter decided to move on. Perhaps, he hoped, by some chance of fate someone living on this avenue had left their car keys in the ignition, or a page of detailed hot-wiring instructions complete with diagrams.

Funny stuff. After three blocks he came across another car that had its windows down, a dark sedan that may have been black, brown, maybe blue. Peter went around to the driver's side, knowing that the lights were on in the house—and it wasn't a bad-looking place—but becoming too worried about Darbi being alone to search any farther. He silently clicked the door open. The dome light came on, and he stuck himself in and quickly eased the door shut.

Fine, he thought, scowling at the steering wheel in the dark. Here we have a very nice vehicle, old but well cared for, traces of cleaning fluid and upholstery polish drifting up from the seats and carpet, a car that appears to be as deeply Chevrolet as that damned Chevette had been, and it will take a brain surgeon to dissect the billions of wires that are behind the dash. It occurred to him that he could go back to the Holiday Inn and Darbi, wait for morning, and buy a car, but his take so far from the robberies was short enough of its goal that to part with even a thousand or two for some junkheap might mean the difference between winning and losing his battle for Darbi's future.

He sighed, momentarily at a loss, worked the bottle of Jim Beam out of his back pocket, and was tipping it back when something hard and cool—a small pipe, he thought at first as adrenaline squirted into his veins and put his heart in overdrive—was jammed against the back of his neck. Cancel the pipe idea, his brain told him immediately, because that is the barrel of a gun and nothing else.

He raised his hands and the bottle. A hand reached over his shoulder and disengaged it from his fist. It was withdrawn and began to gurgle. In the rearview mirror Peter saw only the black shape of a head with the bottle stuck in its mouth. "Ahhh," the head said. Peter realized in a dim and stupid way that it was a man—what else?—and that the man certainly did like Jim Beam.

The bottle was handed back. "Drink deep, brother," a coarse and gritty voice said, the voice of a man who has smoked too many cigarettes and talked too much while doing it. "Matthew twelve, sixteen. Hallelujah."

Peter accepted the bottle, his pale David Letterman eyebrows forming one long line above his eyes as he frowned. Hallelujah? Matthew what?

"Drink, brother, drink! Your salvation is near at hand. Romans nine, four. Damn good whiskey, by the by. Give me your wallet."

Peter felt suddenly very anxious to do as he was told; the gun against his neck felt like a cannon. He dug his wallet out and handed it back. "Damn," the man said, flipping through it, "you're almost as broke as I am. Got any rings, a watch maybe?"

"Got a watch," Peter said. His voice was wavering, his throat dry as sand. He stripped his Timex off his wrist and offered it.

"What did this cost you?" the man demanded after a bit, sounding irritated. "Two-fifty at your local K-Mart?" He handed it back to Peter. "Perchance you could part with the keys to this temple, my brethren."

Peter turned to look at him. He saw white eyes, teeth, shiny cheeks. The man was very black and the gun in his hand was very big. Peter was able to choke out one word: "Temple?"

"Wherever I put my weary frame, there I find my temple.

Luke seven, nine. If you will hand over the keys, I will be on my way. Thank you in advance for the usage of your vehicle on this dark and lonely night. I believe this is the first time I have tried to borrow money from a man poorer than myself, and I do apologize, but instead of sleeping in the temple, you have convinced me to drive it." He tossed Peter's wallet back. The cold barrel left his neck. "Borrow not money from the meek, as Our Master taught. Genesis four, seventeen. He said, however, nothing about cars."

"No keys," Peter said immediately. "It's not my car."

"Ah. You too have learned from the Master. Hot-wire this fucker and drive, my son, and I'll go back to sleep. Take the freeway west, and make haste."

Peter's heart began to resume its normal speed. "Hey," he said, his voice still shaky, the memory of the size of that gun etched in his mind, "are you a preacher or something?" Perhaps better to make small talk with a man like this than simply get out and bolt.

"Indeed I am. I am the Most Reverend Abraham Maharba. It is a palindrome, and I am an enigma."

"Palindrome?"

"Name no one man. Madam I'm Adam. Same thing, backwards and forwards. Abraham Maharba."

"Fake name?"

"Extraordinarily fake. Now, about this hot-wiring business—shall we proceed?"

Peter could only shrug. "I'll probably need some light."

Maharba snorted. "Suffer the blind to come unto me. Acts four, sixteen. Move your ass." He opened the door to his right and began to clamber out. As he moved through the weak light cast from the house Peter caught a glimpse of a crucifix earring winking bits of light, and saw a round white collar that encircled Maharba's neck. Preacher and petty crook, Peter thought. What a combo.

Past him then as he stood, Peter saw with a start that the front door of the houe was being opened, casting a broadening wedge of light across the grass, and that a man was standing in that light speaking to someone inside, his hand on the doorknob, ready to go. His bald head was pink and shiny. He was carrying a briefcase.

"Trouble," Peter hissed. He found the bottle top and screwed it tight over the Jim Beam, ready to abandon ship.

Maharba clicked the rear door loosely shut and opened the front. "I suggest," he said urgently, "that you exercise your talents and get this buggy rolling."

The man in the house was done talking; the screen door opened and slapped shut. A blocky shadow came down the walkway.

"I don't know how to hot-wire," Peter whispered as he put his hand on the door lever. "Have a nice life, Preacher."

Maharba grabbed his arm. Drops of sweat winked on his smooth forehead. "What kind of goddamn car thief are you, man? On this kind of Chevy you use the red and black wires to get electricity, and the heavy yellow one to get it started."

Peter jerked his arm free. "I wish you luck, but I really have to get going."

The man named Abraham Maharba growled and ducked his head under the dash. "Move your goddamn feet," he hissed. "Get me some light."

Peter opened the door a few inches, not knowing if he should get out or stay put. Now the shadow had stopped and was looking at the car. "Who's there?" the man called out. "See here, who's there?"

"I don't like this very much," Peter said, and swallowed. The panic was trying to come back, but this time it at least had a good reason. Between his shins Maharba started jerking wires, making the dash rattle. The shadow on the walk advanced a few steps.

"What are you doing in my car?"

"Preacher," Peter groaned, "we are almost out of time."

Maharba pulled his head away and sat up, his shiny dark face creased with annoyance. He had dropped his pistol to the floor between his feet, and bent down now to get it. He levered his door open, stuck his arm out, and shot at the sky.

The noise was sudden and monstrous, a thunderclap announcing doom. The shadow on the walk backed up, tripped, fell in a sprawl on the grass, then got up and charged back to the house.

"Dumbass," Maharba growled, and went back to the task at hand. Red lights appeared among the gauges; a second later the starter began to grind. The motor came alive, idling smoothly. Maharba pushed himself back up, panting, the whiskey smell of his breath filling the car with an aroma like bad pickles. "I suggest a hasty exit," he said, and Peter couldn't agree more. He mashed the gas pedal down almost hard enough to punch it through the floor. In an instant the tires began to scream while the rear end of the Chevy wagged and jerked like a fish on a line. A block away he slowed and fumbled the headlights on, shaking, sweating, feeling the beginnings of a fresh attack of anxiety that had little to do with the car or the man on the lawn, brain circuitry senselessly opening and shutting electrical routes normally reserved for pure terror. Bad time, bad time. It was always a bad time.

The bottle was between his legs. He started to lift it, the only medicine available, but Maharba snapped a hand over, grappled for it, got it. He tipped it back and took four gigantic swallows. As soon as he lowered it Peter grabbed it back, needing it desperately, and drank until it felt like he had swallowed a handful of Fourth of July sparklers on full burn. Within a minute the approaching panic had been detoured to nowhere, the miracle of alcohol, but his stomach would be in flames most of the night, and tomorrow, when the booze had filtred itself out of his system, his nerves would be raw and jangling worse than ever. Then again, he thought, they had no chance of getting better until Darbi was in Rawlins and until Braine's business partner, name currently unknown, had turned her into a large multicolored ice cube.

"That one was too damned close," Abraham Maharba said, wiping his foread. "Gimme that bottle back."

Peter did, with a certain measure of annoyance. "Where

do you want me to drop you off?" he said, gruff and inhospitable and utterly not giving a damn.

"Drop *me* off?" He sneered at him, his face a patchwork of light and shadow and large white teeth. "I believe I was in the temple first, friend. You, however, may get out any fucking time you want. Me, I need some sleep. Let me sleep the sleep of dreams. Ruth twenty-one, six."

"I can take you to a shelter or something."

"It is my mission to spread my message of salvation across the land," he said. "Thus I was commanded by God to spend my days in poverty, ever on the verge of destruction, unsupported by the charity of Caesar. Render unto Caesar that which is his. Luke fourteen, nine." He pocketed the bottle. "I'm hungry."

"I'll take you to a diner."

"Eat not from unclean plates."

"McDonald's."

"Thus did God set his bow in the sky, that it will never flood that bad again. Seek not after gold and arches. And I prefer Chinese food."

Peter steered the car to a quick, noiseless stop beside the curb. "Look," he said wearily, "I'm in too much of a hurry to put up with this kind of bullshit. Either shoot me, or get the hell out. The choice is yours."

Maharba looked at him, the white circles of his eyes glittering wetly against the glare of a streetlight half a block ahead. The smell of sweat and extremely cheap cologne shrouded him. Peter sensed his hands moving. Steel clicked against steel.

"Brother," Maharba said softly, gently, "this car is mine."

Peter felt fear. It was a fear so suddenly inconsequential, so puny, that it was little more than a tickle of apprehension at the base of his belly. When the panic hit during an attack it was a fear of everything, a terror that had no focus and was all the more terrifying because of it. Here, all he had to be afraid of was one broken-down faker with a big revolver. He found, with a sense of nothing more than dull surprise, that the threat of a bullet through his head was less frightening than the thought of watching Darbi die, almost laughably less. In a sense, the bullet would bring a release from this nameless agony of mental illness, a release at last.

But Darbi needed him. There was no one on this planet to take his place.

Peter let his shoulders slump, let his chin drop until it was resting against the bones of his chest. "You can have the damn thing," he said quietly, and clicked his door open.

Maharba worked himself across the seat. Peter let the door fall shut and surveyed the night, the unfamiliar streets, the pitched and buckled sidewalks. The air was heavy with moisture, even the smell of it strange to him. Not for the first time he felt insignificant, unwanted, lost. There were stars overhead competing with the glow of the city, alien lights shining down cold and stern on this alien part of the country. He wondered how to get back to the Holiday Inn, how long it would it take, if what he was doing made any sense at all.

"Hie thee hence," Maharba tooted gleefully. "Leviticus eighteen, two." He revved the motor, cackling. "Remember," he chortled above the noise, "the red and black wires for electricity, the heavy yellow one for starting. And oh, do I wish you luck!"

Peter swung sideways without knowing he was going to, grappled for one of Maharba's arms without knowing. He felt vaguely surprised, watching his hands take hold of Maharba's left wrist, watching them jerk his hand off the steering wheel and twist it tight. His own hands, his own self, seemed to belong to a stranger suddenly. His mouth opened up and these words fell out of it: "I'll rip your arm off if I have to, Preacher Man." It came to him again that he and Clint Eastwood had very much in common.

Maharba grunted. Things crunched as Peter twisted his wrist. "Jesus K. Christ!" he shrieked. Peter sensed that his free hand was scrabbling across the seat for the pistol. The motor roared insanely, filling the night with noise, victim of a foot gone spastic as Maharba jerked and flopped against the pain of having his hand unscrewed.

"Take the frigging car!" Maharba screeched. The pistol clattered on the pavement. "Motherfucker, *take it!*"

Peter let go. A distant part of himself felt a twinge of disappointment; that part would have gladly ripped the bastard's hand off and slung it across the street. "Get out," he said to Maharba, panting, shocked at himself. Why the sudden desire for blood? More fun stuff from a brain already fried by despair?

Maharba massaged his wrist, grimacing while the motor wound down to a respectable idle. "Lord in heaven, brother," he groaned, "for a skinny man you are very strong."

Peter snatched the gun up. "Out."

"No problem." They exchanged places, Peter in, Maharba out. In the weak glow of the streetlight Maharba looked bent and defeated now as he worked his wrist and stared at it. Peter wondered how old the man was, a hint of guilt twitching at the edges of his mind. He had been pretty rough on him.

"Look," he said to Maharba, heeding that guilt, "I do have a little money. Here." He dug in his pants pocket and pulled out a wrinkled twenty. "Get yourself some food, find a better place to bed down. I've got a daughter sitting alone in a motel, and without this car we're both in trouble."

"Do tell," Maharba murmured. He took a step closer and reached for the bill with both hands. Peter jerked back; too late. Maharba's hard, dry hands clamped around his own. "All's fair," Maharba grunted, and twisted. Peter reached instinctively with his other hand, close to howling from the pain, but succeeded only in handing Maharba the pistol.

"Rank amateur," he sneered, and let Peter go. "Now you give me the rest of your money and get out, no chapter, no paragraph, no nothing, or I will surely kill you dead and dump you in the street."

Peter doubted it, but not enough. He got the rest of the money out of his pocket as he stood, and handed it mutely over. He knew that if he wasn't so tired and so frazzled he could have won this absurd little war, but it was not much consolation. "Two, three, four hundred fifty," Maharba said, grinning as he snapped the bills through his fingers. He stuck them in the breast pocket of his minister's outfit, and patted it twice. "Blessed are they who give freely of themselves. Luke twelve, six."

He got in again and slammed the door, revved the motor a few times, and stuck his head out the window. "You take care of that daughter of yours," he called as Peter trudged away. "No finer love has a man but for his children. Moses four, nine."

Peter ignored him. A moment later the big Chevy roared past him with its tires wailing. He saw a hand poke out and wave an almost-empty bottle of Jim Beam at him, heard a mad cackle of laughter, and then the car was nothing but red taillights dwindling away in the dark.

He began the long walk back to the motel feeling cheated and unlucky, and the cars and people that happened to pass him on the way were occupied with their own business and did nothing to help him, or hurt him, doing him the greater favor of ignoring him entirely.

It was almost eleven when he got back. The band had cranked it up for the late evening crowd, and the entire front section of the motel building echoed and vibrated with drums and bass and loud singing voices pounding out from the lounge. Peter's only intention was to pass all this ruckus and go to his room, reassure himself that Darbi was all right, perform the much-needed washing-up, and fall asleep while his clothes soaked in the sink. By now the hesitant quarter moon had gained confidence and climbed to the top of the sky, and was casting a pale glow over St. Charles, turning the trees and fields of tall weeds between the buildings on this sparse side of the city into silver and black shadows that moved and danced under the pleasant night breeze. The honeysuckle was close again, a sweetness that drifted in the warm night air and the currents that flowed with it, tantalizing and rich. Peter stopped in the shadow beside the motel, breathing the smell that tried to pull him back into memories of childhood, leaning against the sun-warm bricks with his closed eyes turned to the sky. There had been a time, these flowers told him, a time when he was young, a time when . . .

He straightened, frowning. A time when? No. There was nothing but now, nothing but this night and the hard reality of the ones that would follow, nothing but a thousand hard miles between here and Wyoming and the future Darbi had paid for and would have, the new future he had ransomed his sanity and her life for. He wondered as the flowers and the night and the smell of them both took their rightful place in the distant areas of his mind, was John Braine outraged at this public rampage of robberies from the father of his newest client, Darbi? Would he refuse to treat her if Peter ever managed to get her there, money or not? He had insisted on perfect secrecy. He was a middle-aged man on the verge of paranoia, Peter had recognized very quickly, a man conducting his business with the watchful eyes and haunted heart of a dealer in deadly drugs. I've had you checked out, he had said. The results were absolute zero, he had said. But how can you possibly afford this?

It had been on a Sunday, just one week ago, that now seemed so distant. Peter's psychiatrist at the Dutchess County Mental Health Center in Poughkeepsie, the good doctor named Fredrickson, had arranaged the meeting between Peter and Braine during one of his twice-weekly sessions a few days before. For the first time Fredrickson had asked Peter, directly and with no hem-hawing or bullshit, what he was going to do when Darbi died. And she *is* going to die, he'd said. She really is.

"Have her buried if I can afford it," Peter had said, tossing him this casual answer while his guts tightened up and tears knocked on the doors of his eyes. "If not, she'll be cremated. I understand it's much cheaper."

Dr. Fredrickson simply nodded. "Just bury her or burn

her," he said, walking that pencil between his endlessly moving fingers. "Junk her like a piece of bothersome trash."

"Not quite that cold," Peter said, gripping his knees. "When she dies, I'll go on with my life. There's not much else I can do."

Fredrickson nodded. "Going to finish school then?"

Peter made an unhappy sound through his nose. "Yeah, sure."

"Find a woman, remarry, have more kids?"

"Yeah. Sure. Yeah."

"Forget about Brenda, forget about her daughter Darbi, shuck it all aside and go for the gusto."

Peter nodded. "I think that about covers it."

"To hell with them and the painful memories they left. You deserve better."

"I think I could believe that," Peter said through teeth that had gritted themselves and jaws that were beginning to hurt from the pressure.

"You never deserved such bad luck in the first place, did you? Brenda and Darbi have done nothing but hold you back."

"Yeah—yeah. You said it. I'm still young. The future lies ahead, and I'm going to . . . going to . . ."

The tears were starting to come. His sinuses felt hot and full of pressure.

"Going to what, Peter?"

He hung his head. "Nothing."

"Going to what?"

"Nothing."

"Going to—do what you've deserved for so long? Going to—join the family?"

Nothing.

Dr. Fredrickson leaned forward in his chair, making it creak. "What is it going to be, Peter? A bullet? Pills? Razor blade to the wrists? A hangman's rope?"

Nothing.

"Have you decided yet?"

He raised his head while tears that seemed the size of BBs slid and rocked on the inside edges of his eyelids. He was desperate not to let them fall, desperate. "Darbi's doctors say a cure might be found in the meantime."

"And you believe that?"

"Well, I—"

Fredrickson snorted. "She's going to die, Peter. *Die!* How are you going to handle it? How?"

His teeth hurt, his jaws hurt, his mind hurt and hurt. "I am going to," he forced himself to squeak through a throat that had shrunk to a pinhole, "I am going to bury or burn her and then I will go on with my—"

"Bullshit, Peter. What will it be? Bullet? Pills? Razor blade?"

"It will be none of—"

"Which is it going to be?"

His hatred for this Fredrickson man was suddenly huge and unbearable. "I'm going to stand in front of a speeding truck if I have to!" Peter shouted, leaping to his feet. "I'm going to throw myself in front of a train if I have to! Bullets! Pills! Razor blades! *Who in the fuck are you to try and stop me?"*

Fredrickson locked eyes with his. "You know what, Peter?" he whispered in the frozen, pregnant silence. "Do you know what?"

"What?" Peter said, sick of this and everything else, standing like a preposterous wooden Indian with one finger pointing up and his other hand a self-righteous fist under the doctor's nose. He had never hated the doctor before today.

"You are as good as dead," Fredrickson said. "The only thing between you and eternity is the small bother of the method. Sit down."

The words seemed to unlock his bones. He fell back into his chair and nearly tipped over.

"This is against my better judgment," Fredrickson said as if to himself, staring at Peter in his chair with eyes that had no focus. "Against my better judgment."

Peter waited, not caring one iota what the doctor's judgment had to say.

"I know a man," Dr. Fredrickson said haltingly, "a man who knows how to do certain—things. I met him many years ago, and then we lost touch, but I happen to know he is back in business." He leaned forward and pressed his hands together as if to pray, and rolled the pencil between his palms. "Peter, in all honesty I consider it nothing short of a miracle that you have not killed yourself already. Depression is as dangerous as cancer, is a disease of the mind that is very often fatal. Your daughter Darbi has kept you alive these five years since you were afflicted. That she is going to die is fact. As your doctor, my primary responsibility is to keep you alive long enough to make you well. You were making good progress before this catastrophe hit Darbi, though you might not believe it or remember it."

Peter shrugged, not believing it as predicted.

"I know a man," Fredrickson said again, frowning deeply, "a man who knows how to—postpone—death. Are you familiar with the term cryogenics?"

Peter shook his head.

"Simply put, it is the science of freezing human bodies for an indefinite period, and hopefully resuscitating them in the future when a cure for the bodies' sickness has been discovered. My—friend—is on the cutting edge of modern cryogenics. I understand he works with a man who was nearly awarded the Nobel Prize for his research into cryogenic technology some years ago. My friend's operation is very hush-hush, and though no one has told me straight out just *why* it is hush-hush, I have made some assumptions." He looked up. "Are you interested in this at all?"

"Depends on where it's going, I guess."

"Okay. If I am right, the main problem facing the science of cryogenics is that natural death is allowed to occur before the freezing process begins. I have no doubt that the future will bring huge advancements in medicine, technology, psychiatry for that matter. But I do not believe a cure for death will ever be found. When you're dead the electrical activity that made you alive in the first place is gone. Your brain is instantly emptied of memory, intelligence, even the essence of personality. Unlike a car, a brain cannot be jump-started, and if it could, the brain would be utterly blank, even more blank than that of a baby, who is born with a degree of instinct, the ability to suck and swallow, blink its eyes, cry. A corpse electrically resuscitated would not even have the innate ability to perform peristalsis, which is the constant movement of stomach and intestines that drives food through the body. The best one could hope for would be a living brain in a bottle of nutrient solution, but the brain would be as blank as pure vacuum. Stripped of all sensory input, unable to die, the brain would take the only route left to it. It would go insane."

Peter lit a cigarette, feeling chilled. An insane brain floating in a jar of warm gruel, not even able to scream, to die—God, what a horrow show that would be.

"It is my belief that my—friend—has sidestepped this inevitability. He freezes people alive. That's why it's all so secretive."

Peter winced, frowning. "That is absurd."

Dr. Fredrickson smiled. "I find it all too plausible. And so does my friend, if I'm right. The question is, would you want Darbi to undergo the procedure?"

Peter pushed his open hands toward the doctor as if to ward him off. "No. No way in hell."

"She'd be alive, Peter. You would have every reason in the world to keep living, because when she is awakened she will need you."

"No. What good would I be for her if I'm ninety and she's still six?"

"You might be thirty. A cure for cancer could be discovered next year. Would you deny Darbi her only chance to live?"

Peter pulled his cigarette from his lips and tapped it on Fredrickson's pedestal ashtray with fingers that shook.

"What's to prevent her becoming a brain in a jug of Ovaltine, Doc? What if it's a hundred years from now and I'm too dead to prevent it? Absolutely not. No way will I allow this, not in a million years."

"You think about it for a while," Fredrickson said. "We'll talk more at your session next Thursday."

And slowly, perhaps inexorably, the idea began to grow more plausible even as Darbi slipped closer and closer to death and Peter closer and closer to suicidal despair. And after a while, the idea was oh-so-very attractive, was downright magnificent in a sick and deadly way.

And in the end, of course, Peter decided that Darbi's future did not lie in this century, maybe not even in the next one, and that when she woke up hearty and healed a thousand years from now, her world would be a very fine place indeed.

Peter pushed himself away from the hard warmth of the brick wall now, and was starting for Room 126 when the dark Chevrolet piloted by Abraham Maharba cruised past him at a slow idle. The reverend was craning his head around, obviously looking for whatever room he had been assigned; his eyes met Peter's and his face metamorphosed into an instant expression of dumb surprise. He stopped with a short squeal of tires and leaned over to roll the window on the passenger side down. "My good friend!" he called out as if happy about this. "Fate has again cast our lots together, just as the Romans cast lots for the Master's robe. Luke nine, five. I'm in Room One-twenty-eight. Where might you be?"

Peter went to the car and leaned through the open window. On the seat beside him was a white bag that had Wok-King printed in flashy red letters on the side.

"Eating Chinese tonight, are we?" Peter said, his voice thick with bitterness. "Just how can you afford such an expensive meal?"

"A beloved grandfather passed away and left me a tidy sum," Maharba said gravely.

"Care to give me my money back, or what's left of it?"

"Oh, and how I would love to grant that request, my man, but unfortunately I spent the last of it buying this fine footwear." He pulled one leg up into the light, wiggling his foot where a large and new zipper-on-the-side boot gleamed dark and mellow. "The finest that K Mart had to offer, though I'll admit they were somewhat peevish about my arrival at closing time. Fortunately one glimpse of my mighty cannon convinced them to open the doors for me. I even received a tremendous discount."

"That I can imagine," Peter said. He opened the door and sat inside, looking for the pistol but not seeing it. "I believe this is the scene where you hand me my money back and get out," he said, feeling strangely in charge of his life again. It was the nights, always the nights, when the demons of rapidly approaching insanity left him alone for a while. "Do it fast before that guy behind us starts to honk."

"Guy behind us?" Abraham's eyes flickered up to the mirror. He took a sharp breath. "I hate to say this, old friend, but that happens to be a cop."

"Cop?" Peter looked back and saw, dimly, the bar of lights stretched across the top of the car. His heart gave a single, heavy *thump* and seemed to freeze in his chest, utterly dead. "Drive," he whispered to Maharba, almost strangling from the effort of pushing the words out. "Be very casual."

Maharba had different things in mind. He threw his door open and jumped out. "Help! Help! Police!"

The doors on both sides of the police car flew open. The Chevy was still in gear and began to drift slowly away with Peter captive inside, an ice sculpture with wide blue eyes and greasy hair that was nearly standing on end. This jig, his senses told him in a high, panicked voice, is just about up.

"Stop the car!" one of the cops shouted, a black shadow in front of the unbearable lights. Peter heard the police revolver click as it was cocked. He imagined himself jerking over to the driver's seat and mashing the gas pedal to the floor, peeling out in a cyclone of smoke and noise, doing a cannonball run all the way to the Pacific, but unfortunately Darbi was not with him. Yet maybe, he thought as he moved behind the wheel and pressed the brake, her absence is indeed fortunate.

"Get out of the car with your hands raised!" he was told. He put the car in park and climbed out. Maharba was busy shouting something about kidnapping and child abandonment. Shut up, shut up, Peter wanted to scream, but the cop stepped behind him and he was pushed hard against the car. It only took a few moments for him to be frisked and handcuffed; he was spun around and marched past Maharba to the police cruiser.

"Serves you right," Maharba barked. "Trying to kidnap an old man and a minister of the gospel to boot. God may forgive you, sir, but I shall not."

"Shut up," the other cop said, and handcuffed Maharba. "You have the right to remain silent. Anything you say can and will be used against you in a court of law. You have the right—"

"This is a breach of justice," Maharba howled. "I was taken at gunpoint by this, this common *thief!* How *dare* you—"

"Shut up. You're standing in the evidence, mister, because not fifteen minutes ago the K Mart on Grant Street was held up by a preacher and a pair of boots was stolen. Even better, that car is stolen too. You have the right to have an attorney present. If you desire an attorney but cannot afford one—"

"He robbed me," Peter said, watching his chance to talk himself out of this mess rapidly spiraling down the toilet if he did not speak up now and be very damned good at it. "His gun is hidden in the car somewhere."

The cop that had arrested Peter hustled over to look for it. The other one finished reciting Maharba's Miranda rights and put him in the car, ignoring his indignant protests. The Chevy was driven away and parked in the slot in front of Room 104; the policeman killed the engine and ducked out of sight. When he got out he locked the doors and ambled back over carrying the pistol and the sack of Chinese take-out. "Midnight snack, Andy," he said, hoisting the bag. "Put him in the car and let's get the hell out of here before it gets cold."

"Wait," Peter said as the back door got jerked open and hands began to push him inside. "I had nothing to do with robbing any K Mart and nothing to do with stealing that car. The preacher held me up, stole my money, invented this whole scheme."

"We'll straighten it out at the station," he was told. "In."

Maharba leaned across the seat. "Officer," he said quickly, "that man has abandoned a child somewhere in this fine Holiday Inn. He confessed this much to me while begging absolution for his crimes."

The cop paused and looked Peter in the eyes. "You got a kid here?"

"No. He's lying."

"A little girl," Maharba said. "His daughter."

"Well?"

Peter shook his head, where sweat was beginning to form on his hairline. "The man's insane," he said, but the cop had already leaned down and was patting his sweat-stained shirt, his jeans that were stiff with dirt. The cop reached a hand inside one pocket and pulled out the key to 126 on its plastic hexagon. He gave Peter a nasty look and threw the key to his partner. The partner went off to find Darbi and no doubt the Hefty bag of money; this was the end of the line, Peter knew with a cold and dismal certainty, and found to his surprise that he felt almost relieved that this burden of banks and guns and ice was about to be taken from him forever.

The partner came out of 126 and shut the door. "Nobody," he called out. "No luggage, nothing but a bathtub half full of water and a first-aid kit on the dresser."

Peter feld a wild moment of happiness. Darbi had hidden herself, probably under the bed with the money, and the cop had not bothered to look. Smart girl.

"I did find one unusual little thing, though," the cop said when he was back beside the car. Peter saw that he had a fold of white toilet paper in one hand. He peeled it open and showed his partner what was inside. They looked at Peter with expressions of revulsion stamped on their faces, maybe even fear, but Peter did not care because he had stood to see what it was too, and the certainty that Darbi had hidden herself vanished, because he knew she was gone now, had run shrieking into the night, and that he would never see her again.

Nested in the toilet paper was one of Darbi's ears, the black one. It looked very small and very rotten.

They shoved him wordlessly into their cruiser again and slammed the door. As they drove out of the Holiday Inn lot one of the cars parked there sprang to life, and its headlights came on. Peter saw this, saw the driver and the glittering mirror sunglasses on his face, saw that he burned a little rubber hurrying to follow. Braine's man, he thought, and found that he was not very concerned, for without Darbi this trip—and its danger to Braine's brand of secrecy—had ended. And then yet another car came alive and followed, a little red Ford, forming a short convoy. Peter saw it, but it meant nothing to him. If the policemen noticed, they weren't saying.

It took about fifteen minutes to drive downtown to the police headquarters, during which time Abraham Maharba alternately howled his outrage, begged for freedom, or berated Peter for getting an innocent man in such trouble. When the cruiser pulled to a stop and the cops hauled them out, Abraham had reached the pinnacle of his rage, and was hotly insisting that Peter had stolen the boots and forced him, at gunpoint, to put them on.

"Aw, shut up," the one named Andy said tiredly, and they began to walk up the steps that led inside the building, Maharba being practically dragged while screeching about his ministry and his flock. Peter went willingly enough, drained of everything but the smallest hope that someone at the motel had seen Darbi run away, maybe even helped her somehow. He heard a set of tires barking back down on the street, heard a motor accelerate. He glanced back and saw the big dark car, the same one he had seen in Effingham, complete with driver in sunglasses. Peter only thought one thing as the car picked up speed, about to sweep past: Buddy, you're going to go blind if you keep wearing those sunglasses at night.

Weird orange lights flared out of the side window, colorful flashbulbs popping alive and instantly dying, reflecting off those sunglasses and the face behind them. Peter saw the barrel of a very large pistol, bigger even than Maharba's hardware. Someone—one of the cops, Peter thought in a daze—screamed and spun around. The cop holding Peter's elbow dropped down on the steps as if felled by an ax. Small bursts of thunder pounded out from the car while Peter watched with his mouth hanging open and his face blank and stupid. He saw Maharba's head jerk around as if he had been slapped. A warm drizzle of blood sheeted across Peter's face, getting in his mouth, getting in his eyes. It smelled like stagnant water. He stood gaping, too confused to move, watching Abraham perform a slow, unsteady tango as he tried to stay on his feet, but then he collapsed on the steps. Something hard and hot slammed against Peter's shoulder then, making the world a swimming, murky place all of a sudden, and he slipped easily into the comfortable net of unconsciousness, thinking dumbly as he sank that perhaps, perhaps now, he would get some real sleep at last.

TWO

THE SIXTH DAY

SEVEN

IT WAS FAIRLY WELL KNOWN IN CERTAIN AREAS OF ST. CHARLES that Delbert Simms was one of the stupidest men who had ever lived, at least in this town and this century, as the old geezers liked to say. The old geezers were the men of the Canterberry Nursing Facility, where Delbert Simms worked as a day janitor. It had been the center's intention to hire Delbert for the night shift, but when he'd told the supervisor, during his initial interview, that he was a-scared of the dark, the supervisor had relented and given him the day shift. There was more than pity involved, though. Delbert was ecstatic to hear that he would make two dollars an hour and never have to pay taxes and stuff.

It didn't take long for the men and women inhabiting this home to realize that Delbert was missing something between his ears, and though these old people were well aware that making fun of the less fortunate was sinful, it became, as the weeks rolled by, a real torture test to be kindly to young Delbert, who was such a pitiful sight as he tried to change light bulbs in the fixtures and lamps, forever screwing them the wrong way, then both ways before he figured it out, or trying to push his giant four-foot floor-duster through a three-foot doorway, banging it again and again with an expression of vapid stupidity locked on his broad face, and then coming to himself and realizing his error. At one time some months ago, in February, Delbert had attempted the monumental task of changing the water bottle on the water dispenser at the far end of Corridor Six. The service vendor had left the giant bottle on the floor beside the dispenser, and apparently forgotten what he was doing or been called away on some other mission, and it hadn't taken long for the Corridor Six people to get riled about this. Some nurse's aide had trotted to the office and informed the supervisor of the situation, and the supervisor, busy with other things, had suffered a brief mental lapse and told the girl to find Delbert and he would attend to it.

After asking around, she found Delbert scrubbing the men's room floor with a brush and a bottle of Johnson's Wax, which happened to be notoriously ineffective on cement floors, though it did produce a bit of a shine and just enough slickness to cause the elderly geezers traipsing inside to slip and break yet another new and interesting bone. She took his wax away and told him to put the water dispenser in Corridor Six back together, and Delbert trotted off to do it, reeking of wax and urinal deodorant cakes, one of which was still in a pocket of his white uniform, the others dropped into the toilets and promptly flushed away.

As he neared the dispenser and observed its condition, alarm flared in his mind. Never before had he seen the giant bottle separated from its resting place, and it was a frightening new enemy in his endless battle to do things right. His footfalls slowed as he approached this new problem, yet his heart sped up until he feared it might burst in his chest. Old folks were coming on their canes and in their wheelchairs as word spread that Delbert was going to put the giant bottle on its dispenser stand. Money was furtively passed as bets were taken. It didn't take long for a sizable knot of Corridor Six dwellers to assemble into a murmuring crowd. They did maintain their distance, however, in expectation of the flood that must soon come.

There was an orange rubber stopper in the snout of the bottle. An expectant hush fell over the crowd as Delbert tried to wrestle it out. It came free with a hollow *boomp,* left his hand, and hit Barney Smith squarely on the forehead, knocking him over. Friendly hands hauled him back up, and money changed hands again. Two lucky men had made bets that this would happen; the rest had thought Delbert's aim would be poor.

Delbert went into a squat and wrapped his arms around the bottle. It stood two feet high, was some eighteen inches in diameter, and weighed nearly eighty pounds. It was his intention to turn it over and mount it on the stand with such lightning speed that the water would have no chance to escape. The fact that it was the dispenser that needed inverting until the bottle was seated and sealed, at which point the entire contraption could be set upright again, did not occur to Delbert. He hoisted the bottle, took quick aim at the hole, and turned it upside down.

The gush of water was immediate and gigantic, distracting Delbert from his intentions. His pants took the brunt of the onslaught, the floor the rest. Delbert danced and twirled with his strange glass partner, slinging water against the walls. The crowd began to cheer even as they retreated. The soles of Delbert's shoes, still shiny with fresh wax, performed a hopeless clog dance as he began, inexorably, to waltz down the corridor. The crowd parted to let him pass. Barney Smith, still woozy from the encounter with the stopper, wasn't fast enough and got plowed into. As he fell he reached for the nearest support to grab onto, and that support turned out to be Delbert's belt. Even as his pants were yanked down to his ankles, exposing a rather soiled-looking set of Fruit of the Looms, Delbert was gaining speed, headed westward toward a large window and a magnificent new blunder. Silence reigned as he slid past Room Seven, where a lady named Martha Perkins had been awakened by the commotion and was wheeling herself out in her wheelchair. Delbert landed in her lap and together, in mutual panic, they screamed as they zipped to the window and crashed through it. It turned out that Delbert was all right, but Martha, already feeble, was dead before she hit the ground, even though, Delbert would later protest, the drop had been only four feet, not four stories. Only one person really profited from this catastrophe, and that was Ira Goldman, who had bet an even seven dollars that Delbert was going to kill somebody if he wasn't stopped.

Branded with shame, unemployed, Delbert had wandered around town trying to find a new job. He was a haggard and depressed man, verging on suicide if he could only figure out a good way to do it. He wanted to hang himself, but couldn't afford rope. Guns were out of the question, as they cost even more. Slashing his wrists would work, but he was afraid he might cut a tendon and really be in trouble. That left jumping off a building, but heights made him dizzy. Overdose of some kind? Get real. Pills cost a lot of money.

He was defeated once again, and his self-respect began to dwindle. His eyes grew purple bags and his hair began falling out. A haunted vagabond, he lived in boxes and dumpsters and back alleys, slowly metamorphosing into a creature of the night despite his fear of the dark.

And then, just six days ago, as Peter Kaye was beginning his cross-country trek, Delbert tripped over a garbage can and wound up in the hospital's charity ward with a mild concussion and two bruised elbows. When he was well again he told the doctor his tale, and the doctor, taking pity, arranged a full-time job for him as a night attendant in the hospital's morgue, or as Delbert called it, baby-sitting stiffs, which were never allowed to be alone, though Delbert couldn't imagine why.

Thus it was, on this early Saturday morning, that Delbert was sitting in a hospital chair attempting to read a Daffy Duck comic while four or five stiffs rested in the cooler. The newest arrival had been a young child in a pink dress last night, and when Delbert had spotted her being carted in on a steel gurney, already black on one side where the blood had settled and congealed and pasty white on the other, he'd almost fainted. Especially when he'd had to help load her onto a slab and slide her into the cooler. But she was tucked away now, his shift was almost over, he had managed to read two whole pages of his comic, and it was almost time to head home to the YMCA and catch a little shut-eye. He rolled his comic up and waited for his relief.

Something bumped inside the cooler. Delbert's heart jumped into his throat and began hammering away. One cooler door, the one where the kid on her slab was, popped open slightly, pushed from inside against its magnetic latch. Delbert's stomach dropped into his shoes and he very nearly wet his pants.

Bumpity-bump. The door hinged wider. Delbert caught sight of a black foot spastically pressing the door open, and then he knew, oh yes he did, that night work was not for him.

But then the door levered itself shut and there were no more sounds. Delbert's mouth was horribly dry, his head spinning. With a burst of courage he opened the door and slid the girl out on her steel tray.

Nothing. Dead. She even smelled bad. Delbert studied her, frowning, trying to overcome a fright that was almost spiritual in its depth. How the heck had this little corpse done that, that moving and bumping stuff? He bent down and put his ear to her mouth. No breath, nothing. He put on a shaky half smile, ready to push her back into the dark and the cold, telling himself without much luck that he had imagined it all, when her eyes jerked open, shining a stunning blue, and she took one huge, shuddering breath. She sat up partially and her blue lips spread away from her teeth in a dry, hideous grimace. *"It hurts again,"* she warbled in a voice that was bobbling and unhappy. *"Daddy, why does it hurt so bad?"* She slumped down again, her head banging against the tray with a dull, fleshy thud, her eyes falling shut, but by then Delbert had already charged out like a man in flames, never to be seen in this morgue, or any other, ever again.

Kim Marden drove home as dawn was beginning to color the sky with pink and gray slashes, blinking away sleep while her car radio crackled out an unrecognizable tune through a speaker full of dust. She had not used the radio in ages but it seemed necessary now, was a nice diversion from the black and damning thoughts that had been slipping through her mind since the incident at the hospital. The little girl dead for ten, maybe twelve days? It was the first time since high school that something made absolutely no sense whatsoever, and the feeling that accompanied it was very much similar to the way she had felt battling her way through her first geometry test. Nothing had made sense then, and nothing made sense now.

At her apartment building (actually just a big old house on Beech converted into five flats) she parked against the curb and saw that Nina and her car were already home. Eager to repay the debt of hours, Nina had manned the front desk while Kim tried to catch a nap in Gwendolyn's office, but no nap was forthcoming, because every time Kim rested her head on the desk and shut her eyes she saw a white square of cloth with the shape of a little girl beneath it, or failing that, she saw a white square of paper that was supposed to be her resume. Gwendolyn arrived at five-thirty and told Nina to head home, lucky Nina; then she sat up talking debits and credits with Kim as if she had an interest in the motel's profits, which she didn't. Just after six Kim was released from bondage, and counted herself lucky that her Nova had even bothered to start.

She got out now, bone-weary but ready to jump and run if a police car prowling about for Margaret Mason happened to cruise past. It was, to her way of thinking, a miracle that they had not traced her to the motel and pounced on her with questions, the biggest one being, of course, why the hell did you use a phony name at the hospital? She clumped up the wooden steps tacked to the front of the building, glancing around herself apprehensively, and went in wanting only a quick bite to eat, her bed, and about twelve hours of sleep. A light was on in the kitchen when she went inside, stepping high over the birthday clutter, and Nina was there poring over the damned Ouija board again.

"Jesus," Kim snapped at her, "you haven't even gotten

ready for bed yet, girl. That Ouija board is nothing but trouble. To bed with you and to bed with me."

Nina looked up, smiling. "I'm going to miss you," she said dreamily.

"Huh?"

She put a finger on the Ouija pointer and slid it aimlessly around the board. "While you were taking your nap Jerry stopped by. He wants me—he's been bugging me to move in with him. As usual I told him he was insulting my maidenly honor, and he said he'd be by early today with his dad's pickup truck and get my stuff no matter how much I complained, so I said okay."

Kim gaped at her with that strange nothing-makes-sense feeling draping itself over her like a shroud. "Yuh—you what?" she stammered.

"I told him yes." She cocked her head to look up at Kim, her eyes blank and far away. "You know I've been horsing around with the idea ever since he started asking me." She looked down at the board. "Besides," she said softly, "I'm thinking it might be the best offer I'll ever get."

Kim dropped into one of the chairs. It grumbled underneath her, foretelling collapse, as usual. "Nina," she said, frowning deeply, "you're rushing into something you might regret. Jerry's never struck me as being all that serious. You could ruin what you two have together—you guys could be at each other's throats within a week or two—know what I mean? Are you sure you want to take that chance?"

Nina nodded. "Like I said, it might be the last and best offer I'll ever get."

"Impossible. You're only twenty-two!"

Nina picked up the pointer and folded the board shut. "Look at me, Kim," she said. "I don't happen to be graced with Hollywood blond hair and wicked green eyes like you. Half the time I look like a heap of rat shit, my hair all screwy, bags under my eyes. I'm ten pounds overweight and my feet are too big. You've got dimples and I've got jowls. You've got a real bust and I'm a walking advertisement for double mastectomy. I know Jerry's no prince, but I'm not exactly Sleeping Beauty either."

"Oh, quit it," Kim said. "You are a very pretty woman. And have you stopped to think what this will do to me? I'll be lonely as hell here, I won't be able to afford the rent, and I'll have to either move or find somebody to room here."

"I believe that is the condition you were in when I came along last year, *n'est-ce pas*?"

"That's irrelevant. Back then I was pulling night shift at the packing plant, swimming in bucks. I'm a pauper now, Neen, and so are you, but together we've always managed to make it." She reached over and squeezed her hand. "You can't break up the Two Musketeers, can you?"

To her surprise Nina's face fell together and her eyes became shiny with tears. Kim hurried to get a paper towel off the roll above the sink, and handed it to her. "I'm sorry," she told Nina softly. "I didn't mean to make you cry. I guess I just can't believe you'd want to leave."

"Want to? Absolutely not. I think I have to. I think maybe this is the only way I can hang on to what I've got. Do you remember what my mom looks like?"

"Yeah. So?"

"She's fat as a blimp, Kim, and she drinks too much and smokes too much, and she walks around all day in a bathrobe while the TV blasts out soaps. I'm going to be like her, Kim, I can feel it. When I look in a mirror I see her at twenty-two, just starting to swell up to Goodyear size, picking up nasty habits, giving up the battle to look good because it's obviously impossible. If I wait two years, maybe three, I'm going to be so hideous that no man will want me, except maybe some pizza-faced porker with his pants buckled under his chin and his shoes on the wrong feet."

"That's ridiculous."

"Then I'm being ridiculous. I'm also being very serious."

Kim stood up, at a loss for words, and got herself a glass of water. An idea struck her. "Hey, I've got it. Why not invite Jerry to live *here*? Since we work nights and he works days, it'd be like living here in shifts. I'm sure we wouldn't step on each other's toes."

She shook her head. " 'Fraid not, Kim. Jerry's buying his trailer on contract, remember? He'd have to put the thing on the market, and why should he do that? It's really a nice house trailer."

"If you happen to like living in a trailer, I suppose."

"Millions of people do, you know." She picked up the folded Ouija board and began to fan herself with it. "Millions."

Kim was surprised to find herself growing irritated by this nonsense. "You can do better, Neen," she said crossly. "You can do better than some decrepit old trailer and you can do better than Jerry, for that matter. You haven't even bothered to check out other guys, and all of a sudden you want to get married."

"Just live together. And what the hell do you have against Jerry?"

"Nothing. It's not my fault he's so . . . Joe Average."

"Average?" She jumped up, fanning herself in fast-motion, her hair tossing in the breeze she was making, eyes glittering. "I suppose you think Wayne is some kind of special guy."

"No, not that at all. Look, Neen, I'm sorry I said what I did."

"I would hope so. If you ask me, Wayne's a drunk and he looks like an idiot with that stupid hat on all the time."

"I can't argue with that. But at least you don't see me moving in with him."

Nina's face softened, and the angry shine left her eyes. "We must both be dead tired to argue like this," she said, "but there's no sense of me going to bed. It won't be long before Jerry gets here, I'd imagine." She flopped the Ouija board on the table and dropped the pointer on it. "You know," she said quietly as she sat back down, "I'm kinda afraid somehow. Do you think that's silly? I mean, I've known Jerry for two years. I should be used to him by now, don't you think?"

"It's like I said, Neen. You're risking ruining your relationship with him."

Nina scowled, thinking hard. "At my age, it's time to get some security in life. Jerry has a good job."

Kim almost laughed. "Sometimes you're just dingy, did you know that? If you live with Jerry, then decide to get married, then have kids, you'll turn around one day and be thirty and living in so much damned security you'll hate it. I think it'd be a crime to tie yourself down when you're still this young."

"Better that than miss the boat entirely."

"There's a dozen boats waiting out there. You've got your pick."

"Sorry. I've already picked."

They stared at each other. "We agree," Kim said after a moment, "to disagree."

Nina nodded mutely. The silence stretched long while the grimy clock on the oven ground on, buzzing. Through the kitchen window the morning sun began to toss its first warm rays against the glass, promising another scorcher of a day.

"I suppose," Kim said, deciding to surrender now and see what happened, "that I ought to think about getting together with Wayne on some kind of arrangement. I can't afford to live here alone. And you know as well as I do that he wants me there. I'm not saying I'll ever marry the guy, but hell, we might get along all right."

Nina started to nod, then stopped herself, her brows arching while her eyes grew large. "Kim, no!" she blurted out, and reached out with both hands to grasp Kim's forearms. "There are things you should know before you ever, ever do that. Things that—things that Jerry told me."

Kim wrapped her hands around Nina's forearms; they looked ready to engage in some kind of Indian strength test. "Jesus, Neen," she said, "what is it? Don't have a heart attack on me."

Nina stared down at the table. "I probably shouldn't tell you this, but—no. No, I can't."

"Huh? Now you've *got* to tell, or I'll die of curiosity. It must be about Wayne."

Nina nodded miserably. "Something Jerry told me. It's really rotten, but before you go any further with him I think maybe you should know."

"Hold on a sec," Kim said. "My mouth is getting dry already." She stood, picked up her glass, went to the sink, and filled it. She took a drink and turned around. "Go ahead."

Nina took a huge breath, let it out, stammered some nonsense, breathed again. "Can't do it."

"Courage, girl. Remember the Alamo."

Nina giggled nervously into her hands. "Don't do that, Kim. This is serious."

"So what is it?"

"Okay. Jerry told me that Wayne told him, and a bunch of other people, that you are, uh, uh, a dead fuck."

"Pardon?"

"It's what he said."

"A dead fuck? What the hell is that?"

"It means you just lay there while he does all the work. Him and his friends were laughing about it at the Quarter Moon. And he has other girls, all the time. He says if you weren't so damn good-looking when you're—naked—he'd dump you."

Kim turned back to the sink and propped a hand on the rim, clutching her water glass hard enough to turn her fingertips white, staring past the rusty drain into the darkness and muck below. She had no doubt that Nina wasn't lying; Wayne was about as faithful as a Times Square hooker. But to make fun of her, to *slander* her like that, to his other *girlfriends* of all people . . .

She dumped the water in the sink and placed the glass on the counter.

"I'm sorry," Nina said gently. "I thought you should know

before you make some kind of fool out of yourself with him."

Kim turned. "Well, I'm going to hit the sack, Neen. If you need help packing just wake me up. And you know, I really hope you and Jerry make the perfect couple. I guess he's a lot nicer than I thought."

Nina gave her a nod and stood up, smiling awkwardly. She seemed hugely embarrassed. "I think I'll go on over and wake him up," she said. "Be back, you know, after a while."

"Sure," Kim said. "Sure."

Nina went out. The door thumped shut. Kim walked over and stared dully at it for a full minute, feeling parts of her soul flake and crumble inside her like weatherworn paint, wondering why so many things had to turn out so badly. That reminded her of the little dead girl, and she wondered what kind of secret things she had taken with her when she died twelve days ago, and how she had managed to resurrect herself from the dead long enough to scare Kim to the bone while breaking her heart.

She went into her bedroom, pushed the scatter of curlers and dirty clothes left from yesterday off the bedspread to the floor, and fell onto the bed deflated and exhausted, wanting only to sleep and escape. But of course sleep did not come, no matter how many times she ordered her mind to empty itself of reality and fill instead with dreams.

EIGHT

POLICE SERGEANT ANDREW NORTON WOKE UP HALF DEAD THIS Saturday morning, a morning so new the sun had barely begun to tinge the St. Charles Sky with the colors of dawn. He frowned, displaced, confused. He had no pillow beneath his head, was, in fact, lying facedown with his nose mashed into a hard mattress covered by a laundry-fresh sheet. Something to his right was beeping; a cool breeze was drifting down on his back accompanied by the pleasant hum of air-conditioning. Everything smelled new and strange.

He raised his head. A cold swift sledgehammer of pain pounded down on the small of his back, boom, boom. He dropped his head, panting, the beginnings of a good fright trying to coalesce in his mind. He knew only that he had been riding shotgun with his partner Dave Youngblood in Car C-12 and that they had picked up a couple of oddballs at the freeway Holiday Inn; it had happened no more than twenty minutes ago, as he recalled it.

He heard a groan of pain, and needed a moment to realize that the groan was his own.

"Andy?"

"Whuzza?" His lips were too dry, his tongue a useless lump. "Groot."

Instantly someone was beside him, someone who bent over and was laying a warm hand on his shoulder. He tried to raise up again and the sledgehammer found its mark, slamming down on the base of his spine with the force of a wrecking ball.

"Andy, relax!"

He did, dropping his head back down with yet another groan, his nostrils filling with the aroma of foreign bedclothes and his mouth oddly pasty, as if coated with glue. The light was dim and seemed vaguely red.

"I'll get a nurse," the voice said, and Andy realized that of course it was Mercer, Lieutenant Mercer of the St. Charles Police Department, District 12, his superior in the precinct, a very stern and capable man. So what the hell, Andy wondered, is he doing here in my bedroom? And where is Joan?

"Don't try to move," Mercer said. His voice had always seemed, to Andy Norton, a bit too high for a man his size. But he was good, yes, you can bet he was good. He sat on the edge of the bed while Andy tried to piece together the puzzle lying before him, worried perhaps most of all that the lieutenant had found his way to the bedroom and somehow made Joan go away. And just where were the kids?

Something was clicking. Andy turned his face and saw a man's hand with lots of black hair between the knuckles, one thumb of the hand repeatedly pushing a button hooked to a fat cord that ran to the wall above the bed. And the red light, he noticed, was coming from a computer-looking doohickey that was tracing Matterhorn shapes on its screen, blipping a faint noise as it built its foreign mountains and let them fade.

A wedge of light opened across the floor, winking off Lieutenant Mercer's shiny black service shoes. Andy smelled perfume, a strange brand, nothing like Joan would wear. Lights stuttered on overhead, and he saw, he saw.

Hospital room. Bad news for anybody. Especially bad news for a cop. He tried to raise his head, and the pain hit, and he groaned. "Lieutenant," he was able to gasp when his cheek was safely on the mattress again. "Lieutenant?"

Mercer stood up quickly from the side of the bed, making the mattress bounce back into position. Andy almost screamed.

"You're going to live," Mercer said. "Keep that in mind. Nurse, he's awake finally."

"Thank you," Andy heard her say, and wondered why she was not being the slightest bit sarcastic with him. Of course he was awake; of course he was going to live. There was the small matter of a hatchet buried in his spine, but hey, one thing at a time. "You smell good," he said, and was able to grin when she ducked her face into his line of sight, smiling at him. The auburn hair pinned under her crisp white hat sported errant wisps that were pretty spiderwebs beside her ears; she was in her twenties and smelled like eighty dollars an ounce of something French. "How bad off am I?"

She pressed her lips together, hanging onto that smile, but it seemed strained. "It's too early to tell, Officer Norton. You were—" She looked away, her eyes shifting up to the lieutenant. Andy tried to turn his head farther to see what the hell they were staring at each other for, but the pain roared back and he had to give up. She dipped back down into his level of sight. "You were injured. Dr. Simpson will be in very soon."

"Simpson? He's the guy who did my wife Joan's slipped disk and pinched nerve two years ago, to the tune of twenty percent that I had to pay on top of the insurance. Why would I want his greedy ass?" He knew he was being a little crabby, but hell, who wouldn't be? There was a hot charcoal briquet sizzling just above the crack of his ass, getting worse by the second. "My doctor is Barry Raymond. Family practice. Where the hell is Joan?"

Lieutenant Mercer leaned down to look in his eyes, making Andy feel extraordinarily bedridden. "Joan's asleep in the hallway, Andy, she's been up all night. Her sister is watching Tony and little Bill."

"Watching the kids? Why? Just what in the hell . . ." His mouth snapped shut of its own accord, and he knew. From the deepest part of his being, he knew. "Oh, Christ," he whispered, "there was a guy shooting at us, right on the front steps of the station."

Mercer nodded. Andy was filled with a horrible black

cloud of new certainty. "Youngblood? Is Dave all right? Did Dave get, get . . . killed?"

Mercer looked at the floor, nodding almost imperceptibly. "Yeah," he whispered. "Yeah, he did. I'm sorry."

Andy's face was suddenly too hot; a cold weight formed just as quickly in his bowels, a heavy clump like a swallowed mouthful of dirty snow. "Who did it?" he was able to gasp. "Who got my partner?"

Now Mercer shook his head. "Drive-by shooting. That new rookie Michaelson was just coming outside, thought he saw dark hair and reflective sunglasses, the car was anything between a '78 Monte Carlo and a '90 Cadillac. The weapon was a large-caliber pistol, turned out to be a .44 Magnum according to ballistics, with something they'd never seen. The bullets had to be homemade reloads, some weird spiral-shaped steel set on a full wadcutter, making the thing heavier than two slugs put together. It was like shooting a damn corkscrew weighted down with pure lead. We spread the APB's all over St. Charles and eastern Missouri, you can bet your next paycheck on that. What I really need is your recollection before the doc comes in and throws me out, and just maybe we can get this bastard." He dropped down to his knees, looking keenly in Andy's eyes. "I know you hurt, Andy, but for God's sake tell me what I need to know."

Andy nodded, the whisker stubble on his cheek scraping on the fresh sheet. He took a preparatory breath; his back was being jumped on now by a heavy dwarf wearing cleats. "Me and Dave answered the call at the K Mart on Grant Street, might have been ten-thirty. We were too late to see the perp walk out, but we did spot a stolen car that had been radioed about fifteen minutes before, cruising away from a Chinese restaurant. Black guy was driving, dressed like a preacher, turned in at the freeway Holiday, stopped, and this white guy walks up and sits inside. We flagged them, not much resistance, found out the black guy was the K Mart suspect, got them both cuffed, drove back to the station, got out."

"Yeah?" Mercer's eyes were bright. "That's when it went down."

Andy would have shrugged; in lieu of it and the pain it would bring he raised and lowered his eyebrows, wondering in some dim and frightened corner of his mind if he would spend the rest of his life in a bed. "We'd just pulled the two out, were heading for the steps, then boom. Dave dropped down—I thought it was just a defensive move, and you know how fast he is. Bang bang, that's what I heard. I was just going to drop and spin, and then, well . . ." Tears were forming, hot and unwanted. "Did he suffer, Lieutenant? Did he die on an operating room table or get it over with quick? He's my friend, you know."

"I know," Mercer said gently. "Dave was killed instantly, bullet through the back like you, only that freaking corkscrew bullet chewed through his heart. Your wound is, well, I guess you know better than I do."

"One slice above my ass," Andy said. The tears he had not wanted were sliding over the bridge of his nose, pooling in his other eye, and dropping down on that alien sheet. "Am I paralyzed?" he asked. "Lieutenant, am I paralyzed? I can't feel my feet, and not much of my legs."

The young nurse ducked down again. "Dr. Simpson will be here soon. I'm sure he will answer all your questions."

"Touch my foot," Andy said. The tears were leaving him alone, but the fears were sprouting too fast to handle. Here lies the paralyzed victim, he thought while cold terror wrapped its deadly fingers around his heart, making further thinking difficult. Here lies the paralyzed . . . victim . . . awaiting the words that will alter his life forever.

She slipped out of his sight and slid the sheet away—this much he heard, and was able to feel on his right calf—and then there was nothing.

"Do it," he said. "I can take it."

Silence. The air conditioning hummed its gentle snore and the computer thing, the ECG unit, beeped its beeps, making red sketches of scenery. He could hear the faraway zip of her fingernails scraping over the whorls and loops on the sole of his foot, but the nerves below his lower spine rerouted the message to nowhere.

"Jesus God," Andy said, cold with terror, his cheek on the mattress pressing hard against his teeth. "Jesus God."

The nurse came back in view. "That was just a minor prelim," she said, as if such words could possibly be reassuring. "After Dr. Simpson gets that bullet out and you've mended for a few months, well, we will know then, won't we? And there's always physical thera—"

Andy saw quite clearly the shadow of Mercer's hand as he waved it above Andy's line of vision like a warning flag. The nurse rose, vanishing from his sight, then ducked back down, reappearing, a fledgling magician. "Dr. Simpson will be here shortly to explain what happens next."

Gone again. "Lieutenant?" Andy said. "Lieutenant?"

"Right here, Andy."

He was starting to breathe too fast. "Those two guys we were bringing in, the preacher and the guy in the dirty clothes?"

"Uh-huh."

"The preacher was belligerent, kind of odd for a man of the cloth. The other dude was funny. I mean, he was pretty weird. He had a room at the Holiday, and that preacher said there was a kid abandoned there, a little girl, I think." He paused, chugging shallow breaths in and out. "Dave went in, didn't find her, but found a, um, an ear."

"What?"

"It's weird, like I said. He found a really small ear in the bathroom sink, according to him, and it looked like a human ear, cut off some way, by then pretty rotten, smelly. Dave came out of the room with it."

Mercer was frowning. "I haven't ordered a search of your patrol car yet. In fact, I didn't give it much thought. Drive-by shooting, two officers down, I didn't expect much physical evidence in the car besides the bullet holes. Know where the ear is now?"

Andy could only raise his eyebrows. "If it was in one of Dave's pockets, I suppose somebody would have found it already. Might be in the glove box, might be under the seat."

"I'll have it checked. Any idea why it was there in the first place?"

Andy shook his head; his spine submitted a small complaint. "Only thing I know is that both of those guys, the preacher and the whoever-he-is, know each other, and aren't all that friendly. Somebody in that stolen car had a gun, two expended casings in it smelling very recently fired, but the only thing the suspects would do was accuse each other of shit, and none of it made sense."

Lieutenant Mercer leaned closer. "What kind of shit, Andy? What kind?"

He searched his memory, detouring past the part of his mind that loudly insisted PAIN was the only name of this game, and remembered that there was nothing to reveal but petty bickering between the two men, simple stuff with no value at all. "I almost hate to say this," he said, "but if those guys are involved in big-time crime, they're new at it. Very klutzy men who got surprised unawares, I'd bet my badge. Did you get any results on their prints?"

Mercer nodded. "One set, the black guy's index and thumb, courtesy of the computer identifying a Malcom Stiles as our preacher. Of course, he's no more a preacher than I am, though I'll be damned if I know where he got the clothes. Anyway, his record is the usual long-as-my-arm job, petty stuff when he was a teenager, heavier stuff the older he got. He's served a bunch of years here and there, prisons all the way from California to New York. His probation ended a year ago. With the armed robbery charge and his record we can probably get him put away for ten or twenty years."

"Good. How about the other dude?"

"Absolutely nothing. His prints might as well be blank. We're holding him as an accomplice in the auto theft, but it's weak and we won't keep him long. When you two picked him up he already had a wound on his thigh that looked like a bullet could have done it. Incidentally, the black guy got a deep scrape on his head, and the other guy took a clean hit through the shoulder. Whoever was doing all that shooting wasn't very picky."

"So who was he after?" Andy asked. "Us? Them? Who?"

Mercer shook his head. "We're just hoping they can tell us when they come to. As far as that ear goes, I'll have it checked out. Maybe the guy is one of those flipped-out Viet vets who collected body parts in 'Nam as souvenirs. Weirder shit has happened, I suppose."

Andy heard the door sweep open. He watched black crepe-soled shoes walk to him, and Lieutenant Mercer get up. Dr. Simpson, who had wrought expensive miracles on Andy's wife Joan and her back trouble two years ago, ducked down and smiled at him. "Nice to see you again, Andy," he said. "How's the back feel?"

Andy grunted. "It's been better. Am I paralyzed?"

"We're going to wheel you into surgery as soon as I scrub up. The bullet sure looks strange in the X-rays, I'll tell you that, a real original. As soon as I'm done, we'll know what the story is, and we'll figure out where to go from there."

Andy frowned. "What does that mean? When you get the bullet out and I heal up, I'll be done with it, right? Right?"

Simpson nodded. "Sure, Andy. I'm going to have Miss Kuhn start up an IV now, and when you wake up we'll see where we stand."

"Stand?" Andy barked out a sharp and angry laugh. "Will I be able to stand, or do I get to wheel myself around the rest of my life?"

"Just relax. Nurse? Let's get him started."

Her uniform rustled. After a bit she stuck something into a vein in his arm, minor pain came and went, and after that the world began to gray out.

"I'll see you later," Lieutenant Mercer said, but already

the voice was dim and far away. Andy slid into a cold and dark species of sleep where his dreams were fragmented, dreams of wheelchairs and corkscrew bullets and a partner named Dave facedown and bleeding on a stone stairway that went up, and up, forever.

NINE

PETER WOKE UP, OPENED HIS EYES, AND BLINKED TIREDLY AT the white ceiling overhead, feeling drowsy, maybe drugged. It came back to him that he was under arrest and in jail, and he turned his head with a groan, looking for the bars, the other criminals, the jailer. What he saw was a room full of beds in a nice straight row, chrome hat racks on little black wheels with plastic bags of clear fluid hanging from their branches, tubes dangling from the bags and dead-ending in human wrists. Sunlight flooded in through the many windows here and made the whole scene a study in white. He recognized it as a hospital ward, and just as swiftly remembered a part of what had happened last night after he was arrested.

Somebody had shot him. Somebody had shot a *lot* of people.

He turned his head the other way and was stabbed in the right shoulder by a hot pitchfork of pain. He yelped involuntarily, his eyes squeezing shut, wondering if this kind of pain could actually be caused by a bullet no bigger than a cigarette butt. Frowning, he realized something else. The gun had been huge and black, the bullet probably *much* bigger than a cigarette butt. He had seen it clearly under the light cast by . . . by . . .

His memory ended there. He had seen a gun. He had been shot with it. Maybe he had tried to escape and one of the cops had had to shoot him. But somehow that didn't sound right.

He looked at the man on the bed to his right, and saw skin so dark it was nearly shiny, contrasted sharply against the whiteness of the bandages that were wound around his head. Ah yes, my archenemy Maharba, Peter thought. He got shot too. He recalled dimly that last night a spray of blood from Maharba's head had sheeted across his face, getting in his eyes and his mouth, tasting salty and thin. The noise of gunfire had been deafening. Likely it had been some kind of shooting spree against the police, maybe based on an old grudge or the like; if not, it was John Braine's stern and invisible hand reaching across five states to show his displeasure at Peter's very public road show. Yet he had struck Peter as a gentle man with little capacity for anger.

Through the open door of the ward he could hear a doctor being paged, and the sound of many feet coming and going. The smell here, he noticed now, was not much different than the smell of that first-aid kit the pretty girl had given him, antiseptic and warmly sterile. And something was strangely absent; it took a moment to realize his body odor was gone, that he was clean again. Somewhere there was probably a nurse's aide to thank. He tried to sit up and found that he could. His shoulder was thick with bandages and tape, and dull pain was clopping along with the beat of his heart there; he had a blue plastic gizmo stuck in a vein on the top of his right hand, but it was not connected to anything.

He disengaged himself from the sheets and thin summer blanket, saw with distaste that he was wearing some kind of timeworn blue smock, and swung around to put his bare feet on the floor. His sense of balance faded instantly as he stood and he was suddenly swimming in a world that had too many ups and downs. He slumped back onto the pillow before his stomach had a chance to get into the act and eject its contents, if there were any.

Maharba shifted on the bed beside him. His eyes fluttered lazily open and he turned to look at Peter. "Can't you keep it quiet?" he grumbled.

"Sorry," Peter replied. "Are you awake?"

Maharba tried to sit up, shaking and wobbling, and gave up. "What in the hell happened, brother? Oh wait, I remember. Jesus." He raised one hand and touched the turban of bandages, dragging an IV tube as he moved. "I believe one of us has a lot of enemies, my man. Where'd you catch it?"

"Shoulder. How's your head?"

"Exploding." He yawned into his fist. "Whatever that sleeping pill was, I'd sure like a bottle full of them. What time might it be?"

"I don't know." Peter turned and looked out the window behind his bed, where hot sunlight streamed through the glass. "Pushing noon, I'd say. Do you remember exactly what happened last night?"

"Do I remember? You bet your white ass I remember. Some dickhead followed us from the motel to the police station, and as soon as they dragged us out of the car he started blasting away. One of the cops was hit in the back on the first shot, and keeled over. Then you started screaming and dancing around, and then the other cop got shot, and then, then . . . hell, I guess that's when I caught one." He touched his turban again. "Ow. How the hell could I take a hit to the head and still be alive? It must be a miracle."

"Did they catch him?"

He performed a slow shrug. "That I cannot remember, as God often takes our painful memories away, yet leaves to us the pleasant ones. Matthew eight, five."

Peter looked through the open door at the traffic in the corridor. "I wonder if we're being guarded or not."

"I think," Maharba said, "that you can count on it."

Peter sat up again, clutching the edge of the mattress while the world dipped and canted. "I've got to get back to the motel," he grunted. "My daughter's all alone."

"Whoa," Maharba said. "Your daughter, if you have one, was not in that room last night. Remember? And there was something strange one of the cops found inside, but I didn't get a chance to see it."

Peter nodded. "Oh, yeah."

"What was it?"

"I don't remember," he lied. "Maybe I'm in shock."

"Sure. Help me stand up, will you? If we work together we might be able to make it out of here."

Peter emitted a snort. "When the hell did we become the Bobsey Twins, Preacher? You worry about you and I'll worry about me. Deal?"

"You're a real prince today, brother man. Help me up."

"Help *you* stand up?" He laughed without humor. "Sure, watch me go." He stood up and immediately had to sit back down. "Stop the carnival," he muttered.

"Aftereffect of the drugs they pumped into us. Try keeping your head down, stare at the floor. You'll fool your balance into thinking you're lying on your stomach."

"For sure, Doc." He hung his head and stood up. He was wobbling, but he stayed on his feet. He supposed all the other fellows in this oversized room were watching him, and found that he did not give a damn. He would run naked through a convent if it meant finding Darbi before more of her parts dropped off. But as he thought this he quickly realized that unless someone at the motel had seen her go, the chances of finding her were abysmally low. New despair coursed through his mind. She might very well be dead in a ditch somewhere. He shuffled over to Maharba's bed and took him by the arms, hoisted him up to a sitting position, and pulled his legs out of bed. Maharba jerked the IV tube from its connector on his hand, spraying clear liquid in drops, and Peter stood him up on the cool linoleum floor, head still down as was Maharba's now, a pair of very strange-looking characters indeed.

"Doorward," Maharba said, and arm-in-arm they made it to the door while watching the slow progress of their own feet. The intercom was making doorbell noises and requesting a Dr. Pierard, code blue. Peter had seen enough doctor shows on TV to know what that meant. The Grim Reaper was hovering over some poor sick slob, skull face grinning, bony hands ready to swing that long, deadly scythe and part his soul from his body forever. Too bad the guy doesn't know John Braine, Peter thought crazily. John Braine with his money, and that other guy, the sawbones, that Harold Glass fellow who had bored a hole in Darbi's skull and clipped the sacred link between her and mortality.

"I'll take a peek," Maharba said, and unhooked himself from Peter's grasp. Holding the door frame, he leaned out and cranked his head around. There was a thin splotch of blood on the right side of his turban, Peter saw. Perhaps the bullet was still rattling around in his head.

"Hello there, Officer," Peter heard him say in a curt and friendly tone. "I was just checking the hallway for intruders. After what happened last night, well, you can't be too careful, now can you?"

"Get back in there," Peter heard the guard growl.

"Certainly. I was wondering, however, how serious my wound is. I'm having trouble with my balance, you see."

"Balance? One officer is dead, another one is up in ICU recovering from a bullet in his spine, and you're having trouble with your balance. I weep for you, mister, and I weep for your friend who did this, because every cop in this city is looking for him, and when they catch him, he won't have long to live. And if you tell some civil liberties nut I said that, I'll deny it and within ten minutes you'll be missing your teeth. Get me?"

"Mercy me. Am I being charged with a crime?" Maharba asked, sounding meek and surprised.

"You bet your life you are. Did you think just because Norton had a .44 inside his spine his mouth don't work? You happen to be facing charges of armed robbery, grand theft auto, conspiracy to commit murder, and drunken driving. Your pal in there isn't much better off until we find out if the hit man was his or yours. Plus he's got a lot of explaining to do, or so they tell me. Something about an ear, human sacrifice, or the like. Now you get out of my face before I lose my temper."

Peter felt himself go weak with an odd sort of relief. What

he had feared for so long—being unmasked as the new John Dillinger—hadn't happened yet. The charges against him now were more or less absurd. It would be his word against Maharba's word as far as the car theft went, and it was not preposterous to think the man might have some sort of criminal record already.

Maharba drew back from the doorway and pointed wordlessly to their beds. Watching their feet again, they walked slowly back and eased themselves onto them. Peter remembered the pain of the flesh wound on his left thigh, his keepsake from Effingham, and realized that it hurt no more. Either the pain in his shoulder had outbidden it in his bodily auction of aches and agonies, or the doctors here had treated it and made it better. Medicine these days is a strange and wonderful thing, he thought, closing his eyes against the groggy way his mind made pictures appear in his head and then let them drift away, recent memories of people and things that had brought him this far, here to the end of the line. Behind his eyelids he saw a brief snapshot of John Braine, a man in his early fifties whose dark hair had not yet surrendered to gray, wearing a white suit like a Southern gentleman, his eyes dark and piercing, almost menacing. Peter saw another quick picture, a man who had been introduced by Braine as Dr. Harold Glass, his personal physician, an elderly man who looked foggy and confused behind his thick spectacles. Peter saw him, saw Braine again, and as this strange new drugged type of sleep dragged at his mind and threatened to overwhelm him, he began to dwell on the things that seemed so far away now, the things that had happened last Sunday, the day the time clock of fate began ticking its way toward this hopeless day, signaling the beginning, and the end.

"Explain the procedure to him, Harold," Braine had ordered. Peter's psychiatrist, Dr. Fredrickson, had arranged this meeting one day before Darbi slipped into the death that had baited her for so long. Peter's grumpy old Gremlin was parked outside the mansion beside Braine's Mercedes, a stark contrast of rich versus poor, a very ugly thing on the beautiful hundreds of rambling Pennsylvania acres Braine called Inselford Estates.

"I want to make it clear," Glass said, "that this is an experimental procedure that up to now has been performed only on monkeys and rats. If you decide to allow it to be tried on your daughter, I must make it clear that I will in no way accept responsibility for what follows. If you think for one moment you can take me to cour—"

"Harold," Braine interjected, wagging a finger, "I believe Mr. Kaye is a man of his word. Besides, I've had my lawyers come up with an ironclad agreement that absolves both you and me of responsibility. You know that." He turned to Peter, who was sitting nearly paralyzed with doubt on a black leather couch in Braine's spacious den, which was full of books and potted plants, heavy with the scent of pipe tobacco. His doubt was well-founded. Would he go through with this? *Could* he go through with this? He did not yet know.

"I must admit to you," Braine said, "that many years ago I and my cryogenics business ran into an immense amount of trouble with the law. It had nothing to do with Harold's procedure, which is a recent invention and very much a secret until the time comes, if it ever does, to go public with it. It had only to do with faulty machinery, a problem that has been corrected now. Still, I must insist on total secrecy. I was, in fact, very surprised that Fredrickson referred you to me, but he has made his motives clear and I don't fault him for trying to do his best for his patients. He tells me you may become suicidal after your daughter dies. True?"

Peter felt himself shrink a little. Whatever happened to patient-doctor confidentiality? "I've had some psychiatric problems in the past," he said uneasily.

"Minor depression, Fredrickson tells me."

Peter relaxed inside, glad that the doctor hadn't unloaded the whole sorry mess in Braine's ear. "Yes," he said. "I take an antidepressant."

"So you're not actively crazy, in other words."

"Correct."

"You can be trusted with secrets."

"Yes."

"Go ahead, Harold."

Harold Glass tapped a finger behind his right ear. "In this section of the occipital lobe, approximately two centimeters past the inner wall of the skull, is an occipital area of the brain that has long defied medical explanation. The entire section, no larger than a sugar cube, appears to be a dead spot utterly devoid of electrical activity in both humans and animals, though of course in animals it is much smaller."

Peter had reached into his shirt pocket and withdrawn a cigarette, but was hesitant to light it. Braine nodded an okay, and handed him an ashtray.

"Nearly by accident," Glass went on, "I discovered the purpose of that small area of brain matter, which I now call the Mortis Centrum, or death center."

"Actually," Braine said, smiling proudly, "I was the one who came up with it. I've been fascinated by this subject ever since Harold removed a cyst on my fanny eight years ago and asked me if I would consider funding his research. Since he had a scalpel in his hand and I was caught with my pants down, I said yes." He laughed, his flabby stomach bouncing. Peter coughed out a few noises that he hoped might resemble chuckles.

"I had removed the then-unnamed Mortis Centrum from a laboratory chimp for study," Glass said. "The chimp's behavior after the procedure, both learned and innate, was not affected. As usual, under the microscope the brain tissue was tissue, nothing more or less. I was getting pretty damned discouraged. And then I got lucky, and the monkey got unlucky. What happened was fortuitous for me, and for all humanity as well."

"Picture it like this," Braine said, leaning forward, his face bright and eager. "An old man, let's say a real old man, is healthy in every way, no diseases, no injury. Suddenly one night he dies in his sleep. An autopsy shows no heart attack, no stroke, nothing. The old geezer just died, no explanation. His body simply decided to shut down—and of course it's the brain that does the deciding—and his heart stopped, and he died. Yet did you know that when your heart stops beating, you have in actuality the ability to remain alive for a few minutes—two or three? Still, people that are shot through the heart—a soldier, we'll say, or someone in front of a firing squad—die instantly. Why? There's still oxygen in the blood, though it's quickly depleted in the brain. Take a large-caliber weapon, a .45 or the like, and shoot a man in the stomach. Surprisingly, in most instances the victim dies instantly. Why, you ask?"

Peter nodded, recognizing his cue. "Why?"

"Because the Mortis Centrum quickly activates to review the damage, decides if it is critical or irreparable, and switches the brain off forever if the injuries merit it. Of course this does not happen every time—people can and do die slow, lingering deaths—but eventually every brain has to make itself shut down forever." He paused, tapping his chin with a finger, then ducked his head apologetically. "Harold, go ahead, and I'll try to keep from interrupting."

"Fine. The chimp was pretty tame, pretty good-natured. After the operation to remove his Mortis Centrum I let him have free run of the laboratory, named him Chester, spoiled him rotten. And one day he got out, the rascal, and was run over by a car on the street in front of the lab. His stomach area was utterly crushed, both hips broken, one paw nearly torn off. I wrapped him in a blanket and carried him inside, very much in shock, already wondering where I might bury him. Only . . . he wasn't dead. His injuries were massive and should have been instantaneously fatal, but weren't. Rather than let him suffer, I injected an overdose of epinephrine directly into his heart. It went immediately into B-fib and stopped."

"Creepy, isn't it?" Braine said, and Peter nodded, seeing no hope for Darbi in this mad-scientist hocus-pocus.

"Since my primary research was cryogenics," Glass went on, "I immediately realized what I had stumbled across; I could see the futility of modern cryogenics as currently practiced. Freeze a corpse, and that's all you have when you thaw him out—a corpse. But perform my procedure on a living person *before* their disease has a chance to kill them, freeze them alive, and when the time comes when we have the cure for cancer, as in your daughter's case, she can be released and repaired, so to speak."

"And you've never done this to a human before?" Peter asked. "It sounds so, so *weird*."

Braine nodded, and broke his promise not to interrupt. "The entire field of cryogenics might seem weird to laypersons, Mr. Kaye. Since we have entrusted this much information to you, I think I'll be safe in telling you a bit more." He looked at Glass, who shrugged. "You see, Mr. Kaye, at my new facility there are five people frozen already. They are all friends or associates of mine, very brave and determined men and women, and all volunteered to be frozen alive."

"Jesus," Peter whispered. "Did they get that Mortis thing done first?"

"Actually, no. The Mortis Centrum procedure is useful only in cases where a fatal disease or injury is already present. I've been wanting to try it for a long time, so maybe it's lucky for us all that your shrink arranged this meeting. What Harold will do is remove your daughter's Mortis Centrum so that she will not die, which I understand she is very close to doing. The procedure itself is a very minor operation, I assure you, which will be performed in the hospital while the door is guarded by some of my people, for secrecy's sake. This will give you enough time to get her to my facility in Wyoming without having her die in transit."

"For curiosity's sake, why the hell Wyoming?"

"My partner lives there, for one thing, and the state has a very minuscule population in comparison to its size. Wide-open prairie, so to speak, lots of it. Also, Wyoming's state laws are much more lax than any other when it comes to cryogenics—in fact, they have no prohibiting laws whatsoever."

Peter nodded. "Okay, is there any way you could fly her out there? I don't—" He stopped himself, realizing he was about to say *I don't have any money,* which would bring these proceedings to a quick halt. "I don't like to fly. Claustrophobia and all that."

Braine squirmed a little. "I'm afraid I may be under surveillance by the FBI," he said. "I can hardly risk transporting her myself. You, on the other hand, have freedom of movement that I no longer enjoy." He opened his desk and withdrew a slip of paper from the drawer. "This is the number of my partner in Wyoming who will do the actual freezing procedure, as well as a code word you must use when you telephone him once you are safely in Rawlins; else he will ignore the call. Please memorize this and destroy it."

Peter took it, frowning. "So after Darbi has this—center—removed, she can't die?"

"Not for a while," Harold Glass said. "In my research I have learned that when her actual physical death takes place, the heart rate and blood pressure will drop dramatically, very nearly to zero, the heart occasionally not beating for minutes at a time. Brain activity is slowed, but not gone. For reasons I do not understand yet, circulation is limited almost exclusively to the superior vena cava and internal jugular, feeding the brain a bare minimum of blood while ignoring the limbs, by and large. Unfortunately the process of decomposition begins immediately, even seems to be hastened dramatically. I honestly cannot tell you why. Technically the patient is quite dead, though some random spastic twitches can still occur as long as two or three weeks after brain waves are not detectable."

"God," Peter breathed, sickened, wondering what new horror he was visiting upon Darbi.

"There is one more area that my research has not yet been able to remove the cloak of darkness from, though of course

I will win in the end," Glass said, looking very much irritated with himself. "In otherwise normal chimpanzees, commencing almost exactly ninety hours after physiological death should have occurred, the subjects become increasingly hostile, even aggessive. They utter strange noises. In one case the chimp under scrutiny bit its own tongue off while I watched. It bled to—"

"It's not really as grisly as it sounds," Braine said, shooting Glass an expression of cold annoyance. "If Harold's work with animals has taught us anything, it is that the procedure itself causes no physical pain. But for safety's sake your daughter must remain refrigerated until she arrives at my facility in Wyoming."

Peter felt ill. "What made the monkey bite off his own tongue?"

"It was not kept cool, as your little Darbi will be," Braine said. "If there was any way I could arrange the transportation myself, I would have her flown out West on my private jet. But as I said, I have no freedom of movement. I feel sure, however, that you could take a commercial flight with her, but I doubt very much that you could explain the ice away."

Peter stabbed his cigarette out in the ashtray. "I guess I'll have to drive her there. I could probably make it in forty-eight hours if I eat enough No-Doz."

Braine chuckled. "You are very devoted to the child, and I applaud that. I do intend to accompany Harold to Poughkeepsie and witness the operation myself, since it's a first. That is about as far out on a limb I can let myself go."

"I understand." Peter started to rise, but Braine waved him back down.

"I will require five thousand dollars immediately as earnest money," he said, "and the remaining two hundred thousand after the procedure is completed to your satisfaction." Peter saw that he was looking at his clothes and scuffed old Nike tennis shoes with an expression of doubt; Peter himself could feel the blood draining from his face and heart and pooling in those shoes. Two hundred thousand? Darbi was doomed after all, doomed. Unless . . .

"I'll have the earnest money with me tomorrow and arrange for the rest shortly afterward," he said. "Should I pay your man in Rawlins when I get there?"

"Just make sure and get a receipt from the old buzzard," Braine said, and laughed. Glass looked on sourly. "Fine then," Braine said, and stood. "Dr. Glass and I can be at County Memorial at three o'clock tomorrow afternoon. Fair enough?"

"Very fair," Peter said, and shook his hand. "But when I get to Rawlins, how will I find the right place? Is it a building downtown, maybe? Don't I get an address?"

"Hardly," Braine said. "Just dial that number, give the code word, and wait. My partner will usher you from there."

Peter smiled, though his face seemed to have lost all feeling. "Thank you," he said. "Thank you very much."

On the long drive home he suffered a major attack of nerves, and nearly drove his wretched puke-green Gremlin into a Pennsylvania ditch.

Later, after visiting Darbi (who slept all the time now), Peter sat in the heat of his small apartment on Spackenkill Road in Poughkeepsie, trying to formulate some kind of plan that would whip up two hundred thousand bucks in seven days or less. He was immediately struck by the absurdity of it all. It was taking all his resources—a frantic phone call to his father for money, a hasty loan from the college credit union—to amass a measly five grand for the Mortis operation, let alone two hundred thousand for the rest. His father had doubtless scraped the bottom of his barrel to come up with the three thousand that he promised was on the way. How about a really big loan from the bank? Peter thought. Oh, chuckle-chuckle. Why not just go ahead and rob one?

Or two . . . or three . . .

No, he thought, no. Anything but that. He would be cheating himself out of his own future, no matter how dismal it might be. He had little desire to spend the next fifty years in prison as somebody's boyfriend, and Darbi would still be just as dead. For the sake of her life and future, he would have to find a different way.

He pondered as the clock on the floor beside the bed ticked on toward midnight, and was still pondering when one o'clock came. His head ached with failed ideas. His thesis lay on the countertop beside the antique typewriter, a neat and useless pile of paper about an inch thick. He stared at it for quite a while. By two o'clock he had boiled everything down to the only possibility that had a chance of actually working: rob a bank. It scared him to the bone, but it was all that was left.

He went to bed and lay awake all night, sweating in the dark.

Braine and Glass showed up at the hospital the next day precisely at three, tailed by two other fellows—Braine's bodyguards, Peter supposed—one of them looking very nice and a little boyish, the other a big man wearing those annoying mirror sunglasses that didn't allow anyone to see his eyes. The bulge underneath his left armpit spoke loudly of concealed weapons. They stood watch at the door of Room 104 while Harold Glass worked his dubious magic. It only took ten minutes. Peter counted himself extremely lucky that his loan had been approved and the check disbursed earlier this morning, and that the mail had brought his father's check at noon. These were cashed and Peter was pleased to press five thousand dollars in hundred-dollar bills into Braine's hand at the conclusion of this business.

Braine and his people went back to Pennsylvania, and Peter went back home after a glance at Darbi, who had slept through it all. He ate a bowl of tomato soup in the heat of his shabby apartment and pondered how to get her out of the hospital without being seen. He assumed they would frown on him just packing her out in her condition, whether she was his own daughter or not. Without her injections the pain would soon become enormous, critically so. It came to him with the force of a slap that once he spirited her away, she would be leaving all her shots and pain pills behind. He wondered if he could do that to her.

He decided that he could.

It was three-thirty when he left his cruddy little apartment to walk through the relative cool of the night. His overused Gremlin took some cranking and cursing, but it got him to County Memorial. His heart thumped in his throat like a hot, dry tumor as he went up the limestone steps and into the hospital, almost ready to swoon from fright. The halls inside were dim, and only a few nurses were on duty. He slipped past them and went into Darbi's room in the pediatrics ward.

She was gone. There was a spot of red blood on the pillow. All the breath left his lungs in a wheeze and he nearly dropped to his knees, too light-headed to stay on his feet anymore. When it passed and he had not collapsed, he swung the door to go out, to somehow find out where they had moved Darbi, and nearly collided with a nurse coming in, one he had never seen in his many trips here. She had folds of clean sheets draped over one arm. "S'cuse me," Peter mumbled.

"What are you doing here this time of night?" she demanded.

Feeling guilty, he admitted to the crime of visiting his daughter. This softened the nurse up considerably. "Was she in this room, then?" she asked.

"She was this afternoon."

"I'm sorry," she said, and began to fidget nervously. "I don't quite know how to, to *say* this, but your daughter—well, she passed away at about five o'clock. I'm very, very sorry."

Peter's heart threatened to lock up. The procedure, the operation, the five thousand dollars—all a cruel joke, a scam. He tried very hard to convince himself that it was all part of the plan, that she was not dead and would not be for at least a week.

"Do you know where they took her?" he asked, his voice suddenly thin and squeaking.

"The basement, I would imagine."

"Huh?"

"The basement. The . . . temporary resting place until the coroner opens shop tomorrow."

"You mean she's going to have an autopsy?" His mind shifted his mental processes into high panic, with visions of a living Darbi being slashed to pieces on a cold steel table with drains in each corner.

"Only if the coroner finds a reason," the nurse said. "I can assure you, though, that no reasons exist at all. She passed quietly, in her sleep."

Not quite right, Peter told himself without truly believing it anymore. She might look dead and act dead, but she was secretly alive, the embers of her existence glowing dim, but not going out. "I want to see her," he said. "Please."

She shook her head. "You really don't want to, Mr. Kaye. There's nothing left of her but the shell. Her eternal soul is already in heaven, where you will meet her again one day."

He tried to push past her, a woman with the simple belief in an afterlife that brought no solace at all, but she pressed a hand flat against his chest. "Mr. Kaye, this isn't the time. It's the middle of the night, and she's not going anywhere. You need to sleep and make funeral arrangements and do many other things, I would imagine."

"You really expect me to sleep?" he almost shouted. His voice boomed down the corridor, echoing slightly. So much for secrecy, he thought, and dropped his tone down to a harsh whisper. "Darbi is my baby and my life and the only thing I have left. Why separate us now?"

She put on an expression of deep and genuine sympathy. "You don't want to see her."

"Damned if I don't."

"She's not—well, she passed away so quietly, we didn't really discover that she was dead for several hours."

Peter gaped at her. "What?"

"She slept all the time. It was hard to tell."

"Jesus. What kind of outfit is this?"

"We do our best," she replied awkwardly. "We have many other patients to worry about."

Peter gave her a grim and humorless smile, tired of this useless conversation, able to feel the beginnings of a headache. "I want to see her *now* or know the reason why I can't."

"If you feel you have to know," she said, obviously tired of the bullshit as well, "then I will tell you. Your daughter was lying on her side when she passed. Her blood naturally drained to the lowest possible level."

"So?"

The nurse took a long breath. "Dead blood turns nearly black."

"And?"

"Darbi is not pretty to look at."

"Meaning?"

"One side of her body is black. Now, the mortician can hide that very well. I don't think you should see her until he's had a chance to . . . fix her up."

"Is that all?"

"I think it's enough."

"Fine."

He moved forward and she let him pass this time. He went out to the parking lot, listened to the crickets chirp and chatter for a while, smoked a cigarette, then went back in, slinking around corners, sidling through shadows, moving quiet as a snake.

The hospital morgue was indeed downstairs, not hard to find. The basement area contained only shadows and the sharp scent of fresh paint; Peter needed thirty seconds to let his eyes adjust to the gloom. Some kind of machinery was putting out a steady, throbbing hum, which he identified as the gigantic air conditioner that kept this place halfway cool. Pipes wrapped with bulky insulation sleeves lined the walls and jutted out of the ceiling. He had little doubt that the building had stood when his own grandfather was a child.

He saw a door on the left of the corridor, where a square of light shone out of a small window. He went to it and stuck his face close to the glass. There was a different kind of hum now, a closer one. That, he decided, would be the cooling unit for the morgue and its unfortunate guests. Almost everything was brilliantly white inside, well scrubbed. There was a steel table on wheels nudged against the far corner, a wall that had four square doors the size of the average kitchen oven door built into it, and an empty wooden chair with a *Playboy* magazine on it. Peter craned his head, trying to see sideways. He believed there was a law or rule of sorts that required morgues to have someone on watch, for reasons even the dead couldn't know; whoever had been in here had abandoned his *Playboy* and was, in all probability, occupied in the nearest rest room. Peter's already pounding heart began to beat faster. It was now or never.

Something scraped in the darkness to his right, and he quickly drew away from the door and pressed himself to the wall, beginning to sweat. The air conditioner might do its job upstairs, but none of it was sinking down here, where the invisible janitors and maintenance people that kept this place running performed their missions in semidarkness. Peter strained to see, but there was nothing but corridor and overhead pipes. He edged to the door again and pushed it open slightly, peering inside where the light was so bright. He saw nothing but walls and those spooky oven doors. After a mental shrug, he went in.

Heavy feet tromped somewhere in the corridor and stopped at the entrance of the little morgue. Peter's head swung around even as he wondered where the hell he could hide from the watchman in this sterile little cell, and he got a brief glimpse of a large face that had two oval mirrors over its eyes, staring inside. It stayed there a moment, the mirrors showing twin reflections of Peter's face and gaping mouth, then swept out of sight.

Braine's bodyguard, Peter thought, not very sure about it. But if he's Braine's guy, what the hell is he doing here? Peter scrubbed an arm across his face, panting. This was getting too weird, this late-night grave robbing. His hands were shaking worse than ever and his mouth tasted strange things—the sour taste of fear perhaps, or his own blood from constantly chafing his lower lip with his teeth. He had to battle the urge to run out of this catacomb of spies and death, run from here and into the safe and cool night, but a vision of Darbi—so cold and helpless inside one of these awful crypts—made him stop, made his feet turn him around and propel him to the wall and its burden of doors. He reached out a shaking hand and opened the first one.

It was the smell that registered first: a cold, slimy odor like wet seaweed. He ducked and looked inside. The refrigeration fans were roaring, tossing a cold breeze through his hair, but it was empty. He tried the next one, stooping to look for Darbi. He was staring at the pale and wrinkled soles of someone's large feet. There was a tag on the big toe. He eased the door shut and tried the next one.

Empty. He cursed and whipped the next one open, the last one.

Empty.

He heard someone whistling outside, coming closer, but his mind refused to register it for a moment. When his mental alarm finally sounded he froze, imagining someone in charge coming in all full of indignation and questions he would prefer not to answer, even though he had a question of his own: *Where the hell is Darbi?*

The whistler came to the door. The whistler stopped. He changed his tune to something vaguely familiar. He walked away. Peter breathed again, feeling exhausted and drained by these endless comings and goings of strange worries and new terrors. He was bending to recheck the body tray in number four when something shuffled and bumped inside somewhere to his left. He jumped sideways and yanked the third door open, but it was dark and empty. He shut it and reached for the one beside it.

Someone screamed inside. Peter's hair nearly stood on end as shock raced up and down his body like an electric charge. If Darbi wasn't here then who or what in the hell . . .

He snatched the third door open again and looked inside. Too dark, nothing. He pulled the metal slab out on its creaking little wheels. Darbi rolled out into view with it. Her eyes were open, shocking blue against the absurd colors of her face, her black and white face, and her mouth was wrenched open and she was still screaming. Instinctively, Peter bent down to hold her. Her skin was cold and damp under his hands, somehow strange and slick. She smelled like fresh fish.

"Daddy's here, baby," he said, and her arms came up to encircle his neck and hold him tight. She was crying. And God, Peter thought, it is no wonder. Stuck in a horizontal refrigerator, the darkness complete, a corpse to her left and an empty slab to her right, the noise of the fans, the whole rotten mess . . .

He worked his arms beneath her and hoisted her off of her slab, this frail child who had shrunk like a mummy under the endless onslaught of the cancer. She couldn't weigh more than thirty pounds. He held her while she sobbed into the hollow of his collarbone, Peter stroking her back and crooning apologies. The door of this morgue swung open and a chunky little man dressed in white clothes and black shoes came in, and stared at him with his mouth hanging open. "Hey," he said. "Hey."

Peter pushed past him, knocking him against a wall while his protests gained strength and volume. With Darbi flopping in his arms he scuttered down the hall and charged up the steps as fast as he could move, shoes slapping out a fast beat while the orderly shouted behind him. Then Peter was skidding to an awkward stop at a set of double doors that were the freedom gates that would let him out into the night.

They were locked; Peter decided he must be at the service

entrance at the back of the building. Sorry, no deliveries till dawn. He kicked them. The windowpanes rattled. He kicked them again. Somewhere behind him a woman shouted, a nurse who had heard the commotion. He heard rapid footsteps coming from two directions, behind him and below on the stairway. He kicked through the thick glass, which broke and crashed down in huge and noisy shards to the floor. Using his right foot to scrape the pointy knives of remaining glass out of their frame, he rendered it passable while slicing irrevocable gashes in his shoe. He ducked through with Darbi draped bonelessly in his arms and ran into the dark and moonless night. He did not stop until he was around the building and at his car. When the motor was running he left Poughkeepsie and New York behind for what he thought might be a long, long time, but which turned out to be forever.

TEN

I HATE THIS, FBI AGENT STEVE RAFTER THOUGHT, LOOKING across the street to the ornate building there that housed all of the St. Charles government offices, and was the headquarters of the local police as well. I hate this worse than I hate Newell Jackson's stupid ass.

Jared Brooks was sitting beside Steve in the little red Ford, casually leafing through a newspaper that contained a story about the so-called John Dillinger II on the sixth page. Steve had already read it, and was not happy to see that an Illinois state trooper had vowed to catch the guy or die trying. Just what Steve needed: a mad dog on the trail of the man they were trying so hard to protect. But the story on the front page was an account of the reckless shooting spree that left one cop dead, another with a bullet in his backbone, and two civilians in the hospital.

"It's almost one," Jared said, looking at his watch. "You told the lieutenant you'd meet him at one. Want me to do it?"

Steve shook his head. He was tired to the bone and hungry too, but he supposed that between the two of them he looked impressive enough to get what he wanted here; nothing against Jared, but he was a pretty shrimpy guy. Steve rubbed his eyes with his knuckles; they hurt from staring through a windshield that had two huge bullet holes in it. Both he and Jared had been very surprised last night when the man in the black car cruised past the government building and began shooting people, Peter Kaye among them. Steve had spun the Ford in a panicky 360, 180 over the mark, which had not been his intention, and he and Jared had found themselves facing the same direction again—namely, straight into the line of fire. Both had ducked, the bullets had crunched through the windshield, the Escort had attempted to climb the steps that led into the building, and by the time Steve had recovered the mystery man had gone, taillights blending in with distant traffic. Steve had decided to make a hasty exit, not wanting to become entangled with the cops who were streaming out of the building and into the night. And he very much had not wanted Newell Jackson to hear about this mess.

Fortunately, according to the paper, Peter Kaye was not dead, though nobody knew his name yet. According to the paper, an unnamed man was said to be in good condition despite a clean shot through the right shoulder. The other man had been shot in the head.

"Here I go," Steve said, still hating it.

Jared folded *The St. Charles Mirror* up and put it on the dash. "Like I said, I'll do it, if you want."

"Nah." Steve got out and stretched. "God, this heat wave sucks," he muttered, then slammed the door. "Keep an eye on the money, Jared."

"No problem." He bent and patted the big black Hefty bag between his feet that was loaded with Peter Kaye's stolen money. They had rescued it last night before the police could have a chance to make a thorough search of Room 126 at the Holiday, local cops looking for things they shouldn't find. Steve had fully expected to find the corpse of Kaye's daughter inside, but she wasn't there. That, he'd decided, was a mystery for later contemplation.

Now he ambled across the street, dodging traffic, his hands stuck deep in the pockets of his slacks, feeling grumpy and depressed. It occurred to him that he could put a quick stop to this unnatural assignment by simply telling the police lieutenant, that Mercer fellow he'd called to make this appointment, what Peter Gary Kaye was really up to. Then he and Jared could zip back to NYC and a more palatable mission. But orders were orders.

He saw that the steps still bore faded stains that had been fresh blood last night. That made him wonder, not for the first or last time, just *who* in the hell had been doing all that shooting. He supposed it was someone involved with Braine. And, he thought as he reached the huge doors and pulled one open, it was no big mystery why the guy was after Kaye's hide. Braine's operation was very close to being spread wide open, splashed in the papers, all that sort of stuff. If he was really freezing people alive, Braine was a man in a big and ugly mess of trouble.

There was a directory on the wall. It told Steve where Mercer's office was. He tromped up a wide and echoing stairway, able to hear this place mutedly humming with activity, typewriters clacking, people talking. It seemed to be air-conditioned but was still too hot. He battled the desire to rip his tie off, battled it successfully because he'd have to be very convincing and very professional and very believable if this was to work.

Mercer's office was beside the actual police department, where the noise of people, typewriters, and ringing telephones was a constant and distracting roar. He was behind his desk, talking on the phone. He looked up at Steve when he came in, and pointed to the chair beside the desk.

"Just keep them there," Mercer was saying, nearly shouting. He looked weary and haggard, an officer in his late thirties undergoing pressure that Steve easily assumed was enough to drop an ordinary man. Some people got just lucky enough to become a cop. A few others joined the FBI. Maybe they all wound up going nuts.

Mercer dropped the receiver onto the cradle with a bang. "God," he snarled, and looked at Steve again. "You're the guy who called me."

Steve nodded. His tie was a warm vise around his neck. "Steve Rafter, Federal Bureau of Investigation field agent.

Nice to meet you." He showed Mercer his badge, then stuck out a hand. After a pause it was shaken.

"Go ahead," Mercer said. He picked up a pencil and began to tap it on his desk, a fast metronome ticking away the little time Steve felt sure he would get. He cleared his throat. "Lieutenant," he said, "you have two wounded civilians from last night's shooting. Have you been able to get any pertinent information from them yet?"

"No," Mercer said. "Why is the FBI interested, anyway?"

"We're only interested in one of them. Did you get any names?"

"Yeah, we did. One guy's name is Malcom Stiles, though he claims to be a direct descendant of the biblical Abraham and wears the same name. The other guy says he's Pete Jones. Neither one had any kind of ID whatsoever. Stiles is a petty crook, a drifter who screws up once in a while. The Jones character doesn't have any kind of record."

"Pete Jones, huh?" Steve breathed an inner sigh of relief. At least Kaye hadn't been stupid enough to use his real name. "Is he the one who got shot through the shoulder?"

Mercer nodded.

"Any connection between the two?"

"Don't know yet. Personally, I doubt it. Stiles stole a car, robbed a K Mart. All we know about Jones is that in his motel room we found a severed human ear in the bathroom sink."

"Huh?"

Mercer smiled grimly. "It wasn't anything fresh, I'll tell you that. We got the forensics lab working on it, and they figure it's been, uh, amputated for a long time. No, not amputated, but torn off. It belonged to a kid, or a dwarf, hell, who knows? All I can hold Jones for is possession of a human ear, which curiously is not listed in the lawbooks of this state as a crime."

Steve emitted a courteous chuckle, then coughed into his fist. "Has this Jones fellow offered any more information? Confessed to anything?"

Mercer shook his head, frowning. "Nope. What do you think he should confess to?"

"I'm working on a difficult case. Your man Jones is a key player in something we think is highly illegal. You're right in your assumption that he isn't a criminal—not yet, anyway." This was, of course, a brazen lie, but the time for niceties was just about over.

The phone rang, making Steve jump. Damned nerves. Mercer snatched it up, listened with his frown deepening, grunted a few words, and smashed the phone back together. "Cocksuckers," he growled.

"Trouble?"

"Trouble? What makes you say that? Just because the commissioner is screaming for results I can't give him? Pompous bastard. You're with the FBI. Know anything about this that I should know?"

Steve shook his head with the calm dignity of a man who knows very well how to pull the wool over just about anybody's eyes. "Pete Jones has no connection with the shootings," he said smoothly. "Jones is not guilty of any crime yet, as I said, but is an important figure in a nationwide criminal organization that we are determined to penetrate. You could even say that Jones is unwittingly on our side."

Lieutenant Mercer put the pencil down, leaned back in his chair, and hooked his fingers together on top of his head. "You want me to release him."

Steve nodded, still very dignified.

"How about the other man, that Stiles guy? Want him released too?"

Steve started to say no, then reconsidered. What did he really know about Stiles, besides nothing? It might be possible that he was somehow connected to Braine, or even Peter Kaye. "Yes, I would like to see Stiles released," he said. "It is likely that they are both deeply involved in this."

"Just like that," Mercer said, sitting up straight again. He snapped his fingers. "Two men are picked up on charges that are relatively severe. As soon as the patrol car gets to the station, some bastard starts shooting, kills one of my men, wounds another so bad he comes within an inch of being paralyzed—we can count our lucky stars that he isn't—and wounds the two crooks. You expect me to just snap my fingers"—he snapped them again—"and bingo, they're released. Mr. Rafter, what would be your reaction if I told you to go to hell?"

Steve put his hands together, studied them. He had not expected this to be easy, and he hadn't been wrong. "I'm afraid I'll have to insist," he said.

Mercer was silent for a long moment. Phones rang and people talked, somebody laughed, somebody slammed something hard onto a desk and began to shout. Orderly chaos. Steve wished very suddenly that he was back in the New York office where he belonged, even if it meant putting up with more of Marilyn's wifely bullshit every evening when he got home.

"Give me a reason," Mercer said. "That, or something to prove you have jurisdiction in this case."

Steve went ahead and loosened his tie. Mercer wasn't even wearing one; perhaps a casual approach was needed here. "Jurisdiction?" he said, feigning surprise. "Interstate criminal activity is always a concern for the FBI. If you don't release Jones I'll have to go back to the Big Apple with my hands empty, my job on the line, and about a million dollars of taxpayers' money wasted. You can have Stiles, but I want—I *need*—Jones on the loose again. He is our only lead in a case that's over twenty years old."

"Twenty years?" Mercer said. "I haven't seen the Jones guy yet, but from what I hear he's fairly young. Are you sure we're talking about the same man?"

"Quite sure. Mr. Jones is unknowingly leading us on the trail of a crime that began and ended over twenty years ago. But now it's happening again, a new location, one that Jones knows of, but we don't. I can even tell you this. After we're done with Pete Jones he could be facing charges much more serious than what you have in mind for him."

Mercer leaned forward, looking eager despite the fatigue that charted his face with premature valleys and rifts. "Such as?"

"Such as?" Steve thought it over, wondering how much he could safely tell without this Mercer cop getting rabid about having caught the biggest bank robber of the decade, and ruining everything. "Murder," he said.

"Ah, yes," Mercer said softly. He picked up the pencil again and drummed out a fast beat on the desktop. "I guess I could tell the commissioner that Jones is such a big-timer the FBI came in and hauled him out." He blew out a long sigh, looking suddenly relieved. "I like it," he said. "Jones is yours for the taking. He's at St. Mary's Hospital, probably in fairly bad shape with the shoulder and all, but he's yours. I'll call and have the man on duty there allow him to leave with you."

"Dynamite," Steve said, smiling, "but I'd prefer if you just let him walk out. Like I told you, we're tailing him. And incidentally, have you gotten any word here about a, an, uh . . ."

Steve, what were you about to say? Something about the corpse of a little girl?

"Never mind." He stood up and extended his hand. "Lieutenant Mercer, I appreciate this very much. I think we've managed to get both of our butts out of the sling, at least for now."

Mercer was nodding and smiling as he pumped Steve's hand. "Just keep that fucker out of my town."

"Sure. But what's your decision on Stiles?"

"Him I'll keep. The charges against him have some merit, I think. We'll can his ass for ten or twenty years, get him off the streets."

As Steve was about to reply the phone rang, and whoever was on the other end had to be mighty important, he knew, because as soon as Mercer picked it up he was already unloading the new FBI-took-the-bad-man story into the ear of either the mayor, or the commissioner, or somebody from the press.

Steve left the office and walked back to the car, thinking in a vague way that he had accomplished something important, but feeling almost as depressed and gloomy as he had been before. He got to the Ford, went to the passenger side and made Jared get out, then dumped himself inside. It was Jared's turn to drive, whether he liked it or not. Steve tried to catch some sleep as they motored to the hospital, but the sun was too bright and the car's air conditioner was too loud. His mental pictures of a small human ear lying in a sink were even more troubling. When the car stopped at the hospital he did doze off for an unknown tick of time, but then Jared was nudging his shoulder and he had to open his eyes. They seemed full of sand, bloodshot enough to bleed. A glass door at the top of the steps that led into the big brownstone building swung open and Peter Kaye, the key to this whole weary undertaking, came out looking pale and weak and tired, wearing his ratty jeans and filthy T-shirt, a tall and pale young man who transmitted just the slightest hint of insanity behind the gleaming blue of his eyes.

"Here we go again," Jared said, and started the car again.

There they went.

When Peter came out of the hospital and into the heat and the sunshine of this broiling Saturday afternoon, he was little more than a functional robot. The injections and the pills had turned his mind to senseless mush; the sky seemed too high, the ground too low. One arm was in a sling. His right shoe, the one that looked as if it had made a journey through a sawmill, had decided to lose part of its sole, and he could see his toes poking out, feel the heat of the steps and the grit of their surfaces as he tromped drunkenly down them. The authorities had returned to him all of his belongings not five minutes ago, then tossed him out. The cop on guard outside the hospital room had been furious.

He came to the base of the steps and stopped. He was

frowning, wondering through the murky fog of drugs what he should do next. There was a small red car among the others of the parking area, the only one with people inside, he saw, and the only one with bullet holes in the windshield. The two men in it were staring at him, looking about as sleepy as Peter felt. He raised one hand in an idiotic gesture of hello—thank you, drugs—and suddenly the two were busy staring at their laps.

It came to him again that for some strange reason the cops had actually let him go. Maharba had not been happy about this at all, and for a reason he could not understand, Peter felt bad about leaving the man behind. "Abe, my friend, sometimes life just sucks," Peter had told him, and shambled out, bumping into walls and doors, wearing his decrepit old clothes and a silly grin. And now, standing in the heat, no money, no car, no idea where the Holiday Inn might be, no way of finding Dee, he knew that he must find a phone and let his fingers do the staggering for a change. He swiveled his head and saw only cars and oceans of asphalt and unhealthy heat shimmering the air, no phone booth. But he had seen one—where was it? He made himself turn, and struggled back up the steps. Immediately inside was a pay phone; he had seen it but had been too high to remember it clearly. He grabbed the phone book on its cable and slapped it apart, looking for motels in the yellow pages. When he located the Holiday Inn whose address sounded good ("just off I-70, pools, phones, cable TV, lounge open until one A.M. daily") he belatedly felt his pockets, and found to his everlasting joy that he had no coins on himself at all, and that he had forgotten to demand the money Abraham Maharba had stolen from him, which the cops doubtless now possessed.

He went to the admissions window, where a man and two women wearing hospital whites were busy writing the secret things hospital people write. He tapped the glass and one of the ladies looked up. "Could I borrow two dimes or a quarter," he asked her, and she looked puzzled. The window in front of his face had a hole cut into it absurdly low; he stooped and asked her again.

"What for?" she shouted.

He made motions indicating talkie-talkie on the phone. "Emergency," he barked into the hole.

She reached down, retrieved a purse from under her desk, and found a quarter.

"Thanks much," Peter shouted at her, and winked as she thrust it through the hole. He knew, and she had to know, that he would never see her again, never repay that quarter, so sorry about that. At least it reminded him that there were some kind strangers on this earth; not everybody was a John Thomas Braine.

But damn, in Pennsylvania the guy had seemed so *nice*.

He went back to the phone and called the motel. Nice or not, one of Braine's bodyguards was tailing him. Peter believed he knew why—Christ, he thought, even an idiot would know what the guy in the sunglasses was up to. When the road was open and clear, no problem. But when it looked like the whole mission was being blown apart by cops, Braine's man was there to kill him.

He turned and saw a clock on the wall inside the admissions office showing that it was shortly after one. He remembered that the pretty girl at the Holiday had given him an extended departure, all the way to two o'clock. If anybody saw Darbi running around in terror, with luck they would have reported it to the desk, and to the pretty girl behind it. It was a slim chance, but the only chance available. What had been that girl's name anyway, that chick with the blond hair done up so nice, the one with those green eyes that had tried to snatch him away from his mission with sheer charm?

Kim. Yes, Kim was her name.

Holiday Inn go-getter. God, Peter thought as he pushed the quarter in the slot and listened to the connection boop and beep its way down the wires, there we have one giant temptation, but don't forget Brenda, don't forget the way she looked, the way she looked that night in the lodge, so quiet and pale, and so soft and so warm, and then she got bloated and large with our first child, and how we laughed with the knowledge that we were immortal and our child would be a genius.

The phone on the line buzzed twice in Peter's ear, then was answered. A pleasant-sounding female voice said, "Holiday Inn. May I help you?"

"Kim?" Peter asked.

"Kim's not here now. This is Gwen. Is this Wayne?"

"Wayne? No. I need to talk to Kim. Is she there?"

"Not right now, but she'll be here at six. Could I help you with something?"

He brought a hand up and slid it down his face, breathing against it, confused. "Uh, was a little girl found there last night, a girl who looked kind of, well, strange?"

"Not to my knowledge, sir."

"May I ask who was in charge then?"

"Sure. It was Kim. Also a girl named Nina. Could I ask what this might be about? Do you mean you lost a child here?"

It only took a second to think about it. "Yes, I did, actually. I had to go to town for some food. When I got back my daughter was missing."

"Have you called the police?"

"Not yet," he said. "I've been thinking I should talk to Kim first."

She hesitated. "Are you saying Kim had something to do with this? She's a really nice girl. What's your name again?"

"My name? It's, uh, it's Myron Gleason."

There was no reply. Peter heard a pencil being scratched over paper. "Your phone number?" she asked after a few seconds.

"I live in Florida," he replied. "I'm a trucker and I only get home five days a month, so I'm on a pay phone downtown. Did this Kim say anything about a girl?"

"Once again, she did not. I talked to her last night, business-oriented stuff, and she said nothing at all about a little girl. Do you want me to dial the police for you? They could be here in a few minutes."

He bit at his lower lip. No, not that, lady. The cops and I have parted ways forever. "Could you please give me those two employees' phone numbers? I need to know if they saw anything. Can you do that for me?"

"Sure can, but I think we should get the police."

Peter's thoughts began to get cloudy, tangled inside a rising surge of panic; he remembered the bag of money. At two o'clock a maid would go into Room 126, begin cleaning, and find one peculiar Hefty bag under a bag. "Um, I have a sister who lives here. Maybe my daughter walked to her house. You know, I'll bet she did. But could I have those phone numbers anyway? Please?"

"Oh, all right. Hold on, please."

"You bet I'll hold on."

"And let me know what happens," she said.

"I will."

She put the phone down and was gone for a long time. Peter could hear the distant click of shoes on tiles, people talking, the door wafting open now and then, letting the noise of traffic enter the lobby of the motel. He took quick stock of himself to pass the time, a daily ritual of his, knowing that the mental crap would start itself again pretty soon, was in fact already gathering strength. The pleasant drugs that had been pumped inside him were wearing off, abandoning ship, leaving him alone and unarmed to wrestle the legions of mental soldiers and a shoulder that throbbed and screeched with pain. For a tiny piece of time he wished Clint would reappear and take over. At least when he was around, overcrowding Peter's mind with his blustery presence, all the other inconveniences vanished for a while.

The lady came back and gave him Kim and Nina's previously mutual phone number, and their previously mutual address on Beech. Peter forced himself to remember it all, thanked her and said good-bye, pushed the chrome hook lever of the telephone down with a finger while softly mumbling numbers, and dialed. Nothing happened. He clenched his eyes shut. Coins required.

He looked back to the office and the people working there, already feeling his face grow hot with embarrassment. He started toward them, stopped, and went back to the phone, chewing his lower lip.

He called collect. He no longer had any idea which alias he had used last night, but decided it didn't matter much anymore. He told the operator to tell whoever answered, Kim or Nina, that it was a collect call from the little girl's father.

It rang three times, then was picked up. A sleepy-sounding woman answered. "Collect call for Kim or Nina from the little girl's father," the operator said dutifully, and a long pause followed.

"This is Kim." She sounded guarded, even a little scared suddenly. "What little girl's father?"

"Darbi's father," Peter informed both Kim and the operator.

"Darbi's father," the operator repeated.

There was the sound of a harsh, quickly drawn breath. "Oh, my God," Kimberly Marden said. "Oh, my God."

"Will you accept the charges?"

"Yes." Her voice was wobbly and faint. "Yes, I'll accept the charges."

It turned out they had a lot to talk about.

ELEVEN

WHEN THE PHONE RANG, JOHN THOMAS BRAINE RAN OUT OF HIS den, waving away his elderly butler James, who was plodding to the ornate porcelain-and-brass telephone on the oaken stand beside the couch, and answered it himself. "Braine here."

"Mr. Braine." The call was long distance, the voice masked in hissing electricity and loud traffic noises at the far end. "Ready for this?"

Braine took a deep breath, staring through the huge picture window in the south wall of his mansion without seeing the riotous greenery of the woods outside, or the heavy mists of humidity that hung like thin gauze over all of Pennsylvania. He was a bit overweight, his hair free of gray but rapidly falling out, looking very much like Colonel Sanders of chicken fame in his white suit. At this moment all he could see was himself in chains. Harold Glass was in the den, doubtless thinking similar thoughts.

"All right, Trumbull," Braine said. "Let me have it."

"The cops grabbed Kaye last night."

"Jesus." Braine sat down. He immediately stood up again. "Where is he now?"

"About a block away from me. I'm in a booth in downtown St. Charles. He's in the hospital. Nope, nope, cancel that. He's walking down the steps."

"What the hell is he doing in a hospital?" Braine snapped.

Trumbull sighed loudly into the phone. "The fucker leads a charmed life, Mr. Braine, I swear he does. Last night I unloaded six of my little specialty rounds at him, nicked him a little, shot up a few cops, killed one . . ."

Braine's knees unhinged and dropped him on the couch. "You *what?*"

"Hey, they got in the way. You said to take him down at all costs if he gets caught, but don't worry. There's no chance I was seen for more than a second."

"A second might be all it takes, Trumbull, but if he got caught, why the hell is he walking around? Didn't you say you can see him?"

"Sure, yeah, I see him. He's wearing a giant bandage on one shoulder where I tickled him."

"He's been released, then?"

"Sure looks like it. I might be able to drop him from here. Should I?"

Braine thought it over, trying to picture Trumbull shooting at a hospital from a phone booth a block away. Trumbull was not a stupid man, but his overeager attitude wasn't very helpful in delicate situations. "Do not shoot," Braine said firmly. "If he's been released we are still in luck. What did he do with the girl?"

Trumbull hesitated. "I really can't say, Mr. Braine. He left the motel around ten last night by himself, so I tailed him, and lost him some damn place in this screwy city. I went back to the Holiday Inn—"

"The Holiday Inn?" Braine almost shouted. "He spent the night in a Holiday Inn? Jesus!"

"Yep. See, I figured he'd have to come back eventually, which he did. He came back and this car drives up with some black dude at the wheel, and then there were the cops."

"Hold it." Braine stuck a shaking hand in his breast pocket and pulled out a half-eaten tube of Rolaids. He popped two in his mouth, grimacing at the sweet-chalky taste, and put the rest back. "Then what?"

"Well, then the cops hauled him in."

"So what about the girl?"

"No sign of her."

Braine found that he was able to stand up again. "Okay, Trumbull, listen. Stick close to him. If I'm any judge of character he's got only one thing on his mind, and that's keeping his daughter close by. Chances are good he stashed her in the motel, stuck her under a bed, in a closet, who knows? So stay with him."

"Like a shadow, huh?"

"How you do it is up to you. Report back the very second he finds her, because he won't be wasting time. Time for him runs out tomorrow or so."

"Why's that?"

"Nothing that concerns you. And this time don't keep me waiting by the phone so long."

"You bet, Mr. Braine. Anything else?"

"No." He started to hang up, then jerked the receiver to his ear again. "Trumbull?"

"Yeah?"

"If you have to kill him, for God's sake make it quick and painless. If you kill him, I want you to put a bullet through his daughter's head, and her heart too. Quick and painless."

Trumbull hesitated. "Kill a little girl? Isn't that kind of—severe?"

Braine shook his head. "You may never believe this, Trumbull, but it will be the most merciful thing you've ever done. Now get back to work."

He hung up, wagging his head with exasperation, sickened by this prolonged catastrophe. A quick mental calculation told him Darbi had been dead six days almost to the minute. That translated into 144 hours. The longest the monkeys ever made it was ninety hours, and then they got so, became so, so . . .

He pushed the thought away. Peter Kaye was no dummy, and Darbi was a human, not a monkey. She was iced, she had to be. Because if she wasn't, he was going to be in for some very ugly surprises.

He went back to the den, shut the door, went to his desk, and dropped his bulk into the chair behind it. "Brandy?" he said to Glass, who was sitting on a recliner between the potted palms, staring out the bay window with an almost childish sort of glumness clouding his face.

"No, thanks," he said dully. "What did Trumbull have to say?"

"Nothing good."

"Kaye's still on the road, then?"

"Yeah." Braine put his hands flat on the blotter, looked at it, frowned, then got up and took a cut-glass bottle of brandy from the liquor cabinet. He poured himself a snifter while the bottle and glass in his hands rattled against each other. "Damn nerves," he grumbled, putting it back. "Trumbull says the cops got him, and now they've let him go. You figure it out."

"Can't. I guess we have another day or two of this to endure."

"Yeah."

Glass turned his head. "John, let's just kill him." He raised a hand as soon as Braine opened his mouth to speak. "Hold on, I know," he said. "We're not in the business of murder. But look at the risk we're facing. If Kaye makes it all the way to Rawlins—and I'd like to see how he does it with the little time he has left—he might well be trailed by all sorts of authorities. If they find the site, they might not make us unfreeze any of the clients, but they will surely bar it and seal it and our chances to use it ourselves go down the drain."

"I know," Braine said, sniffing the brandy without smelling it, too lost in troubled thoughts. He drank it down as if it were water, no grimace of appreciation, no snort against the taste, no eyes filling with tears. He poured himself some more. "Harold, I made a deal with Peter Kaye that I still consider to be binding, no matter what the risk. I promised that for five grand you would do the Mortis extraction, and for an additional two hundred thousand I would take care of Darbi. Kaye's absurd method of getting the money does not negate the contract."

"Even if it means we get shut down? Austerwahl's planning on becoming a client next year. I'm not getting any younger, and if you keep drinking like that you won't make it to sixty. You would risk our futures for a girl who by now is probably semi-skeletal, maybe having the Mortis reaction already? John, have Trumbull kill Kaye. End his daughter's suffering as well. Trumbull is good at what he does."

"Yeah?" Braine barked out a cold burst of counterfeit laughter. "Then how come he lost Kaye last night? Why doesn't he know where the girl is? Why did he . . . never mind. The man is just the slightest bit on the dense side, Harold, and I am becoming less and less satisfied with him. If Peter Kaye makes it to Rawlins in one piece, I will have Austerwahl finish the operation on the girl. This is—was—my intent. I'm now reconsidering."

"That, at least, is encouraging."

"I much prefer the original idea, though."

"Even if it means exposing us?" Glass stood up, his normally dull brown eyes taking on a bright sheen of anger. "You frighten me, John. I do not want to become maggot food."

"That's certainly a scientific statement, Harold."

"There's nothing scientific about being dead and turning to foul-smelling mush in a rotting wooden box either. I intend to bypass that ugly reality, but I can't if you blow the whole thing over some stupid kid and her idiot father."

"Idiot? No. We were the idiots. You don't need the five thousand bucks, and I don't need two hundred grand, wouldn't even notice if I had it or not. We were so busy trying to close our first new open-market business transaction in cryogenics, skillful contracts, tidy sums of money, everything a neat semi-legal package, that we forgot what the whole idea was about."

"Oh?" Glass put on a little sneer. "What idea might that be?"

Braine sat down again. He stared into his snifter, rolling it in his hands. "For the sake of the dying children, if no one else, we need to accept charity cases. Do you have anything against that?"

Glass frowned, looking confused behind the thick lenses of his glasses. "Well, I guess not, but it is currently illegal to freeze living beings. And consider this. If Kaye manages to get us exposed and shut down, how are we going to treat those dying children, those charity cases?"

Braine sighed. "I hate logic. Until the law changes, we can only legally freeze corpses, and you know how useless *that* is." He slugged the brandy down and smacked his lips. "Harold," he said, "we have got to make a decision here. I'm tired of this risky, horrible business of trying to gun Mr. Kaye down at the point where he's been caught and is about to tell things. It puts Trumbull right at the scene along with the police. And I really can't live with this kind of anxiety. And by the by, Trumbull killed a Missouri policeman last night, wounded another, and only hit Kaye in the shoulder. Kaye's already been released from the hospital. Still think Trumbull's so great?"

Glass lowered himself back into the recliner as the few traces of color in his wrinkled face faded to white. "Oh, no. No, no. Don't blame that on me. It was your plan. You're the one who sent Trumbull off with those orders."

"I suppose you'd rather I said just shoot him and get it over with."

Glass cleared his throat. "Um, I don't know. You know, technically what I did with the girl is not illegal. I am, after all, a medical doctor."

"And quite true to your Hippocratic oath, I'm sure." It occurred to him to apologize for the caustic remark, but he let it drop. "Do you expect me to coldly order the murder of Peter Kaye and his daughter?"

"As I recall, you did last Monday when you sent Trumbull off."

Braine swallowed. Yes, he had done that, told Trumbull to follow that car, gun the sucker down if the heat shows up. What a wonderful humanitarian he was. "That's beside the point," he snapped. "What we have to do now, right here, is decide. Do we let Kaye keep trying, or do we stop him dead, and I mean dead, have Trumbull gun him down and execute his daughter?"

"And dump her body someplace where it will never be found," Glass added, then frowned. Braine could see that he had amazed even himself with such a cold statement. "I mean, dispose of her body with dignity, if possible. An autopsy would reveal the surgery, so we can't have her found, can we? We can't. Agree?"

"Agree? I thought you said your surgery is lawful. Why the hitch suddenly?"

He looked at the floor between his feet. "Kaye should have signed an agreement authorizing experimental surgery to allow me to do it."

"Ah." Braine nodded. "We forgot that little detail, didn't we? What would they do to you?"

"I'd lose my license. Plus I'd be branded as some sort of Frankenstein. It's not all that awful, I suppose."

"But unpleasant, I'm sure."

"Yes."

Braine got himself more brandy, starting to feel his responsibilities in this matter being shifted a little more evenly between him and Glass. A result of the brandy, maybe. He assumed that if he drank enough, he would feel absolutely marvelous, and then instead of being a murderer, he would be a drunken murderer. He sat down again. "About the decision?"

Glass raised his head. "I don't think we've gone over the details of this enough. There must be other facts involved, other ways to approach it."

"So you agree it's a life-or-death decision?"

"Without doubt."

"Then vote. Make your choice. Raise a hand or something." He almost chuckled at this unfunny remark, then cut it off before it had a chance to get out. Jesus Lord, we're sitting here discussing murder, he groaned inwardly. At least we could do it with some compassion.

"We need more time," Glass said. He ran his shaking hands through the remains of his gray hair. "More time."

"No. Trumbull could call back in an hour, or in twenty-four hours. Now is the time. So far I've managed to botch everything, so the decision rests with you."

"But what about Austerwahl? He should have to do this with us."

"Screw him. All he knows is that he's getting a phone call and a code word. He's still so skittish from the disaster of 1968 the mere mention of the law puts him in a panic. This stuff would kill him."

"But we need more time . . ."

"Vote, dammit!"

"But I—"

"*VOTE!* Stop dillydallying. Which will it be?"

Glass rubbed his face with his hands. "Kill them. I mean, no, don't! But we . . . Kill them, I don't give a damn, just get them out of our lives!"

Braine leaned back in his chair, making it squeak, and folded his hands on his large belly. "I believe you have made the only decision available to us, Harold. Keep in mind, though, that the girl is already dead, technically dead. That leaves only Mr. Kaye, who might get gunned down by the police anyway."

Glass got up and wandered to the liquor cabinet. "So you do agree with me? They have to be stopped?"

Braine nodded, and felt a large piece of his soul and his sanity slip away from him to spiral down some dark crack in reality that could lead only to hell. But it had to be done. There was just too much at stake, and he had as little desire as Glass to spend eternity in a soggy box.

"When Trumbull calls again, I'll tell him," he said. "I'll tell him to kill them both. End of discussion?"

Glass nodded as he poured himself a drink, and was able to spill just a few drops before getting his fingers back under control. "End of discussion."

TWELVE

KIM STEERED HER AILING CAR INTO THE ST. MARY'S PARKING lot just off Harrison Street while the afternoon sun cooked down through a thin, damp haze. The Chevy's motor was backfiring and belching much too loudly for this well-marked *Quiet—Hospital Zone.* Kim nervously turned her head this way and that, looking through the heat waves for the man who had told her that his name was Peter Kaye. He'd said he would be waiting out front, that she couldn't miss him, but gave a brief description of himself all the same. Kinda tall, kinda thin, wearing jeans and a black T-shirt and a brand-new sling. Didn't she remember him from last night?

Of course she remembered him from last night. At that time he had been Olsen. Albert Olsen. His filthy clothes and unwashed smell had made him stand out in her memory, despite her job, which turned all customers' faces back into strangers' faces as soon as they left the motel. This Peter had joined that group when he walked out on his daughter and this mess early last night. She thought she remembered handing the guy with the Swedish name a first-aid kit—he'd seemed overwhelmed by her kindness—and then she remembered having seen it on the dresser when she went into Room 126 to investigate the screaming.

Today Peter had called her just after one, the clanging phone on the kitchen wall rousing her out of what snatches of sleep she'd been allowed and getting her out of bed. She hesitated to tell him where Darbi was, too afraid of what he might do, too tired to think straight because even though she had been in bed since about seven, all she had done was remember and remember and remember. Darbi in her bath of ice. The ear in the sink. Darbi falling asleep in bed and never waking up. Darbi covered with a sheet, dead so long. Just as she thought the memory was conquered and was about to drift off, in came Nina and Jerry, thumping and bumping things as they cleared Nina's belongings out. They were done by ten. Nina bid her an apologetic farewell, standing in the bedroom doorway while Kim tried to focus on her with eyes full of swimming grit and bloodshot veins. She gave Kim a promise to see her again tonight at work. Then they left.

She tried to sleep again. Ugly visions of Wayne drifted up from memory to give her a review of their entire relationship, from the start many months ago when his awful hat was between the ashtrays and she was charmed by him, to the present nasty finish, the whole unpleasant Main Attraction overshrouded by the gigantic circus tent of his derby. She knew with intuitive certainty that there would be no final and dramatic showdown between them. He would probably just laugh in her face and run to the nearest secret girlfriend with the hilarious news, and even if he didn't, there was still no point in trying to extract emotional vengeance from such a turd. As she lay in bed with her curlers strewn across the threadbare green carpet of her expensive bedroom, she insisted that all this be shoved aside for at least a few hours. It almost worked. Just this side of a bad dream the phone rang.

"Collect call for Kim or Nina from the little girl's father," the operator said, and instantly Kim was afraid, knowing exactly who it was, more afraid, maybe, than if the cops had called and demanded information she couldn't give.

"This is Kim," she said as her heart began to pound. She felt as if she were being strangled; the kitchen was much too small, not enough air inside. "What little girl's father?"

It was the man who answered. "Darbi's father."

"Darbi's father," the operator said mechanically.

"Oh, my God," she gasped at this confirmation of what she already knew. "Oh, my God."

"Will you accept the charges?"

"Yes," she said. "Yes, I'll accept the charges."

"Thank you for using AT&T," the operator said, and then it was Kim and Darbi's father alone on the line.

"This is Peter Kaye," he said. "I lost my daughter from Room One-twenty-six last night. Did you see her? Do you know anything about where she went? Did anybody else see her and tell you?"

"I know," Kim said.

"You know what? You know where she is?"

"Yes."

He breathed a long sigh of relief into the phone. "God, tell me where."

That was when she hesitated, trying to think clearly between her fatigue and her fright. What would this guy do when she told him Darbi was currently in a morgue? What if he got mad about her own unintended intervention last night? But . . . Darbi had been screaming. Anyone else in Kim's position would have done just the same. Besides, he didn't even know where she lived, did he? Why be afraid of him?

Maybe because he could always find her later at the motel.

She called on her never-used reserves of courage. "I have a lot of questions first," she said.

"They'll have to wait," he barked. "I need her *now*."

"What is wrong with that girl?" Kim demanded, trying, and failing, to sound authoritative. "I have to know that first."

He paused. In the background Kim heard something like a doorbell, heard a doctor being paged, and the murmur of busy people. "I don't have the time to strike bargains with you," he said evenly. "Darbi is getting worse every second that you make me wait."

"I kind of doubt that," Kim replied. She could well envision this Peter man frowning, getting mad, and even though Darbi was his daughter, Kim felt she had a right to know *something* about her weird condition. She had, after all, driven her living corpse to the hospital.

"What do you mean, you doubt it? What could you know?"

Kim took a measured breath. "Mr. Kaye, Darbi is dead. She was screaming in your room, I got her out of the tub, and she died in bed. I'm sorry."

"Oh, great," he snapped. "You took her out of the ice. You put her in bed. When she gets warm she usually conks out."

"You mean dies."

No response, just the rush of his breath.

"What's really wrong with her?" Kim demanded.

"As if it's any of your business, lady. Tell me where she is."

"Not until I get some answers," Kim said, amazing herself with this tough-guy routine that was so unlike her. Maybe working with the public had stiffened her ability to be firm, she thought, because as everyone knew, get ten or twenty people together and there'll be an asshole somewhere in the crowd. The guests of the Holiday Inn were no exception. "Well?" she insisted.

"Who asked you to stick your nose in this? Where is my daughter?"

"I was just doing my job," Kim said in measured tones, "and please don't shout at me. You may think I'm awful, but I need to know what was wrong with her, how she could be alive when the nurse said she'd been dead ten or twelve days, and I don't think I'll ever be able to sleep again after what I've seen unless I know."

She could fairly hear him grind his teeth. "I can't tell you over this phone," he said, able to whisper and growl at the same time. "Please tell me where she is, and then I'll tell you the whole miserable story." He hesitated. Then, timidly: "Please?"

"Where can I meet you?" she asked. "Where are you now? It sounds like a hospital."

"It is. It's St. Mary's, but don't ask me where it's located in this city. Where's Darbi?"

St. Mary's? He's standing right on top of her. "I'll meet you there in fifteen minutes. Where will you be?"

He sighed. "All right, dammit. Out front somewhere."

He gave her his description. After that she had thrown on some jeans and a white blouse and her expensive pair of Reeboks that had taken a month to save up for, rushed out, and coaxed the Nova back to life. Here at the hospital these few minutes later, she prowled up and down the lines of parked cars, looking for a space, her car idling jerkily while the muffler rattled underneath, her face sheened with sweat and her blond bangs stuck to her forehead in wet strings. The huge hospital was bright and white under the afternoon sun, too bright to look at for long, but yes, there beside one of the Virgin Mary statuettes that guarded the walkway was Peter Kaye. He had not mentioned anything about looking like a man with a severe case of battle fatigue. She drove over to him and stopped at the base of the walkway, and he opened the door and sat inside.

"Okay," he said. "Where?"

She looked him over; he didn't seem homicidal, just pale as fresh bone. "Promise you won't get mad, beat me up or something?"

He scowled. "I don't beat people up. Where is Darbi?"

She glanced in the rearview mirror; a car was waiting behind her. "I have to park first," she said, prodding the gas pedal and resuming her search for a space. "Do you remember our deal?"

He was trying to adjust his arm in the sling, pinching at the white canvas, blinking and jerking against the pain. When he was done he said, "Yes, I do remember it well. You go first, though."

She shook her head. "My dad always used to tell me not to

trust a man wearing a shredded shoe." She almost expected a laugh, maybe a smile; what she got was a cold stare.

"Tell me."

She decided to drop the innocent-girl approach, realizing for the first time, and with a measure of surprise, that it was one of several fraudulent personality types she often used in uncomfortable situations, something like the way a soldier would use camouflage. "Mr. Kaye," she said as she tried to shake off that feeling of being a phony, "I brought Darbi to the emergency room here last night around ten or eleven. I thought she was asleep. The nurse there said she was dead, had been dead ten or twelve days."

"More like six, actually."

She blinked. That made about as much sense as everything else today, which was no sense at all. "They covered her with a sheet. I thought they'd made a mistake. I checked her breathing, which was not there, and her pupils. I'm no doctor, but for me if a pupil doesn't shrink under bright light, you're dead. The lady in charge told the orderly to wheel her downstairs. That's where the—morgue—is."

"So she's in the morgue?"

"Right. I remember the nurse saying something about adding her to the coroner's pickup sheet."

"Jesus." His head dropped like loose dead weight until his chin was on his chest and his teeth had snapped together. "What time does the coroner arrive?" he mumbled. "Do you know."

"Uh-uh. But I think she said something about tomorrow afternoon, which would be right now." She found an open slot and steered into it. Two men in a small red car in the space to her left were busy examining something in the distance. Even they looked tired and frumpy. Kim decided it had something to do with the weather, maybe the moon and the planets. "What happens if the coroner gets her?"

He raised his head and turned to look at her, his eyes puffy and red. She decided he looked as tired as she felt, and a twinge of sympathy flitted through her mind. The poor guy looked ready to collapse. “He’ll probably cut her up,” he said dully. “Standard autopsy, pull her guts and brain out, check them over, dump the whole mess including the brain inside her abdomen, and sew her up with thread as thick as shoestring.” He bit at his lip. “Only problem is, she isn’t dead. He’ll wind up killing her.”

Kim made a face. “But that doesn’t explain anything. How can she be dead and still be alive? That’s nonsense.”

He nodded. “That’s what I thought. There are only three people on this earth who know about this, and I’m one of them. I guess you get to be number four, but I advise against it. There are a few very angry people after my hide.” He moved his arm slightly, the one in the sling, and winced. “Ouch. This is a trophy from last night, and I was lucky to get off this easy. Are you sure you want to get involved?”

“Involved? I just want to understand it. Besides, nobody will know.”

“Oh?” Her smiled at her, grimly. “I have no doubt that I’m being watched. Even now. See the two guys in the car beside us? I haven’t got the slightest idea who they are, but I first noticed them in Pennsylvania, and here they are in Missouri. I imagine they just about shit their pants when you parked here.”

She turned and looked at them. “They don’t even notice us. Are you sure it’s the same men?”

He shrugged his good shoulder. “Same car, I know that much.” He leaned toward her, staring at something outside. “Hey, Kim, check that out.”

“What?”

“Look at the windshield.” She did, but the angle was bad. There appeared to be two round patches of cracked ice stuck there.

“So? What is it?”

“Two bullet holes, from my count.”

She craned farther, then nodded. “I’ll be.”

He emitted a sound that came out as an unhappy snort. “If

they're out to kill me, they're not so hot at it. The guy in the sunglasses almost killed them last night, by the looks of it."

She was starting to feel jumpy. "What guy in sunglasses?"

"The man that shot me, and shot a guy I met, and two cops as well. One of them died. Don't you read the newspaper, watch local TV? It's a pretty big thing. So big, I hope, that the guy will give up."

She started to turn off the motor, then stopped herself. "Is it safe to sit here like this?"

He shrugged both shoulders this time, and let out a little yelp. "I don't know what's safe anymore, Kim. I'll go try to find Darbi. Do you have any idea how to get to the basement without being seen? A service entrance, maybe, where they unload trucks and stuff?"

"No. I've only been here once myself. Just go inside and find an elevator, punch the B, presto. You're in the basement."

"How easy that sounds. I hope nobody will get upset when I carry her out that way."

"Sorry," she said, feeling stupid, but cloak-and-dagger stuff had never been her specialty. "I guess I just wasn't thinking, Mr. Kaye."

"Peter," he said. "When they nail me, you'll be the only one who knows what name to put on my tombstone."

That struck Kim as being funny in its own gruesome way, and she smiled. To her surprise Peter smiled back, and as he did a bit of color rose into his face, pushing away some of that sickly paleness. Once again she was struck with the idea that if he wasn't dressed in dirty rags he might be quite handsome, though a little slimmer than she preferred. But then, Wayne was not a bad-looking guy, had a nice build, a winning smile, and a heart as cold as wintertime. So much for looks. Her next man would have a soul, maybe even a brain.

"Kim?"

It came to her that she had been staring at him. She flinched, feeling the color rise in her own face. "Yes?"

"How did Darbi lose her ear?"

She found that she did not know, and was puzzled for not wondering about it before. "It must have happened before I got there. See, she was screaming. That's why I went there in the first place."

"Oh. Did she lose anything else?"

She grimaced, envisioning that dead black ear on that shiny drain. "No, I don't think she did. And that reminds me of the original point. You still haven't told me what the deal with Darbi is."

He looked at her curiously. "You still want to know?"

"Sure. If you're being watched by these men I'm already in trouble, right? Right?"

He gave her a little nod. "Yeah, I guess so." He took a breath. "I'm going to have to make this quick, so listen up. Darbi developed stomach cancer in February. At the time I was still in grad school, utterly broke, and I had already had some psychiatric troubles, which of course did not get any better when she was diagnosed. I have about three separate, um, problems. Mental problems." He looked at her, obviously expecting a reaction. Kim kept her face carefully neutral, not wanting to spoil this. "The worst is the anxiety, I think, which is pure torture. Then the damned depression. It keeps me suicidal. To top that off, not long ago I began developing an alternate personality. I call him Peter the Second, sometimes Clint, because he's real tough, the opposite of me. Does any of this frighten you? I really don't think I'm dangerous. Clint either. Sometimes I get the feeling that another one is on the way, another new me, but there's no way to predict it. He could come from heaven, or come from hell." His gaze shifted down to his lap. "Does any of this bother you?"

She regarded him. There was nothing in his face that indicated danger. "Doesn't bother me," she said, though in reality it did bother her more than she wanted to acknowledge. It was her first encounter with someone who could freely admit that something was wrong with his brain, as if it were as ordinary as chicken pox. "Go on," she said.

"Okay."

She listened with growing unease while he detailed what had happened in the last six days, and the short period before he went on the road, when he struck his deal with a man named Braine. There was a point where she was sure that he was utterly insane, that there had never been any bag full of money and there was no mysterious John Braine and his crazy cryo-whatever-it-was, but her thoughts kept jumping back to Darbi, who really was dead and really was still alive, and this strange Mortis operation explained it quite neatly. The only thing she found hardest to accept was the bit about the money, the hundred grand collected in five states and hiding under a bed at the motel.

Be that true or not, she decided, it didn't alter the fact that Darbi was either still in the morgue or in the hands of the coroner. With any luck, she was still in the lowest depths of this blinding hospital, but it might only be a matter of a minute, an hour, maybe two, before she would be transferred, autopsied, her guts shoveled out, her living brain scooped from the pot of her skull. "God," she said to Peter when he was done. "I didn't *know*. How could I have known something so—hideous?"

He was getting antsy, checking his watch again and again, nibbling his lip. "Call it what you want, but it's the only thing keeping me going." He levered his door open. "Just do me one favor," he said. "Just one."

She didn't have to think very long. "Okay. I guess I owe you anyway."

"Wait for me at the door. I'll find my way to the morgue, try to find the service entrance, then come back and tell you where to meet me with the car. All right?"

She frowned. "Couldn't we wait until it gets dark?"

"Nope. The time factor, remember? Tomorrow is the last day, Darbi's last chance."

"Oh. Okay." She shut the motor down, opened her door, and got out, glancing furtively into the little red car where the two men sat looking old. There was a folded newspaper on the dash, a litter of paper cups and Hardee's bags strewn on the floor. There was a black garbage bag on the back seat. As she passed she saw the bullet holes clearly, holes the size of dimes, a spiderweb of cracks radiating from them. As she began to follow Peter she made sure to leave plenty of distance between him and herself, and couldn't help glancing over her shoulders while she walked, feeling a little foolish, but watching for hidden assassins all the same.

Peter stopped at the base of the steps, where the white statuettes began their climb on either side. "Damn," he grunted when she caught up.

"What's the matter?" She swept her gaze around, spinning in a clumsy circle. There were people busily going in and out; none of them seemed to be armed. "What is it?"

"Those damn drugs they put into me, they make me forget things." He looked at her sharply. "What time do your maids clean the rooms at the Holiday?"

She had to think for a moment. "Well, checkout is at eleven, and the maids start in shortly after that."

"Yeah, but you told me I could stay until two o'clock. What time would that room be cleaned?"

"About two-oh-five."

For an uncomfortable moment she thought he was going to cry at this dismal news. His face screwed itself up and he began to shake. He looked at her as if she had suddenly become a stranger, looked around himself as if these surroundings were new and ugly. He began to sway on his feet. "Peter?" she said, alarmed. "Peter?"

"Oh, shit," he muttered. "Here it comes."

"Huh? Here what comes?"

He was visibly shaking. Sweat began to track down his forehead in thick lines. A young couple, the woman huge with pregnancy, paused long enough on the way up to the doors to stare at Peter. "The mental shit," he wheezed. "What I told you about a minute ago. My mind has to blow off steam once a day or I'd be *really* crazy." He brought his free hand up and knuckled one of his eyes. "God, everything's so damn bright." He dropped himself onto the first step and hung his head to his knees. Kim hovered over him, bewildered. He was obviously in a hell of a lot of pain, but what do you do when somebody's brain hurts? Feed them aspirin?

"Is there anything I can do?" she asked helplessly. "A glass of water, maybe? Do you have any medicine you take?"

His head bobbed up and down. "The cops took it away. I had to tear the label off because it had my name on it. They must have thought it was illicit stuff."

"What's it called?" she asked. Sweat was dripping all over his knees. "Maybe I can find some here."

"Don't bother, Kim," he panted. "It never worked anyway."

The people walking past all gave him a concerned glance before going on about their business. Kim could imagine that they thought he was indeed crying, soaking the knees of his faded Levi's with tears. She went into a squat in front of him. His hand snapped out and caught hers, and began, slowly, to crush it. His seizure that's the only way Kim could describe this strange attack with any degree of clarity—traveled through the bones of her hands and spread up her arm. Her teeth began to click against each other.

"Ow, Peter," she said. "You're hurting me."

"Don't leave me!" he nearly shouted. "Everybody leaves me!"

She looked around guiltily. "I'm not leaving you," she whispered. "But you're crushing my hand."

He eased up, but still held her hand with the strength of a vise. He raised his head slightly and she saw that he was indeed crying now. "Don't worry," she said, and stroked the back of his hand. "I'll go to the motel and find that money." She stood up and tugged at him. "Come on, Peter. Back to my car."

He shook his head. "Why? Why bother? I've tried and tried to do my best, but it's never enough. Darbi's probably in chunks by now, the money's gone, I'm a wanted man, and somebody is trying to kill me." He snorted and snuffled. "Don't look at me, Kim, just hold onto me until this goes away."

She moved around and sat on the step beside him while the sun baked down and the shimmering traffic on Harrison Street droned endlessly past. Hesitantly, she draped her arm over his quaking shoulders; he turned his head and pressed his face between her breasts, sobbing. She was aware of feet clopping by, people murmuring things, but now she didn't feel so awkward, because she realized that just because his sickness was in his brain, it was no different than a bum ticker or a ruptured appendix, so why be so damned embarrassed about it?

After several minutes his shaking tapered off. In a while he was able to sit upright again. He mopped his face with his hand, looking so exhausted Kim wouldn't have been surprised if he simply keeled over. He gave her a shaky, lopsided grin. "Quite a show, huh?"

She pulled her arm away; it was soggy with his sweat. Her heart was going a little too fast still; this episode had been downright scary. "Are you going to be okay now?" she asked.

"About as okay as I ever get, I suppose." He stood up, squinting at things, shielding his eyes with a hand, obviously self-conscious about his display. "What were you saying about going back to the motel?"

She got to her feet as well. "We can look for the money. Maybe the maid will be late or something. Or maybe she turned it in at the desk."

He looked at her with a ghost of a smile shaping his lips. "Do you really believe anybody who works for minimum wage would return a hundred thousand dollars some fool lost?"

She reddened slightly. "Well, maybe. Maybe, you know."

"Darbi has to be there tomorrow," he said. "I don't have time to, uh, *borrow* from another two dozen banks. So what

I'm going to do is get Darbi out of here, and then I will take her to Wyoming and do everything I have to to convince whoever it is out there that he must do the process on her or face my wrath. He might even believe I actually *have* wrath. At least I could borrow some time for her that way, hammer out some new kind of deal later, start making time payments, or maybe I could volunteer for indentured servitude."

Kim frowned, confused. "But Peter, what's to keep them from thawing her out as soon as you disappear?"

He wiped his forehead and slung the drops on the cement. They evaporated instantly. "All I can say is that I believe John Braine might take pity on Darbi. His men are following me and trying to kill me; as far as his cryogenics business goes, it makes perfectly good sense to eliminate me. I'm the one who lied, broke promises, negated contracts when I knew very well how secret this was supposed to be. I only hope he can understand why. And I think, but am not all that certain, that he does." He made a fist and tapped it gently against his lips. "I wish I had a better answer, Kim, I really do." He thought for a moment, then started up the stairs. "Wish me luck."

"Sure. Good luck. I'll be waiting out here."

He waved a hand in a bye-bye motion and tromped up the steps. When he was inside Kim pretended to admire the statuettes, wandered back and forth on the narrow sidewalk, tried everything possible to look nonchalant, but her anxiety level was increasing in a steady tide. She wondered what kind of crime she might be committing, if any. Seemingly none. She was just the wheel man, the guy in the getaway car. Besides, Peter was snatching his own daughter. Try and prosecute him for *that*.

She waited. Minutes dragged past like hours. A dull green van with one stark word written on its side bounced off Harrison Street and up onto the higher pavement of the parking lot, startling her. It slid past her like a dark portent of bad news. The word written in black on its side said, simply . . .

CORONER

. . . and Kim found that further introspection was not necessary; time for some action. Only—she really had no desire to entangle herself any deeper in Peter's trouble. It struck her now that there was nothing stopping her from simply hopping in her car and going away. Who would blame her? Peter was a certified nut, a bank robber (maybe), a shaky guy with one very strange little girl. Kim decided she should simply go home, lounge around until six, go to work, forget this nonsense, find a new roommate, work on that pesky resume some more, ditch Wayne, enjoy life and the serenity of not yet being twenty-two.

She took a step. Her feet turned themselves to the right and she hurried to follow the van. It went immediately right, wound down something that resembled a curving little lane, and stopped at a high chain-link fence whose single sign proclaimed deliveries must be made before eleven A.M. This was what Peter had been looking for, she knew. It seemed obvious that this van had no deliveries to make. Someone wearing a plain gray work uniform, a janitor perhaps, ambled out of the building and to the gate, where he went to work on a large padlock. Kim trotted close to the van, already sweating but expecting more, glad that she did not know what she was doing because if she did, she might stop herself.

The gate jangled as it was hauled open. The van moved forward, going slightly to the right, closer to the building. Kim followed, her knees almost knocking against the van's shiny bumper. She was quickly seized by a certainty that the man in gray would shut the gate again and see her, but knew if she ran beside the van to stay out of his sight, the driver might see her in the rearview mirror. She was already dreaming up a thousand nifty excuses for being here (got lost topping the list), but the van ambled on at walking speed, and the man in gray was on the other side barking howdy-doos to whoever was inside. Kim breathed a little easier. So far so good. The exhaust smelled lousy and sweat was trying to drip into her eyes, but it was victory sweat. She had, at last, managed to do something so foolhardy even Wayne with his rakish manner would be impressed. She had followed a van through a gate. Well, maybe he wouldn't be all *that* impressed.

The van made a huge left turn and stopped. Gears clunked. It began to back up toward a short, descending stairway that led to what had to be the basement. The janitor was still making chitchat. Kim shuffled backward, looking over her shoulder, examining the door behind her. It was barred, but the big hasp had an open padlock dangling from it. She turned and jumped down the steps in two exaggerated hops. She pushed the door open, slipped inside, and pressed it quietly shut again. The janitor was still talking and laughing. She heard his feet grit on the stone steps, and turned to run before he could come down and see her.

It wasn't necessary. Immediately to the left of the door was a mobile clothing rack where dozens of white coats and pants hung on ordinary clothes hangers, awaiting their trip topside. A somewhat sinister-looking corridor branched off in multiple directions before her, growing dim at its farthest reaches. There were no directional signs at all. In here she could hear clangs and rattles and detect the rusty odor of steam. What in the hell am I doing here? she wondered, panicked. The barred door squeaked open. Kim hustled around the rack and wormed herself in behind the clothes. Her heart was beating wildly in her chest and her breath was rushing up and down her lungs too fast, hot as fire. Something gave a loud metallic crack; she heard small wheels squeak. A gurney, collapsible stretcher, whatever. The coroner was here for a pickup.

The noises and voices drew close, went past her, then continued on down the corridor. Kim was suffocating in a world of white clothes still warm from the mangle, and the only smell was the dry and woody aroma of baked starch. She forced herself to stay there. Less than a minute later (Kim would swear it was ten) she heard those squeaky wheels again, and the rattling gurney. It was probably a pity that whoever was riding on it was dead, but that person might keep the janitor and the van driver occupied long enough for Kim to find the morgue. She knew it lay off to the right somewhere because that was where the men and the gurney had gone to make the pickup.

The driver and the janitor sounded like longtime buddies as they came back. One of them was talking about some guy named Delbert something. Kim listened in, had no choice in the matter really. "So I asked Morty when he was coming on shift, where the hell is Delbert? The kid's only been here a few days, and already he's cutting out. I'd heard some weird things about that boy, that Delbert."

"He sure looks funny, I know that," the other said. "Doofy."

"Yeah. So anyway Morty hunts him down and he's in the nurses' lounge sitting on a chair with his feet all drawed up and a look on his face as if he'd laid eyes on the devil himself. Morty tries to talk to him, but all that dip Delbert had to say was *Get her away! Away! She's dead!* all high and squeaky like that. Morty figures he got a bad case of the spooks. New help gets that sometimes. Two, three nights alone with the stiffs, then they can't take it anymore. That's what happened to Delbert, I do believe."

The gurney kept rattling forward. Sweat stung Kim's eyes.

"I got it," the other man barked. "Delbert Simms, that's his name. I seen him at Canterberry's old-folks home many a time. Last I'd heard, they booted his retarded ass 'cause he killed some old lady. Pushed her out a window, he did."

"Damn! You mean the stupid shit's a murderer too?"

"That's what they say."

"No wonder he wigged out. There weren't nothing in the freezer but a few grampas and this here little girl, and God knows she ain't fun to look at, but it ain't so bad you'd lose your mind over it. Must have been him feeling guilty about killing that old lady."

"That's my guess too."

They trudged up the steps, taking their opinions with them. The gurney banged and rattled, and then the van's back doors complained as they were pulled open. More things clunked.

Kim had pressed a knuckle to her mouth, her thoughts racing in the stifling cubbyhole she had made behind the clothes. That had been Darbi, almost within touching distance. She would not have to worry about getting her out of the morgue because she was no longer there. Maybe now it was up to Peter and no one else. All she had to do was wander outside, claim she was lost—no law against that—and go on her way. The worst she had to contend with now might be a cranky janitor.

The van's doors thudded shut. Kim ducked out from among the clothes, saw that the door here was still open, and meandered casually to it, feeling everything *but* casual. The hot outside air draining in through the doorway blew coolly across her damp face, and with a certain degree of apprehensive grace she climbed the stairs and went past the van.

The driver wasn't in it yet. She stopped, heart thudding again, and saw that both men were taking a smoke break and a short walk toward the farthest fence, where wooden pallets had been thrown in a careless pile.

Don't

She put a hand on the door handle.

do

She popped the door open.

anything

She got in.

stupid, stupid.

She started it, dumped it hard into drive, and roared out of the fenced enclosure. The van bounced wildly, tires barking and smoking as she screeched into a left turn, then another, and then she was on the narrow driveway that crossed in front of the hospital.

Peter was standing there at the bottom of the stairs, looking angry and bewildered. Kim wormed a hand in her pants pocket and pulled out her keys as she manhandled the van around the corner. As she passed a few feet in front of him she threw them at him. They hit him on the chest and bounced to the sidewalk. Peter's head snapped around, he frowned at her, and then recognition flashed on his face. He picked the keys up and ran into the parking lot.

Kim went left one more time, hanging onto the big steering wheel while Darbi's gurney slid and bumped in the back, the van's engine roaring insanely, two angry men waving and shouting inside the enclosure as she passed it for her to get the hell back here that's government property. Everything was noise and confusion, but it was not dull motel work, it was not lonely nights alone in an apartment that cost too much, it was not Wayne and it did not wear a derby, no, it did not. It was, Kim decided when she had time to catch her breath, the first stupid and impetuous thing she had done in her entire life, and God, did it feel good. Even the hot air blasting through the open window beside her seemed new and fresh.

She looked back when she was safely on Harrison Street, and saw that Darbi's gurney had come to rest lodged against one of the van's steel walls. Darbi was mercifully wrapped in some sort of green plastic. To be honest, she was starting to smell very, very bad.

In the side mirror Kim saw her old jalopy pull away from the hospital with Peter Kaye behind the wheel. It was jetting huge blue clouds as he hurried to catch up. She glanced back at Darbi again. It was, she thought, miraculous that she had not fallen off the gurney, whose canvas straps dangled from the chrome runners, unfastened. Thank Lady Luck, Kim thought, and got back to the business of getting on the freeway, ditching this incriminating van, and using her own car for the rest of the trip. A part of her mind was reprimanding her for this brash foolishness, but the new side of her, the Kim who might actually make something out of herself one day, was happy enough to shout. She was finally getting out of that town.

Happy, grinning, sweating like a wrestler, Kim did not notice or hear when Darbi punched through the plastic sheet, her hands pressing it out weirdly until it split. Kim did not notice when Darbi slowly disentangled herself from the tatters. She did not notice when Darbi sat up, turned, and put her bare feet on the floor, swaying with the motion of the van as she stood. She was a small thing, Darbi was, and was able to walk erect with the top of her stubbled head barely brushing the van's ceiling.

Kim did not really notice anything about her at all, except that the smell was growing stronger despite the open window. She turned her head and was nose-to-nose with a shocking black and white face whose blue lips were drawn up in a hideous, leering snarl.

"He always liked Mommy best," she hissed. The cold outrush of her breath was all ruin and decay, her eyes woven with crisscrosses of black capillaries. Kim opened her mouth to scream, scooped in a breath to scream, but Darbi's fingers were in her hair, dragging her backward, and Darbi's teeth were on her scalp, biting, biting, seeking purchase.

THIRTEEN

PETER SAW THE GREEN VAN BEGIN TO PITCH AND SWERVE. Fortunately Harrison Street was broadening from two lanes to four as it arrowed westward, but unfortunately the van was headed for a stoplight that was most decidedly red. Cars were honking, dropping back as the van screamed into a wild broadside skid. The tires on the driver's side lifted away from the street, spinning out thin gray smoke as the van tried to tip over. Peter caught a glimpse of Kim's white blouse, saw her arms valiantly working as she tried to steer back on path, wrestling the wheel. He thought for a baffling moment that she had no head, or that she had fallen asleep and her head had tipped back and out of sight. Heart pounding with new fear, he hurriedly changed lanes and followed the van as it bounced back down and skidded backward through the intersection and its stoplight. Southbound traffic locked brakes almost in unison. The noise of honking blasted from four directions. Peter saw two cars spin out of control; one jumped the sidewalk, screeched past two kids who were gaping at the sudden and noisy carnage, and smashed against the steel pole that held the traffic signal suspended over the intersection. Peter shot through just as the entire structure crashed to the street, the big yellow traffic signal bursting into ragged chunks of metal and plastic while digging a crater in the heat-softened pavement. Shards of red, yellow, and green glass sprayed to both curbs. An ancient orange Plymouth went into a sideward skid and wrapped itself messily around a telephone pole, dirty chrome winking and flashing under the brutal sun.

He looked forward again just as the van spun in a full circle, tires howling, and still Kim was there, valiantly spinning that wheel, still with no head. For a moment they were facing each other head-on as the van swung in its tortured circle, and he saw that her head was raked back, her pale neck too long and white, her nostrils twin dark holes. Something was having at her, seemed to be trying to pull her out of the bucket seat. Then the van showed its taillights again, beginning to slow, jerked hard to the right, and lumbered up onto the sidewalk. It clunked to a stop against a yellow fire hydrant.

Peter pulled over, smoking his own tires a little, amazed at just how hard it was to drive a car with only one functional arm. He jumped out and cracked his head on the Nova's door frame. Ignoring the pain, he ran to the van with his hand mashed on top of his sweaty scalp. The van was still idling, but going nowhere with the immutable hydrant blocking its way. Still it rocked on its springs, and Kim was screaming somewhere in the back. He ran around to the rear, giving traffic a glance, not seeing any cops yet. He levered the doors and pulled them open.

Kim was flat on her back on the cargo floor, squirming and bucking, grunting with effort. Darbi was sitting on top of her like a large discolored toad, jerking wildly at her hair. Streaks of blood were smeared on the walls and floor; Kim had several bald patches on her head that were oozing blood and clear fluid. Peter's breath left his lungs in an asthmatic wheeze while his heart gave an unhealthy lurch in his chest. Darbi had jerked handfuls of hair out of Kim's head. Bloody tufts of it were scattered around like abandoned confetti.

Darbi stopped, and swiveled her head to look at him. Her eyes sparkled with savage intelligence. Her lips spread, and she grinned. Blond hair was stuck between her teeth like hillbilly corn silk. "Hi, Daddy!" she said in a cold and syrupy voice that had never belonged to her before, perhaps the voice of someone whose vocal cords had begun to decay. "Why did you leave me alone so long? Why didn't you kiss me good night?"

She lifted her white hand to her mouth, took the dark side of her upper lip between her thumb and first finger, and tore it away. Brown slime leaked out and stained her teeth, which were hideously exposed where the flesh was gone. She puckered what remained of her lips and made smacking noises. "Kiss me, Daddy," she said. "Kiss me and I'll go to sleep."

She threw the piece of lip aside while Peter gaped in horror. It stuck to the van's green wall like a moist black garden slug. She lunged at him, quick as a bat, flopped against him with her arms and legs coiling around his neck and waist, and clung to him like a large squid. She mashed her face to his and began kissing him. Peter tried to push her off, but she was too strong and he only had one hand to work with. She wormed her tongue between his teeth; it tasted like rancid pork. He jerked his head away. "Darbi!" he screamed, staggering in circles under the burden of her weight. "Darbi, for God's sake! Darbi!"

One of her flailing legs slammed him hard in the crotch. The pain in his testicles was stunning, enormous. He folded together in a spasm, eyes bulging, madly batting at her with his open hand. The bandage on his shoulder acquired a red stain in the middle of the flawless white gauze.

"Read me a story!" she howled. "Read me Donald Duck!"

He dropped to his knees, unable to breathe, unable to dislodge her. He dimly was aware of some rickety metal thing clacking. He popped his eyes open long enough to see Kim bumble out of the van with shiny red blood dripping down her face in lines. In her hands she held one end of the folded gurney. She hoisted it clumsily and swung it in a large semicircle. One of the wheels caught Darbi above her right ear with a distinct *crack*! She fell off of Peter and plopped to the sidewalk. Peter buckled again, his forehead bonking on the cement, a volcano of agony nested in the base of his stomach. He heard Kim panting.

"What in the hell was that?" she screamed at him. She had let go of the gurney; it was rolling merrily down the street while cars played duck and dodge with it, tires squealing. "What the hell is really wrong with her?" she shouted, and Peter looked up. She was shaking, pale with fear and rage, hands balled into fists while traffic whizzed by on the street behind her. Her white blouse was splotched and stained with crimson flowers.

He shook his head, barely able to speak. "Don't know," he grunted, but oh, oh, yes, he believed that he did know.

Darbi stirred. Kim stepped back, her remarkable green eyes growing bright with fresh terror. "Not again," she moaned. "Please not again."

Darbi pushed herself up on her hands. Peter heard a siren, one of those damned sirens that had so often announced the hunt was on. This time he thought the destruction at the last intersection would keep them busy for a while, enough time, as happened strangely often, for him to get away.

"Daddy?" Darbi moaned. That thick brown fluid was dripping from her ruined mouth and down her chin like a horrible shade of decomposing lipstick. "Daddy?"

He lifted himself upright and regarded her, still on his knees. The pain was subsiding, allowing him to breathe normally again. "Darbi?"

She began tearlessly to cry. "Daddy, where are we? Daddy, what happened to you?"

He waddled over to her. She had a large slit the shape of a grin above her right ear where the gurney's wheel had hit her. The skin had peeled apart to expose a shallow white canyon of bone. Peter pulled her to her feet while tears and sweat dripped off his chin onto her dress, unaware that he was crying. The smell of her was okay; he could come to live with it. She was shivering, though her skin was warm. The big toe of her left foot was a pointy bone now; she had lost the meat of it. He held her tight, aching with love and outrage.

A shadow fell over them as they huddled together under the blinding light and heat of the uncaring afternoon sun. Peter looked up; Kim was looking down, her face ghost-white, her features stained with an ugly blend of revulsion and fear. "You tell me what that was," she demanded, her voice hollow and shaky. "What made her do that?"

Peter realized in a dazed sort of way that Kim smelled good, was wearing nice perfume of some kind that the breeze from passing traffic urged into his nostrils, something that reminded him of her last night when she was so nice. It seemed to have happened a year ago. "Maybe when she woke up she was scared," he panted.

Kim spat out a laugh. "That's bullshit, Peter. She was everything *but* scared."

He eased Darbi away and looked at her. She seemed somehow bloated, oily. The whites of her eyes were becoming yellow; the black mapwork of veins there stood out in shocking relief. He had worried so much that without her pain medicine she would be in agony, but the Mortis thing seemed to have made that worry senseless. He wondered if her tumor was still growing, then stopped himself. Wondering about such things made even less sense. What was done was done. He looked back up at Kim. "She's okay now," he said.

"Yeah? For how long?" She touched her fingers to a bloody patch on her scalp, wincing.

He stood up. Darbi hung onto his legs, swaying, bobbing as her knees gave out and she locked them back in place. "We just need to get her iced again," he said, and groaned. The thunder in his shoulder was gigantic. Even the scratch on his leg had begun to speak up again. He looked hard into Kim's eyes. "What made you do that?" he asked. "What made you steal the van?"

She ducked her head, seeming embarrassed. "I guess I just lost my mind," she said to the sidewalk, then raised her head and met his gaze. "No, that's not true. I did it because I, um, I want to help. This is the strangest thing I've ever seen in my life, and I kind of feel like I'm a part of it." She shifted her gaze away from him to look at the tangle at the intersection, and Peter followed her eyes. Four police cars and an ambulance had converged on the debacle with their lights blipping and winking. It was Peter's cue to get moving. He disengaged Darbi from his legs and bent to pick her up. "Come on, baby, hop on," he said, hooking his arm around her tiny waist. Her attempt to jump was nothing more than a weak jerk. He was able to hoist her a few inches, then thought her skin might tear and put her back down. "Can you take her, Kim? This business of having one arm sucks."

She hesitated, looking down at Darbi. Doubt was stamped on her face, where the lines of blood were drying to brown in the heat.

"Are we on our own now, Kim?" he asked gently.

She rattled her head as if coming out of a daydream. "And leave me here with the van? No, thanks." She smiled at Darbi and held out her hands. "Come on, Darbi," she said. "We're heading out West. I just hope your daddy has a credit card, Texaco or something."

Darbi nodded, looking sleepy, her eyes wandering in their sockets and her eyelids fluttering. She took a shaky step as Kim reached out to her, and pitched over on her face. Peter jumped as if kicked and managed to catch her in both arms an inch away from the sidewalk, saving her from a new catastrophe, his sling suddenly an odd drapery of white canvas hung around his neck and swaying at his chest, a sling without a purpose. He had no idea how his arm had escaped it so fast, but didn't have much time to wonder, because the pain was really showing its stuff.

He barked out a short yelp without wanting to. There was a hot spike hammering through his shoulder, the price of catching Darbi and maybe popping some stitches in the process. They had told him at the hospital that the bullet had entered and exited without even striking a bone, as if he was supposed to consider himself a lucky guy. Fat chance. He passed Darbi to Kim, too unsteady to hold her, and she took her with hands that had begun to shake again. Peter leaned against the van's hot green skin, waiting for the pain to become bearable again, vaguely wondering just what they *were* going to use for gas. Robbing gas stations sounded very unsafe, especially without a gun.

"I'm sorry," Kim said, cradling Darbi in her arms. Her emaciated limbs dangled as lifelessly as strings. "Peter, Darbi is a sweet and lovable girl, and five minutes ago she tore a few big chunks of my hair out and almost managed to kill me. Don't you have any idea what went wrong?"

He was putting his arm back in the sling, flinching whenever it hurt too much. "All I can do is guess," he said as he worked. "According to Braine and his pal, a guy named Harold Glass who's a doctor of some sort, if you wait too long after that Mortis thing I told you about, you get, um, kind of crazy, I think. But that was with monkeys and rats, dogs too. Darbi is the first human who ever had it done. They told me not to worry about any reaction from the operation. I guess they didn't know what to expect."

"Or else they lied to you."

He nodded. "Possibly. But I didn't have any other alternative at the time. I still don't."

"What about Darbi's mother? Why isn't she helping? Did she leave you when things got so bad?"

"Brenda?" he said hesitantly. "She died giving birth to Darbi." He was done with the sling; things felt a little better now, at least physically. A glance down the street told him the cops were still occupied, but that wouldn't last long. The ambulance was leaving with its siren warbling. He armed his face to dislodge the buildup of sweat there and said, "Let's get out of here before somebody tells the cops about the van. It's not exactly a low-profile getaway car."

"Has Darbi ever gone crazy like that before?"

"No, of course not." He stared at her; she looked as if an insane barber had assaulted her with the clippers. She also looked very dubious. "Believe me," he said. "She is a very gentle girl."

Her frown deepened while the sun sparkled in the green of her eyes. "Peter, until today I didn't even believe in life after death. Now I'll believe anything."

"Good enough," he said. "Let's get out of here."

She hobbled to her car and lowered Darbi onto the back seat. Darbi looked like a corpse not very recently exhumed, and there seemed to be more flies here than there should be. Peter felt a twinge of outrage. Now the insect world had declared war on her.

"Peter?" Kim called out, still bent across the seat with her fanny sticking out. "Peter, what is this?"

"Huh?"

She pulled herself out and dragged a battered-looking black garbage bag with her. She shoved a hand inside and pulled out a fistful of money. The hot breeze snatched one bill free and sent it pinwheeling across the street, where passing cars sucked it along. "You're not as crazy as I thought," she said wonderingly.

He stared at it dumbly. How in the hell . . . ?

A siren wound up to a shriek at the intersection. Kim's and Peter's heads both jerked around at the noise.

"I'll drive," she shouted, and pushed the bag back onto the rear floor. Peter hurried over, slipped past her while she worked, and dumped himself in the passenger side. She scurried around the car, hauled the door open, and stuck herself behind the wheel.

"It's about twenty hours to Rawlins," Peter said, starting to breathe too fast again. The adventure just never stopped on this tortured road. A glance back showed him, to his relief, that that particular cop was headed the other way on some new mission. They both slammed their doors shut. "We need to get some ice first," he said. "Then take 70 West, if you can find it."

"I'll find it," Kim said. "At least now we don't have to worry about gas money, do we, Mr. Dillinger?"

He nodded agreement, suppressing a smile. She dropped the shifter into go, gave it gas, and went.

"It's the heat," Steve Rafter said, stuck at the head of the giant traffic jam Peter and his new girlfriend had just made. He had to give them this much: It was a spectacular mess. Despite the wreck he had no worries about catching up to Kaye and his unexpected partner in crime, name unknown. What had him troubled was what he had seen not two minutes ago, after the green coroner's van had lumbered to a stop against a fire hydrant a block up the road and Kaye had pulled in behind it driving the girl's old Chevy. Kaye had jumped out and run to the van, hauled the doors open, and then, and then . . .

"Just the heat," Steve murmured again.

Beside him, looking ill, his partner Jared nodded agreement. "Heat stress can cause hallucinations," he said for the tenth time. "It's just the heat."

"Yeah." Steve didn't believe it, but he was trying to, was desperate to. He and Jared had watched as Peter Kaye's dead and discolored daughter had leaped out of the van like a lunging shark and attacked her own father, nearly knocked him over. They had watched as the unknown female partner stumbled out of the van and brained the dead girl with the collapsible stretcher thing, while blood ran down the woman's face, visible even from here. Steve had felt sure that Kaye's trip was now at an end. The intersection was alive with cops, people were out of their cars, arguing, shouting, pointing. A cop had walked hurriedly past Steve's open window, shouting at another cop to go check out the green van up the road there. Steve had jumped out. "That's not the same one," he had shouted, and pointed south down the street. "It went thataways." For some inexplicable reason the cop had believed him, and radioed his troops to concentrate on South Barclay Avenue. Steve had decided the show wasn't quite over yet.

They watched as a young man was pulled out of his

ghastly orange Plymouth that was now shaped like a horseshoe, and put into the ambulance. It was Kaye's first real casualty, but at least the man appeared to be alive still. Steve had already decided that, important mission or not, as soon as Kaye killed somebody his trip was over. Whenever Jared's turn to drive came, the only thing Steve was able to do as he tried so hard to sleep was run mental movies starring Kaye as the bad guy, Steve as the good. As it unreeled he saw Kaye in his gun sight, Kaye getting shot, Kaye falling over, dead as he deserved to be.

"Maybe just the heat," Jared said dully.

Steve nodded without replying. It had galled him to the bone to put Kaye's stolen fortune back into the car and into his hands again, but he and Jared had both agreed that without the money he really didn't have much reason to keep going. But now, now—his daughter wasn't even dead anymore. Oh, how Newell Jackson was going to shit bricks when they told him about this.

They watched the Nova pull away from the curb and charge westward, still on Harrison, heading for the freeway and the open country beyond. Ten minutes later a team of wreckers had removed the litter of smashed cars, some courteous cops had procured brooms somewhere and swept paths through the glittering shards of headlight glass, and Steve and Jared were under way again, shaken, wondering, though Steve, at least, was strangely willing to see this ugly thing through to the end now.

It had been no hallucination, that thing with Kaye's daughter. He believed that quite firmly. He couldn't wait to find out how Kaye had fooled everyone into thinking she was dead when she wasn't, and why, for that matter, he thought it necessary to fool anyone at all. Steve also wanted to know one last little thing too.

He wanted to know what had turned her so damned vicious.

* * *

Morris Trumbull was at the tail end of the jam, hot, fuming, cursing, really laying on that horn while sweat dripped down the lenses of his mirror sunglasses. He did not know what had caused such traffic. He only knew that Kaye was someplace he was not. In a way he felt it would not be hard to find him again; Morris Trumbull had watched, stunned, as a green van shot past Kaye at the hospital, the girl inside threw some keys at him, and he ran to a crappy-looking Chevy Nova. Zoom, he was gone, but Trumbull already had a make on the car. He had held off chasing him, instinctively waiting so as not to cause suspicion, even though Kaye would have to be a moron not to know Trumbull was after him. Trumbull also waited to see if others were trailing Kaye. A little red Ford flew after him, and Trumbull supposed he had seen it before. His only solution to this possible mystery was that Braine had sent the two men after *him*, to make sure he did his job. Last night at the police station he had gotten two quick shots at them, blowing holes in their windshield, then spent the rest of the night worrying if Kaye was dead, worrying if he had managed inadvertently to kill one of his own boss's men. In reality, as he'd found out soon enough, nobody was dead except one cop.

Well, he had thought sullenly more than once since then, Braine was the one who said to drop Kaye at all costs. It was *his* fault the cop got killed, not Trumbull's.

He looked at his watch now. Ten minutes had passed since Kaye hit the road in that junkheap, yet here Trumbull still sat, accomplishing nothing. He laid on the horn again, making useless noise. He was barely one block from the hospital; he'd be better off walking. Well, he decided, fuck this.

He dropped the car into reverse and gave it gas, watching the mirror. His rear bumper clunked against the bumper of the car behind him, some innocuous-looking dude with thin glasses behind the wheel. Trumbull got honked at.

"Screw you," he growled, turned the wheel hard left, and tried to make a U-turn. The corner of his front bumper thudded into the rear bumper of the car in front of him. The woman driving looked back at him, frowning. "You too, lady," he muttered, and backed up again. By performing this unkind maneuver three times, he was finally able to get Braine's big black Plymouth turned around. Burning rubber, he drove back to the hospital lot, parked, and clambered out, cursing under his breath. He walked to the same phone booth he had used barely a half hour ago to talk to the boss, went inside and flapped the squeaking door shut, dumped a quarter inside the phone, and told the operator to connect him to Braine, collect this time. The last call had set him back twelve quarters.

The phone was quickly answered. John Braine accepted the charges.

"Mr. Braine," Trumbull said. "Got a new development."

"A good one?"

"That's up to you," Trumbull said. "Kaye seems to have a little girl helping him now."

"Little girl? You mean his daughter?"

He shook his head. "Uh-uh. Some pretty chick, about twenty. I don't know where in the fuck she came from, though. She stole a coroner's van that must have Kaye's kid inside, and he's wound up driving a car that must belong to her. Do you follow that?"

Braine blew a sigh into the phone. "This is getting screwier by the minute. Glass and I have made a decision."

"Yeah? Can I come home?"

"Pretty soon, Trumbull. We want you to kill Mr. Kaye without delay. For God's sake don't go shooting in public like last time. Kill him, then put two bullets in his daughter, her head and her heart. Got it?"

He scowled, frowning stupidly. "I've never killed a kid in my life, Mr. Braine. Can't I just—pick her up or something? Bring her to you for the dirty work?"

"Impossible," Braine said. "After they're both dead, dispose of the bodies somewhere. Bury the man, throw him in a ravine, toss him in a lake, I don't care. But I want you to burn the girl."

"After she's dead."

"Right. After she's dead."

"Okay, I guess. Would this mean a raise for me, you think?"

"Do it right, and we'll talk money then. Now listen. After you shoot the girl in the head and heart, go ahead and get rid of her no matter what she might say or do."

"Huh? She'll be dead."

"Right. If she keeps moving for a while, ignore it."

Trumbull shook his head again. "This sounds too spooky," he said. "What's so special about the girl?"

"You have no need to know," Braine said heavily. He sounded to Trumbull like one very nervous fatman.

"What about the girl?"

"I just told you!"

Trumbull waved a hand. It was stiflingly hot in this booth, making steam collect on the top edges of his sunglasses. "Not the little girl, Mr. Braine. The big girl."

"Oh. Hold on." The phone was covered; two muffled voices carried through. Braine came back, sounding tired and dull. "Kill her too."

"Just like that."

"Don't start getting accusative, Trumbull. I don't like this any more than you do."

"Then why are we doing it?"

Braine heaved another long sigh. "Just do it. Phone in when it's done."

"Okay, Mr. Braine," he said. The line went dead. "Fucking rich bastards," he muttered, slammed the phone back together, and made his way back to his car, his black suit soaking up sunlight and making his shoulders hot. He jerked the door open, still grumbling, wormed his bulk inside, and started the motor again.

Something warm and round was pressed against the back of his neck. He froze, then slowly turned around, expecting one of Braine's men here to solve a little personal grudge. What he saw was the faded blue of a hospital gown, a head wrapped in a white turban, and a large and shiny police revolver in a very black hand. The man holding it smiled at him.

"I am Abraham Maharba," he said. "That is a palindrome, and I am an enigma."

THREE

THE SEVENTH DAY

FOURTEEN

HENRY AUSTERWAHL HAD A CRICK IN HIS BACK AND WAS ABOUT ready to give up this foolishness, gold or no gold, Edith or no Edith. His knees were wet and aching. His hands and feet had turned white as pearl, the skin as wrinkled as old prunes. It was not even noon this Sunday morning and already he'd had a bellyful of this crap.

"I think I'll take a break," he called to Edith on the other side of the creek, the shallow Two Flash Creek that runs south in a swift zigzag between Rawlins and Rock Springs before dumping itself into the larger Bitter Creek. They had left early, Austerwahl and his elderly lady-friend, so early it had been dark still, ghostly patches of pink vaguely visible in the fabric of the eastern sky, a cool and serene predawn that became, after sunrise, one hot son of a bitch. Tired of the heat, tired of a lot of things, Austerwahl tossed the big shallow miner's pan on the rocky bank of the creek, a pan that had produced only gravel and grit in the six weekends Edith had dragged him out here to pan for gold, and staggered across the slippery rocks to the weeds and dust beside the creek. He sat down with a groan, drew his knees up, and clasped them in his arms, rocking a little to massage his weary tailbone. God, but this was boring.

"You might miss that first nugget," Edith sang out. She was sitting cross-legged on the mud and rocks of the far bank, dipping her pan (which Austerwahl suspected had been a wok at some point) in the water, swirling it, fingering the contents, finding nothing as usual, and scooping up some more worthless dirt. Six weeks ago, which Austerwahl recalled was just after he'd met her for the first time at the Veterans' Hall in Rawlins, this panning thing was fun and adventurous. But every weekend, every Saturday and Sunday, to get up at the crack of dawn and drive for an hour to this wretched little creek? It was no longer fun, but Edith had terminal gold fever and was not to be stopped.

He silently begged God to let her find a fleck of gold so they could get out of here. A man his age, unhappily in his middle sixties and headed for disease and death not far down the road, with his luck—a man his age should not be forced to do this ridiculous stuff, roll up his pants to his knees and wander around on slippery rocks that could easily escort him to a broken leg, broken hip, trench foot, whatever.

He looked sourly at his watch. Eleven-twenty. They'd been here since five.

He rearranged his face into something almost pleasant, drawing a breath to shout at Edith. The sun directly overhead was a blowtorch on the thin skin of his bald scalp, where sweat made running rivers unimpeded by hair. Shade was not available anywhere out here on the Great Divide Basin, unless he decided to crawl under his Bronco and let oil drip all over him. The damn thing ate a quart a week, though it was barely two years old. "Let's take a break and eat lunch," he called out. The hot breeze pushed a tumbleweed past him, making him jerk away with a gasp. He had found himself growing increasingly nervous lately, ready to jump at shadows. And no wonder. The cryogenics business had never treated him very kindly before, and he had very little desire to face prosecution ever again. But at his age, he would reason on those long sleepless nights when the image of his own mortality stood before him like a ghost, a Grim Reaper knocking ever harder on the door of his soul, he felt it was time to take action. That, or die like everybody else. At times in bed he would hold his pale arms out to catch moonbeams, and imagine them as fleshless skeleton arms, gleaming white bone where his own familiar meat and skin used to reside. The idea that he would someday be a skeleton bothered him a lot. What was that line from Shakespeare? Woe, that this too, too solid flesh should melt? Something like that. Even the Bard had had a healthy dislike of death.

Sitting on the bank, Austerwahl shivered despite the heat. To die, to die—how would it feel? Pleasant? Not likely. Scary? You bet. Probably a lot like drowning, he supposed, a titanic and useless struggle to stay alive when the brain decided to shut down in spite of protests to the contrary. Overwhelmed, as it were, by a tidal wave of fear and pain.

Edith went on panning, studiously examining the contents of her wok. The tumbleweed skittered across the rocks and the sparkling water that surfed its way southward over them, a hairy basketball. The current caught it finally and it floated away, slowly sinking. "Edith," Austerwahl said. "Oh, Edith?"

She looked up. She was in her middle fifties, which made her an infant in Austerwahl's eyes, and had maintained her figure fairly well. Her black hair was shot through with stripes of gray, her dark eyes nested in a webwork of wrinkles, but not very deep ones. Austerwahl had never been married, for no particular reason, and supposed he would exit as he had entered, unencumbered and childless. "What?" she said.

"Picnic time. Take a breather with me."

She frowned. "Just one more, Henry. I've got the feeling this will be the one."

She went back to work. He scowled at the top of her head. Dizzy dame. Two Flash Creek had not come by its name by accident. Supposedly, about eighty years ago, a miner had pulled two healthy nuggets of gold out of the water when he saw them flash in the sun. Two flashes, two nuggets. Since then the creek had been panned and sluiced almost to death, without result. A town of sorts had sprung up, a few rattrap wooden buildings and a hitching post; people had come to pan and wound up empty-handed and starving, and the town had died. The buildings were husks now. Austerwahl had the feeling the whole thing had been a hoax.

He got to his feet, pressing a hand into the small of his back, trying not to groan out loud. He padded to the 4 x 4, having to hurry a little because the sandy dirt was hotter than hell under his bare feet. He opened the door and scurried inside, where the temperature had climbed high enough to bake a pie, maybe. Gasping, he opened the wicker picnic basket on the seat, rummaged through its overheated contents, slammed it shut, and fished a Coors Light out of the cooler on the floor. He popped it open, waited for it to settle down, then took a long drink. His esophagus became nearly frostbitten, and tears formed in his eyes, but man, was it good. He decided panning for gold was no longer on his list of hobbies. In its stead, copious drinking would be performed every weekend.

He drank, watching Edith through the heat waves with his eyes squinched down to little slots against the glaring floor of the desert, aware of the musty aroma of sagebrush and the factory smells cooking out of the truck's upholstery. He drained the beer, grimaced against the cold and the pain it brought, fished another one out of the cooler, and went at it more leisurely, thinking. Thinking about death—his lifelong obsession—cryogenics, and of course John Braine. Braine had called him last Sunday and told him about their newest client, a little girl whose father was to hand him two hundred thousand dollars when they arrived. Dad and daughter hadn't been there by Wednesday, so he'd called Braine to see what the holdup was. Braine had seemed confused and uncertain. "The deal is still on," he had said. "They're headed west."

This was fine with Austerwahl. The only person he was truly concerned about getting frozen in time was himself, but he was still too afraid of the process to go through with it. What if the Acme Tool and Die nitrogen compressor failed like the Bradforde's had? What difference did a simple change of corporate name make? Who was going to keep the show running for the next few hundred years? He began to contemplate the idea of waiting for his natural death before being cryogized, as he had come to call it over the years, but he knew as well as Braine and Glass how useless that was.

Then Braine had called again yesterday, just as Austerwahl and Edith had returned from another unprofitable Saturday panning. "The deal is off," he'd said, and told Austerwahl some of the indelicate details he had omitted before: the Mortis procedure used for the first time on a human, the series of bank robberies being committed, the girl probably putrid by now. They'd discussed the possibility that even in her doubtless ghastly condition, the cryogizing would work, but what kind of future technology could restore a body turned to mush, a brain decomposed into gray sludge? No one could know what the future held, but they had to be realistic. The little girl would be better off dead.

"So how are you going to accomplish that?" Austerwahl had asked.

"Accomplish what?"

He made motions in the air. Edith was not far away, dinking around in the kitchen making iced tea. Austerwahl cupped his hand around the receiver. "Who's going to kill her?"

Braine hemmed and hawed. "Don't concern yourself about it, Henry."

"But I *am* concerned, John. I don't even want to be within a thousand miles of that girl if what you and Glass did to her is illegal. Understand? I won't go through that kind of hell again."

"We're not sure if it's legal or not. Just like we're not so sure about freezing living beings. Until Congress tackles this issue, we have to stay undercover. So don't concern yourself."

Austerwahl rubbed a hand over his sweating head. "What do I do if he makes it here with the girl after all? Proceed, or not?"

"He won't make it there," Braine had said. "I guarantee you that he *will not* make it."

Austerwahl had nodded. "Say hi to Trumbull for me,

John. And tell him to stay the hell away from me. Stay the hell away from Wyoming too."

They hung up without saying good-bye. Austerwahl had a bitter taste in his mouth that reminded him of the catastrophe of 1968, the trial, the whole mess. It was the taste of fear, bright and sharp as hot chrome. He wandered into the kitchen and killed it with tea.

And now, he decided ruefully, he was killing it with beer. Today was the last possible day that the Kaye girl could be cryogized with any hope of future technology resuscitating her and making her whole again. Robot bodies by 2100? Brain restructuring? How could they attach new muscle and skin onto the framework of her skeleton? Most likely Braine was right. It would be better for her to be dead.

Edith was wading through the creek now, arms outstretched for balance, her pan in one hand, the water around her full of flashing diamonds of sunlight. She tromped up the bank. "I wish you wouldn't drink so early," she said as she got inside. "It's bad for your liver."

He looked at her, his face a blank. Just who in the hell, he thought, does she think she is? If I need a mommy, I'll put an ad in the paper.

"I hope the sandwiches didn't get stale this time. I double-bagged them, just in case." She flipped the basket open. "This time I brought peanut butter and jelly, kind of like we were kids again."

She handed him a sandwich. The bread was whole wheat, the kind with full kernels of wheat baked inside. These invariably got under his dentures, which made eating a lot like chewing barbed wire. And he happened to loathe peanut butter and jelly, even worse than he loathed liver, which was the type of sandwich she had packed last weekend. Liver on whole wheat. She was rapidly slipping on his scale of tolerance.

"Save your beer for later, Henry," she said, and disengaged it from his hand. In two minutes, he knew, the damn thing would be warm and flat with this overheated breeze charging through the truck. He unwrapped his sandwich and tried to look eager, then wondered why he was maintaining this charade. He enjoyed her company but he hated panning for gold and he hated being told what to do. Maybe, he thought, that is why I never did get married. Ain't nobody out there I care for.

"I've been wondering something," Edith said. "You work at Op Base Twelve, don't you?"

He nodded.

"I've heard that's where they make poison gas and stuff for the military. Are you involved in that?"

He shook his head. "Operations Base Twelve is a government distribution center, Edith, nothing more. You know those ads you see on TV all the time for free publications from the government? That's what we do."

She frowned. There was a blob of peanut butter in the corner of her lips. Austerwahl's stomach performed a slow flip-flop. "Then how come people are always protesting about it? And what about the livestock that gets gassed to death every few years? How do you explain that?"

He wagged his head, the famous I-don't-have-a-neckbone routine that Braine found so queer. "I think it's UFO's," he said gravely, and she laughed.

"Oh, you government supersecret types." She raised the can and drank a large swallow of stolen beer. "Eat your sandwich, Henry. You can't pan if you don't keep your strength up. Come on." She clasped his hand and guided the wretched sandwich to his lips. He took a bite and chewed it. "I packed some bean sprouts somewhere," she said, and rummaged through the basket, coming out with a Tupperware bowl. She pried the lid off. Instantly Austerwahl smelled hay. She pinched a bundle together and stuck it under his nose. He opened his mouth, where peanut butter was permanently lodged, and let her shove them in. He began to pity both himself and the cows of the world. The sprouts tasted the way old lawn clippings smelled.

"Nummy," he said, and she left him alone, reflectively munching her sprouts while Austerwahl fought a duel with his gorge. His urge to abandon this fruitless panning and go back home was becoming overwhelming. Besides, this was that Kaye fellow's last day, and despite Braine's reassurances, where something could go wrong, it would. If Kaye did show up, what then? Freeze the girl? Refuse? What?

When Edith was done with her lunch she hopped out, picked up her pan, and walked to the creek. The back of her jeans was a solid splotch of mud. He looked down to where she had been sitting. The seat was smeared with it. He clenched his teeth. At least it was vinyl, but Lord, oh, Lord, he was starting to dislike her more and more, even though she was talented in various other fields besides panning. The trouble was, how could he disengage her from his life when she seemed so damned fond of him? The motherly routine was probably a remnant of her former marriage, though she hadn't talked about it much. The guy had upped and left her. Austerwahl knew why.

He was reaching down for a fresh beer when he heard her shriek. He straightened, and almost laughed. She had slipped and fallen in the shallow rapids there where the rocks were slippery and the water was white foam. She was pushing herself up on her hands while continuing to bellow, her hair wet and stuck to her face, her blouse pasted to her skin and bra—suddenly a wet T-shirt though no contest was under way, he thought with a grin. He leaned his head out, laughing for real, and shouted at her.

"The sign says no swimming!"

She turned her head. "Help! Henry, help me!"

He stuck his sandwich under the seat and got out. The desert sand cooked into his soles as he hobbled to the creek. Edith had dragged herself toward the bank, and Henry thought he saw that the water chasing behind her was somehow reddish. He waded in, took her arms, and hoisted her up while she whimpered. "Where does it hurt?" he asked, but already his eyes had swiveled down and he saw.

The shattered end of her broken shinbone had stabbed through the skin and was bubbling blood in a bright crimson froth. "Jesus," he whispered, bent, and snatched her into his arms. She screamed at the movement and dug her fingernails into his neck and back. He waddled up the bank and ran to the truck, settled her inside, and got in behind the wheel.

"The pans," she moaned as he turned the key.

"Don't worry about the damn pans," he said, shaking. Blood was starting to pool on the floor around the cooler, smelling somehow like weak iodine. He backed up in a swift curve, spraying sand while sagebrush thumped and scraped under the truck. He found a forward gear and roared across the prairie, sending ground squirrels scurrying madly for their holes. Edith groaned, almost screamed, at each lurch and bump. Austerwahl had become a pale and thin race driver, bouncing down inclines, dodging washouts, actually becoming airborne for one frightening second. It took ten minutes to find the freeway, I-80 West, and fortunately because the truck could make its own road, he was able to get on the highway without benefit of a ramp that would cost too much time to find.

The closest town, he decided quickly, was Rock Springs to the west, perhaps ten or fifteen miles closer than Rawlins here in the middle of the parched basin near Patrick Draw. He had often wondered just how fast this baby could roll, and by the time the motor was wound up to its full screaming pitch, he was doing ninety-five while the big knobby tires sang their howling tune on the hot pavement. Edith's face was the color of eggshell, and her eyes were closed. He found that he did in fact care for her, because if she bled to death he would feel very lonely, and very guilty indeed.

It took half an hour to get there, and another five minutes to find the hospital. By the time he had carried her into the emergency room and let the pros take over, he was almost too weak to stand, his thick glasses perched low on his nose, sweat drenching his upper body. He collapsed onto a bench in the corridor outside the ER, fumbled a Winston out of the damp pack, and lit up even though all the signs said No Smoking.

Edith was in there for quite a while. By the time they had reassembled her leg and put it in a cast with a hole where the stitched-up exit wound was, she was swimming in a world of painkillers and sedatives, and didn't recognize her Henry as she was wheeled past him to her room.

His watch told him it was almost three. He decided to stick around Rock Springs until Edith was coherent, maybe grab a motel room for the night and drive her back to Rawlins tomorrow, if they'd release her.

In the meantime he bought some cheap shoes to replace the ones left in the desert, drove downtown, found a respectable tavern, and went inside to calm his frazzled nerves with a drink or two.

Trumbull honestly believed he had never hated someone in his life as much as he hated this Maharba fellow. It wasn't just because Maharba had hijacked him and Braine's car at the hospital yesterday, or even that he kept his stolen Police Special permanently jammed in Trumbull's ribs as he drove. What he hated Maharba most for was his goddamned mouth.

They were in Cheyenne, two hours away from Rawlins as the sweltering afternoon sun dawdled in the excruciating blue of the big Western sky, the Plymouth's air conditioner blasting, barely keeping pace with the heat outside. Abraham Maharba's Police Special was indeed stuck against Trumbull's ribs just above waist level as he drove. And Morris Trumbull's own huge pistol was jammed against Abraham Maharba's ribs, just above waist level.

Trumbull was not extremely fond of this situation, this tête-à-tête that had been going on since about midnight last night. Maharba had gotten sloppy—maybe because of the hole in his head, Trumbull could assume; he had ordered Trumbull to stop at a rest area, and tried to swap his nightgown for Trumbull's clothes. Bad idea. Trumbull had made a move to take his suit coat off, reached under it instead, and presto, he'd been pointing his gun at Maharba's enigmatic head, but to his dismay Maharba had been pointing *his* pistol at him. No clothes had changed hands, the two had gotten back in the car wary as cats, and off they'd gone. Maharba had wanted to stop somewhere and catch some food and sleep and boot Trumbull out. Trumbull wanted to keep going, *had* to keep going if Peter Kaye was to be dispatched along with his daughter. There were times in the night when Maharba had become woozy and incautious, but the barrel of his gun had stayed where it was. Over and over Trumbull tried to envision how he could end this ridiculous and unbearable stalemate, but he knew enough about guns and death to persuade himself not to do anything just yet. Sure, he could blow a hole in the black man with his nifty corkscrew bullets, but even if it killed him instantly he could still pull that Police Special's trigger in a spastic motion. Trumbull was fond of being alive, too fond of it to take such a chance. But as the hours drilled by and Maharba failed to shut his yap, Trumbull began to think that maybe death wasn't so bad after all. If he heard one more quote from the Bible he just might use his big gun on himself.

"So there I stood," Maharba was saying. It wasn't a very big secret that he was talking to keep himself awake. "Alone, me against the burning house, the fire department too terrified of the rioters to enter the neighborhood. Of course I was a younger man back then, sturdier of body and mind, like the Master. Rosecrucians four, nineteen."

Trumbull ground his teeth against each other, filling his head with crunching noises. He swore never to look at a Bible again, as if he ever had.

"I formed an impromptu bucket brigade, that is what I did," Maharba went on, pausing to yawn. "The rioters suddenly found themselves helping not only me, but their friends and neighbors as well. A sense of camaraderie developed. My house was saved, the tensions eased, everyone began to work together as a team motivated by mutual respect, mutual love, very much like the message our Lord brought us from heaven. Love one another, brother, so for God's sake stop somewhere for a hamburger. Ishmael one, nine through eleven. Praise be."

Trumbull turned his head. "We are not stopping until we

get to Rawlins, mister. If you were looking for a luxury cruise you sure picked the wrong car."

Maharba nodded. His eyes were puffy, shot through with red. "Such is my fate. Don't you ever eat or sleep?"

"When the time comes, I will."

"What's the rush, anyway? Getting married today?"

"I told you it's none of your business. Ask me one more time and you die."

"Mercy me. Do you, by chance, have to urinate as badly as I do?"

Trumbull frowned. Did he ever. "When the time comes, I will. Morris Trumbull one, two."

"Heretic."

"Huh?"

"Where was I? Ah, the Detroit riots. Summer of sixty-eight. A city in flames, a tragedy, people on the edge of anarchy. Where was I really?"

Trumbull's head dropped. "Please," he muttered. "Just shut the fuck up. Let me stop by the road, you can get out, find yourself another ride."

"Nope. Not dressed in this peep show of a gown. We trade clothes, I go on my way."

"I'm not gonna get bare-assed for you or anybody else. I have business to conduct."

"What kind of business?"

"None of your—oh, shut up. Just shut up."

"Fine." Maharba tapped his chin with his unoccupied hand. "I was in the Navy for four years, did I tell you that? Of course it was a long time ago. The fifties, matter of fact. I was the first black crewman on a destroyer who was not a cook. I was a gunner. We had these huge, ridiculous helmets so the casings from the ack-ack guns could bounce off our heads without killing or burning us. Have you ever handled a fresh ack-ack casing? No, not you."

"Shut up, Maharba. I'm warning you." He pressed his pistol harder against Maharba's ribs.

Maharba pressed his own. "Listen to me, Trumbull. I'm warning you."

Trumbull sighed, aching with fatigue, his bladder an overstretched balloon, his stomach a growling pit. He took the gigantic left turn off 25 North onto I-80 West. A sign told him Rawlins was 140 miles ahead. The giant spires and crags of the Rocky Mountains loomed in the shimmering distance, furry with pine forests, capped with unbelievable snow. Trumbull could estimate, though it was a challenge with his brain full of cobwebs, that he was no more than ten or fifteen minutes behind Kaye and his little troupe, and he could thank Maharba and that irritating traffic jam for the delay. The possibility that the wreck Kaye was driving had died somewhere on the road and he had managed to get another one was too unhappy to dwell on. The only way Trumbull could find him was to spot that car. He knew well enough that Kaye was headed for Braine's weird freezing joint; he also knew well enough that Kaye did not know where it was.

Trumbull realized suddenly that he did know one other location in Rawlins that Kaye couldn't, though he had only been there once before and it was a couple years ago, about the time he went to work for Braine as chauffeur and general heavy who specialized in anti-union projects. A problem-solver, in other words.

He knew where that screwball genius Henry Austerwahl lived, if he hadn't moved. Trumbull decided he would go there, take a piss and eat some food and wash his sweaty hands and kill Maharba and give his gun to Austerwahl, and then the two of them would sit down and figure out just how to proceed with the timely murder of Peter Kaye, his daughter, and his new girlfriend.

Maharba went on talking, but now that Trumbull was sure these words would be his last, he didn't mind that much.

FIFTEEN

KIM, BEHIND THE WHEEL OF HER CAR, SAW RAWLINS APPEAR ON the western horizon at about the same time Peter began having another major attack of nerves. She was exhausted, full of aches, her head pounding from the sunlight and the heat, almost too spent to even think anymore. Peter was in worse shape, she assumed, because he had been on the road seven days now, compared to her one. She could scarcely imagine how he must feel. He looked more dead than alive, she knew that much: face sallow, eyelids drooping, his blond whiskers sticking out at weird angles as if he had slept on them wrong. His eyes were dull, adorned with puffy bags the color of plums.

In the back, buried in a slushy mountain of ice, Darbi was asleep or really dead, Kim didn't know which. She had not stirred all night.

Peter began to breathe too fast, no preliminaries, no warning at all, his free left hand clutching his knobby knee in a crushing grip, unwarranted sweat rolling down his forehead, which was knotted with pain. Kim reached over and coaxed his hand into hers, and this time he was careful not to crunch the bones of her fingers together. He began to shiver violently, gasping, moaning. Kim's heart ached for him, but there was nothing she, or anyone else, could do.

She took the first Rawlins exit, battling the cranky steering wheel with one hand, pumping the brakes. The city was spread out on a huge flat plain under the dome of the sky, where it seemed she could see a thousand miles in any direction. Despite the buildings, the houses, the general air of civilization, she felt as if this town was too small, was trying, and failing, to compete with the vast and endless prairie, a temporary and unwelcome settlement that time and the desert would eventually swallow. The Nova shuddered to a stop at the sign at the bottom of the ramp while Kim tried to shake that creepy feeling. Wisps of steam were rising from the motor. She acknowledged sadly that the old beast was about ready to go belly-up.

Just to her left was a run-down gas station whose sign declared that it was Wyoco, whatever that might be. She pulled in and drove past the station's single pump, and stopped beside a decaying telephone booth in a square of welcome shade. Peter's forehead was on his knees now; he seemed to be coming out of it, no longer shaking. She gently pulled her hand away from his. "We're in Rawlins finally," she said, and he looked up. She had never seen such an expression of fatigue and raw misery in her life. "Make that phone call," she urged him. "We're really here."

He cranked his head around and stared dully at her. "You better do it," he croaked. "I don't think I could remember the directions he's going to give." He stuck a hand in her doorless glove compartment, wormed it around, and pulled it out. "God, do I feel strange. What happened to the gas money?"

"I spent the last handful in Denver. Got a quarter?"

He checked his pockets. "Nope."

She smiled. "If I wasn't so tired I'd laugh. We've got a bagful of money buried in the back, and you don't have a quarter."

"There's some change in there somewhere, I think. In one of the canvas bags."

She opened her door. "Never mind, I've probably got one. What's the guy's number?"

He closed his eyes. "Okay. It's 684, uh, 9181. The code word is Salamander."

"Pardon? Salamander? Why?"

He frowned. "Don't ask me, Kim. I just take orders."

She got out, stretched hugely, tweezed the back of her damp jeans away from the skin of her fanny, and ran a hand through her windblown hair, which no longer resembled Patti Page's old hairdo, did not resemble much of anything anymore. She got a quarter out, mumbling the number, and ducked into the flat and stifling air of the booth. She dumped the coin inside, and dialed.

It was answered on the fourth ring. "Hello. This is Dr. Henry Austerwahl."

"Yes," she said awkwardly. "Salaman—"

"I'm not able to come to the phone right now, but if you'll leave your name and number, I'll get back to you soon. Thank you."

Beep!

"Son of a bitch," she muttered, and hung up. She pulled the folding door open and stepped out, wiping her wet bangs away from her eyes. Peter had gotten out and stood swaying on his feet, looking around as if lost. She walked to him and leaned against the car's hot fender. "Nobody's home," she said. "Sorry."

His upper body gave a tremendous lurch, as if he had been electrically shocked. She looked at him, wondering what new torture he was about to undergo. He looked back at her, one eyebrow raised, then slid his glance down to her chest. "Hey-hey," he said in a voice that was too deep, somehow distant, as if it came not from his mouth but from the recesses of his chest. "Look at the little lady." He whistled. "You're some prime Grade-A beef, honey."

Her jaw dropped.

"Tell you what," he said, leering at her. "Let's get back in the heap and find us a motel. I could use some good pussy about now."

"Peter!" she barked, backing away. "What are you saying?"

"Peter? Fuck Peter. He's a wimp, a faggot. What you're dealing with now is the real item." He pulled his arm out of the sling, worked it over his head, and tossed it aside. He swung his arm in circles, grinning. "You can call me anything you want to, but that wimpy buttfuck calls me Clint, and I think I like that." He advanced on her, his haggard face bent and twisted into a stranger's face, the merciless sun painting his features with furrows of shadow and light. Kim fell back, alarm flooding her mind. Peter had told her this might happen, but seeing him now, seeing Clint now, she felt a cold finger of fear stroke the base of her brain. He'd told her he could be Clint. He hadn't told her how to make Clint go away.

"Peter," she said evenly, "Darbi needs you to come back. *I* need you to come back. Are you . . . inside somewhere?"

He stopped. His head tipped back, and he laughed at the sky. Through the yellowed glass of the station's windows, Kim saw a grimy little attendant look over. "Peter is dead," Clint said, chuckling. "Man, how I've waited for this moment. Hey, isn't that a song?"

She narrowed her eyes. "Clint, you are not real. You are Peter, and Peter is you." She had no idea how to deal with this. Hell, who did? And how come there was never a roving psychiatrist around when you needed one? "Peter, please come back! Think of Darbi!"

He glanced over to the back seat, sneering. "That little shit has been dragging us down for years, her and her idiot mother Brenda."

"Us? Who is us?"

"Me and the wimp. Me and the wimp and whoever else happens to be crawling around in his head. Now, how about that motel? You look like you need it." He reached out and brushed her cheek with the back of his fingers. They were not trembling anymore, Kim noticed, and then remembered that Peter had told her Clint was full of talk and nothing else, apt to disappear when the nitty got gritty.

"All right," she ventured after some hesitant thought, "I think I could use a . . . a quickie . . . but I demand the best. Let's . . ." She swallowed. "Let's see your hardware, Clint."

"Super," he said, reaching for his belt buckle, but his

voice was now warbling and unsure. His smile vanished and an expression of pure confusion took its place. "Huh?"

"Peter?"

"Yeah." He looked around dazedly, then pressed his left hand against his bloody bandage, swaying on his feet. "Jeez, what in the hell is going on?" He tapped his fingers against his forehead, and those fingers were shaking. "Clint," he moaned. "Jesus Christ, Kim, this is a lousy time for me to start wigging out. What did they say on the phone?"

She breathed a great sigh of relief. "Answering machine. We'll have to wait."

He sagged against the car. "Swell." He straightened so fast it was almost a jump. He spun around and looked inside at Darbi.

Kim stepped closer. "What's wrong?"

He looked up. "Thought I heard her move. Just ice shifting, I guess."

Kim looked in at her. Her eyes had sunk deep in their sockets. Her mouth hung open, a ragged black hole in her face with a stray ice cube or two sitting on the blue-brown knot that was her tongue. The bones under the skin of her face were sharply angled, as if the skull were trying to push through. Peter reached in and skinned one of her eyelids back with a thumb. A yellowed eye looked up at him with the mindless flat stare of a department store dummy. He slid her eye shut and looked helplessly at Kim. "Are you sure she didn't respond to light before? She looks absolutely dead now."

Kim frowned, wiping a trickle of sweat off her forehead. Quite a scare, that Clint thing. "Peter, at this stage I don't think it even matters. As soon as your pal answers his phone, it will all be over."

"Pal?" He coughed out an unhappy laugh. "I don't even know his name."

"Does Henry Austerwahl ring a bell?"

"No." He slumped back against the car. Kim did the same, aware that on top of being red-eyed and sleepy she was hungry as well. She looked to the squat cinder-block station and its flaking coat of white paint and saw an ancient pop machine and a rack of candy inside. The attendant was still staring out the window. She trotted over to where Peter's sling had flopped to the ground, and took it back to him. Grunting, he put it back on. His bandage was soaked, ready to drip.

"Let's get some candy bars or something, Peter. I'm famished."

He nodded, not seeming interested. "Need a handful of money?"

She looked over at the street where a sign on a bent pole informed her that it was Mallard Street, and at the traffic droning by. A little red car was parked beside the curb a block away, two men inside it, two bullet holes in the windshield. "I don't think this is a good place to be waving it around. I've got a buck or two. Come on."

They went inside, jangling a cowbell over the door. The dirty little attendant stared at Kim, then at Peter's sling. "Hi there," Kim said to break his trance.

He blinked. "Howdy doody. Need gas?"

"Don't think so." She examined the candy that was slowly melting on a rack beside the gumball machine. After some hesitation she chose a Kit-Kat. Peter stood by, watching. She glanced at him. "You ought to eat something," she said. "You're going to drop dead at this rate."

"Sounds reasonable." He got himself a Kit-Kat as well. Kim was handing the attendant a dollar when the little man frowned and turned his head.

"What in the fuck is that?" he breathed.

Kim jerked her head around.

Darbi was clawing her way out of the ice, trying to squelch out the window. Her little face was twisted and insane, her eyes rolling in mad circles, ruined lips turned up in a grimace of effort. Kim dropped the dollar and the candy bar and charged out. Peter followed, clanging the overhead bell shrilly. His candy bar wound up on the dirty floor.

Darbi had wormed herself almost free, was doubled over the door with her fingertips scraping the ground. Kim took her by the shoulders, lifted her, and tried to shove her back.

"No!" Darbi shrieked, batting at her arms. Even though her skin was cold under Kim's hands, the smell rising off her was ghastly. "I need my daddy!" she screamed, writhing, clawing. For a weird moment she went suddenly stiff as a plank, then jerked as if a high and deadly voltage of electricity had slammed through her. When she screamed again her voice was a hideous squeal, a combination of animal howls and piglike grunts. "I'll kill you! I'll *kill* you!"

Kim was being battered in a frenzy. Darbi hooked her fingernails into the soft flesh under Kim's left eye and jerked downward, splitting the skin in four lines all the way to her chin. Kim screamed and dropped back, eyes blurry with tears of pain. She thudded into Peter and nearly fell.

"Gotcha!" Darbi shrieked, cackling. She dropped out of the window onto the hot cement with a bony smack, then pushed herself up onto her feet. Kim's blood was red and shiny on her hand, crescents of her flesh packed under her small, sharp fingernails. Hadn't Kim heard once that a dead person's fingernails keep growing for a while? It seemed to be true.

Her eyes sparkling with glee and hate, Darbi brought her hand up and licked it, then spat a slimy red blob on the pavement. Her tongue flicked out and bobbled at Kim like the tongue of a snake.

Kim spun around, stunned with terror. "Peter! Don't stand there like that, *do something!*"

He regarded her with mild eyes. His sling was gone again. "Ah, these women," he said with a smirk, and walked around the car, skirting Darbi as if she weren't there. She jumped for him and he slapped her easily away, and for a moment Kim believed she could see an expression of surprised indecision on the wreckage of Darbi's face. He made the driver's door screech open, leaned inside, and brought out the sack of money from its protective crypt in the ice.

"Do yourself a favor," he said as he thunked the door shut. "Get rid of the kid. She makes too much noise."

He walked away toward Mallard Street, the bag swinging from his fist and bumping his knee, whistling while ice cubes slid off the plastic and spatted wetly on the street.

"Peter!" Kim shouted, but then Darbi slammed into her, all arms and legs and teeth, and she fell backward, hitting her head on the cement while Darbi's hands clawed at her and momentarily seeing bright stars of pain. Cloth ripped; Darbi had torn her blouse open. Tiny white buttons rolled away in a scatter. Blood was in her eyes, in her mouth, thin and salty. She bucked and heaved, but Darbi had become as clinging as a spider, biting at her, biting at her neck, her nose, her chin, grunting and snuffling.

"Help me!" Kim screamed. Darbi burst her brassiere apart with one gigantic tug, slung her head downward, and bit her titanically hard on the right nipple. She screamed again.

Darbi raised her head. "You'll never take him away from me," she hissed. Blood dripped leisurely down her chin, Kim's blood. "He's always been *my* daddy."

Kim got both hands against her chest and shoved. Darbi's fingernails were dug into the flesh of her breasts, crushing them; now as Kim pushed her away her small fingernails dug furrows in the skin that filled instantly with blood. "Get away!" Kim screamed, drunk with terror, and was able to throw her off. Kim staggered to her feet, gasping, drooling bloody spit, and ran for the station, where the attendant still stood, watching everything with an expression of dumb surprise. She was almost at the door when Darbi jumped on her back and clamped her teeth on the hard knob of bone at the base of her neck. Bright pain shafted down Kim's spine and she heard, dimly, the crunch of teeth against bone, her bone, her backbone. She screamed and spun in a crazy circle, off balance, her legs wobbling and scissoring. "Help!" she shouted, and crashed against the glass door. The thick safety glass cracked in a starburst pattern, but held. She was able to push against it, the door swung open, and she was inside while the cowbell jangled merrily overhead.

The attendant jumped back, eyes large with wonder. His dirty hands flew up and clapped over his cheeks, dragging his mouth downward in an exaggerated clown's face.

"Hit her with something!" Kim shouted at him. Darbi was trying to chew through her spine, maybe even succeeding. The little man stood frozen.

"Hit her!" Kim screeched, becoming woozy, but then Darbi's teeth were gone, leaving a black hole of pain. She hopped down with the agility of a monkey and scurried over to the statue that had been the attendant.

"Make her go away," Darbi howled at him. Blood was dripping from her chin to her wet dress, forming thin elongated splatters of red against the pink. She danced a furious little two-step. "Send her to bed without supper! Sometimes my daddy did when he thought I was bad, but she's just as bad! Worse!"

Kim staggered against the wall, weeping, groaning through her clenched teeth. There was a rack at her feet that displayed two rather dusty Emerol car batteries. She bent and hoisted one up, unaware of its tremendous weight, stumbled over to Darbi, and dropped it on her head as she screamed her insanity at the attendant. It bounced a little and cracked on the floor, spilling water and acid. Darbi lurched sideways into the cash register, reeling, holding her head, her eyes dull and glassy. The register slid off the counter and crashed noisily to the floor, spilling change that rolled on edge to the walls. Darbi recovered and snarled at Kim like a terrier, ran at her, and shoved her off her feet. Kim fell against the gumball machine; it heeled over and the globe exploded, spraying glass and gumballs in a colorful tide.

Kim pushed herself back on her feet. The floor was slick with blood and battery acid; her feet scooted away and she fell again. Her teeth snapped shut over her tongue. Foul-tasting, bitter blood filled her mouth.

"You're not my mommy," Darbi growled, and came at her again.

"Why are you doing this!" Kim screamed, spraying blood in a mist. *"Why!"*

"I hate those tubes in my nose," she whined, and jumped. Kim tried to roll away, but that clinging spider was on her again, biting her face. The smell of blood and decay rolled off her like a gas.

"Help!" Kim screamed for the last time, drowning on her own blood. She heard a bright *crack!* and then Darbi stiffened, flopped epileptically on top of her for a drift of time, and was still.

Kim heaved her away. The attendant was standing over her with a rusty tire iron in one shaking fist. His baggy pants were darkly stained on the crotch and inner thighs. Kim realized dimly that he had wet himself. She was able to push herself up, hands pressed to the wall behind her for support, hurting in a thousand places, leaving red handprints in a track up the wall, ready to swoon for the second time in her life. The man hobbled over to a telephone in the abrupt silence, sliding and skating on glass and gumballs, picked it up, and stared at the dial.

Kim covered her bleeding face with her hands and screamed into them while the attendant gathered his senses together finally, and called the police.

Steve Rafter was feeling very old for a man of forty. Life had handed him many unpleasant surprises over the years: banal looks, no muscles to speak of, a wife who had gone to night school majoring in nagging. A receding hairline. Premature wrinkles. Newell Jackson and the humiliation he caused. And here, as he sat a block away from the Wyoco station watching Peter Kaye and friends do mysterious things, another nasty surprise had been dished out. The little girl had sprung to life again in order to baffle him and Jared, and had attacked the young lady while Kaye himself stood by idly taking off his sling. Then he'd taken the bag of money and walked casually away. The girl had gone at the pretty young lady in the white blouse again and practically torn her to pieces, ripped her blouse open, torn her bra apart, and done awful things before they'd both gone into the station. Under better circumstances both he and Jared would have enjoyed that little striptease, especially since they both had pocket-sized binoculars for better viewing. But pretty or not, that lady was not pleasant to look at with blood streaming all over her face and naked upper body.

"We should have jumped in," Jared said, fingering his throat while looking ill. "Nobody deserves that kind of treatment."

Steve had to shrug. "It's hard to tell, Jared. We might have screwed something up. This whole thing is getting very strange."

"Wonder why she's colored like that?" Jared mused, not for the first time. "Is she supposed to look dead or something?"

"I don't know. I don't know anything anymore."

They had watched Kaye as he ambled past, watched him push through some raggedy hedges that encircled a collapsing house in this seedy part of Rawlins, walk across what had been a lawn, and vanish into the anonymity of the bad apartments and deserted homes that greeted westbound travelers here.

"Want to follow him?" Jared asked. "Or do we stick with the girl?"

Steve frowned, too tired to figure out what was what. "Which girl?"

"The grown-up girl. She's still in the station." He leaned his head out the window slightly. "She's still screaming, Steve. What should we do?"

Steve ground his teeth. "Shit, our job is to follow Kaye, not some pretty girl with big tits just 'cause she's better-looking." He twisted the key and the car rumbled alive. He put it in first, then hesitated. "Where do you suppose he went, Jared? We can patrol around and maybe spot him, but without that car he won't get far."

"Oh?" Jared laughed unhappily. "What happened in P.A.? What happened in Ohio and Indianapolis? The guy's a master at hot-wiring, maybe as good as I am."

Steve doubted it. "Those cars were running when he snatched them. What we have to do now is outsmart the bastard." He put the shifter in neutral and turned to Jared. "Okay, what just happened at the station over there?"

"Kaye walked with the money. His daughter attacked the pretty girl with the messy hair, and beat her up pretty bad."

"Right. Now let me ask you, why?"

"Why to which part? None of it makes sense."

Steve concentrated, looking studious, a tactic that often really did produce results. "Kaye and the little lady had a fight. He stomped off in a huff. His daughter got pissed at this. She attacked the girl. Daddy is now looking for a car to steal. In other words, the pretty lady is out of the picture. Make sense?"

Jared nodded slowly, frowning as he pondered. "Sounds likely, yeah. But why didn't Kaye just boot her ass out of the car and keep running? Why risk traipsing around a strange town with a hundred grand in a trash bag? Why leave his daughter behind like that?"

Steve tapped his head. "Gimme a minute to think this out, Jared. I'm so damn tired I could sleep for a year." He turned the motor off and tried hard to concentrate. Jared worked himself deeper into his seat, crossed his arms, and closed his eyes. Steve envied him for that. He could sleep through a nuclear explosion.

Minutes passed. Steve heard a distant siren, ambulance or police or both, but ignored it. Just what was Kaye up to? A little display to throw Jared and him off the trail? Surely he knew they were here; hell, he'd parked right beside them at the hospital in St. Charles. How embarrassing *that* had been. But anyway, why this sudden move? Why the change of plan?

Maybe because Rawlins is his destination. Maybe the journey is over.

He liked that, liked it a lot. He nudged Jared, then shook him awake. "We'll be going home before nightfall," he said, starting the motor. The siren was closer now, so close that Jared turned to watch for lights. Now he nudged Steve.

"The plot thickens," Jared said dourly.

"Huh?" Steve turned his head and watched the pretty girl, now a torn and shambling red creature with huge shell-shocked eyes and clothes in rags, carry Kaye's daughter to the car and work her onto the back seat. She stayed bent inside the car for a long time, and by the motion of her arms, it seemed she was moving things around. Steve remembered what he had seen in Effingham two days ago when Kaye's stolen car had exploded. In the melee a few bags of ice had fallen out of the car before it blew. He slid his binoculars out of his pocket now, snapped the case open, and settled them to his eyes.

No bags of ice. Just ice. The girl was shoveling it with her hands. She stood up, and Steve saw with puzzlement that she had a length of steel rod in one fist. She used it to jab at the ice, then shoveled some more. When she was done she dropped the rod on the front seat, trudged around the car, and got in. Steve put the binoculars back in his pocket. "I think," he said, "that it is time we find out just what is going on."

He engaged the clutch and drove to the station. A city police car with its lights flashing and its siren howling beat him to it, but not by much. The cop shut the siren down and got out, looked around while adjusting his gun belt, and went inside the station. Steve frowned as he wheeled to a stop beside the decaying old Nova. The pretty girl had ducked out of sight. He stepped out, stood, and saw her huddling on the seat. She looked up and their eyes met. She was indeed a woman made of blood, her face slashed in lines, her eyes huge, red foam bubbling between her lips. The peep show was still in full swing, still unpleasant to watch. He saw a wet and rusty tire iron on the ruins of the seat. Her hand flashed over and turned the ignition key of the old Chevrolet. It rumbled alive, farting dense smoke.

"Hey," Steve said as he looked into the back seat and saw the kid buried in bloody ice. "Hey!"

Too late; she was already backing up, tires howling and jumping, and by the time Steve had hopped back in the car she was taking a right on Mallard, blending with traffic, vanishing. The cop hustled out of the station as Steve found reverse.

"Hold it!" the cop shouted, and jerked his gun out of its holster.

Steve held it.

SIXTEEN

MORRIS TRUMBULL BELIEVED HE HAD ENDURED HANGOVERS IN his life of hard drinking and fast cars, but this one was the worst, *the* worst, and he had not touched a drop in days. Behind the shiny blanks of his sunglasses, hidden in shadow, his eyes were seamed with bright red veins, and behind them, inside his skull, his overtaxed brain was functioning with all the speed of a shorted-out computer. The ache in his head throbbed in cadence with his weakly thudding heart. His left forearm was stiff and aching from holding onto the steering wheel alone, his right arm a length of dead weight from holding his pistol against Maharba's ribs the last twenty hours. Though Rawlins was a pretty easy town to navigate, he got lost again and again as he tried to find Henry Austerwahl's house by memory. He knew it was an average house with a brick front and pale blue aluminum siding around the rest. There were some hedges sprouting near the front door that were impressed even more firmly in his mind; last time here, while Braine and Glass sat around discussing all kinds of boring scientific crap, Trumbull had snatched a bottle of gin from Austerwahl's liquor cabinet and gotten loaded on the front porch, pissing at least a dozen times into those handy hedges.

The damn gun stuck against his ribs wasn't helping his memory much either. Maharba was in some kind of daze, some foggy zone between asleep and awake beneath his preposterous turban, but Trumbull was still not willing to shoot him and risk the chance of being shot back even as Maharba died. Somehow, once he found those familiar hedges and that house, he would get the jump on Maharba and kill him.

Austerwahl's house turned out to be on Lincoln Lane on the western edge of town, where the streets dead-ended in sagebrush and sand, awaiting new settlers. Trumbull pulled onto the driveway with a grateful moan, and killed the engine. The silence was genuine and smooth, no more road noises, no more roaring motor, no wind leaking through invisible cracks between the car doors and their frames. He let himself slump a bit, and closed his burning eyes. Thin whispers beckoned him toward sleep, soft interior voices that made no sense but were compelling nonetheless. He forced his eyes back open, feeling drugged, and looked over at Maharba.

He didn't look very healthy, but he was awake. Perhaps, Trumbull hoped, his wound would get the better of him and he would simply drop dead, but it hadn't happened yet. No sense hoping for favors from above on this rocky road of life, he knew. To get lucky, you had to make your own luck.

"Where are we?" Maharba grunted, looking dully out the window.

"Timbuktu," Trumbull snapped. Already the car was heating up without the air conditioner roaring. He cracked his door open, letting in the sounds of desert life—bugs, crickets, a screeching bird angry somewhere out on the endless prairie. "I don't know about you, but I'm getting out."

Maharba opened his door too. "Okay, we've practiced this at gas stations," he said, and stuck his pistol under the breast of his gown. Trumbull moved his inside his sport coat. Now the guns were hidden, but they were still aimed in the right directions. Both men eased out, and slammed their doors in unison. Keeping wary hawk eyes on each other, they made it to the front porch. Trumbull thumbed the doorbell, and dimly inside it gonged.

They waited. Trumbull tried again. No answer.

"Oh, this is just peachy," he growled. "Open the damn

screen door, Maharba, and I'll kick the fucker in. I gotta piss like a racehorse."

"At last." Maharba pulled it open. "You know, if you're a door-to-door salesman," he said, "you certainly have a peculiar way of getting into your customers' houses."

"Shut up." He stepped back, glancing from Maharba to the door and back, raised a foot, and crunched it with a grunt against the door, near the ornate knob. It jumped immediately open; Trumbull was no slouch in the weight department. He pulled his pistol out of his jacket and trained it on Maharba. Maharba did likewise with Trumbull as the target. "You first," Trumbull said.

Maharba shook his head. "A true gentleman always enters last, friend. Romans one, forty."

Trumbull's jaw worked back and forth, grinding his teeth against each other. "Wiseass." He backed through the open door with Maharba following. The first thing about this house that struck him was the fact that Austerwahl was a cheapskate. The air conditioner wasn't running. And the place smelled like a cigarette factory, just like last time. It was dim and uncluttered, a museum of middle-class taste in furniture. He moved aside and drew the drapes apart, letting light flood in through the plate glass.

"Charming," Maharba said, eying the place with the practiced eye of a veteran cat burglar. "Now, who gets to use the potty first?"

Trumbull deliberated. This was getting too bothersome. "Tell you what," he said. "There's a sliding glass door that leads to the patio and the backyard over this way. Let's go there, put our guns down someplace on the lawn, and try to act civilized for a while."

Maharba's dark face wrinkled into a doubtful frown. "It has merits, your idea, but I'll go even further. There's no reason anymore for you to kill me, and my only desire has been to get some real clothing and get on with my life." He stooped and cautiously lowered his pistol to the floor, watching Trumbull. "Peace treaty," he said. "Willing?"

Trumbull hesitated, then shrugged and lowered his pistol to the floor.

"On three," Maharba said. "One, two, three."

They stood up. The guns stayed on the thick blue carpet. Maharba kicked his toward Trumbull's, then scooted both under Austerwahl's nice blue couch. "Okay," he said, letting out a long breath. "Go ahead and use the bathroom. I promise not to touch the guns."

Trumbull rolled his eyes. "I wouldn't trust my own grandma with this. Come with me to the bathroom so I can keep an eye on you."

"Why, sir!" Maharba exclaimed, feigning shock. "Do I not look like a man of his word?"

"I'll let you answer that."

He nodded. "Okay, let's go."

They both tromped down a hallway, located the spotless bathroom that reeked of Glade wintergreen air freshener, and went in to do their business. For Trumbull, nothing had ever felt so good as this unloading of the gallon or two of piss he had carted around with him since yesterday. When he was done Maharba took his turn. They went back into the living room. "Okay," Maharba said. "Point me to a bedroom and some clothes."

"You'll have to scout around," Trumbull said. "I've only been here once myself."

"Why, by chance, are we here at all?"

"Personal business. Go on, find some duds. I won't bother you. I'm gonna locate me some liquor and some food before I fall over."

Maharba wandered away. Trumbull found the liquor cabinet. It was locked, but he had no time for such inconveniences. He got a kitchen knife and pried the doors apart. Inside he found bourbon, vodka, Gilbey's gin. He took the gin for old times' sake. When the first swallow blasted its way into his groaning stomach he became giddy with thankfulness and pleasure.

The phone rang. Trumbull stiffened, bottle in hand, the

lines on his face deepening, his eyes locating the phone on a table beside the sofa. Would that be Braine, checking on him? No, no, that was paranoid thinking. It was just one of Austerwahl's local buddies, maybe a phone solicitor, some pesky bastard out to bother Austerwahl on this Sunday afternoon.

He let it ring. After the fourth ring something clicked. Henry Austerwahl said, "Hello, this is Dr. Henry Austerwahl," through a machine parked behind the phone. "I'm not able to come to the phone right now, but if you'll leave your name and number, I'll get back to you soon. Thank you."

Beep. Another voice, a woman's, crackled metallically through the machine, accompanied by remote traffic noises. "Oh, damn. Uh, this is, uh, Salamander. I'm at, let's see, I'm at a phone booth, and the number is 684-0048. Please call the second you get home, I'll wait here. I have, um, oh, jeez, I've got the girl, and Peter's gone. Um, ah, hell . . ."

Click. The machine made noises, then shut down. Trumbull stared at it, his tired mind flaring alive again, processing what he had just heard. A smile crept over his features, making him look younger, almost handsome in a dark way. He went to the sofa beside the phone, sat, played back the message (along with one from somebody named Bob Stadler who wasn't going to make it to work tomorrow, had the flu), and dialed the number of the phone booth, 684-0048. It was picked up on the first ring.

"Salamander?" Trumbull said, trying to sound wheezy with the beginnings of emphysema, like the four-pack-a-day smoker Austerwahl.

The girl drew a sharp breath. "Yes, yes, this is Salamander! Dr. Austerwahl?"

"Speaking," he said. "Sorry I've been away. Family matters. Did you say that Peter's gone?"

"Yeah. He's, uh, he's not well. But I've got Darbi iced in the back of my car." Her voice lowered a notch. "She's pretty bad, Doctor. Is it too late for her?"

Trumbull frowned. Who gave a shit about the kid? Braine

and Glass, that's who. Shoot her through the head and heart, they'd said, as if ordering a pizza or a bucket of chicken. Well, if they wanted a six-year-old kid executed, they could damn well do it themselves. Peter Kaye was a different story, fair game, a clever son of a bitch and probably very dangerous. "I'll have to see her first," he said. "Uh, who is this, please?"

"My name is Kimberly . . . Mason. I'm a friend of Peter's."

"Fine, Kimberly. Any idea where we might find Peter? I'll need his help to assemble my data."

"Assemble?" she said, sounding confused. "Data?"

"To update my files," he responded, pulling this junk straight out of his ass. "Where are you located now?"

"Well," she said hesitantly, "from here I can see I'm on Rawlins Avenue, and it's pretty busy, so I guess it's the main street or something. And I can see down a street called Sitting Bull. I'm at the intersection, but off a little to the, ah, the east, if my directions are right. Do you know where it is?"

He gritted his teeth again. Fuck, no, he did not know where it was. He would have to ask some local how to get there. "Sure," he said. "The phone booth at the corner of Rawlins and Sitting Bull, no problem. I want you to stay there, don't move. I'll be there in, say, twenty minutes, half hour at the most."

"Good," she said, and now Trumbull could tell, to his own amazement, that she was on the verge of tears, her voice thick, wavering. "Thank you," she whispered. "Please hurry."

"Calm yourself," he said. "I'll be there soon."

She hung up, and so did he. He mulled things over for a tick of time, reached under the sofa, and felt for the guns. Maharba had shoved them too deep. Grumbling, Trumbull got on his knees and stuck his arm under the sofa, found one and dragged it out, and saw that it was his. He had set the bottle of Gilbey's on the table beside the phone, and picked it up now. He could hear Maharba bumbling around down the hall, hear clothes hangers twanging. "Hey, Maharba," he called out. "Maharba!"

Bare feet brushed across the carpet in the hallway. He appeared with dark slacks and a white shirt on, working to knot a tie around his neck. "What's up?" he said.

Trumbull raised the gun. "Nobody hijacks Morris Trumbull and gets away with it," he said softly, and pulled the trigger. The noise was huge. Maharba catapulted backward and slid across the smooth linoleum of the kitchen, slamming to a stop under the table while chairs clattered over on their backs. His head was cocked at a strange angle, eyes closed, a thin line of blood trickling out of his mouth, down his chin. Gunsmoke was thick in the air.

"Sucker," Trumbull said, and went out.

Happy hour at the downtown Sitting Bull Tavern started at four o'clock, Clint discovered with glee as he happened to cruise by on his search for a new life in the former cow town called Rawlins. He liked being here, liked the aura of a frontier town perched in the wilderness surrounded by a desert so vast that you could get lost just by making a wrong turn and spend the last days of your life crawling toward mirages. He felt that Rawlins fit his image, fit himself, fit his future. He had a ton of money in the bag he carried, enough to put him up in the finest hotel here for twenty years, enough to buy himself all the booze and T-bone steaks he might desire. He had a permanent sneering grin nailed to his face now, and as he looked through the red-tinted windows of the tavern, it came to him that he had been on the road for a long time and deserved some magic waters to clean the dust out of his pipes.

He swaggered to the door, wishing he had cowboy boots on, boots with tall heels and spurs that would go jingle-jangle-jingle, just like the real Clint's did. As he pushed the bat-wing doors apart and stepped inside onto the wooden floor that clunked very satisfyingly under his feet, he decided that he would also get himself a gun too, and one of those flat-brimmed cowboy hats Clint had made famous. And what if somebody in this lean and hard town decided he looked funny dressed that way? High noon for that fool, Clint thought, grinning inside and out. High noon.

It was dim inside, but he was able to make his way to the bar without falling over a table. He slid professionally onto one of the tall wooden stools, and the bartender, some goofball wearing a Bon Jovi T-shirt and a red Budweiser cap, ambled over and asked what he'd like.

"Some competition," Clint said, pressing his lips together to keep from laughing. God, but this was magnificent! No worries. No cares. No brat to hold him down, enough money to buy this place. Maybe best of all, not one of the sickening mental diseases that wimp Peter carried around, like Atlas struggling alone with the world on his back. Freedom, yeah, freedom.

"Drinkwise, I mean," the goofball said tiredly.

Clint thrust a hand out, lightning-quick, and took a handful of Bon Jovi in his fist. "Look here," he growled, "don't fuck with me, boy. *Nobody* fucks with me. Got it?"

The man's eyes were now large and mystified. People were staring. "Sure, yeah, sure." He was either terrified or queer, Clint didn't know which, didn't care all that much.

"A bottle of your finest firewater," he said, and shoved him away. "Pronto."

The young bartender hurried away. Clint flopped the trash bag on the slickly varnished wood of the bar, making coins inside rattle, and looked around, smirking. Three guys were bellied up to the bar to his right, minding their own business now; a guy and his slutty girlfriend were over at a table; two clowns were trying to play pool underneath a mellow bar of lights that proclaimed the goodness and quality of Busch beer. The air was dry with heat and the memory of cigarette smoke. In a corner musical equipment stood idle; the bass drum had a hand-painted logo on it that announced this band called themselves Roadhouse. Clint blew through his lips, flapping them noisily, unimpressed. He could probably pick up that guitar and play better than the band, better than Bon Jovi himself, for that matter, even though Peter had once tried to master the thing and given up when his best attempt at a bar chord was a dull buzz, nothing distinguishable, nothing remotely hopeful.

The bartender came back and carefully set a bottle of Wild Turkey in front of him, and a shot glass. "Best we carry," he said. "Seventeen-fifty."

Clint frowned. "What about happy hour?"

"Beer and mixed drinks only."

Clint grinned, and pulled the bag open. "What you get is what you keep, barkeep. Test your luck, but no peeking."

The bartender fidgeted. "Look, friend, I'd love to play along, but rules are rules. Seventeen-fifty, you're happy, I'm happy. Deal?"

Clint stared at him, eyes alive with good humor. "Fine, fine," he said, relenting, and shoved a hand in the bag. He drew a crisp bill out, snapped it flat, and winked. "Your lucky day, amigo. The big five-oh." He flipped it toward him; it helicoptered to a soft touchdown on the bar. "Keep the change, barkeep, and buy yourself some new duds. This is the Wild West, ain't it? Yeah. So try to look like it, okay? I'll be a regular here now, so don't piss me off. Last guy who pissed me off? I got this bloody trophy on my shoulder out of the deal, but the guy's pushing up daisies. Get my drift?"

The bartender nodded, entranced by the fifty-dollar bill that had come to rest in front of him. "You're new in town, huh?" he asked as he swept it up. "Welcome to Rawlins. Where might you be from?"

Clint chuckled. "You ain't gonna believe this, son, but I was born a week ago and just now grew up." He laughed, the young bartender laughed, and the world was a fine place to be. "Tell you what, sonny," he said. "Go rustle me up a pack of Marlboros and some matches. Can do?"

"You bet." The bartender hustled off to can do. The batwing doors swung apart and two cowboys came in, real cowboys in boots and hats and Western shirts with pearl buttons,

Levi's brown with dust. The doors flapped shut as they ambled noisily over, boots drumming out a slow beat, their voices full of laughter and drawling Western accent. They sat to Clint's left, ignoring him, too busy swapping stories about home on the range to notice anyone else. The bartender swung past Clint and put a pack of cigarettes and a pack of paper matches on the bar, then got the cowboys two tall beers without asking, and they drank up without paying.

Clint felt a hot flicker of anger flare alive in the base of his stomach where his emotions resided, barely in check. Those two fellows were regulars here, probably stopped by every afternoon, knew every patron here by name, but it would take many weeks, maybe months, for Clint to get that far. He recalled that back in New York, Peter had managed to ingratiate himself with some cute chick of a bartender at some foppish college hangout. She'd often slipped him a free beer now and then, aware of his poverty, not doing much better herself. But Christ, it had taken two, maybe three months of steady attendance to be admitted to the magic circle of regulars there and enjoy the benefits of membership. Clint wanted to be a regular *now,* wanted to be liked and admired *now,* not six weeks from now when his abundant finances had attracted a following.

He unscrewed the bottle cap, ignored the shot glass, and got busy stuffing himself full of Wild Turkey. It burned all the way down, stinging his chafed lower lip like a hot match, sliding down his swallow-pipe like steaming lava, nesting in his empty stomach and glowing cheerfully there. He stifled a gasp when he stopped for air. Not bad, he noticed. The bottle was already one-quarter gone. With no food to soak up the alcohol, no damn useless drugs in his blood to mix with the booze and put him to sleep, he intended, and expected, to be screamingly drunk within fifteen minutes. Then he would buy a gun and boots and spurs and a hat, and come back to drink another bottle. He knew there was no limit to the things he could do, whether it was drinking, screwing, playing pool, playing guitar, you name it. He was the alpha and the omega, the beginning, the middle, and the end. It would not surprise him, he mused as he tore the cigarettes open and lit one, if he reached up with his hands and found a crown on his head made of gold and red velvet, Imperial-margarine style. This tremendously witty idea made him laugh out loud.

One of the cowboys glanced over. Clint looked hastily away, a cowardly remnant, he supposed, of his days and years as Peter the Faggot. He tipped the bottle back again, even angrier now, mad at the cowboy and Peter and his own self for having looked away, thereby losing the battle of wills before it started.

The bartender ambled over. "Everything okay, partner?"

Clint put the bottle down with a bang. People stared. He ground his teeth, Peter's teeth, which had not seen a dentist in eight years because he was so damn poor, the Milquetoast wimp. "No," he growled, "everything is not okay. This—this whiskey has been watered down."

"What?"

"The fucking whiskey," he shouted, and became instantly embarrassed, looking around with a criminally haunted expression, seeing too many faces and eyes aimed his way. He glared at the bartender, his face burning. "It's been watered, boy, it doesn't take a genius to figure that out. You either replace it or give me my goddamn money back."

"That's impossible," the bartender said, and sniffed the bottle. He picked up the plastic cap and showed it to Clint. "Tax tag was still in one piece when I gave it to you. That bottle hasn't been opened since it left the distillery."

"Ah," Clint muttered. "Calling me a liar then?"

The bartender waved his hands in front of himself in a calm-down gesture. "This is a peaceful place," he said coolly, "and since you're new in town, I hafta tell you I've got a shotgun filled with double-ought handy nearby, and it's been used before, yes it has. It looks to me like you've got enough hurts going for yourself, and you don't need another one. The whiskey's straight Turkey, you've got my word on that. Good enough?"

Clint swept his head left and right. They were looking, all of them were, blank faces, shiny eyes, waiting to laugh at the bum with the chewed-up right shoe and the soggy bandage dripping blood down his arm where they had cut his sleeve off, a bum with a trash bag that most likely held old cans or bottles headed for recycling, a bum who kept the streets free of hard litter for the simple purpose of making a pauper's living.

He rose up, heels on the bottom rung of the stool, swinging his head to include everyone. "What are you staring at?" he shouted, almost in tears for reasons he could not fathom. "I'm Clint, you fuckers, *the* Clint! Chew on that for a while!"

"Sit down," the fan of Bon Jovi ordered. "We'll take some shit here, but not a lot of it. Either sit and shut up, or get out."

Clint lowered himself down, jaws clenched tight with unbearable rage, eyeballs bulging with insane hate. It was hot, even here in the semidarkness, and sweat was rising up on his skin as he chewed his lower lip hard enough to shred it while every available muscle in his body strained taut and hard against his bones. "I—am—Clint!" he screeched through his clenched teeth, and tears were slipping down his cheeks, detouring through the hills and valleys of his distorted face. "I—am—*Clint!*"

"Fine, Clint. Can you shut up now? The crowd's gonna get bigger and you're gonna be awful unpopular if you keep it up."

Clint placed his knotted fists on the bar and stared at them, screaming inside, his forearms greasy with sweat and sticking to the varnish. His tears were hot as they tracked down his face, splotching the bar in random patterns. The bartender pushed the bottle back to him. "Clint," he said, keeping his voice low, "everybody has tough times once in a while. Just don't take it out on my customers."

Clint swiveled his head up while his neck bones creaked

and muttered like old hinges. "You're just a kid," he said between panted breaths. "What the fuck could you know? What are you, fresh out of high school?"

The bartender smiled. "I own this place, partner. At least, I get to make the payments."

"Oh." This struck Clint as extremely unfair. What had Peter managed to do with his life these twenty-nine years? Work endlessly toward a fag doctorate in mathematics, worry himself sick about his daughter, pine forever for an eighteen-year-old girl whose face he could barely picture anymore without a photograph to fill in the details? He'd only done one thing of merit, and the results were in this black plastic bag.

"Peace, then?" the bartender—*owner!*—said, and held out his hand.

Clint nodded. Instead of shaking his hand, though, he reached into the bag and withdrew a fistful of bills. He thrust them at him.

"Whoa," the owner said, big-eyed once again. "What in the hell are you doing with all that cash in a goddamn trash bag?"

"Making friends," Clint said calmly, and slid off the stool. He walked toward the two cowboys, dragging the bag along the bar. They looked over when he stopped, deeply tanned faces open and questioning. "Go fish," Clint said, and held the bag open under the first cowboy's nose. He frowned at Clint, then looked inside. "Smells good, don't it?" Clint said. "Go fish."

Hesitantly, with a glance at his partner, he stuck an arm inside and pulled out a crinkled clot of greenery. His eyebrows rose up almost high enough to touch his hat. "Holy, holy," he whispered, just surprised enough to make Clint feel magnanimous.

"Line up," Clint shouted, flapping the open bag, and this time he got not only eyes and faces but whole bodies converging on this strange vending machine of money. "One at a time," he warned them, smiling, ready to laugh once more. Life was getting good again.

The first cowboy tried to reach for another bundle. Clint ducked good-naturedly away. "Only one per person, it says right here in the rule book. But you may get your friends and neighbors together, and try your luck once more."

The tavern got empty in a hurry. Clint ambled to the door and looked out into the sunshine, smiling. Someone, one of the cowboys maybe, was shouting something about money money money, and pointing to the tavern. Clint nodded, pleased. Screw six weeks making pals, he thought, satisfied. I've made a bunch of pals already.

The owner called out to him. "Hey, Clint?"

He turned. "Yo."

"Is there anybody I can call? Anybody that knows you?"

He grinned. "Nah. I'm doing fine by myself."

The owner nodded, and went to the phone anyway. Clint heard him dial, vaguely concerned about it, but then the doors were swinging open and more people were flooding in, eager hands flexing, faces bright with greed. They assaulted the bag, almost tearing it out of his hands, while he laughed and beamed at them. "My name's Clint," he shouted again and again above the noise of the growing crowd. "I'm a regular here!"

He gave in to another urge, pushed his way outside, and began throwing handfuls of money to the sky. Traffic stopped; people gathered in a gleeful riot. Blood ran down his right arm from the red sponge that had been his bandage. Drops flipped and spun through the hot afternoon air, tainted the money, made splotches on the sidewalk, but he was Clint and it was happy hour at the Sitting Bull Tavern and he had never had so much fun in his life. But as he'd told the owner of this fine bar where he was now a regular, he was only a week old anyway.

SEVENTEEN

By four o'clock Henry Austerwahl had exceeded his own estimation of how many drinks he would have at this very nice Amber Club lounge, where a lady wearing a sequined dress was tinkling at the piano with a glass globe stuffed full of money perched on the ebony expanse of the grand piano's upper deck, taking requests, not stymied by even the oldest or newest of songs. After a few drinks had loosened him up a bit, Austerwahl was able to stop worrying about Edith and her broken leg, which was, he admitted, a pretty commonplace injury and certainly not life-threatening. When he was working on his fifth martini he gathered enough false courage to request a song, secretly hoping to stump the lady and get a free drink, which was the way things operated around here; if she indeed knew it, he'd be obligated to put some money in the pot. It was a fun little challenge, and he thought he had the capper.

He turned on his stool and raised a finger. "Play 'Rock Lobster,'" he called out, becoming just a bit embarrassed. The lounge was very much crowded for this time of day, but he'd discovered fifteen years ago when he moved here from California that Westerners of this region had a very casual attitude about drinking, spending more time doing it than worrying about it.

She smiled at him, her dress shafting sparkles into his eyes. "Are you sure you want to hear punk rock right now? The B-52s are a little gross for this crowd, wouldn't you say?"

He chuckled, pulled out his wallet, and walked to the piano. He stuck a five-dollar bill in the globe. "Do me a favor," he said. "Don't play the song until I leave. I wouldn't want to get lynched."

She winked at him. "Gotcha."

He wandered off to the rest room while she tapped out a more palatable tune, did his business, then called the hospital on the pay phone in the corridor. He was transferred to Patient Information, and was told that Edith was still drugged out of her mind, or words to that effect. He hung up, frowning, wondering if he should go back to Rawlins or stay here in Rock Springs, maybe get liquored up and skip work tomorrow. But he'd have to call the project director and lay down some smooth lies, which he was not good at doing, or Bob Stadler would have to cover for him, which he was not good at doing either. Ah, he decided in the end, to hell with the booze, and left the bar, squinting in the harsh sunlight outside, overwhelmed by the dry hot air. His truck in the Amber Club's parking area looked like a thing made of dust with bony fingers of shattered tumbleweeds masquerading as a front grille. He got inside, sweating already, settling himself on a seat whose brown skin was close to the melting point. Gasping, he started the motor and backed out, barely able to touch the burning circle of the steering wheel. It was days like this that made him look forward to winter, but the winters here were so numbing, so full of snow and wind, that he invariably found himself wishing for summer. The thought of retiring back to California seemed pleasant, but he was slated to retire in an aluminum-nickel-alloy coffin filled with circulating liquid nitrogen, if he ever got the nerve to go on with it. He was able to see the irony in this. The mad scientist who'd created the process was too afraid of it to have it done on himself.

He drove to a Sinclair station, had the tank filled to the tune of nineteen dollars, stopped by a McDonald's and got a double cheeseburger with fries and a Coke, found I-80 East, and settled in for the long drive home, reflectively picking his false teeth with his tongue when the food was gone. A thought struck him, and he leaned forward, one hand digging under the seat. He got ahold of the disgusting peanut-butter-and-jelly sandwich on whole wheat, hard as granite now, rolled his window down, and pitched it out.

In the rearview mirror he saw a handful of huge black crows settle on it, and hoped they like it, because he sure as hell didn't. Then he realized that at least one very good thing had come of this day.

There wouldn't be any more panning for gold for a long, long time, and he could get back to his lazy, hazy weekend schedule, which consisted of doing nothing, nothing at all. He would start tonight, just as soon as he got home.

He laid on the gas, bringing the truck up to eighty, then eighty-five, because on this desolate stretch of Wyoming highway the chances of running across a cop were zero.

Kim Marden believed that she was finally able to understand something of what Peter had endured all these years since his collapse, which he had told her "was spectacular" without giving many details. Uncontrollable shaking. Choking on air, vomiting beside his bed. Losing eleven pounds in eight days, unable to eat. Heart pounding out of control. And the endless crying, of course, for the wife he had lost, for the mind he was losing.

Kim didn't think she was losing her mind, though the thought had occurred to her before. She knew she was breathing too fast, sweating too much, her heart a galloping pony beneath the bones of her chest. Fifteen minutes had passed since she'd talked to Austerwahl on the phone, and she was doing as told, staying put, sitting in the steaming Nova at the intersection of Sitting Bull and Rawlins Avenue, quite possibly illegally parked, burning with anxiety. Every few seconds she glanced back to the ice mountain, imagining she had heard Darbi move. She kept the tire iron in one sweating hand, ready to bean the poor girl if she came back to life, crack the thing across her poor head to quiet the madness that had taken control of her.

Why are you doing this? she asked herself, raising her head to look at her face in the mirror. Her cheeks and forehead were nicked with a dozen small, crescent-shaped cuts that had bled red teardrops, the work of Darbi's fingernails. There was a perfect circle of teeth marks on her chin and nose where Darbi had bitten hard enough to draw blood. The horrible slashes from her eye to her chin were going to need plastic surgery, she knew with a cold internal breeze of despair. And her breasts, her breasts—Wayne had once manhandled them too hard when he was drunk, and she'd believed then that he had done permanent damage before she could bat him away. Those had been love squeezes, nothing at all compared to what Darbi had done. Kim opened her blouse and inspected the damage, which was awesome, deep trenches in her flesh still merrily bleeding, a ring of deep punctures around one nipple. She covered herself back up, sickened, and held the blouse together with a fist. In the space of one minute the madness within Darbi's decomposing brain had destroyed her looks, maybe for life.

So why are you doing this?

She knew why, in a vague sort of way. It was because she was mad—angry, as they seemed to say on television all the time, as if mad still had its old definition—she was mad but not insane. She had left her life behind for this bizarre journey, finally doing something new, exciting, getting away, forging a new life from the pitiful debris of the old one, a new and improved Kimberly Marden on the road to a new future. She was not mad at Darbi—Darbi was the ultimate victim in all of this—and she was not mad at Peter. She was mad at Clint, the swaggering phony who had snatched Peter away, but even more she was mad at the devious mental abnormality that allowed Clint to exist, and the merciless disease that had ravaged an innocent child. Kim knew that this ghastly Mortis thing, that brain extraction, had put Darbi into some brutal wasteland between death and life. The only way to end Darbi's suffering now would be either to crush her head and its degenerating brain with some heavy object, maybe put her on the ground and run over her with the car a few times, or get her frozen and let future technology rebuild her a thousand years from now when death had been abolished and sickness banned from the earth.

Ice sloughed behind her. She whirled, tire iron ready, eyes huge, but it had been just a small glacier of melting cubes sliding off the mountain to plop to the ocean on the floor. Darbi was a distorted image in black and white and pink, sunken eyes closed, a new split on her scalp where the gas station man had hammered her with the tire iron. Kim's heart ached for her, this living tragedy who should be laughing and giggling at a playground somewhere, free of cares, free of pain. The future might give her that.

Kim looked past the ice to the dirty rear window, watching for the cop she had so narrowly escaped before, watching for Dr. Austerwahl, who would lift this entire burden from her. As far as the money went, it was the end of the line. Clint was roaming the streets with it, probably doing battle for control with Peter in the confines of their mutual skull. If Peter could regain possession, there might be a chance. Until then, Austerwahl would just have to take a rain check.

Unusual motion to her left made her turn her head again. On Sitting Bull Street two blocks away, a riot was in progress. She frowned, straining to see, idly massaging her bleeding tongue against the roof of her mouth. It looked like some kind of streetfest, like they had in St. Charles every July to limber people up for the real fun of the Octoberfest. But the streets weren't barricaded, no police cars were keeping watch, people weren't ambling around carrying tin pails of beer. Here, some of the people were running, abandoning their cars where they stood, joining the fracas, what seemed to be a very happy crowd assembling out of nowhere. Kim saw a boy charge past with both hands clamped over a sizable bundle of money; a man not far away was cramming the pockets of his jeans full of bills. When the bills were all tucked away he turned and jogged back to the riot, rejoining it with a fevered grin.

Who the hell was giving away all the money? Kim thought of banks, and of bank robbers, and of a certain idiot named Clint who was liable to do just about anything.

"Jesus," she muttered. She put the tire iron on the seat and got out. She crossed the street at a jog, holding the tatters of her blouse together, worried that her car might get towed away, worried that someone might look inside, worried about Austerwahl showing up and finding no one. She came to the rim of the logjam of people and forged her way inside, elbowing a path, getting insulted and barked at. The hot street was littered with money, some of it bloody, and for Kim there was no more doubt about it.

"Clint!" she screamed, badgering her way to the center. One more shove and she was through, and there stood Clint with the deflated trash bag tucked under one arm, jamming money into the sea of hands surrounding him, his face wet with tears or sweat, blood from his shoulder worming down his arm in multiple streams, shockingly red against the paleness of his skin. She drew up to him, jostling with the crowd, and shouted his name again.

He looked at her and his grin faltered. Other people looked at her, this battered woman drenched with blood, and a magic sort of calm rippled through the crowd as they gaped at her in wonder.

"You son of a bitch!" she shrieked in his face, destroying the sudden quiet. *"Get the hell away from Peter!"*

She slapped him hard enough to spin him around. His shiny eyes went momentarily dull as he fell against his admirers, was caught and heaved back like a punch-drunk street fighter, and regained his balance. He opened his mouth to say something—probably something nasty, Kim thought—but then the unnatural contour of his face softened, transforming him. "Ah, God," he moaned, looking at the faces, the reaching hands. "Kim, get me out of here before the cops show up."

She took him by the hand and dragged him along, teeth clenched hard enough to hurt her jaw, rudely pushing her way past people, ready to do battle with anyone who got in the way. A disappointed murmur rose up as the crowd began to loosen, and suddenly everyone was busy picking up the bloody money that until now had been small change, not enough to bother with.

"God, I'm sorry, Kim," Peter groaned when they were free and being ignored, hurrying to the car at a trot, hand in hand.

"You couldn't help it," she said. "I just hope Austerwahl doesn't think we chickened out."

"Who?"

"The guy who's not your pal. The doctor, Salamander and all that."

"You got ahold of him?"

"Yes, and he's on the way, might even be here already. Come on." She let his hand fall, and broke into a dead run with Peter following. She could see that the Nova was still there, and that it was indeed in a no-parking zone, the curb painted yellow, as any idiot and traffic cop could see, but there were no cops snooping around yet. They came to the car and slid inside, panting. Peter got on his knees on the front seat and checked Darbi over, shoveled a few handfuls of ice, then sat back down. He looked at Kim, his tired eyes full of apologies.

"Darbi did this to you, didn't she?"

She nodded.

"Why are you sticking around, Kim? There's nothing in this for you."

She touched her fingers to her face, wincing. "Too late for that, Peter. I've already paid the price, and I'm going to see this thing through to the end."

He laid a warm hand on her arm; blood dripped off his wrist to the trash bag on the seat between them. "If there was any way I could repay you, you know I would." He looked in the bag. "About half gone, I'd say. I hope this Austerwahl guy will go ahead and do it. Maybe I can promise to rob a few more banks. Hah!" He shook his head. "I think you should abandon ship now, Kim. You're consorting with a felon, and that's a serious offense. I think I can handle it from here."

She almost laughed in his face. "Really? How about Clint? Can he handle it too?"

He looked morosely at his knees. "Never mind."

"I told you I'm in this thing to the end."

"Okay."

She looked at her watch: four-thirty. "It's been almost half an hour," she said. "How far away does this man live?"

"Don't know," he mumbled.

A shadow passed between Kim and the sun. She turned with an involuntary gasp. A stocky man wearing a rumpled suit was staring at her, stooped over, his face inches apart from her own. "Salamander?" he asked with a sympathetic little smile.

"Yes!" Kim half shouted. "Dr. Austerwahl?"

"Nice to meet you." He looked at Peter. "Looks like you two had a hard trip."

They both rolled their eyes; hard wasn't the word for it.

He looked in the back seat. Kim saw something flare in his eyes, a twinge of disgust maybe. Odd bedside manner for a doctor, but she had to admit that Darbi was rather startling at best. "Shall we take my car?" he asked, and Kim shook her head.

"We can't take Darbi out of the ice. She's pretty, well, pretty far gone."

He nodded, looking around uncertainly. "Have you been followed?"

Kim hesitated. To lie, or not to lie? "There's a little red car dogging us sometimes, with two men inside. We don't have any idea who they are. That won't—screw up the deal, will it?"

He gnawed his tongue for a second, frowning. "We'll

have to throw them off, if they're still around. Just follow me, do what I do."

"Is it far?" Kim asked. "We're low on gas."

"Not far. Just out in the boonies a ways."

The noise of a siren had been building in the east. A police car surged around the corner of Rawlins onto Sitting Bull, tires squealing, lights stabbing Kim's eyes with red and blue flashes. She felt herself go weak. Two minutes earlier and Peter would have been arrested, and he was certainly in no shape to face charges today. "One more thing, Doctor," she was able to squeak. She lifted the trash bag for him to see. "Is it enough?"

He looked perplexed for a moment. Then: "Money isn't an issue here. It's the child we have to worry about."

Peter leaned forward, staring past Kim at him with large eyes. "What do you mean, it's not an issue? Do you know what I went through to get it?"

"No."

Peter slumped back. "I don't know whether to laugh or cry."

The doctor exchanged glances with Kim. "Ready?"

"Damn right we're ready." She turned the key, the earthquake hit, making ice scatter and clatter, and fresh steam rolled out from under the hood. The doctor eyed the car doubtfully, then walked back to his own. When he pulled away Kim slotted herself in behind him, getting honked at in the process, and glanced down at the gas gauge. One hair above the E.

"Finally," Peter said. "It's almost over."

She nodded. "Almost over."

They followed the big black Plymouth, heading out of town, out to the deserted prairie where this business could be finished unseen.

Abraham Maharba opened his eyes and saw the bottom of a table. Pain encircled his midsection and blood was sour in his mouth. He sat up, groaning, and pressed a hand over the bleeding hole in his white shirt. The house was rocking like a boat on bad seas. It occurred to him that he had been shot. It occurred to him that the big tough bastard without a name had done it. In his life Maharba had pulled a lot of stunts, conned a lot of people, stolen a lot of things, but never had he been beaten to the punch when it came to breaking an agreement. It should be the big ugly man walking around with a bullet in his gut, the son of a bitch.

He wormed out from under the table, got to his knees, then to his feet. He tottered to the sofa, dropped to his knees again, and fished for his pistol underneath. The pain was white-hot, searing, flaring with each move he made. Grunting, he pulled the gun out and made it to his feet again. He stumbled to the open front door trailing blood, reached for the knob of the screen door, and became woozy, then sick, vomiting a huge amount of blood and meaty clots of his own ruined stomach onto the threshold.

He fell over, his head banging the door. He tried to push himself up on his hands, thinking only of the big man and how good it would feel to watch him die. His palms slipped in the cherry-colored vomit, and this time when his head hit the floor he stayed there while his fading imagination conjured up pictures of the man in the black suit suffering in agony, the man in the black suit cowering and cringing in fear and pain and remorse, the big man in the black suit being dumped into a coffin. Abraham Maharba on top once again.

Pretty soon the visions slowed. His mind began to shut down. All became black, blacker than a suit, blacker than his own born-again hide as his blood and his life oozed out to stain the pretty blue carpet of this nice Western home.

EIGHTEEN

RAWLINS'S BUSY STREETS THINNED OUT TO BECOME ONE-LANE country roads to the north of the city, where Kim was guiding her balky Nova in an effort to keep pace with the black Plymouth. Why paved roads were here at all was a mystery to her. Everything was the shimmering mirage of a desert, complete with distant counterfeit rivers and lakes the color of steel. Just beyond the doctor's speeding car the road became water where it met the rambling horizon, water that kept its distance no matter how close she got. Though her car was churning steam in thin clouds, as yet the idiot light in the dash that was supposed to glow red when the motor overheated remained calm and dark. Whether it worked or not was a good question.

"He's driving in circles," Peter said, eyes narrowed against the light.

Kim nodded. "He's trying to shake whoever might be on our trail. I just hope the gas lasts."

As she followed the doctor she was taking every ounce the Chevy had to offer in the way of horsepower, making it skid around curves on its smooth tires, wind up to seventy on the straightaways, take bone-rattling bumps and potholes that sifted most of Darbi's ice to the floor and jarred Kim's teeth in her head. In this new world of limitless desert she had the feeling that the car was actually standing still, the landscape moving like an Atari game beneath the wheels. All she had to do was dodge the obstacles.

The asphalt became gravel; the gravel became what

passed, in this area of the country, for dirt. It was more like talcum powder, and for her the world became a pale brown fog that washed through the open windows, collected in her eyes, and coated her teeth with grit. She dropped back, knowing she could follow at a distance of five miles and still see the plume of dust the black car was raising. Navigating her car through this stuff was tantamount to driving through wet snow in Missouri. Even at her new, slower pace, she could feel the car slewing from side to side, the treadless tires captured by the dust, skating in directions Kim didn't intend. Peter had his hands hooked in the defroster vents in the dash now, holding tight, the sweat on his face attracting dust that became dark grime below his nose and on his forehead. Kim blinked, momentarily blinded, and then two small, cold hands fastened around her neck, the fingers pressing into her throat, and she pushed out a noiseless scream as her windpipe was crushed shut.

Peter was knuckling his eyes. He dropped his hands, blinking furiously, intent on the road. Kim swung out a hand and hit him on the arm, her vision beginning to go haywire already, everything too shiny, too bright. Peter lunged at her with a squawk and tried to peel Darbi's fingers away from her throat, his face distorted in a grimace of effort, succeeding only in making Darbi squeeze harder, too hard for a sick little girl, as hard as a vise being screwed shut. The car drifted off the road. Sagebrush thumped underneath. Something clunked, and the motor took on a new, deeper tone. If she was able to look back, she knew she would see the carcass of her muffler bouncing to a stop in the brush. Right now, as she began to slip into oxygen starvation, it seemed wise to leave the matter to the folks at Midas.

The Nova went into a wild broadside skid, no screeching tires, just a wicked high-speed float on the loose desert soil. For reasons Kim would never know, the horn, which had not made a sound in years, blared alive and stayed that way, adding noise to this noisy mess, sounding like a dwindling siren as her consciousness drifted away.

She tried to go for the tire iron, and got a handful of money instead. She jerked the bag off the seat and threw it. The car filled with a cloud of floating and pinwheeling bills, caught in the jet stream of hot air blasting through the open windows. While the world went from too bright to too dark, Kim got her fingers around the warm steel. She tried to raise it but Peter's arms were in the way as he went on uselessly trying to pry Darbi's hands away. The horn shouted its unlovely music as the car spun onto the road again. It rattled to a stop in a tidal wave of dust.

Kim heard a very distant Peter screaming at Darbi, begging her to let go. Kim shoved the tire iron onto his lap while the four hands around her neck wagged her head in furious circles. Well, she thought dimly, I don't care, 'cause it's time to check out.

Peter picked up the tire iron and swung it. Kim heard it crack against Darbi's skull. Her hands fell away and Kim took a long, sweet breath of air and dust, her heart pounding, her head full of noise and unbearable pressure. She coughed and retched, her throat a band of agony, her larynx hot, maybe swollen. With pleasure she collapsed against the steering wheel, panting. When her chest hit the horn it immediately shut down.

"Goddamn little shit," she heard Peter grunt. His door screeched open. "Fuck this routine."

She jerked upright. "*Noooo!*" she screamed, and her bruised throat screamed back. She hurled her door open and jumped out, wobbling on her feet. "You son of a bitch!" she shouted at Peter's back. His T-shirt was a sweaty black rag, but he surely didn't mind, because he wasn't even Peter anymore. This was happening too often, too fast. This time, she knew, he might never come out of it. "Clint!" she shouted, enraged.

He turned his head as he walked. "Fuck you."

She smashed her door shut. The Plymouth was approaching, going backward with the husky doctor twisted around inside. He stopped with a flare of taillights and got out.

"What's wrong?" he called to her. "Where's he going?"

Kim opened her door again and leaned inside. Darbi had collapsed in an awkward heap on top of the dwindling bed of ice. The tire iron was on the front seat. She snatched it up and drew herself out. "He's Clint again," she called back.

He hurried over. "What?"

Clint began to jog back toward Rawlins, his shoes kicking up puffs of dust. "I'll explain it later. We need to stop him." She hefted her miserable weapon. "I just hope I don't wind up killing him. Shovel some ice on top of Darbi, will you?"

The doctor's face was a mask of confusion. Kim ran after Clint, shouting for him to stop. He did, and turned to face her, legs spread, fists on his hips, mouth twisted up in a sneer. She charged at him, waving the tire iron over her head. When she was close she swung it at him, but he stepped out of the way easily, stuck out one leg, and tripped her. She thumped facedown into the dust and skidded a few feet. Jumping up, sizzling with rage, she charged at him again. This time he swung out and hit her on the mouth with his fist, mashing her lips against her teeth, knocking her over backward. Her head bounced on the hardpack beneath its layer of brown powder, and she saw familiar stars. She got to her feet again, her mouth a bleeding gash in her face, her eyes bright with rage. She threw the tire iron at him. It went end over end and bounced off his chest, knocking him backward a few steps. He looked at her, no longer sneering, his lips twisted with pain.

"Peter?" she said, moving toward him. "Peter?"

He leered at her. "I'm going to kill you, bitch."

She groaned, a bundle of pain from top to bottom, tired beyond repair, tired of trying and trying, hurting and hurting, tired of tasting her own blood. She fell back as he advanced, his hands jerked into claws, blood dripping off his right arm in a steady pulse to be swallowed immediately by the dust.

She saw the doctor hurrying to help. "Try *him* on for size, Clint," she said, and Clint turned.

The good doctor had a very large gun in his hand. He stopped and aimed it at Clint.

"Good!" Kim shouted, and ran to the doctor. He stared at her with his eyebrows high and questioning, jaw hanging slack.

She reached out and jerked the pistol out of his hand, turned, and aimed it at Clint with both hands. "Last chance, hotshot," she said, aimed it downward, and shot between his feet. Dust jumped in a spurt, and Clint jumped with it. When he touched down he put out his hands as if to block her.

"Got more where that came from," she snarled. The trigger had been hard to pull, and the recoil had nearly knocked her down. Her ears whined from the enormity of the blast. Some pistol this.

She aimed it at his chest. "Clint," she said, "I am tired of this bullshit, and I am tired of you. Put Peter on the line, or you are one dead man."

He frowned, opened his mouth, then seemed to forget what he was going to say. He jerked, and his face relaxed. His shoulders slumped. "Oh, God," he moaned, and staggered toward her.

"Peter?"

He nodded. "It's going out of control, Kim. I can't fight him anymore."

She handed the pistol back to Austerwahl, and took Peter's arm. Together they walked back to the car. It did not occur to her to wonder why a doctor would carry a gun in his car. If it had, she would pass it off as just another unusual thing in this unusual part of the country.

Following behind them, the man who called himself Austerwahl raised the pistol, and sighted in on the back of Kim's head. He lost his confused frown and his face went curiously blank, then spread wide in a grin.

His finger tightened on the trigger.

Dr. Henry Austerwahl was nine miles from Rawlins when the impossible happened. Patriotic lights, red, white, and blue, flashed into existence in the mirror of his dirty Bronco as he sped toward home and nothing to do. He backed off the gas immediately, amazed, feeling a sharp twinge of panic somewhere between his stomach and his chest, a feeling he had almost forgotten about. It was the same feeling he'd had every day from 1968 to 1971, when New Future Cryogenics was being investigated by the Feds as they tried to figure out who to put on trial. For a moment, as those flashing lights drew closer, he was able to fool himself into believing the cop was after someone else. The fact that there was no one else around killed that idea. He dived deeper into panic, thinking that no, no, this cop was not after a speeder, he was after a mad scientist of dubious reputation who had recently frozen five people alive.

The cop in his black and white Wyoming State Police car drew up so close Austerwahl thought their bumpers must lock, and hit his siren for a second, ending all doubt of his intentions. Austerwahl applied the brakes and pulled over, his mouth too dry, his palms wet enough to leave smears on the steering wheel. It was all over. He would spend the rest of his life behind bars.

The cop got out, his tan uniform stiff and perfect, and marched over. Austerwahl rolled his window down, intending to beg for mercy; he was an old man with a bad heart, a virgin as far as prison deviations go.

"Afternoon," the cop said, looking at Austerwahl, then at the dusty insides of the truck. No, Officer, I am not smuggling drugs. "Could I see your license, please?"

Austerwahl got it out with shaking fingers, managing to dump everything in his wallet onto his lap. The cop looked it over, then ambled back to his car and sat inside. Austerwahl saw him use his radio. His heart gave a huge lurch and began to gallop, thundering in his chest, making him woozy. What a way to end such a successful career, such a good life. He would kill himself before he let them put him in prison.

After a few breathless and intolerable minutes, the officer came back. He handed Austerwahl's license over. "I clocked you doing eighty-six miles an hour, Mr. Austerwahl. The speed limit is sixty-five, as is clearly posted." He handed him a ticket as well. "Because you were twenty-one miles per hour over the limit, this is not payable by mail, sir. You'll have to appear in court at the date and time indicated."

Austerwahl stared at the ticket in his hands, stunned. "Is that it?"

"Sure is. From now on, watch your speed."

"I will," he said, nodding his head in a blur. A lousy speeding ticket, that was it. No arrest, no handcuffs, no trial, and no jail. "Thank you," he said, faint with gratefulness.

The cop looked at him strangely. "I don't usually get that," he said, and went away. Austerwahl reassembled his wallet, still shaking, unable to quit grinning. From now on, he decided, he would leave the paranoia to the paranoids of the world.

He put the Bronco in gear, brought it up to sixty-five, lit a Winston, and continued on, noticing that aside from the heat, it was a very nice day here under the blue Western sky.

"This is stupid," Steve Rafter said.

"Better than doing nothing at all," Jared replied.

Steve turned one of the giant pages of the book in front of him. Here in the basement of the Rawlins City Hall, surrounded by endless racks of oversized record books, it was too dim and smelled too much of dust and old paper. Some of the plat records went back as far as 1868, when settlers were claiming stakes and dutifully registering them with the local authorities. Unfortunately, the persons who had been in charge of these records over the years had done a lousy job of keeping them in proper order; Steve found a 1960's entry sandwiched between one that turned out to be the record of a property exchange in 1898 and another dated 1981. What a mess.

His eyes ached from reading dead clerks' handwriting, the ink faded and smudged. Starting in 1938, the gigantic pages went from handwritten to typed pages glued on top, but the numbskull who'd typed the entries had used a typewriter whose teeth were clogged and whose ribbon was dry. More eyestrain. It was very doubtful that even if Braine had actually purchased local property for his new cryogenics venture, it would be recorded. Braine was rich and records clerks were poor. It was even possible that Austerwahl had made the land purchase, maybe under a false name. It wouldn't be hard.

The cop at the gas station had detained them just long enough for them to lose the trail of the Nova entirely. After seeing their ID and badges, he had tried to get them to tell who had wrecked the station and what exactly in the fuck was going on. They'd begged off, national security and all that, but Steve had had a brainstorm and asked if a man named Braine or Austerwahl was known to own any property hereabouts. You can check with city hall, the cop had told them, obviously pissed off. So here they were now, destroying their eyesight checking every entry in every book, and there were a lot of books. "Christ," Steve hissed. "Here we've got everything from A to Z and it's not even alphabetized. The entries start at 1914 and jump all the way to the late fifties and back." He levered the cover shut; the books were the size of an open newspaper, each one weighing about thirty pounds.

"Ten down, fifty more to go," Jared said, watching him.

Steve put his elbows on the wobbly cafeteria table that passed as a desk here, and dropped his chin onto his hands. "What if they're headed out of town, man? Who can guarantee Rawlins is the place? You checked the phone book yourself, right? No Austerwahl, certainly no Braine. They're using aliases. Fuck." He got up and exchanged the book for another one whose cover was old and flaking. Hell, he thought, it might have entries all the way back to the dawn of time, with a few brand-new ones mixed inside without any scheme at all. He dropped it onto the table with a bang.

"Maybe we should hit the road," Steve grumbled. "This sucketh."

"Do tell."

He sat down and opened the book, looking for Braine, Austerwahl, Austerwahl, Braine. If he could find the entry of property sale or exchange, it would tell very specifically where the property was, and they could go there, and they would be done and finished with this piece of shit of an assignment. For all Steve knew, he admitted unhappily, Kaye might be holding up a bank in town right now. Strange thing was, he had made it from St. Charles to Rawlins without knocking over one bank at all. Maybe he had enough dough now.

"Here's one," Jared said suddenly, tapping his finger on the entry. "Record of property sale, purchaser Harold M. Braine and wife Nancy."

"Huh? I don't think he's married. What's the date?"

"Oops. 1954."

"Hell, Braine was a teenager then. Better luck next time."

They went at it again, but Steve's attention span was lagging. The specter of the little girl buried in ice still haunted his memory, made him wonder about a lot of things; topping the list was what in the hell she was doing in all that ice. Then came questions about her color, her insane assault on Kaye's girlfriend, the demolition of the gas station, and why Kaye walked out in the first place.

"Ah, shit," he mumbled, tired, hot, dirty, mad. What he'd give for a long cool shower and a meal that didn't come out of a bag. He went back to the book, able to foresee a bit of the future. They'd have to report to Newell Jackson that they'd lost Kaye, couldn't find the site, were as incompetent as he secretly suspected beneath his facade of friendly impartiality.

Steve heard footsteps coming down the wooden stairway into this semidark chamber of records. He leaned sideways, peering past one of the metal book racks where these dusty monsters reposed. It was the lady he had talked to upstairs, the one who'd pointed the way for them, very impressed by their badges. "Hellooo," she called out as she came to the table. "Any luck yet?"

"Not yet," Steve said. "Isn't there some kind of filing system to speed this up?"

She cocked her head, this lady who reminded Steve of every grandma he'd ever seen. "Well, once we tried putting all this on microfiche, but it was such a mess it would have taken ten people a hundred years to sort it out by date and alphabet. Probably a good thing too. Microfiche is ancient history now, since we have computers and things."

He brightened. "You have all this on computer?"

She laughed, and swept an arm to indicate the whole room. "Mercy me, heavens, no! It would take ten people a hundred years to sort it out by date and alphabet. We've only got the newest deeds registered, the newest abstracts."

"Yeah?" He stood up. "How new?"

"The last two years. I thought you said this purchase might be fifteen or twenty years old."

"I've changed my mind." He folded his book shut, and nodded at Jared. "You keep it up down here," he told him. "Ma'am, lead the way."

He followed her upstairs, not really expecting any miracles, but damn glad to get out of that basement. She led him down one of the corridors, where his heels clicked out a lonely beat on the marble, and to an office. At the door she wished him luck, and left.

He went inside. A pretty young thing, maybe twenty-five, was tapping on a nice big NEC computer with glowing green letters on its screen. She looked up and smiled. "Help you?"

He thought maybe she could.

NINETEEN

As Kim put out a hand to open the Nova's door, it was rammed open from the inside, bursting the latch into bits of jagged metal that buzzed away like shrapnel. The impact of the door crashing against her legs pushed her off her feet and hurled her a remarkable distance away, where she crashed headfirst into a huge sagebrush. The prickly parts of the scratchy bush shallowly pierced her scalp in a dozen places as she slid deep into it, hurting like needles of fire, while dust and a powder of old twigs rained down on her face. She sat up with a jerk, wiping her eyes, her knees ablaze with pain that thundered in her kneecaps, knowing without seeing that Darbi had ejected herself from the car. She could hear her crazy, howling voice as she screeched the insanity of the demons that the Mortis operation seemed to have planted in her brain.

Kim opened her eyes, fully expecting to see Peter imprisoned in her unearthly clutch, but it was Austerwahl this time. Darbi had her arms and legs hooked around his shoulders, her stomach mashed against his face, biting his head and his neat, dark hair, screaming nonsense. He was stumbling in small circles, arms waving, the pistol in one hand, dust boiling in clouds around his feet, his shadow under the blinding sun a wavering black puddle. Peter sprang over and took hold of the back of Darbi's dress, pulling at it, but he might as well not have bothered, Kim saw, because in her condition—or despite it—Darbi was as strong as an enraged pit bull.

Kim got herself up onto her feet. Her shoes were lumpy inside with sand now, oddly heavy as she ran. Austerwahl was behind the car, dancing an awkward tango to the tune of Darbi's screams, while Peter tugged uselessly on her pink dress in a small, unhappy game of crack-the-whip. A host of green desert blowflies buzzed in tight circles around them as Austerwahl twirled and jumped, big as beetles. Kim got behind him and took hold of Darbi's head, both hands clamped on her scalp, trying to push her head back and make her let go. Darbi barked and slavered, filling Austerwahl's hair with frothy bubbles of bloody saliva that dripped down his forehead in pink zigzags. Kim pushed, just realizing that the tire iron was about the only way to end this. Suddenly something gave, and Kim smacked her face hard against Austerwahl's forehead.

She staggered back, stunned, and shook her head to clear it. She look at Darbi, then at her hands, and then she was screaming, shuffling backward with her face drawn up in a rictus of terror, because stuck to both of her hands were large flat slices of Darbi's scalp, stubbly hair a delicate fuzz against the skin of her palms. Darbi's pale right ear was in Kim's left hand. Kim flapped both hands, unaware that she was screaming, only knowing that the disgusting paste that had been Darbi's own decomposing flesh would simply not come off. She looked up with huge eyes, flapping her hands in a frenzy.

Darbi was still going at it. Her head was a gleaming white skull flecked with clinging bits of meat, the remaining skin at the edges of her face wrinkling, peeling. Her cheeks were sunken hollows, her eyes rolling yellow circles capped with shocking irises the color of the sky. Peter was charging down the road, his head whipping back and forth as he looked for the tire iron. Still Austerwahl danced, trying now to hit Darbi on the head with his big gun, his arms wildly flailing, woofing out guttural curses. He succeeded two times, without effect. The sound of gunmetal against bone was loud and thick, the sound of death camps and inquisitions. Kim went into a squat, weak with a horror that bordered on a deep and numbing species of superstition. She scrubbed her hands in the dust, crying now, and the slabs of Darbi's skin lost their grip and peeled away like old, soggy wallpaper. The smell of rot and dust and hopelessness was overwhelming. Kim had a strong urge, a need, to get away from here and her and the thing she had become. She rose up, almost too weak to stand but ready to run anyway, and saw Peter rush at Darbi with the tire iron upraised, dust sifting off it and his hands. His mouth fell open as he approached, his eyes grew huge. He tripped on nothing and fell to his hands and knees, raising dust in brown puffs. The tire iron bounced away and cart-wheeled to a stop between Kim's feet. She clenched her eyes shut, denying all of this, denying that Darbi had ever lived, that Peter was real. She opened them again and nothing had changed.

Austerwahl's pistol went off, a terrific bang, shooting a bullet harmlessly into the sky. Kim jerked at the noise, then bent and picked up the tire iron, hot tears coursing down her cheeks, stripping what was left of the aging mascara that she had applied so long ago, that faraway yesterday in Missouri. She stumbled toward Darbi and her whirling captive, raised the tire iron in both hands, and smashed it down on the top of Darbi's bony new head. The sound was awful, strangely crunchy this time, the sound a cockroach might make when it is stepped on. Darbi went instantly slack, and dropped into the dust behind Austerwahl's heels. He lurched around, pale as bleached flour, his hair standing out in spikes. He pitched backward across the Nova's trunk, eyes bulging, blood rolling down his face like hot war paint.

Kim's hands opened, and the tire iron thumped down beside Darbi's head. She took a staggering step sideways and looked down at her.

There was a crevasse on the top of her head about three inches long, perhaps half an inch deep. Some sticky gray stuff was bubbling out of the cauldron of her skull, salted with bone chips. Kim swallowed, overcome with revulsion.

She turned away and vomited a small amount of clear liquid that the dust ate, and some bitter yellow stuff that could only be gall. The dry heaves kept her bent over for a full minute, face deeply red and gorged with blood from the internal pressure, her entire body quaking.

Peter crawled over to Darbi. He scooped her up in his arms, and laboriously got to his feet. He carried her around the Nova, lurching, a walking skeleton with eyes huge with pain and shock, laid her gently on the back seat, and began shoveling ice on top of her.

Kim straightened, gasping. "Peter!" she tried to shout, but it came out as a miserable whisper. She tried to swallow, tasting vomit and new blood from the teeth marks in her tongue, which had decided to come awake again. She wobbled to the car and stuck her head inside. "Peter," she gasped in a strange new voice that had been invented when Darbi tried to strangle her. "It's all over. Her brain is mush, there's nothing left of her but a shell."

His head levered up, and he looked at her. His eyes were wandering black holes of despair. "She'll be all right," he croaked. "I know she'll be all right. She just needs ice, you know? I mean, Braine said to keep her in ice, right? I mean, I have to keep her in ice, right?"

He went back to scooping the wet slush with his hands, mumbling to himself. Kim opened her mouth, then shut it. She went around the car to the doctor, who was splayed out on his back on the trunk, his feet in the dust. His gun had dropped from his hand and lay on the rusty bumper. Kim bent and picked it up. "Dr. Austerwahl?" she said. His face remained blank. She touched his arm. God, she thought, but he must be hot in that suit.

"Dr. Austerwahl?"

He jerked and slowly worked himself upright, his big hands pushing temporary dimples in the hot thin metal of the trunk lid. He seemed to be having trouble focusing his eyes. She took him by the elbow and guided him to his car. "Do you see any sense in this?" she whispered. "Is there any chance they can fix all this in the future?"

He frowned. "What? What in the hell made her do that? God, my head." He flattened a hand and touched the crown of his head. "Jesus Christ, she *bit* me! Bit me like a dog or something!"

She opened his door for him. "Maybe we should go ahead just for Peter's sake, huh? Do you think he'll be normal again when this is all over?"

He dropped himself inside. Kim saw a bottle of Gilbey's gin on the seat, didn't care one bit. "Rabies!" he said wonderingly. He got his feet inside and reached up to the dash, moving like a slow robot. He picked up a pair of sunglasses and settled them on his face.

"Are you all right?" Kim asked, frowning.

He nodded, still a robot.

"Here." She handed him his gun back. "I don't think anybody is following us. Let's just go straight there, okay? I can't take any more of this, and I'm almost out of gas."

"Yeah," he said. "Yeah. *Rabies?*"

Kim shut his door, hoping he wasn't too dazed to find Braine's secret place, which she pictured as a squat building made of shining steel, maybe camouflaged with big nets the color of sand. She hurried back to the Nova and coaxed Peter into the front seat, started the car, which had died of its own accord, and when the doctor found the right gear and drove off, found her own and followed. Her latchless door drifted and groaned in the wind. She had driven nearly a whole minute when she remembered the tire iron. It was back there, buried in dust. She glanced back at the pitiful remnant that had been a girl named Darbi, not worrying all that much that she would come alive again. Crazy brain operation or not, no child could survive a blow like that, a head peeled clean like that. She had to be dead. Which meant, Kim realized with growing, uneasy despair, that she had murdered a six-year-old girl by shattering her naked skull with a tire iron. It would take some time to get used to that. Maybe the rest of her life to get used to that.

She drove on without hope while Peter swayed and mumbled and Darbi went on decaying in the back.

Henry Austerwahl, the real one, drove his Bronco onto his driveway, killed the motor, and hopped out. He was still feeling elated from the brush with disaster, thinking that maybe his luck would hold for a very long time, long enough to get himself cryogized. He remembered the picnic basket and his cooler, and chalked up another good one from the fates. The cop had not asked to look in the cooler, where at least five or six beers were floating in water and slush; that might have led to a Breathalyzer, and that would have led to incarceration. He hauled himself back inside the truck with a hand gripping the steering wheel for leverage and snagged the basket, walked around the truck and its oversized knobby tires to get the cooler from the other side, and headed for the house. What awaited inside, he knew, would be a lot of heat and a lot of quiet. No sense cooling an empty house, right? Besides, the warmth reminded him of his childhood home in Sacramento, where he had grown up without air-conditioning, just a big box fan whose soothing hum lulled him to sleep every summer evening, better than Nytol, better than Sominex.

He stepped up onto the small porch, and only realized that the door was open when he reached for the knob and it was not there. Broken spikes of wood jutted out of the doorjamb where some fool had kicked the door in. The door itself was fully open. He put his burden down, a fresh squirt of fear injecting itself into his veins. What if the burglar was still inside? He could be, couldn't he?

He put his face to the screen door. "Hello!" he sang out, freezing inside, ready to run. "Hello?"

Nothing, no panicked crook rushing out to slay him, nobody. He swung the screen door open and almost stepped on the man lying there in a big wet stain of blood and gore, the man who had a police pistol in one slack, black hand. Austerwahl froze, sensing police investigations, impossible questions, the uncovering of his secret activity. He stepped wide over the body and the bloody part of the carpet, drifting toward raw panic. He saw that the liquor cabinet had been jimmied open, and that the full bottle of gin was gone. He looked back at the body. No bottle. That would take some figuring out, but first, he had to figure out how to dispose of the body, how to get the stain out of the carpet, how to keep from going insane under this kind of pressure. Was this another good one from the fates? Funny. The fates had conspired to trip him up from the beginning.

He reached for the bottle of vodka with hands that jittered, pulled it out and unscrewed the cap, and took a long, burning drink. Never much of a hard liquor man, barely able to tolerate his martinis, he wound up gagging and choking on this pure stuff. It tasted like hair oil, Vitalis or something. He recapped it and put it back. If it was supposed to soothe his nerves, it sure as hell wasn't working yet. He regarded the dead man, the corpse, a sure omen of his own imminent destruction. Why had he come here, to this neighborhood, this house out of the thousands available? Goddamn luck. And who'd killed him, anyway? Goddamn crooks.

The corpse groaned. It shifted a little. If Austerwahl had hair, he supposed it would be standing on end now. He felt a strange and compulsive urge to take a crap, preferably not in his pants. He edged over to the groaning corpse, squatted a safe distance away from it and its blood, and watched its eyes flutter open. He was struck with a burst of hope. Get the guy on his feet, get him the hell out of here to die someplace else, order a new rug, no more worries. He rose, and with a grimace of distaste took a step with his new shoes squishing in the blood. He bent and pulled the gun out of the man's hand, then helped him upright.

He was livelier than Austerwahl would have guessed, using a lot of his own power to stand up. Austerwahl propped him against the wooden door and held him there by one shoulder, his other hand busy with the unfamiliar weight of the gun. "What in the hell are you doing here?" he demanded without very much authority, despite the pistol. "Who shot you?"

The black man wobbled his head. "Don't know his name. Might be Austerwahl."

"Huh? *My* name is Austerwahl." He wondered immediately if he should have confessed to that, but what the hell, it was too late for regrets. The man breathed in his face, the swampy smell of warm blood heavy on the outrush of his breath.

"Then I guess he knows you," he said. "He was using your phone, called himself Dr. Austerwahl on it. Big guy. Black suit."

"There are a lot of big guys in black suits, mister. Why did he shoot you?"

"Beats me."

Austerwahl's frown deepened. "Who are you, anyway?"

He groaned and pressed both hands to his stomach. "Abraham Maharba," he grunted through his teeth. "That is a palin—ah, fuck it. Gimme my gun back."

Austerwahl backed away, shaking his head. The Maharba fellow stayed on his feet with obvious effort. "I'm not stupid," he said to the man with the odd name. "I'll drive you to a hospital, get you to the emergency room, but for God's sake don't tell anybody you were here. Say you were on the other side of town, somebody mugged you, got nasty, shot you. Can you do that?"

Maharba opened his mouth and a thick clot of blood the size of a quarter oozed over his lower lip and down his chin. Austerwahl's stomach rolled. "Don't fool yourself, Doc," Maharba said weakly. "Nobody survives a wound like this. I've been busy dying, but it hasn't worked yet. Save yourself the hospital bill."

"Don't be stupid. The only thing that's going to kill you is loss of blood, if you want my opinion. Go get in my truck. I'll get a couple of towels."

Maharba waved a hand. "Listen to your answering machine if you want to find this guy, Doc. I heard something come through it, some woman's voice. After that the dude shot me."

Austerwahl hesitated. The last thing he felt like doing was playing detective.

"Please, Doc. Grant a dying man his last wish. If I have to die, that fucker is going with me. An eye for an eye, right? First Corinthians nine—never mind. Just find out who he is, 'cause if he knows you, you know him, and if you know him, you might know where he went."

Austerwahl sighed. "All right. Don't try anything funny behind my back. I'm the one with the gun."

Maharba nodded. "I don't really feel up to a fight right now."

Austerwahl went to his machine, rewound the tape, and made it play. It beeped, and there was Bob Stadler, making up some lame excuse to miss work again. Good thing I didn't stay in Rock Springs, Austerwahl thought stupidly. It beeped again, and a woman's breathless voice spoke.

Oh, damn. Uh, this is, uh, Salamander. I'm at, let's see, I'm at a phone booth, and the number is 684-0048. Please call the second you get home, I'll wait here. I have, um, oh, jeez, I've got the girl, and Peter's gone. Um, ah, hell . . .

Austerwahl grew light-headed, thought for a moment he might fall over. Salamander. The girl. Peter. Trumbull had been here. Trumbull had taken the call. The homicidal idiot had left to meet them, and it wouldn't be for a grand tour of Rawlins. He was under orders to kill Kaye and his daughter. Who this woman was, he had no idea. Yet Braine had promised Kaye would never make it. Time for a new business partner, right, folks?

He turned to Maharba, weak with terror. "How long ago did he leave?"

"So you know the dude, then?"

"Yeah. Name's Morris Trumbull. He's walking bad news."

Maharba snorted. "That I believe. Is that where he is, at that phone booth? It's hard to remember what time he left, but I'd say it was, well, at least forty-five minutes ago, if you can believe a man who is dying. We gotta hurry."

Austerwahl blanched. "Hurry? You're crazy. Trumbull's a hired assassin, among other things. I refuse to get involved any further. I'll take you to the hospital, and that's it."

Maharba's eyes grew narrow. "Ain't you just the concerned citizen," he spat at him. "Fine, get the damn towels, I'll try not to mess up your upholstery while I die."

"Look," Austerwahl said evenly, "you don't know what's going on, you don't know the kind of trouble I could get in. I have nothing to do with Trumbull, never really did. I wash my hands of it."

Maharba drew himself upright. "Spoken better than Pontius Pilate himself, Doc, and I don't even know the verse for it."

"Just get in the truck," he snapped. "And for God's sake don't let anyone see you."

"Sure," Maharba said. "For God's sake."

He lurched out, making red bare footprints as he went. Austerwahl hurried to the bathroom, got a bundle of neatly folded bath towels together, and ran outside past the picnic basket and cooler, making his own set of tracks. He was at the truck before he noticed the pistol was still in his hand. He climbed inside, thinking he could hide it under the seat, but what if a cop nailed him again? Would they look for it? With both of them walking around in all that blood, him in shoes, Maharba barefoot, would they get suspicious? Should he throw it in the hedges?

He didn't know, but the question was made unimportant. As soon as he thrust his arm inside the truck to grab the wheel and pull himself into this high-standing Bronco, his usual method, Maharba reached over and plucked the gun from his hand.

"Damn you!" Austerwahl barked.

Maharba smiled with a mouthful of blood. "We're going hunting for a phone booth."

He eyed him incredulously. "Do you know how many phone booths there are in this town?"

"A few, I'd bet." He wagged the gun. "Get in."

"You idiot!" Austerwahl bellowed, and threw the towels at him. "Trumbull isn't at a phone booth anymore! He's gone out to . . ."

"To what, Doc? To what?"

He closed his eyes. "Nothing. Oh, shit, what does it matter now?" He opened them, climbed in, and looked long and hard at Maharba as he settled on the frying pan that was the seat. "Trumbull is going to kill the man she called Peter. Him and his daughter Darbi, both of them. I doubt if he'll shoot them at a phone booth, though I wouldn't be all that surprised. I believe I know where he is."

Maharba's jaw had dropped open. He shut it with a click. "Peter? Darbi? Pete Jones and his daughter. I can't believe it."

"Jones?" Austerwahl grunted. "No, it's not Jones at all."

"I know." He started wrapping his stomach in the towels. They stained instantly red. "It ain't his name, and it sure as hell ain't no palindrome, but I know him, yes, I do. If you know where this Trumbull dude is, I suggest we get there fast."

"Before he kills them, sure."

Maharba smiled. "I ain't worried about that, Doc. With Pete's luck, he'll probably kill Trumbull before I get a chance to."

Austerwahl shrugged. The pain was making Maharba delirious obviously. He started the truck and backed out onto the street, praying that Maharba would go from delirious to unconscious, because he had little intention of getting within ten miles of Trumbull and the catastrophe Braine had let drag all the way from New York to here while he dillydallied about what to do. Drive around aimlessly for a while, this was Austerwahl's hasty plan. Wait for Maharba to lose enough blood to pass out, dump him at a hospital, come home and get to work on cutting out that stain, snipping the carpet piece to bits, and flushing the bits down the toilet. Good-bye, evidence, good-bye, danger.

He headed for the country hills and the prairie, taking his time, going the wrong way.

TWENTY

PETER'S EYES WERE BECOMING DULL, HIS EYELIDS FLUTTERING up and down as he rocked with the motion of the car. Kim kept glancing at him as she drove, afraid now that his fragile sanity had broken into too many bits to ever reassemble. It was like looking at a man-shaped, burnt-out fuse, a husk that had once contained life and purpose. For all she knew, he might be dying right beside her, succumbing to loss of blood, loss of hope, too many miles, too many horrors.

The doctor had picked up the pace now, probably because he had come out of his daze and was ready to get Darbi's corpse frozen and end all this, she thought. She kept her distance from his car, following the cloud of dust he was churning to the bright blue sky, knowing full well that her gas gauge had bottomed out, that the Nova was running on fumes, ready to gasp its last any second.

The road split off into a Y-shaped divergence, one road aiming straight toward a series of steep hills crisscrossed with motorcycle paths, where she could see one lone man at the peak of the highest hill—in Missouri, she knew, these would be called mountains—standing astraddle his colorful dirt bike while the dust of his climb unwound in the wind, staring down at them, king of the hill. The dust storm that contained the black Plymouth angled left, where the road followed the base of the foothills, and Kim followed, marveling at her car's ability to run without fuel. The road held some surprises in the form of invisible little inclines, where the Nova would suddenly become airborne, with the tires an inch or two off the ground while Kim's stomach rolled, then slam down, jarring the car to its frame, making metal things clatter. Her speedometer registered eighty-five. Austerwahl was one dedicated doctor, she had to admit, but to keep this furious pace, he had to be crazy.

The road branched again, and this time he took the one to the right. Kim laid on the brakes, feeling her car drift in that frightening way, and when the air had cleared a bit, the doctor had pulled off the road at the base of a hill that had no motorcycle paths, just two parallel trails that climbed straight to the peak, car tracks. At the top she could dimly see some kind of wires heaped in a tangle.

She drove up behind the Plymouth, stopped, and turned the motor off. Silence descended as the dust washed past. She raised her hands to the ceiling and stretched, yawning hugely, very pleased with herself despite the hundred hurts that yammered at her, forgetting for just this moment that she had killed the girl she'd brought here to save. Then the sky was blue again, the sun a burning lamp, the trip over. She pushed her door open and stood up. Almost as an afterthought she clamped her blouse together with a fist. A pleasant breeze blew through these damp clothes, deliciously cool against her skin. She watched Austerwahl get out, and smiled at him, unable to see his eyes because of his mirror sunglasses. He still had his big gun in his hand. He strolled toward her, grinning.

Something clicked inside her, several loose connections suddenly bonding. Fright seized her in its cold, stiff clutch. Mirror sunglasses. Black car. Gun, for that matter.

She ducked back in the car. "Peter!" she hissed, and he turned his head, fastening incredibly weary eyes on her.

"Huh?"

"Is he the guy who shot you?"

"What?"

She turned. He was only a few yards away. "Peter, look at him! Is he the one?"

With unbearable slowness, he turned to look. A bit of

sharp understanding came into his dull eyes. "Oh, my God," he breathed.

For a second, one long second, Kim was unable to move, frozen in an awkward posture, too filled with understanding and terror to unlock her bones and loosen her muscles. When she did, finally, she dropped herself inside, and cranked the key. The Nova's aged starter began to grind. Austerwahl—or whoever—stopped. He lost his grin.

Kim pumped the gas pedal, her naked breasts heaving, knowing quite well that she shouldn't pump a hot engine, and the starter kept on grinding, at times slipping with gears clashing loudly before falling back into place and doing their job. The few gauges and idiot lights in the dash that still worked flashed dull red messages, predicting doom. The motor caught, belched out a brief cloud of blue smoke and one monstrous backfire that shook the car, and went back to being dead, grinding, slipping, grinding.

The man raised his pistol, found his grin again, and aimed the gun directly between Kim's eyes. Against the bright sunlight the dark bore of the barrel seemed huge, an empty hole big enough to crawl into. Kim pumped the gas, moaning, ducking down, numb with certainty and fright. She could sense the battery becoming weak, sense Auster-whoever-he-was walking closer, shoving the gun through the open window, exploding her head with a bullet the size of a jumbo crayon.

The motor caught again, igniting the gas she was dumping into the flooded cylinders and passing into the broken exhaust pipe, a tremendous, noisy blast that jarred the car as if hit by a wrecking ball, and shot blue fire out the rear. The starter slipped, ground, slipped, tired and worn out, slipped, ground, caught. The motor rumbled to life.

Kim dropped it into reverse just as the pistol was fired. She heard glass burst at the same time something, some big bug or the like, zinged past her ear with a curious low buzz. Bits of decayed foam padding blew out of the back of her seat from a fresh hole in the Naugahyde, and powdered down on her head. She jammed the gas to the floor. The car hobbled backward, engine roaring, rear wheels jumping up and down in the slick dust. She spun the steering wheel hard to the right, and the car swooped around in a tight circle. Whoever-he-was shot again, and more glass broke. Peter had ducked down. Gravel made of old windshield bits showered down on his back. He grumbled something unintelligible, sounding dangerously like Clint, who had no business being here.

Kim hauled the shifter down, spun the wheel left, and once again her Nova did a jitterbug as it came up to speed. She raised her head just enough to see over the dash. Open country, sagebrush and tumbleweed, giant hills on her left, the road a ribbon the color of sand. It is still a very nice day, she thought crazily as she battled to keep the car on the road. Such a nice day, such pretty country.

The road angled left where it had angled right before, leading back to that curious long stretch where invisible springboards launched cars and made them fly. She took the corner fast, too fast, fishtailing, spinning in a complete and bone-jarring circle, recovering, charging on, unable to believe she had pulled herself out of a full spin, sort of like Rick Mears had done at the 500 in Indy some years back. He'd even won.

She chanced a backward glance. The Plymouth was taking the corner. It straightened and disappeared into her dust cloud. Your turn to chew on that stuff, she said to herself, and would have enjoyed it if she wasn't so scared. The speedometer was working its way toward seventy. She wondered just how fast this old beast could go, here in its golden years, the twilight of its life. She had the gas pedal mashed all the way down, her leg beginning to ache from the effort of trying to shove it through the floor. Peter sat up, his hair whipping in the wind, his eyes small and puffy.

"I wonder who he is," he mumbled, staring woozily at the floor.

Kim tossed him a short glance. "Braine's man, has to be.

You told me he only shows up when you're in big trouble. Looks like they've changed their plan, 'cause the only trouble here is him." She looked back; nothing but dust. "That, or he's just one dedicated killer."

Peter's eyes had fallen shut. *Don't you die on me,* she thought fiercely. *Don't you dare.* She was holding the steering wheel almost hard enough to twist it into a pretzel, her hair dancing around her head and getting in her eyes, her buttonless blouse open and flapping. The engine was a shrieking locomotive, the speedometer hovering just above ninety. Again the car seemed to be floating, trying to skid into another spin, but she was able to anticipate the movements and counter them. She felt absurdly proud of this, her newest skill in a list of new skills. Driving like a maniac. Dodging bullets. High-speed chases. Shooting a gun. Bashing a six-year-old girl on the . . .

The Nova gave a strange lurch, derailing her suddenly unhappy train of thought. She frowned, knowing it did not bode well for them. Flat tire? Broken axle? She might have a lot of new skills, she knew, but in the luck department she was notoriously short. But the car was fine now. Maybe a piece of something rusty and old had fallen off, something not very necessary to the functioning of a motor vehicle, like the transmission maybe, or a couple of pistons. Hah, she thought. Ha-ha.

It lurched again just as an incline rose up to toss them in the air. The car went into a quick dive, its nose threatening to dig itself in and flip everything and everybody end over end a dozen times, before exploding, of course, and turning them all to cinders. Kim's heart locked up. The car crashed down while the engine noise boiled down to a few squeaks and rattles. The steam hissing out of the hood was misting the windshield, turning the dust into mud, making the glass brown. Kim clicked on the wipers as the Chevy found itself and surged forward again, and immediately regretted it. The wet dust became smeared paste. Chevrolet had of course equipped this beauty with a bag under the hood that held windshield washing solution, but did the squirters work? She squinted through the mess. No way, man.

Another lurch, another surge. They were coming close to the juncture in the road that led back to Rawlins, or went left up the hill, she could take her pick, and she chose not to turn the car into a dune buggy. She started to let off the gas, but it wasn't necessary, because the engine wasn't running anymore anyway.

"Fumes all gone," she whispered in the comparative silence as they coasted to the junction. The speedometer began a downward swing, ticking off the miles per hour she was losing.

What now? she asked herself while fear expanded inside her and tried to turn her thoughts to useless chaos. Here you are, her mind told her as she tumbled toward raw panic, here you are about to be shot to death at the age of twenty-one, never to turn twenty-two and need all that security Nina told you about.

She put on the brakes, going into a skid that didn't matter anymore. The car drifted sideways off the road and skated through the sand and sagebrush, and came to rest with all four wheels buried to the axles in this strange, loose dirt. Kim pushed her door open, scraping a wedge of desert smooth. She looked back and saw Braine's man, Mr. Sunglasses, burst out of the last cloud of her dust. He looked over, sunglasses winking sunlight, and slammed on the brakes, which Kim decided had to be some of those anti-skid jobs, because that Plymouth didn't waver one bit.

"We have to run," she shouted to Peter. "He can't follow us to the mountains in his car, and we might be able to find a place to hide!"

He nodded, put a hand on the door handle, levered it, and fell out. She watched him claw his way back up, rocking the car. When he was on his feet he leaned back inside and reached for Darbi.

"Peter!" she shouted at him. "You won't make it ten feet with her!"

He dragged her out and hoisted her into his bloody arms, lurching in odd directions. She was a pink sack of twigs, flopping in his arms as if her bones had turned to taffy. Her naked skull was a shock of dirty white.

Kim jumped out. "Peter, no! You can't!"

His head was wobbling. He couldn't seem to find Kim with his eyes. "Watch me," he whispered. "Just watch."

He made it three torturous steps, just past the front of the Nova, but his knees didn't work right anymore. He hobbled another two steps while Kim watched in helpless despair, Peter slowly sinking, still trying to walk but doing a slow, sad limbo instead, his knees bobbing out of sync with his shoes. He collapsed onto his back in an agony of slow motion, and lay there unconscious, his closed eyes dark and sunken almost as bad as Darbi's dead ones, his blood pulsing in a thin stream through his useless bandage.

Kim heard the big pistol click. She turned around, wanting to run, wanting to stay, wanting to do a hundred things, but all she could do was stand there shivering, watching as the mystery man, the sunglasses man, stalked up to her, swung the gun up and aimed it at her face again, and grinned.

"Good-bye," he whispered sweetly.

Maharba was losing his hold on life, Austerwahl could tell that easily enough. His eyes were glazed with an opaque film. His borrowed towels were soaking. Whenever Austerwahl hit a bump in the dirt road Maharba grunted with pain, and he was hitting every one he could find. He knew roughly where he was, south of Rawlins somewhere, a wasteland where the only visitors were dirt bikers and four-wheelers on this toasty Sunday afternoon.

At last Maharba fell, easing forward until his bloody turban was resting on the red plastic of the dash, jaw hanging slack as if he wanted to speak to the floor mat. The Police Special hung between his knees from one lifeless finger. Austerwahl pulled the Bronco to a gentle stop and looked him over, not smiling, feeling just guilty enough to press his fingers to Maharba's jugular and find the thready pulse there. Nurse, he knew he would say downtown, Nurse, I found this man shot in the hills, but he's alive. My name? Burner. Bunsen Burner. See ya.

He smiled without enjoying the jest at all. He was flirting with willful murder here, he knew that much, criminal negligence and all those fun crimes. It had already occurred to him to shove Maharba out and leave him for the buzzards, but then that would be a real murder, accessory after the fact, whatever else society could charge him with. Overriding these concerns, though, was the fact that he was not a murderer at heart, no matter what they'd said in 1968. He was just a pioneer in cryogenic technology in a society that didn't trust it, much like Pasteur with his germs they didn't understand, his vaccinations they didn't trust.

He reached over and tickled Maharba's ear with a finger. No response. He touched an eye. Zilch.

He gasped out a loud sigh of relief. Unconscious, but not dead. This was according to plan. He turned the Bronco around, taking it easy, taking it slow, thinking about that carpet at home that would need amputation, and the seats in here that would need scrubbing. Well, even if it took until midnight, he would brush, clean, snip, and wipe, until this whole ugly mess was behind him.

Maharba groaned, making Austerwahl's heart squeeze painfully. And damn, he thought as he looked over fearfully, I should have taken the bastard's gun.

He leaned over to do it, took it by the barrel and pulled on it. Maharba pulled back, maybe in spasm, maybe not. The gun went off with a flash of yellow fire, a sonic boom of incredible noise, a burst of gunsmoke that filled the cab like gray fog. The fine upholstery that adorned the inside of the door on Austerwahl's side got a nice neat hole in it just above the armrest, where Austerwahl's arm had been not too long ago. He fell back against the seat, stunned. Maharba woke up.

"Huzza?" he said, and sat up straight. He looked at the pistol in his hand. Smoke was still drifting out of the muzzle. He looked at Austerwahl. "What the fuck were you trying to do, Doc?" he growled at him. "A little mutiny all of a sudden?"

"You shot it in your sleep," Austerwahl lied, putting his attention back on the road.

"Sure." He was silent for a few cranky minutes. Then he said, "We went past those hills once before, Doc." He pointed past Austerwahl's nose. "I remember thinking they looked like two hippos screwing, and they were on my side. Now they're on yours."

"So?" Austerwahl replied nervously. "All the hills out here look the same."

"Where are you taking me?"

He tried to think fast, and wound up not thinking at all. "To where Trumbull is, like we agreed. Yeah, just like we agreed."

"My, my," Maharba said. He stuck the pistol hard against Austerwahl's sweaty right temple. "You're driving all over the fucking place, and you're doing it at twenty miles an hour. I smell bullshit, Doc, and it's coming from you."

Austerwahl swallowed. His dry throat clicked. "What are you going to do?"

"Baby-sit your ass all the way to Trumbull. You're going to put the pedal to the metal, and you won't let up until we're there, dig?"

"But," he moaned, "but the roads are treacherous!"

Maharba smiled. "So am I, Doc." He clicked the hammer back. It sounded to Austerwahl like the click of lifelong prison hackles locking shut, chaining him forever to an iron ball.

"By now Trumbull's killed them for sure," Austerwahl said, desperate to explain his position, to make this man realize what was at stake. "He's probably headed back East by now. Can't you see the danger you're putting me in? Don't you have any compassion?"

Maharba laughed. It sounded genuine, even though it fractured into gasps of pain at the end. "Compassion, Doc? We had a chance to save one dude, and save his little daughter, though I honestly can't say I was all that concerned, since Pete is Pete and luck is luck. Besides, I thought he didn't even care about the kid. Even so, your little scheme might have fucked their chances forever. Don't talk to me about compassion. Just eat up those miles."

Austerwahl kept quiet, wallowing in dread, eating up those miles.

TWENTY-ONE

"I THINK YOU'D BETTER LOOK BEHIND YOU," KIM SAID, MOVING her eyes from that entrancing bore of the big pistol to the hilltop, where the king of the hill, the biker, was watching everything going on here below, his flashy blue helmet dangling by its strap from one hand.

"That," Braine's man responded, "is the oldest trick in the book. Good-bye, little girl, whoever you are."

Somewhere from the depths of her soul, Kim was able to dredge up an uncertain, wavering brand of courage. "Just for curiosity's sake, who are you, anyway?"

"Name's Trumbull, as if it matters."

"Braine's man?"

"What else?"

"Why do you have to kill us?" she asked with a tone that was close to demanding, surprising herself. She clutched her blouse tighter, knowing she had crossed some sort of boundary of propriety between killer and killee. The condemned gets only one last request.

Trumbull waved his free hand. "Enough talking, girl. This won't hurt much."

She pointed over his head, over the tangle of his dirty hair, her little burst of courage about to exhaust itself. "There's a man on top of that hill," she said. "He's on a motorcycle."

"Some people just never learn," Trumbull said. She saw his finger press the trigger, that hard-to-pull trigger, saw his fingernail go white, his fingertip suffuse with pink. She thought about ducking, jumping, attacking, retreating, dropping dead of fright, too paralyzed now with fear to even lower her pointing hand.

The dirt biker kicked his motorcycle alive. The racket from the motor was like a Lawn Boy without benefit of a muffler, *kak-kak-kak-kak-kak,* rolling down the hill and spreading across the prairie in waves. Trumbull turned. The biker was working his helmet over his head. He spun his machine around, throwing a curtain of dust, and started down one of the trails, standing on the pegs, fighting for balance.

"Jesus Christ," Trumbull growled, and lowered the pistol. He looked at Kim, no grin anymore, just a face creased with an irritated frown. "Get those two in my car," he ordered, motioning with the gun to Peter and Darbi. "Then put your own ass inside. I'll take care of that fucker." He turned and jogged toward the road and the hill, coins and keys jingling in his pockets. The biker was halfway down the hill when Trumbull shot at him. Kim saw his head jerk up, saw his face swivel to look at Trumbull. A small belch of dust popped out of the ground below him. He hit the brakes and went into a long, wild skid. Trumbull fired again, but the distance was too much. Kim didn't see the bullet hit, but the biker surely did. He spun in a jerky half circle, gave gas and noise, and barreled back up the trail. He disappeared over the crest.

Trumbull trotted back. Kim got herself going, walking through the dirt with her shoes burying themselves in it, filling them up even more, leaving elongated tracks. She stooped beside Peter and waved the blowflies away from Darbi. Darbi was as rank as a bloated dog dead beside a road. Clamping off her own breathing, Kim picked her up and carried her to Trumbull's car, shielding her own breasts from Trumbull's sight with Darbi's pitiful body, her face twisted up with revulsion. Darbi was a very dead, very skeletal corpse, Kim knew. If Peter was dead as well, at least he had died with his child in his arms, for all the consolation that might be worth.

"Changed my mind," Trumbull said, looking over his shoulder at the hill. He turned his head and grinned at her as she slogged her way back to Peter, blouse held shut again. He aimed the gun at her, lowered his glasses slightly, and squeezed one eye shut, offering no more amenities such as last requests, last words. She dived off to the right. The gun thundered, the concussion making dust jump from the sagebrush. The bullet punched a deep crater beside Kim's waist, showering her with dirt. She went up on her hands and knees and scurried madly toward the Nova and its protection, throwing dirt in handfuls, numb with terror, controlled by a survival instinct that didn't differentiate between courage and cowardice, asked nothing of her but to get the hell away from that gun.

He shot again, a brief and awesome explosion, and a bright metal crease appeared on the Nova's broken door ten feet in front of her. The bullet howled as it ricocheted away. Kim was panting, sweat a hot film on her face, her clawing hands burning in the sand. She heard that *kak-kak* noise again, far away, and turned to look.

The biker was king of the hill again, a lord on high inspecting his domain. "Shit!" she heard Trumbull snort. "Get in the car, dammit," he snarled at her. She got to her feet, blundering in circles, disoriented. She got a glimpse of Trumbull as she bumbled around. He was hoisting Peter up as if he were weightless and carrying him to his car. When he had dumped him inside, he turned and motioned to Kim. She went obediently toward him, functioning on autopilot, her brain humming with disconnected thoughts, crazy emotions. Trumbull got in, started it, and spun the car around.

"Open the glove compartment," he said, getting up to speed a lot faster than the Nova ever had. Kim leaned a bit and opened it, trying to collect her frightened senses. "Green box inside," he grunted. "Hand it over."

She found it, a heavy little box of the requested color. She passed it to him and he began to reload his pistol as he drove. She noticed without wanting to that the bullets looked weird, had some kind of wicked corkscrew set on top. Probably the choice of discerning hunters of the human animal, she thought dully, and put the box back when he gave it to her. He was watching the rearview mirror a lot, wearing a frown again. Kim turned. Nothing but dust. If the biker is following, he sure as hell is going to have lots of boogers, she thought, and almost cackled, her sanity fragmenting quite nicely now.

Trumbull's car held the road a lot better than Kim's had, becoming airborne only once. At the junction that led to Braine's hill he took the curve at fifty miles per, and the Plymouth held on like a cat, amazing Kim even more than her upcoming execution did.

He stopped. Dust killed the sun momentarily. He waited, looking back at the fork in the road, where nothing came and nothing moved.

"Out," he said when a minute had passed. "Get those two out too."

She did as ordered, dazed, ready to obey even the silliest of orders, her will gone, her personality falling apart in glassy shards that sifted to her feet and were gone. She carried Peter first, gasping against his weight, and dropped him in the road in front of Trumbull's car. Darbi went next. Kim stretched her out beside her father. Local flies had heard the news, and were busy with her already.

Trumbull sat down on the hood of the car, gasping a little as his butt encountered the hot metal. He wagged the pistol at Kim, who was standing dumbly beside Darbi, arms hanging slack, her bloody blouse open, and who cared? If Trumbull was enjoying the show he wasn't acting like it. She shuffled around to face him fully, her eyes waxy in her face, a fly ambling unharmed through the raw meat of the slashes on her cheek, which were turning black.

He aimed his gun at her, his own eyes two mirrors of chrome. He reached up and stripped the sunglasses off, but offered no smile this time.

"Third one's a charm," he said.

* * *

Henry Austerwahl had never driven so fast in his life, at least not on roads like these. He could see his Bronco as if from the outside, envisioning it much like Lee Majors's 4 x 4 in that old TV show *The Fall Guy,* in which Lee performed impossible automotive feats such as flying off ramps and smashing though telephone poles, banging his truck around hard enough to snap the wheels off, but getting away clean every time. Well, Lee Majors notwithstanding, Austerwahl had no illusions about the condition of his beloved Bronco now. The steering wheel was rattling from an encounter with a huge bump he had hit some miles ago. It had sounded like an explosion when the Bronco touched back down, and swiftly the truck was pulling hard to the left, something bent—probably something expensive, he knew. The barrel of the Police Special did not waver from its position against his right temple no matter how bad the road got. Maharba looked positively dead, a creature made of blood and pain, but his eyes were open a bit and his shooting hand remained strong.

"How much farther?" Maharba rasped above the noise of the wind charging through the open windows.

"Just ahead, there where the road branches," Austerwahl replied, unable to point because if he let go of the wheel, the damn truck would do handstands.

"Better slow down, then."

He did so gratefully. He took the curve at twenty and immediately rammed into the back of a black car with a terrific crunching bang, shoving it forward a few feet. A man who looked very much like Morris Trumbull somersaulted over the car and crashed down on the hood of the Bronco, denting it expensively. Austerwahl's chest bounced off the steering wheel; Maharba's face said hello to the dash.

"Ah, shit," Austerwahl moaned.

Maharba raised back up. There was a head-shaped depression in the smooth brown expanse of the dash, slowly popping back into shape. He groaned, holding his head with both hands, the pistol pointed at the roof. "You dumb fuck," he groaned, and opened his eyes. He started. "Man, you killed that dude!" His voice was tinged with wonder.

"It's Trumbull," Austerwahl said. "You wanted him, you've got him."

"Trumbull?" He jerked around and stared at him. Trumbull's head had smacked against the windshield, and Austerwahl lamented the new and probably expensive cracks there. Trumbull shifted, making noises. Austerwahl saw that one of his legs was cocked at a strange angle. "Oh, goody!" Maharba said. "One busted leg, but he's still alive!" He opened his door and worked his way out, bloody towels slithering off him like clinging red eels. He walked beside the Bronco and stuck his pistol against Trumbull's temple, a place much more preferable for Henry Austerwahl than his own aching head.

"Get up," Austerwahl heard Maharba say.

Ahead, standing just in front of the black Plymouth, Austerwahl saw a blond girl whose face was a Halloween mask of slashes and dried blood. Her shirt was open, but what was there to see was awful. She skirted Trumbull's car and wobbled her way over to Maharba, nearly falling twice, crying. "Thank God," Austerwahl heard her say again and again. He began to feel sick, even sicker than he already was. This was a disaster that could only lead to violence, death, jail.

He saw Trumbull sit up. He heard him groan. One big hand flashed out, became a fist in mid-flight, and crashed into Maharba's nose with a distinct, bone-cracking splat. Maharba rocked backward, staggering to keep his balance, eyes fluttering while bright blood streamed out of his nose and over his mouth in a sudden crimson splash. Trumbull reached over and snagged the revolver easily out of his slack fist. Austerwahl watched in amazement and alarm as Trumbull shoved the gun against Maharba's chest, still sitting on the Bronco's hood as if out for a quick suntan with his broken leg twisted almost backward, the man amazingly grinning, grinning. Austerwahl heard the pistol thunder, gazing on in horror as Maharba dropped to his knees through a cloud of blue smoke, his face a blank of stunned amazement. Through the open window he heard Maharba say something about Jesus.

And Austerwahl watched, now with his hands clapped over his mouth and his eyes big as eggs, while the torn-up pretty girl edged backward, hands held out in a last defense. Trumbull shot her in the chest. Maharba thumped against the hillside, all full of joints and uncomfortable angles. So did the girl.

Trumbull turned and gave Austerwahl a ghastly wink of satisfaction.

In front of the black car a tall, thin man rose up, a wobbling specter of dirt and blood. Austerwahl sucked in a horrified breath. This was Peter Kaye, the last player in this hopeless mission and its madness. He was looking around in an obvious daze. He ducked slowly back down out of sight. When he rose again he had something in his arms, something heavy enough to make him stagger, something made of bone and colors and the rags of a pink dress.

Austerwahl covered his eyes with his fists. Not the last player then. Darbi Kaye was.

When Austerwahl was able to look again Peter was starting up the trail. Trumbull pushed himself off the hood. He danced on one foot for a few moments, grimacing, and hobbled after him, the pistol firm in his swinging hand, no grin on his face now at all.

TWENTY-TWO

"JUST ONE LAST TRIP, BABY," PETER WHISPERED TO DARBI AS HE left the road and began to climb drunkenly up the narrow tracks that led to the top of the hill that was more like a mountain. He had not heard any shots, had not seen anything except a car lunging at him like a black dragon with savage teeth made of chrome, bellowing its strange, crashing roar. He looked back as the way got steep, and saw that it was no dragon, of course, just a black car with a four-wheel-drive truck of some sort welded to the rear. A man in a suit was hopping past it, gun in hand. Peter turned his attention back to the trail. Sweat was already drizzling down his face and his breath was scorching his throat, here barely ten steps away from the road. Darbi flopped in his arms, chased by flies, her open mouth a dark hole in her rotten face. Peter's legs were jerking and scissoring as the last of his strength drained out of the hole in his shoulder, and his mind began, in this last effort, to retreat down a more familiar road, the familiar one so full of nails and potholes and trip-wires. He knew suddenly that he was going to have the last attack of nerves in his life, right here, right now.

Everything became swiftly bright, too bright to look at. He dropped to his knees with a groan. Darbi rolled out of his arms and thumped hard into the weeds and dust. He clutched his head with his hands as the demons pried open his skull and began to swoop and circle.

He heard something explode behind him. Dust jumped beside his folded right knee, and he knew it was a bullet, this he knew, but it was too late for bullets, too late to fear them anymore. He let himself collapse face-first on the steep hillside, cracking his skull against Darbi's naked one, seeing a brief starshow that was somehow more beautiful than anything he had ever seen before.

Something moved beside his head. Something tugged at his wrist.

"Bedtime for Darbi!" she screamed at him in a cackling, familiarly insane voice. She shuffled to her feet and kicked him on the head, snapping it around on the weary stalk of his neck. *"Donald Duck!"* she bellowed.

He pushed himself up on his hands, shivering from sudden cold despite the furnace of the sun. She went into a squat and laughed in his face, her breath abominably thick with a slaughterhouse stench. "I never knew my mommy," she said contritely, "and the balloons in the hospital never popped. Aaaaagggaa. *Aaaaaagggaaaa.*"

"Stop it," he groaned.

"*Aaaagggaaaa* . . . to fetch a pail of waaaaaa . . ." Some black thing slid out of her mouth like a small horseshoe and plopped on his wrist. Baby teeth stuck out of it.

"Aaaaaagggaaaa . . . before Christmas and all through the aaagggaa . . ."

She began pinching chunks of flesh out of her forearm, flipping them idly away, making her horrible noises. Peter tried to get up on his knees, couldn't do it. He swiveled his head up and looked into the ruins of her eyes. "My God," he moaned at her, filled suddenly with loathing for this creature she had become. "You're not Darbi anymore," he hissed at her. "You're not anything alive."

He rocked back, and was able to put his weight on his knees, swaying. He made his right hand into a fist, pulled it back. "Die," he was able to grunt. "In the name of God, just *die*."

He hit her in the face, pulled back, hit her again, pulled back, hit her. She fell on her back, squealing, arms batting uselessly as he pounded her. He walked on his knees to straddle her, using both fists now, drugged with horror, his own face twisted dark and unrecognizable while the flesh of his daughter came off under his knuckles. "Die," he said, drooling and weeping without being aware of it, without being aware of anything but the thing he was sitting on. *"Die!"* He wrapped both hands around her chalky skull and hammered it against the ground. "Daddy says die, Darbi! Daddy says you can die! I love you, Darbi! Daddy loves you and he wants you to die!"

She stiffened in a spasm. Her eyes fell shut. He pushed himself away from her, sickened, so far past exhaustion that his mind was jumping stupidly from place to place, memory to memory, seeking a pattern, not finding one.

He slumped over and slid a few feet on his face in the dust and gravel, wanting only to sleep forever.

Time flowed past on its unhurried, endless journey, how much time he did not know, but after seconds or days, something tugged his wrist again. He groaned and tried to pull away.

"Daddy, *come on!*"

He raised his head. He saw a fuzzy outline in front of him, fuzzy yellow-white, fuzzy brown-black, overlaid with soft pink. It was Darbi and she was trying to pull him up. The world was a stunning light show but she was alive after all, she was Darbi after all.

"Please get up, Daddy!" Her voice sounded odd, something like a record playing one speed too slow, but nothing like before. "That man is shooting at us!"

He swiveled his head around, face scrunched into a comical squint, and saw Braine's man bent over beside his car, doing something to his leg. Peter staggered to his feet, running on a new energy made of hope. Darbi pulled him up the trail but his feet slipped and he fell heavily onto his injured shoulder. He clamped his teeth over a scream. Dust jumped beside him and a moment later came the bang of a gun.

"Daddeeeee!"

He got up again. Darbi's cold hand was around two of his fingers, pulling him without much energy. He made it two drunken steps and went down again. He doubled over with his eyes squeezed shut, dripping forehead pressed against the ground.

"Come *on!*"

She was pulling on him, her slowly pedaling feet flipping up puffs of dust, skidding. He got up once more to stagger onward with a strength he had not believed he possessed anymore. His fingers slipped out of Darbi's grasp and she spilled forward. She got back to her feet, moving in slow motion. She reached for his hand again, got it, and slipped again.

He reached for her; something was stuck to his hand. He looked down and some sort of moist fleshy glove was wrapped around his first two fingers, and he instinctively jerked and flipped it away. It landed in the dust and flopped lazily open.

It was the palm of Darbi's hand. She was staring at that ugly white starfish so dead on the ground now, her eyes dull and sunken. Peter grabbed her wrist and turned her hand over.

It had become an X-ray picture. Every bone on the bottom of her hand lay white and exposed, nestled in the remaining flesh, glistening wetly under the sun. As he watched, what remained peeled itself away like old sausage wrappings. It plopped to the ground and she was left with a macabre Halloween hand, something sold in cheap novelty shops.

"Aw, baby," Peter moaned. He urged her forward, and the sole of her black foot slid greasily off as she took her next step, a bizarre rubber footprint in the dust bearing the imprint of many small bones, but she wasn't screaming as she used to when she lost something. She was vacuous and displaced, this last burst of energy burning out. Her slow walk became an unsteady stagger.

Another shot, loud. At the same moment Peter heard the bang, he heard another sound, a curious *thup!* A small hole was punched through Darbi's back near her left shoulder blade, knocking her over on her face. Peter dived for her, shielding her from more bullets, but no bullets came and she got resolutely to her feet again, reached back with her remaining hand, and pulled him gently forward. Dark fluid slid out of the new wound. Several black desert horseflies were going at it.

Bang. This one slammed against the back of Peter's left thigh, the bullet loudly cracking the bone in two as it chased all the way through, exiting through his jeans with a jet of blood and meat that sprayed all over Darbi's back. He went down without a scream, without much reaction at all, simply surprised. Darbi helped him up and they continued their slow progress, Peter hopping weakly while sweat cascaded down his paper-white face. He turned his head and saw the man in the suit, Braine's man, throw his gun angrily at the hill. The man began to scout around, inspecting the ground, holding onto the cars as he hopped.

Darbi slipped as her other foot sloughed away, this one dragging behind for a moment like a loose sock before ripping free. She walked on her neatly peeled skeleton foot while Peter's mind shifted into a world of shock.

He fell again and had to drag himself with his arms. Darbi tried to help, but when he wrapped his fingers around her forearm to pull himself up, the flesh tore apart like wet bread and slicked down her arm to her hand before Peter could let go, and she had a terrible new bracelet made of skin and muscle hanging on her wrist.

Time passed, slow and merciless time, no shooting, nothing but the screech of bugs and birds, Peter's grunts of pain, the ugly click of bones every time Darbi put her weight on her skeleton foot. Time passed, uncaring and endless time, and then Peter raised his head and saw that there was a metal gate in front of them full of padlocks, and spreading beside it on both sides were tangles of barbed wire sparkling in the sunlight.

He angled himself toward the wire, crawling faster. Darbi

stumbled through it like an automaton, surrendering chunks of flesh to the barbs, and long strips of her dress as well. Several times as Peter watched she walked headlong into wires that tightened and then pushed her back. She would raise these like a robot and wait for Peter to crawl through. Barbed wire punctured his hands and snagged on his pants, but the pain from these was minuscule compared to the broken leg that dragged behind him spilling blood. His progress was abysmally slow. Though the sun burned down on his back he was getting colder. His teeth began to chatter.

He dragged himself through the last of the wire and on up the hill, laboriously crawling around sagebrush, freezing. Darbi was tottering; he was sure this was the last heat she would ever endure. Her dress was in rags and her remaining skin seemed to wrinkle and sag like an old lady's skin might sag, ready to pull apart on the angles of her bones. She was forging ahead, resolute, bones clacking, her yellow eyes small and full of misery when she looked back and waited for him to catch up. They came to an area that was flatter, here where the hill crested. Peter pushed himself up on his elbows, straining to see what was ahead, perhaps Braine's supersecret cryogenics facility that was Darbi's only hope, if hope was left.

There was nothing there. Dirt, sagebrush, a strong breeze whipping the dust into tornados and making weeds dance in brown waves. Nothing else.

He gaped at the nothing else, jaw slack, the wind oddly cold against his face. It had all been for nothing. He squeezed his eyes shut against the tears of shame for having been a stooge for so long. There was nothing here. There never had been. The whole thing had been some horrible joke, experiment, something. Darbi bent down wordlessly and tweezed at the tatters of his shirt with her remaining hand. He moved his eyes up to look at her, and shook his head.

"It's all over, baby," he whispered, his voice competing with the wind. "It's finally all over."

She sank down and stared at him with eyes that had been bluish with health most of her life, pretty baby eyes that were dry and yellow now. The part of her that was locked in the insanity of death had disappeared, chased away, was gone forever as surely as Brenda was gone, as surely as Peter was going. This he knew; Braine's magic was a flawed magic after all. As he lay he reached for her hand and squeezed it, no longer concerned about what might slough off this time. She began to cry though she couldn't possibly understand what had happened, making throaty mewling noises that did not sound like her at all.

He dragged himself closer. "C'mere, babe," he said, and she slowly scooted toward him. He pulled her down to nestle the bones of her head against his chest, and stroked the remnants of her face that had once been pink and alive. "We'll always be together now," he said, and coughed. The cold was stealing through him, making him want to sleep very badly. "We'll do this one together, just like always. You stay with me and go to sleep, and I'll keep them from hurting you anymore."

She snuggled closer. Her smell was the finest thing he had ever smelled. She pulled away a bit, and in her slow new voice said, "Daddy?"

He caressed her cheek. "What, baby?"

"Tallyho," she said. "Tallyho, okay?"

He smiled. "You bet. Tallyho."

And then he drifted off while his blood drained into the dirt and the cold gathered around his heart, and his dead daughter held him tight.

TWENTY-THREE

KIM OPENED HER EYES.

There was pain, a large flower of pain in the center of her chest, a flower that had dark worming roots and acid tendrils, burrowing through her body and touching everything with agony; her lungs, her throat, even the bones of her rib cage. She blinked at the blank, blue sky, confused, at home in bed, waking up, not in the right place, gravel and rocks hard against her spine, a circus of gnats swarming over her face without sound. There was hot new blood in her mouth.

She tried to sit up, and found that she could if she pistoned her arms just right in counterbalance. The pain in her chest became a heaviness as she sat, perhaps what a person might feel at the beginning of a bad heart attack, and when she breathed, liquid salt misted up the back of her tongue and sprayed her throat. She swiveled her head while bits of rock sifted out of her sparse new hairdo, and saw a man dead a few feet away, his open eyes staring painlessly into the sun. She looked straight ahead and saw a bald man with a red face in the crashed truck in front of her, a nervous man looking around with frightened eyes. She looked to the right and saw Morris Trumbull crawling on his hands and knees in the dust, his black shoes brown now, his dangling tie wiping a shallow zigzag trench as he moved. He was muttering to himself. One of his feet was turned the wrong way, his leg startlingly broken. She frowned at him, though he wasn't looking, and the memory of what had just happened flared into her consciousness. The son of a bitch had shot her.

She thought maybe she should flop back down and play dead, but if Trumbull was on his hands and knees, he sure as hell wasn't doing it for fun, playing doggie or the like. He was looking for something, and that something could only be the gun he had lost in the wreck. She recalled dimly that the one he had shot her with had not been his own, the big revolver, but a smaller version. She happened to glance under the truck from her low vantage point, and saw his monster of a pistol in a puddle of motor oil. It was dripping onto the gun in steady drops.

She rocked forward and fell on her face, then slid onto the road where things were softer, leaving a thin trail of blood. The pain was getting worse. She began to feel strange, somehow cold, things becoming unreal. Her memory kept offering reruns of the shooting, the surprise she had felt, the weird instant when the bullet penetrated her ribs just above her solar plexus, painless, smooth, fast; the tumble into blackness. She began to shiver, and knew what was happening. She had heard of shock before, had never had it before, but this had to be it, and it was threatening to overwhelm her, put her to sleep, a sleep that would never end.

She pounded her forehead on the ground, eyes squeezed shut. She made fists and pummeled the sides of her head with them. The gruesome picture show faded off, became less important. She crawled under the truck, scooted to the puddle of oil, and dragged the pistol away. When it was in her fist, slick as a fish, she crawled backward and got herself back on her feet.

Trumbull was upright now, gamely hopping on one foot with a hand on the truck, searching the weeds and bushes. Kim wrapped both hands around the grip of the gun and pointed it at him, her hands shaking, intending to kill him without warning. Her finger slipped off the trigger and the gun squelched up like a wet bar of soap. She got it back under control and aimed it again. She pulled on the trigger, squinting in expectation of the blast and the concussion, but found she could not bring herself to do it all the way. Trumbull had his back to her, was unaware.

"Trumbull!" she barked.

He spun around and nearly fell. His grimace of pain became one of concern. "Hold on there," he said, hopping toward her while his broken leg jiggled and flopped in odd ways. "It's all over. You've got no reason to shoot me, and I've got no reason to shoot you. So drop it, will ya?"

She shook her head. "It was all over a long time ago, but you were going to kill us all anyway. Is that what Braine told you to do? Kill us all even if we made it here without being followed? That sounds like bad business to me, Trumbull. Now this time, *you* say good-bye."

He smiled, still coming. "Little girl, you can't shoot me or anybody else. It's gotta be in your blood, gotta be something you enjoy doing. Give me the damn gun."

She backed away, shaking her head. "No way. Say good-bye."

"Good-bye," he said, and stopped.

She swallowed. Her trigger finger was under orders to shoot, but it had locked up tight as if rigor mortis had suddenly struck. Damn him, damn him, she thought, and backed away some more, leaving the truck and the man inside behind, moving toward the curve in the road. Trumbull leered at her, and hopped some more, faster. She begged her mind to allow her finger to operate, already knowing what would happen to her if it didn't.

Trumbull lunged. He captured her wrist and twisted it. She shrieked and let go, then shouted to the man in the truck. He didn't even turn his head. Trumbull pushed her over on her back and smiled down at her.

"So, you miserable little bitch," he said, "you want to play cops and robbers, huh?" He sat down on her stomach. She let out a great woof as her breath was forced out, breath misty with blood. She turned and twisted without effect.

"You're the luckiest little shit I've ever met," he growled. "But no more." He pressed the pistol against her lips, worming them apart, and knocked on her teeth. "Open up, or I'll bust them out."

She opened her mouth and simultaneously pressed her eyes shut. He jammed the thick barrel to the back of her throat, making her retch. He cocked the hammer back and she began to gurgle muted screams, wild with fright, trying uselessly to throw him off.

"Nice tits," he said while sweat from his face rained down on them. "Very nice."

She flopped and bucked. The barrel was hard and greasy, threatening to slide past her throat and into her stomach.

Something banged. Trumbull whipped his head around. Kim opened her eyes.

The nervous man in the truck had come out at last. "Trumbull!" he shouted, his eyes huge behind his glasses. "For God's sake, man, don't! We'll all go to jail!"

"Ah, shut up," Trumbull said, and grinned down at Kim. Just as her eyes flew shut again she heard a strange, distant popping sound, once, twice. Trumbull jerked upright, squeezing more of her breath out. She opened her eyes.

A large chunk of his skull was gone above his right ear. Yellow-gray brains were sludging out, plopping on her naked stomach. He fell over, surprised dead eyes staring at the horizon. She screamed and struggled away, clawing the ground. The pistol was clamped in her teeth, protruding like a grotesque Popsicle. She wasn't aware of it.

"Hold it!" someone shouted from a distance down the road. She looked over and saw two men crouched in the dust there. They stood up, pistols ready.

"FBI," one of them called out. "Nobody move."

Crying, filled with dissolving fear, Kim crawled over to Trumbull's body, could not find the pistol in his dead hands, realized it was still in her mouth. She spat it out with a cry of disgust.

"FBI! Put down your weapons!"

She picked it up, tried to get to her feet, fell, tried again, fell, tried again, and made it. She lurched over to the nervous man and stuck the pistol against his chest. "Are you Austerwahl?" she gasped. "Are you?"

He hesitated, then nodded timidly.

"Get your ass going," she said, "or I will surely kill you dead."

She forced him up the hill while the FBI men followed, shouting at her to halt, shouting all kinds of things, but not shooting.

EPILOGUE

IT WAS A BEAUTIFUL AND SUNNY SUMMER DAY WHEN A SLEEK white hospital van drove past the gate of Greater Rawlins Cemetery D-9, followed the winding road for a while, and stopped. A man climbed out of the side door, followed by a little girl, the girl dressed in a fine silver skirt and radiant blouse that shifted from red to pink and back as she walked and the breeze toyed past her. The man had on a plain white jumpsuit, which he hated, but it seemed to be all the rage nowadays. He looked back uncertainly to the van, even after all these weeks surprised that it had no wheels and gently rocked on nothing, and the lady inside pointed, then made go-ahead motions with her hands, smiling.

He searched for it, almost hesitantly. He had both welcomed and dreaded this visit for some time. He absently rubbed a hand over his right shoulder as he walked. It had itched for a while, as his leg had, but not unbearably. There were three small hairless scars on the back of his head, easily covered with a comb. These did not bother him at all.

They found the tombstone not far away. The ground had heaved and pitched and the marker was leaning at an angle that indicated untold years of service through freezing winter and scorching summer. Fortunately the engraving on the stone was easy enough to read still:

KIMBERLY WHARTON

Beloved Wife and Mother

b. January 8, 1970 — d. October 19, 2044

SORELY MISSED BY ALL

Peter stared at it for some time while Darbi skipped across the grass humming a happy tune. He reached into a pocket and withdrew an envelope that was curled and yellow. This was the address:

Kaye, Peter and Darbi
USG Cryogenics Site 194
Greater Rawlins, Wyoming 76234-8787-11

He slipped the letter out, not for the first time, unfolded it carefully, and read the spidery script that was old and blurry and very familiar from many rereadings.

Dear Peter and Darbi,

At my advanced age I have no doubt that when you read this, if ever, I will be long dead. I tell myself I'm over seventy now, but I don't believe it and have to look in a mirror for proof. In my head I am still the twenty-one-year-old girl who took a crazy chance on a crazy guy.

I stayed in Rawlins, as it used to be called before they tacked the "Greater" on, most of my life, never regretting any of it. I went to college for a while, but I was too wild with my new freedom and my new life to make much of a go at it. When I calmed down a bit I happened to meet a man named Roy Wharton, and pretty soon I was married and had three kids and one day I woke up and I was forty. Then fifty. Then I quit counting.

Because of the chaotic conditions of the cryogenics business, it was nationalized about five years ago. That Austerwahl jerk was reliable enough, and you can bet I kept my eye on him after paying him all your— ahem — savings, which I made Austerwahl retrieve from the car before the cops showed up and started confiscating things. He died many years ago, and is probably buried in one of the many cemeteries here. I'll never understand why he didn't have himself frozen. Since then I have dropped in on you and little Darbi about once a year, and I always wished, before the government took over, that I could open up one of those silver coffins of the living for just five seconds, and see you once more, just once more. I have no pictures of you or Darbi, just the pictures in my mind. So sad that they are growing dim.

What Braine had feared for so long happened because of us; he was exposed, investigated, and charged not with any crime involving cryogenics, but for conspiracy to murder us. He was on TV a lot, and like you said, he was basically a nice guy. There was some brief talk about unfreezing you to stand trial, but at the time it was preposterous, sure death for you, so Braine made good every cent you stole, plus tossed a million in the pot to keep you and Darbi going. I believe he died in prison not long afterward.

Remember how we wondered, during that endless night drive from Missouri to Wyoming, how that sack of money got from the motel to my car? It turned out the FBI had been following you all along, helping when they could. Those two agents saved my life, and I think both of them got a promotion out of the deal.

I am glad, in my heart, that I helped you, even though my contribution was almost too little, almost too late. You two were in pretty bad shape on that hill so many years ago, and Austerwahl needed some prodding, but in the end he was convinced he saved you both.

I wish you all the happiness you deserve in your new world, Peter. You must forget the past now, and never allow Darbi to dwell on it. Please leave your demons in the old century and banish them from your own. If there is to be a Peter the Third, as you told me, then he will be the Peter you deserved for so long: a Peter who is alive and well and happy.

Light is fading now as my life draws to an end. If you ever do read this, do me a favor and find out where I'm buried, and drop by, maybe just say hi. I can't guarantee I'll hear, but if I do, I'll be smiling up at you.

Kim (Marden) Wharton

Peter looked away from the letter, and folded it up. "Hi, Kim," he whispered to the ground, and though there were tears in his eyes, they were not tears of sadness or of pain. Darbi flitted about like a happy butterfly, crying, "Daddy! Daddy! While they were fixing you I learned how to do cartwheels! Watch me, Daddy! Watch me!"

He made a move to stop her from dancing among the graves, then stopped himself instead. She had spent too long among the dead; she deserved to dance free and alive in this beautiful new future.

"Show me," he called to her. "Show me a good one!"

She did her best, and when she had tired of that they walked back to the van hand in hand, and the sun shone through the trees on her golden hair and played against his face and hers, and the breeze smelled sweetly of freshly cut grass.